Journey of SORROW Journey of HOPE

Journey of SORROW
Journey of HOPE

Carol Handy

Wilmette, Illinois

Bahá'í Publishing
401 Greenleaf Avenue, Wilmette, Illinois 60091-2844

Printed in the United States of American on acid-free paper ∞

17 16 15 14 4 3 2 1

Library of Congress Cataloging-in-Publication Data

Handy, Carol.
Journey of sorrow, journey of hope / Carol Handy.
pages cm
Includes bibliographical references.
ISBN 978-1-61851-067-9
1. Bahai Faith—Fiction. 2. Religious fiction. I. Title.
PS3608.A713J68 2014
813'.6—dc23
2013044789

Cover design by Misha Maynerick Blaise
Book design by Patrick Falso

Dedication

To the memory of

Hands of the Cause of God
Zhikrullah Khadem and John Robarts,

Continental Counselor Edna True,

and to

Mr. Ali Nakjavani,
Member of the Universal House of Justice (retired),
all of whom have shown us
what human beings can become.

Contents

Acknowledgments

When I remember the forty years or more that have passed since the morning I stood watching the sunrise on a little footbridge in Colorado and promised God I would write this novel—I am overwhelmed. Not only by the time that has passed, but at the number of people who have come in and out of my life and whose gifts have led to this day. They are the authors of this story—they and their wisdom, their encouragement, their advice, and their love.

I cannot possibly thank them all. A good number of them have left us and gone on to a clearer vision and a fuller life in another of the worlds of God. Among them are, first of all, my husband, Claire Handy, who never doubted for a moment (even when I was convinced otherwise) that I would actually finish this effort; my childhood playmate and "sister-in-love" Joan Ernst, who spent hours together with me from girlhood until in our fifties reveling in "God-talk" and who lived long enough to weep with joy over the first uncertain chapters; my closest of Bahá'í friends and companion in travel-teaching, sorrow and merriment, Arlene Jennrich, who spoke of the book as though it were already written; and author and poet, Roger White, who couldn't stay but who promised to help from the next world.

Still in this world with us are Linda Siemiaszko, another very close dear friend without whose gentle nagging this would have never seen the light of day; Christina Rose, a captive friend, who listened patiently to each chapter as it was written; Bahá'í author and theologian John Hatcher, whose work has been invaluable to me both personally and professionally; Bruce Whitmore, who offered very necessary advice and support; Joe Shinnick for efforts well "above and beyond"; my nineteenth-century history professor, who was so patient with all my questions; and my five children, who put up with a mother whose mind was too often in her books. I know I have forgotten other important friends; please do forgive me.

Further, I want to make mention of people in this Faith, living and departed, whom it has been my honor to serve: Donald Barrett, Dorothy Borhani, Steven Ader, and Javidukt Khadem, and most of all for the honor of the year spent serving the Universal House of Justice, seated in Haifa, Israel, on Mt. Carmel, the Mountain of God.

In addition, I want to thank Tim Moore of Bahá'í Publishing for his encouragement when I had almost given up, and my editor Christopher Martin, who has patiently and cheerfully seen us over the finish line.

Carol

Foreword

It is hot on the day of the execution. A young man of about thirty years is being led to the place of His punishment. He has been sent from authority to authority in an effort to convict Him of blasphemy. It is accomplished. Now, he is raised up from the ground and fastened to the instrument of his dying.

The regimental officer is reluctant to give the command that will end in the man's death, but he has his orders.

There is a crowd, curious and excited, gathering to watch. Some are weeping in sorrow and heartbreak. They believe the man to be holy; the long-awaited Messenger of God. Others are grinning with bloodlust. They are laughing and jeering, calling out to the Prisoner: "If you are the Promised One, save yourself!" He ignores them until at last He utters His final words and dies. This is history.

The date was July 9, 1850; the place was Tabriz, Persia—modern-day Iran. Among the nearly ten thousand spectators were Jews, Christians, Muslims, a few Zoroastrians, English journalists, and the merely curious. Those who were mourning most grievously were followers of the young man Himself. They were soon to become the most hated and persecuted group of innocents in what was, at that time, the entire history of mankind.

Immediately following the death of the prisoner, a huge dust storm swirled through the streets of Tabriz, blotting out the sun for the rest of the afternoon. People were frightened and hid in their houses. It was so dark that chickens roosted and goats went bleating into their sheds. Dogs whimpered in doorways. Within days, plagues broke out in a number of areas, and in one city an earthquake struck, so severe it killed seven thousand people.

It was as though nature herself knew how horrendous the crime that had that day been committed and announced to the world her heartbreak and angry protest.

Her cry was only the beginning, for as of that very day, the world underwent the first effects of a huge transition—one that has ended all the ages of the past and set in motion changes that are still today thrusting all of us forward into a new world with bewildering rapidity.

The young man held the title of the Báb, or in English, *the Gate*, and on that day that "gate" slammed shut on the whole of the human past. His "blasphemous" claim was twofold: first, that He was called to prepare the world for the arrival of one greater than Himself. Second, that within nineteen years this divine Messenger would arrive who would be the Promised One of all ages and all religions; who, in Himself, would be the return of all God's Messengers of the past: Krishna, Moses, Zoroaster, the Buddha, Jesus the Christ, and Muḥammad.

From the beginning God has been sending divine Teachers to move His children forward along their path to spiritual adulthood. We have been taught by Their wisdom, learning new patterns of behavior every thousand years or so. In this way we have grown from a childlike creature in the days of Adam, who understood only that God was our Father who loved us and talked with us in a garden of innocence. During that time, we learned—as children must—that we needed to obey His precepts, for refusing obedience would lead only to sorrow and tragedy.

Each divine dispensation brought a deeper understanding of the meanings of God's teachings. Like children in school, we moved from the simple lessons to the more complicated. In every age, the Messengers have repeated the promise that someday we will learn the meaning of life and know the purpose of all the ages of struggle. They have assured us that we will live upon the earth as true brothers in one human family, at peace with God and nature, and that the Eden-like innocence we lost so many eons ago would be restored to us. When this time comes, we will live not as creatures ignorant of good and evil but as a single humanity with our own God-inspired volition. Now, having reached the adolescence of our species, we have been visited again by the latest of these divine Teachers. In 1863, the divine Teacher whom the Báb foretold, entitled Bahá'u'lláh,* whose name means "the Glory of God," announced that the long ages of prophecy were over and that the great and hoped-for Age of Fulfillment stands in the doorway.

As for the Báb Himself—His life was short, His days sorrowful, His mission turbulent, but His sojourn on this earth ushered in the climax of human history, long anticipated as "the Apocalypse," a word that means *Unveiling* or *Revelation.* It opened the gate to a reorganization of society that will last for 500,000 years.

This is a story of the Apocalypse.

---

* Pronounced Bah hah oo lah.

A Word about Martyrdom

The Britannica Dictionary defines a martyr as follows:

From the Greek word "martyr," meaning "witness," almost more at "memory." (We would most likely say "mindful.")

1. (n) One who voluntarily suffers death as the penalty of witnessing to, or refusing to renounce his religion, tenet or a principle.

2. One who allows his life, station, or what is of great value to him, to be taken for the sake of a principle.

3. To martyr: (v) to put to death for adhering to a belief, faith, or a profession of principle.

4. To put through torture or great pain, as from a disease or as a victim of mistreatment.

Nowhere in any of several dictionaries—Britannica, Webster, or Oxford English—is there any indication of martyrdom having any similarity to self-immolation, nor should it be associated in this story with any such practice.

Character List

While this book is a work of fiction, the history as it is told is true. Below is a list of the characters, with notation as whether they are fictional or historical.

Fictional Characters
Shirin and her family
Mírzá Abbas and family
Too-Tee (named Fatima)
Count Nicholas Dolgoruky and his immediate family
Popov and Melikov
Rubin Dubinsky
Edward J.H. Hillhouse III and family
Padre Giuseppe Vittorio
Padre Francis Mario
Francesca Santini
Hamid
Fareshteh

Historical Characters
The Báb ('Alí-Muḥammad)
Bahá'u'lláh (Mírzá Ḥusayn-'Alí Nurí)
Ṭáhirih
Prince Michael Dolgoruky

Vasily Zhukovsky*
All kings and queens, as well as their families and attendants
Pope Pius IX
Cardinal Antonelli, Papal Secretary of State to Pius IX
Louis Catafago, French translator of Bahá'u'lláh's second letter to Napoleon III.

* It is true that V. I. Zhukovsky was close to the royal family and did, indeed, educate both the Tsarina and the boy, Alexander II. It is also true that he was a respected poet in his youth and a close friend of Pushkin's, as well as a friend of a number of the Decembrists. I have, however, taken the liberty of fictionalizing his later life.

Prologue

12 August 1850 Tehran, Persia

To: The Office of Her Majesty's Diplomatic Service in London
c/o His Excellency the Ambassador to Persia: Attention Mr. William J. Smyth, first minister
From: Edward J. H. Hillhouse III, Consul in Persia

* * *

(quarterly report . . . cont'd from page 16)
and as to the matter of the execution of the aforementioned Alí-Muḥammad of Shiraz, called "the Báb": you have been in the past thoroughly informed of the thousands of deaths (at the present time we have no exact number) of what appear to be innocent souls who have placed their loyalty in his teachings. The bloodbath has been such as to bring the most hardened European heart to trembling, and I know I myself find it debilitating to live with these atrocities, as one sees evidences of it every day and never knows where it may appear next. Mobs of rabble, urged on by a fanatical clergy, publicly hack their victims to death with swords and clubs and even cooking knives in the hands of street women. They have cut off the ears of some of the old men who are believers and forced

them to eat them, before dispatching the poor wretches. They have slit the throats of mothers and their little ones, leaving the bodies lying together near the entrances to their houses. They have cut holes in the arms and shoulders of some of the victims and placed lighted candles in the wounds, forced them to dance and run through the streets before hacking them to death. Needless to add, the houses, fields, and other properties of the Bábís (as they are called) have been summarily confiscated, ransacked, and in many instances, burned to the ground.

The Báb himself, following his long incarceration in more than one prison, was taken to Tabriz and imprisoned there, to await his execution.

This anticipated action required the permission of both the clerical leaders—i.e., the mullahs—and the civil authorities. As the Ramadan fast was approaching, one could not help but notice the similarity to the so-called trial of Christ—the back-and-forth activity between civil and religious leaders and the haste to finish it before Passover. It appears that some fear of God hides even within the coldest of breasts.

The night before the execution, the Báb was in his cell with a few of his disciples, including a young man called 'Alí-Muḥammad Zanuzi, who was called 'Anís.' The lad was so devoted to the Báb, it seems that he had begged never to be separated from his chosen master. At that time, it seemed, the Báb had promised the youth, "Rest assured that you will be with Me."[1]

The Báb was, it has been reported, radiantly happy, as he knew that his time of persecution at the hands of men was nearly over. When he commented that he would have preferred to be killed at the hand of a friend rather by those who hated his Cause, young Anís offered to do it for him. The Báb informed Anís that he would die with him on the following day. "This same youth who has risen to comply with My wish," he said, "will, together with Me, suffer martyrdom. Him will I choose to share with Me its crown."[1]

On the morning of the execution, the colonel of the regiment elected to carry out the order, a certain Sam Khán, in charge of a regiment of Armenian Christians, grew increasingly uncomfortable with his orders. It seems he too, was struck with the similarity of this event to the events surrounding the crucifixion of Christ. He explained to the Báb, "I profess the Christian Faith, and entertain no ill will against you. If your Cause be the Cause of Truth, enable me to free myself from the obligation to shed your blood."

The Báb replied, "Follow your instructions, and if your intention be sincere, the Almighty is surely able to relieve you from your perplexity."[2]

It was nearly noon of July 9 by our calendar, while Khán was assembling his 750 soldiers and preparing the stake from which the Báb and young Anís were to be suspended, when a prison guard went to fetch the two condemned. He entered the cell and found the Báb dictating to a friend. Interrupting the flow of words, the guard ordered him to stop what he doing and come with him, for the moment had arrived.

The Báb turned to the guard, and speaking distinctly and somewhat sternly, as one would speak to a student, said, "Not until I have said to him all those things that I wish to say can any earthly power silence Me. Though all the world be armed against Me, yet shall they be powerless to deter Me from fulfilling, to the last word, My intention."[3] The guard made no response but led the Báb and the youth with him to the execution site.

Khan assembled his regiment in three files of 250 soldiers each, one behind the other. One file was seated, the second kneeling, and the third standing. Sam Khán reluctantly gave the command to fire, and when the smoke from 750 rifles had cleared, young Anís stood alive and unhurt. The binding ropes lay shredded from the 750 bullets, and the prisoner himself was gone.

Immediately soldiers were sent scurrying to find him. The crowd was shocked. Amazed and frightened, they muttered and shouted such things as, "The Siyyid-i-Báb has gone from our sight!"[4]

Sir, I must say to you that while I was not there that afternoon, other witnesses with whom I am acquainted were, and saw with their own eyes this thing take place. I have seen executions before firing squads a good many times in my professional life, as have we all who serve government, but I will tell you that these witnesses told me that there was about this event an eeriness that is difficult to explain. To begin with, 750 crack riflemen do not miss a close target such as this. And where had the prisoner got to? And so quickly? It was the same prison guard who, going back into the prison cell, found the condemned calmly finishing the dictation that had been interrupted earlier. The prison guard stood amazed as the prisoner spoke the last words of his message and, turning to him, said, "Now you may proceed to fulfill your intention."[5] The guard resigned his post on the spot, refusing to have anything further to do with this execution.

Colonel Khán was told to proceed, but he refused, saying that he would not fire again on this man, even if it cost him his life. A second regiment was ordered to the task. Again, 750 rifles were readied, aimed, fired. Again, the smoke blackened the barracks square, and when it had cleared, the suspended bodies of the two were so riddled they were fused together as one corpse, except for their faces, which were untouched.

Immediately following the death of the prisoner, a huge dust storm swirled through the streets of Tabriz, blotting out the sun for the rest of the afternoon. People were frightened and hid in their houses. It was so dark that chickens roosted. Soon afterward, plagues broke out in a number of areas, and Shiraz suffered a terrible earthquake.

I am unable to covey to you the sense of fear that seemed to overcome the citizens who had been in attendance that day. Though much of it was undoubtedly due to superstition and ignorance, I myself was deeply impressed with a sense of—what am I to call it?—the supernatural, perhaps. I know only that I will never be able to explain its effect, either on me or the people of Tabriz. There were a multitude of spectators there, several foreign representatives, and a number of English journalists, as well as Frenchmen of some reputation. None was left unimpressed.

More information on this event and its aftermath will follow in subsequent reports as dependable information becomes available.

Respectfully, in Her Majesty's service I remain

your obedient servant,

Edw. J. H. Hillhouse III

BOOK 1

The Bright and Morning Star

"AND I WILL GIVE HIM THE MORNING STAR."

Revelation 2:28

1

THE MEMORIES OF SHIRIN: APRIL 6, 1914, PARIS

A hundred years is too long to have lived. Even so, I am to begin a new century, and tonight they are having a party to celebrate. They are going to drink toasts to my health and wish me "many more years" and apologize for gifts they think are not grand enough. But I am already in possession of the grandest birthday gift I could possibly receive. It is the sure and certain knowledge that I do not have to live another century. I am grateful for that. I am not unhappy, but I am very tired.

Besides which, I have never quite got used to this business of celebrating birthdays. In Persia, we did not keep track of birthdates as they do here in the West, and we know mine only because it was exactly two years to the day before my father's death.

Tonight, on the first evening of my 101st year, the first warm spring evening of April 1914, the past returns so clearly, it is as though someone unseen were softly breathing in the room. I rise, go to the window, and smile into the dusk, inhaling the perfume of hyacinth, lilac, and distant rain. Happiness floods me. Suddenly, to my surprise, there is the taste of salt in the corners of my smile, and I do not know if I am weeping for joy, or for all the sorrow that inevitably followed the joy, and I am struck again with the realization that the sorrows and joys experienced over a lifetime blend into singleness.

At the beginning, it seems, riding on the crest of a wave, racing high above the surface where youth can see forever and recognize nothing but triumph, we call out to the world in laughter. Then the wave races on ahead of us, taking the triumphs with it, and crashes upon the shore, depositing there for other hands the prizes we thought were to have been our own. We are left wallowing in the trough, the bright sky above us forever out of reach, while before us and behind us we see only the heaving walls of gray water and feel the lonely struggle to stay afloat in the deep valleys of the sea where our memory—that always in the past the crest has returned—is our only substitute for vision.

There was a time when I would have—more correctly—*could* have gone running on an evening like this, across a courtyard to meet someone, my uncle perhaps, in the earliest days of my girlhood, returning from a journey, his footsteps raising little eddies of dust behind him. I would hear the sounds of harness, the jink of metal and squeak of leather, joining with the soft call of the creatures and the smells of travel—sweat and mules, horses and dust—blending with the hyacinths, so that now the smell of one calls up, from those years long lost, the smell of the others.

Or I can remember a little girl named Maria, a child from the houses of the Christians who lived not far from us, and who used to play with me, and whom I loved with the fearless wholeheartedness of all first loving, and whom I lost when we grew a little and our elders agreed, without speaking of it, upon the only thing they ever agreed upon, that her Christianity would corrupt me and that my Islam would somehow harm her. They forbade us each other's company. It was the first of all the losses to come in the years since, and each loss had in it something of that first one; either that, or it only seems so, because while each loving is unique, grief is always the same.

Now I am a century old. I look back on this journey of my life and see that, viewed from a distance, the ocean is a single body, and the heights and depths are of no moment. They were only the vehicles; it was the direction that mattered. Whether tears or laughter, whether crest or trough, water is water, the yin *is* the yang and God is one. And why should it not be like this? *Il ilaha, il Allah. There is no God but God.*

Though my uncle remains the most exciting memory of my childhood and Maria the most poignant, the earliest and most precious is, naturally enough, of my mother. Most often I see her in purdah,* moving through the streets of Shiraz, haggling in the bazaar over the price of a fish or some vegetables, or squatting on the carpet in our dark house—making the chelo, washing the rice again and again, counting out the portions into the pot, shaking the saffron into her cupped palm. When she wore the chador** at home, her eyes only were exposed, and even her body motions were largely hidden beneath the voluminous folds of that veil. We children learned early to read those eyes for the subtlest message, and we often responded before anything was said. I remember them bright with exasperation, hard in their punishing, and soft with a tenderness beyond any I've known since from man or child, or will ever know again.

I remember her, too, without her veil as she often was at home, especially when my uncle was gone on one of his frequent journeys, and she and my aunts (my uncle's two wives), worked and laughed, gossiped and argued together. My mother's hair, dark and thick, would be hanging down her back, her smile sweet and girlish, until she laughed uproariously and opened her mouth where, toward the back, the two teeth were missing. "One for each of you," she said of my sister and me, because of course, soon after each birthing, she had lost a tooth. Needless to say, she was to me the loveliest creature Allah ever made, and I remember how, when she touched me, smoothing my skirt or brushing the hair from my face, I felt saddened at how work worn and old her hands were. Yet, they were the hands of a girl compared to my own tonight. Ninety years and thousands of miles between us. I look down at my own gnarled hands here on a windowsill in Paris—and I miss my mother.

My uncle, the Hájí,† Firuz Aliy-i-Shiraz, was a mule driver. He made such a poor living and was gone for so long when he could get work that

---

* Purdah: the full veiling of Muslim women.

** Chador: similar to purdah but without the facial covering.

† Hájí: one who has made the pilgrimage to Mecca.

he remained for me, always, a capricious and exciting interruption in the long monotony of our days. Always he brought gifts for his wives and for Mother and us children. They were simple gifts—a scarf, a packet of spices or a little box of tea, and sometimes . . . oh, sometimes a toy, carved by some old merchant somewhere and traded for a tiny cone of sugar or three for a small coin. For me, the chief joy of the toy was its exotic journey.

Once he brought me a small carved wooden camel. It had a red saddle-blanket painted on its back and two tiny red tassels hanging from either side of its bridle. To think that it had ridden in my uncle's saddlebag all the way from Baghdad or Tabriz far to the north, or even from the east, from across the mountains through the wilds of Afghanistan, and along the edges of the great salt desert and down through the cities of Persia to Shiraz! I would sit and hold it, willing it to share with me the adventures it must have known. It was dear to me, and I believe I would have kept it all my life, but in the years when my children were small, they liked to play with it, and once my little son took it outside and lost it. At the time, it did not seem so terribly important that it was gone. When I remember all that has transpired in my long life, it hardly seems that a carved toy could be very important, yet it surprises me at how often I think of it.

As we grew older we, like our mothers, began to value the stories and gossip he brought home with him, as much or more than the gifts. That interest in the world that he awakened never left me, and when in later years my own husband returned from his journeys, he found in me a ready audience for his tales, and the hours we spent with each other those first nights at home, soft with murmurs and warm with embraces were, for me, the best times of our years together.

In the long years that followed those first homely ones, the years that carried me farther than any little barefoot girl sitting in the dirt outside the door, wondering at a wooden toy, could possibly have dreamed of, that wonder stood me in good stead. More than once, alone and at my wit's end in matters of survival, it was that curiosity only that saved me from despair. I have a great deal for which to thank that uncle who was gone so much and home so seldom. These are my earliest recollections.

Of my father and his death soon after my little sister's birth, I have no memory. I was only two. But my mother said that one day, as she stood holding my sister, she saw my uncle enter the courtyard of our little house. She thought at first that my father was still outside the gate and would appear behind him, happy to be home to his only wife after three months on the road, anxious to see the new baby, hopeful it would be a boy. She knew before my uncle could speak that my father was not there, that he had died on the road.

There had been a sickness, contracted somewhere along the way. He had held on for a time, trying to return, wanting to see the new child and believing that if he could rest in beautiful Shiraz, he would surely recover. But two day's journey from home, he had died with the praise of the Prophet on his lips, and so we went that very night to live in my uncle's household, where our living was always meager. I suspect that was why my uncle never took a third and fourth wife. I suspect, too, that that is one reason we girls were betrothed as early as possible. By the time they were nine, three of my cousins were married and had already left the household.

I was not married until I was thirteen. My uncle said I was a beauty and that by waiting until I had ripened a little, we could make a better match. No doubt he had in mind for me a man who would take in my mother as well, for if a woman is beautiful enough, a man will agree to a good deal for the right to remove *that* veil. But in the end it was not like that. My mother died, and the next year, I was married to a man of thirty-four years who traveled with my uncle sometimes. So I went to Tehran to live.

I wept when I left the garden city, for not only was I leaving all I had ever known, but I heard that Tehran was hot and dry and unlovely—not at all like our beautiful Shiraz, and so far away.

"So far away" . . . that makes me smile now for the simple girl who was uneasy changing cities. After all, almost the only difference it would make in her days would be that she must now steam her rice in the pots of Tehran. But, of course, for me, the whole world was Shiraz and my uncle's tales. We thought the sultan of Turkey and the sháh of Persia were the only kings on earth and as remote in their courts to us poor and unlettered souls as Muḥammad Himself in the courts of Allah, in Paradise.

In those days, I expected I would get to the court of Allah as soon, if not sooner, than the court of any earthly king. If I had known, that betrothal day in 1827 as I wept and embraced my sister and little cousins, promising to return to see them as soon as I possibly could, that not only would I never see any of them again, but that the Tehran I thought "so far away" was only the first step of a journey that would carry me thousands of miles, that kings and courts would be the stuff of my life, and that into all of it, from time to time, there would waft the breezes of that Heavenly Court itself . . . if I had only known, I would have wept indeed—not only in parting and fear of the unknown—but in a wealth of wonder.

In the years of our childhood, we had "played wedding" often. When we were not busy picking the husks from rice, shelling peas or otherwise helping our mothers, we spent hours discussing and quarreling over our latest plans for the next game of "wedding." We would plan out who should be the bride—always the coveted role, of course—followed by the groom, and finally the ladies in attendance. Always, for me, it was the most fun to be the bearded old mullah, who read from the Koran to the groom. I loved to scowl and stomp and give orders. Once I even borrowed the household copy of the Holy Koran to play mullah, and was caught and severely punished. Looking back on it, I cannot imagine whatever possessed me to lift it from its place, let alone to *play* with it, even in its authentic role. I must truly have been very little.

We played at wedding, of course, as a sort of rehearsal for the only life we expected, and what came after the ceremony itself we already knew about—cooking and birthing, nursing and dying. There was nothing else to married life so far as we could observe, but watching our mothers, we were certain it would be boring. But our wedding ceremony itself marked adulthood, the wonderful day when, handsome and mysterious, a youth of Shiraz would cross the city by its main street to claim us as his bride, and we, hidden beneath the decorative folds of the bridal veil, would ride behind him in a handsome howdah, carved of sandalwood. Where the money for all this finery would have come from, we never asked. In the games, our weddings were as fine as the daughters' of the sháh, and each game grew grander than the last. These games were the warp of our little girl lives, woven against the weft of our simple existence.

Yet, when I was told that I would be the bride of a Tehrani and that he was thirty-four years old and possessed of two wives already, and what was more, that there would be no procession through the streets of Shiraz but that I would be taken to his house by my uncle on his way to begin another journey with the groom the morning after the marriage, I was not really surprised. In spite of all the childish planning, we had known it was fantasy, and that for us, life would unfold with a practical expedience. Such is the fate of the poor.

The journey north and inland was hot. I was afraid and homesick for my sister before the end of the first day. The food seemed tasteless, and silently I cried myself to sleep that night. However, by the time we had arrived in Tehran, I had discovered I was a natural traveler, and the longing to see the world, born in those days while contemplating the toys my uncle brought, was reawakened and strengthened on that very first journey. I was interested in every new sight around each bend in the road, and the noise and smell of the cities as we moved north, from Shiraz to Isfahan to Kashan to Qum, each with its own particular flavor and atmosphere, I found exciting. The mosques and shrines, the bazaars and caravanserai, all so alike and yet each so distinctively different from every other, the tantalizing glimpses of someone else's life as we passed by alleys and gates, had me almost dizzy with looking and listening, turning my head from right to left.

Because of the sights along the way, supplemented by Uncle Firuz's anecdotes, the fear was forgotten. So we arrived in the south of Tehran. We came to the house of 'Alí Taqí, my husband-to-be, and suddenly the fear returned.

Well it might have. His eldest wife of seventeen years, almost thirty herself, was sent to help me, and she was cold and unwelcoming. Beyond the barest facts, I knew little of wedding nights or what might ensue. In my nervousness, I finally found the courage to question her about it.

"Didn't your mother tell you anything? You've been a woman for at least three years, I'll wager. Didn't she even instruct you this last month?"

"My mother has been dead for a year," I explained, hoping she might at least take pity on my orphaned state and answer my question in a softer tone. But she didn't. She said only, "Well, what did she talk about before that?" I began to answer, but she didn't listen. Her question, it seemed, had been only a criticism, and then she said, putting up the comb and arranging the folds of my veil once more, "Tomorrow will be here soon enough, and you won't have to ask anymore." With that, she was gone, leaving me standing alone in this strange house, and very, very afraid.

Tomorrow came surely and found me wived by 'Alí Taqí. He was gentle enough and tried not to frighten me with his first lust, though I wept in embarrassment as he began. Before he had sated himself on this fresh girl, I confess that my embarrassment had given way to my ever present curiosity and an interest in my own pleasurable reactions, but ardor was far from awakened when he left me in the still dark, and it was three days before the soreness in my belly went away, and two weeks before I saw him again.

During that time, I came to know the women and children of his household and was beginning to be almost comfortable by the time he returned home from his journey. The older wife, Azarmidukht,* who had dressed me the night of my arrival, was sour and most often silent. When she spoke, it was usually to criticize and instruct in a tone that was none too kind. She had borne three children, two of them girls, one of whom was crippled, having been born with one leg considerably shorter than the other. The second was tongue-tied and spoke unintelligibly when she spoke at all. The third, a boy at last, had died at birth. I once asked 'Alí Taqí why he thought they might have been born like that, and he said that Azarmidukht was no doubt being punished by Allah for something she had done wrong. I asked him why, if Allah were angry with her, did He not punish *her* instead of her children, and 'Alí Taqí got angry with *me*, so I never said anything more about it.

The younger of the two older wives was Sadighe.** She was only a few years older than I, and we became friends right away. She was a plump and happy little person who laughed a lot, and she and I used to make

---

* Azarmidukt. Pronounced Azhar-mi-doe.

** Sahdighe. Pronounced Sahd-i-gay.

fun of Azarmidukht and ape her frowning face and angry walk behind her back, and then giggle shamelessly. Sadighe had two children, a son, age three, and a daughter of a year-and-a-half.

The first evening of 'Alí Taqí's return home, he came to his new bride. In an effort to put him off a little while, I began to ask questions about the journey. He ignored me, however, until like a petulant child, I nervously inquired of his silence, "Well? Aren't you going to answer me?" He turned and stared at me incredulously. In a less demanding tone, I explained lamely, "My Uncle Firuz always tells me all about it."

"I am not your Uncle Firuz," he said, removing the loose shirt that bloused over his arms and waist, "and your purpose in this house is not to be entertained." He glanced over at me then and smiled, as if my child-likeness amused him, and approached. "You needn't be afraid of me," he said gruffly. "I'm not a bear. Are you really so afraid of me?"

"N—no—yes—no!" I wavered in my confusion. I feared his anger, yet I was remembering a story Uncle Firuz had once told of how he and 'Alí Taqí had been nearly killed by highwaymen, and of how they had escaped by sliding down a steep wooded hill toward a rushing rocky stream where it appeared they had surely drowned. Remembering how he had told us of 'Alí Taqí catching his trouser waist on a sharp rock and hanging as helpless as a trussed hen, until the thieves had gone and Uncle Firuz could rescue him, I suddenly began to laugh at him. He mistook my laughter for flirtation and, grinning, began to gather me up in his arms. Then I found myself telling him of it and saying, "So you see, I *am* entertained."

His pride wounded, he scowled, and his eyes blazed with anger until for a moment I was sure he was going to begin to beat me, but instead, remembering it, he suddenly began to laugh himself, and in a moment had begun to retell the rest of it, of how he and Uncle Firuz had hidden breathless in a cold and tiny cave, like lost birds through a long wet night, and where he left out details, I supplied them, until my own eyes were shining with excitement and suddenly he stopped. Gentleness and interest lit his face. "You really like to hear about it, don't you?" He was stroking my hair, touching the line of my cheek. "You know the stories as if you had been there."

"I *was* there," I cried, reaching up and catching his hand in my own in order to remove it from my cheek. "At least I always feel that I was. Oh, please, tell me . . ."

"There *is* one thing you might enjoy," he said, realizing for the first time, I think, that he was speaking to little more than a child, ". . . on the first afternoon after we had left Yazd and were on our way back here. . . ." So he began to tell of his journey, and something in the telling awakened a need to share of himself that he had not known was in him, and over the months ahead, he talked and talked, and I listened, and the listening reminded me of home and uncle, and affection grew and replaced the vanishing fear. With the affection came ardor, so that I looked forward now with eagerness to his returns, and it was almost always to me that he came on the night of a journey's end, our voices sometimes blending in conversation until nearly sunrise.

Azarmidukht was not so heartless as she had at first seemed. She was rather tired and, I imagine, embittered that she could not bear 'Alí Taqí a healthy child. In addition, she was singularly without charm and so aroused in 'Alí Taqí only the most perfunctory interest, and, I came later to understand, ill in that way that only the lonely can be. She died in a miscarriage during my third year in Tehran, her third in less than two years. We all grieved for her, but not intensely, and in a month or two our lives had filled in the spaces left blank by her dying, and I asked my husband with that unwomanly directness that always nonplussed him if he would take another wife. He looked at me with a mixture of exasperation and tenderness in his face. Then he turned away and answered shortly, "Of course." But he never did.

Sadighe and I were like sisters and wonderful company for each other while 'Alí Taqí was away. Once in a while we quarreled, but not often. Because 'Alí Taqí and I could talk together sometimes, and because he therefore spent more time with me, especially when he'd been gone, Sadighe occasionally pouted and once, I remember, when he finally came to her room, she quickly slipped out the door with the key and locked him inside. She would not let him out and shouted to him that since he was finally there, perhaps he would like to stay.

He grew angry and then furious and finally quiet. Still she kept him prisoner until at last he threatened to empty his swollen bladder into her clothes trunk, and so she relented. He would not speak to her for a week, and she and I giggled about it for days.

What happened to me in the next twenty-five years, I can tell in three short statements. I bore three children. Because my husband died, I went to live as a servant to a woman in a wealthy household. I learned to read and write.

But these three events stand like posts in a vineyard, while the vines themselves, the history of those years, and, indeed, all my years to come, wrapped around the posts, their tendrils weaving and tangling in and out of my simple industrious days, absorbing the sunlight, drinking the rain, blooming and fading and fruiting at last, in clusters of royal purple.

By the time Azarmidukht died, I had a child of my own and was carrying another. My little Hasan was a sturdy boy of two and had about him a comical way that brightened the household. It was not what he said or did, but the way he said and did it that could set the whole family to laughing. Now, when 'Alí Taqí returned from his journeys, I had stories for him as well.

The second child was a girl. Taqí named her Fatima, after the Prophet's daughter, and though she seemed healthy enough at first, before she was three months old it was obvious to us all that she was not. Early after the close of her first year, while Taqí was gone again, I woke in the morning to find her lying beside me, pale blue-gray and cold. The shock of waking beside my baby's body hastened the labor for the third child I was then carrying, and she was born a week later, nearly three months early, and we all thought that surely we would lose her, too, she was so tiny and weak and barely able to nurse.

She was called Khadijah,* after the Prophet's wife. We believed even as we named her that these two little namesakes of Muḥammad's wife and daughter would lie together before very long, but she *thrived*, that

---

* Pronounced Kha-di-jay.

tiny thing, and grew and became to me daughter and sister, mother and friend, and is here with me still in Paris. Such are the tricks of life's arrangements. Praised be to God, the best of arrangers.

After that there were no more children. I do not know why. I was always robust well into my middle eighties, and even today feel well enough save for occasional aches and pains, these thickening cataracts, and the terrible weariness. Whatever the reason, it was not health. Perhaps it was because 'Alí Taqí was growing old.

By the time Hasan was eighteen, though still droll, he was less comical. He no longer made us laugh aloud at his manner, but somehow had a way of speaking a word or turning his head that brought a smile or a chuckle. There was joy inside him, and his eyes radiated a kindly amusement at all he saw and heard. Perhaps it was that scarcely contained laughter, as if he knew some delightful secret about life that he was just waiting until the right moment to share, that not only made him seem to be about to laugh, but put everyone around him in a light humor the moment he entered the room. 'Alí Taqí had begun to take Hasan on the journeys by then, and we all missed him dreadfully when he was gone. Hasan was my sunrise, and I knew that when Taqí died, as he must before very many more years, Hasan would care for me, and I looked forward to a later life free of worry and want. So those years of my life's third decade passed tranquilly enough, but much of it now is lost from memory, one of the fees we pay for the years of peace. I came then to my thirty-second year.

'Alí Taqí had not yet made his pilgrimage to Mecca in spite of all his traveling, so when Hasan asked his father one evening soon after the Naw-Rúz of 1263 (or 1847, as I have learned to date here in Europe), at any rate, when he asked if they might not go on pilgrimage during this next journey, as it was to be a long one anyway, deep into Arabia, 'Alí Taqí hesitated for a minute, thought deeply and quickly, and then nodded assent. Hasan was jubilant! The bright eyes danced more gaily than ever, and he was up and pacing the room in his excitement. I am sure he had not expected it to be decided so easily.

The journey to Riyadh for business, then to Mecca, to Medina, and back to the Gulf, and up to Mosul for return business, then East across the Zagros Mountains to Tabriz, and home again would take nearly a year.

Khadijah and I were not so jubilant. We would miss Hasan's bright spirit and Taqí's strong presence in the household, but we were used to it. After all, since childhood I had spent my life awaiting the homecoming of men.

The morning of their departure dawned clear and cool, a good omen we said to each other, and when the moment of leave taking came, Hasan was torn between wanting to stay and wanting to be off, as if he were a lad on his first journey. He grinned down at me, "Mother, think! We shall both be Hájí when you see us next!" With his words, a darkness filled my mind, and I could not reply.

Taqí then came to where we stood. To Khadijah he entrusted my care and promised to bring gifts for her marriage. Then he looked at me a moment and spoke. "You," he said crossly, "are too bold for a woman, and you always speak out of turn." He was scowling, but his eyes were dark with the pain of leaving.

"Hah!" I said, "Just for that I shall spend the whole year thinking up difficult questions that demand answers the moment you return."

"Demand. Demand answers indeed," he growled. "your purpose in this house is . . ."

I smiled a little crookedly at him. "Oh, go. Go traveling, 'Alí Taqí, before you forget the way." I turned from them both, then, so they should not see the tears that fell from eyes that had seen farther than they were meant to on that clear spring morning. I think.

It is hard to know in retrospect whether the feeling that I would never see them again was true foreknowledge, or just a womanish fear that might have been laughed away in relieved chagrin when they were safely returned . . . if they had safely returned. But they did not, and so I do not know about the feeling.

A traveler came almost a year to the day later and told us of their deaths. They had been on their way home, already into Kurdistan (they had made their pilgrimage, and I gave thanks for that as he told me), when they had been asked for protection by two men who then joined them, Turks from the coast of the Black Sea who claimed to be afraid of the Kurds and were uneasy about the way through the Zagros. They were thieves who believed Taqí to be carrying gold, though he was not, and they had murdered them for it in the hills of Kurdistan.

"I had overheard the travel arrangements being made one night in the Caravanserai in Mosul," said the stranger. "I was traveling with a detachment of Turkish soldiers on business for the sháh's minister. Later, I suggested to one of the thieves that perhaps they would feel more guarded traveling with the soldiers; that I would be happy to inquire of our commanding officer if they would not be welcome to join us. He thanked me graciously, but explained that he also wished to discuss with your man along the trail the possibility of hiring him for some business projects of his own in the future. I could hardly accuse him of lying, but I did not feel right about it, and I told the officer of the troops with whom I was traveling, so we followed rather closely to keep an eye on things. We had had some trouble with mules that forced us to remain an extra day in camp before we entered the mountains . . . and well . . . suffice it to say that we came upon them just as they had finished.

"If we had been but one half–hour earlier!" he had said, biting his lip and striking the air with his fist. "They were searching the luggage and saddle bags, ripping them open with knives, and your men were lying there with . . . ah, anyway we caught them and, you will be gratified to learn, the Turkish officer took care of the justice with admirable dispatch."

There was a long silence while we wept silently, digesting this, and Khadijah said with quiet desperation, "Oh, Hasan!" and I thought for a moment that it was not possible that Taqí's gruff voice, hoarse and rumbling, was forever stilled.

"We buried them on the side of the mountain," the traveler said, "on a south slope where the sun will move through the day . . . it seemed a warm place to lie." He watched me. I thanked him. He seemed reluctant to go and leave us with our grief, but we sent him on his way with our heartfelt gratitude and the blessings of Allah.

I think now, as I look back on all of it, that 'Alí Taqí, with his gruff manner and pretended harshness, was probably a better husband than most, though I don't really know, and I missed his capable habits for a long time. He had, however, been approaching his sixties, which I thought then was "very old," and I could not grieve overlong for one whose life had been useful and good.

But, oh! I had not been prepared to lose Hasan . . . not my bright Hasan, the joy of our household and the pride of my motherhood, and sometimes still, when I lie sleeping, after seventy long years, those eyes will flash and I will hear his laughter, boyish still and forever happy, in the safe, sweet world of my dreams.

2

SHIRIN: 1847

Sadighe's children were all grown save one, and as she had a brother in Isfahan, she and her son of eleven went there to live after Taqí's death. We wept in each other's arms that day of parting and commended one another to the care of God. As for me, I was in dismay, wondering what I would do. I thought if I could find a suitable husband for Khadijah, then perhaps I could return to Shiraz. Uncle Firuz had died some years before, but perhaps one of my cousins' husbands might offer me a home. Before I had even voiced these thoughts to Khadijah, the care of God manifested in the appearance of Mírzá Abbas 'Alí, a local merchant known as Abbas, who had often hired 'Alí Taqí to accompany his goods on their shipments around the country. He had heard in the bazaar that we were left alone and had come to see how we were faring. When I told him of my plan, he offered me a place in his household as a handmaid and said, "Bring your daughter with you. She will be useful, never fear." Believe me, I hesitated not a moment, and we gathered our things from the house to wait for the cart he said he would send.

We rode in some style then through the streets of Tehran, and as we moved up the hills to the section in the northern part of the city where he lived, the air became sweeter and the day decidedly cooler. It was like moving to another city altogether.

I was amazed as we approached the house. I had had no idea we would be living in a mansion, and I cautioned Khadijah not to speak unless she had to. I was so afraid something we said would offend someone and that we would be sent packing before our simple belongings were *un*packed.

There was a long driveway along which our carrier approached the house. There were fruit trees, gardens, and even a fountain and pools with goldfish. We drove past the front of the house and around to the back where we stopped at last, and the driver jumped down and unloaded our things.

"Follow me," he said tersely, and off we went, our heads turning on our necks like two ostriches.

The mansion, as I grew to know it later, was in two sections: two large square buildings—each square built around its own central garden and joined together by a covered walkway—and a logia, the front side of which was shielded by a row of tall thin cedars (the ones that look like candles). The view from the back side of the walkway looked out over a pleasant scene of fruit trees and kitchen gardens. In the distance, the Elburz hills rose toward what far to the north became the mountains and forests of Mazindaran. The biruni, the large room where Mírzá Abbas entertained guests, and his private apartment, as well as the sleeping rooms where the male servants and other men of the household lived, were in the eastern building. The arjuna, or women's room, was in the western building, along with a gracious apartment for Mírzá Abbas's primary wife. He had three others, of course, but they lived in houses of his located nearby. There were also lovely little rooms for the children, a schoolroom, and workrooms. Even the living space for the servants, while small, was comfortable and clean.

Khadijah and I were led down the long logia, open on one side to the central courtyard with its garden and trees, to a low doorway. The carter stopped and motioned us inside without speaking and left our things outside the door. We were suddenly alone. I looked into the dim room that was to be our home for the next few years and caught my breath.

It was already dark inside, and as we stepped into what would appear to be a cavern, there, across from us, was a splash of blood-red as the setting sun was framed in a small window. It was to become in the years ahead one of the great joys of my heart, to share with my only remaining child at the end of the day that moment of perfection as the setting sun seemed to halt for a moment each evening as if to bid us farewell once again before the world was plunged into darkness.

We stood then, watching, speechless, mother and daughter draped in purdah, reaching for each other's hands in the strange dark room, interpreting the flash of brilliant light as a sign of good luck in our new lives.

I broke the silence at last. "There must be a lamp about somewhere, or at least a candle." Khadijah began to move slowly toward a little table, as our eyes grew accustomed to the gloom. "No," she said, "there's nothing that I can see."

"Well, help me with these bundles then, and we'll pile them all in the corner and settle ourselves tomorrow."

"May I sleep then? I'm very tired, and I'm hungry too; have we anything to eat?"

"I've some nuts in my scarf, and there is tea as well. . . if I can find my samovar and some water. I imagine there are apricots on the trees out there."

"Are we allowed? Do we dare pick them?"

"Oh, I hadn't thought! I don't know. We'd better wait. Bring the bundles, and we'll just eat the nuts."

"But, Mama, I'm hungry! I want more than . . ."

"We will eat the nuts and go to sleep!" I interrupted a little harshly in my uncertainty. You will dream of rice and vegetables and tomorrow. . . . well, tomorrow will tell us much, and we will not starve. We *do* have a home, Khadijah," I said in a softer tone. "Please be content for tonight. We *are* together."

"And we had our sunset," she added, trying to be valiant. "Good night, Mama."

She had begun to move toward the pallet in the far corner, when in through the doorway came a glowing lamp, carried by a very fat woman who carried also a basket of fruit, a samovar and, locked against her side by her elbow, several slabs of bread.

"The Lady Shaydah sends these . . . she thought you might be hungry," she said. Khadijah gave a little hop of pleasure, and I was deeply moved to think our new mistress would even know we had arrived, let alone be concerned for our comfort.

"Oh, how lovely! How thoughtful!" I said, flustered with strangeness, and bustling uncertainly about, trying to make the woman comfortable in my one, unsettled room. She laughed, showing her teeth, or rather what was left of them, and began to dominate the room, talking all the while at breakneck speed, wheezing at her infrequent breaths. "Here," she said, "you sit and let me help you . . . you, too, young woman . . . you must both be very tired . . . has it been a long day for you? Shaydah Khánum* *is* very lovely *and* very thoughtful . . . a joy to serve . . . you will see. Yes, you will see. Come, come . . ." she said, beckoning to Khadijah, who stood shyly back on the shadow, her childlike eyes dark and huge in the lamplight. The woman chattered away nonstop, all the while managing us both, preparing the tea, arranging the fruit in the basket, guiding Khadijah to the rug in the middle of the room.

When we were both settled comfortably on the rug with apricots and a glass of good hot tea before us, she finally sat down herself, puffing and grunting, and joined us at her own invitation. She broke chunks of bread from the slabs and handed one to each of us.

"Now," she said, with the air of one who has settled in for a season, "You must tell me all about yourselves," and proceeded to continue talking almost without a breath, instead telling us about the household, the master, Mírzá Abbas; the mistress, Lady Shaydah; and of the existence they led here. Had I wanted to, I could not have found a way to squeeze in a word about us. But I was happy to be silent. Tired and hungry, we were content to listen and look about us in the lamplight and hear the pleasant singsong of her friendly gossip.

I was relieved to hear that the kindness of Mírzá Abbas in coming to see after us and bring us here was truly kindness and without guile. I had been a little suspicious of such an unprecedented concern for a mule driver's widow and child but too desperately in need of keeping the two of us together to question over much. It had all seemed a little too good to be

* Kha-noom; a title meaning *Madam* or *Lady.*

true, but in the cool dark of our servant's hut, with my stomach full of bread and fruit and the tea glass hot in my hands, I felt relaxed for the first moment since three weeks before, when the stranger had come knocking at the gate, bringing his tidings of death.

The serving woman's name was Fatima, and, I was to learn, she knew not only everything about everyone in the household of Mírzá Abbas, she knew everything about everyone in Tehran. How she learned anything talking so much, I often wondered, but she must have absorbed gossip and information through her eyes and skin and fingertips . . . for she was a wealth of information. She told it all as soon as she learned it and spread news with the generosity of the morning sun. Her earlier command that we must "tell her all about ourselves," was a mere gesture of welcome, for I found she already knew all about us, and who we were, and where we had come from, and why.

Had she been a mean woman, she would have been a monster of destruction, but luckily she was not; she was merely interested in everybody and everything and blessed, to say the least, with a generous tongue. She was known among the servants as "Too-Tee" (Parrot), and though we called her that only behind her back, it was nevertheless a title of affection.

"Kh́ánum is so beautiful," she said, "you will count yourself fortunate to be near her . . . and as for you, my little one," she said, looking at Khadijah and patting her arm so hard it made Khadijah wince, "you are to be taught fancy work and sewing and beadwork and all such. You will have the best teacher in the world . . . though she's old and going blind. That's why you have her," Fatima grinned and her fleshy body trembled with silent chuckling, "because she needs to teach somebody to carry on when her eyes are gone. She's truly very, very good . . . the best." Fatima nodded, as if agreeing with herself, smacked her lips over a section of orange, was silent for a split second, and then said, "Yes, indeed, the very best. You're lucky."

"Well," she said, heaving to her feet and gathering pits and peels into the basket, "I suppose I had better go and let you sleep. The samovar and the lamp are yours to use 'til you get your own things unpacked. You can pick the fruit from the trees in the courtyard, but not in the outside gardens. The well's outside for your morning tea. Be up at first light, and I'll come get you after breakfast to meet Khánum. Wait 'til you see her jewelry . . . it's as beautiful as she is . . . and her gowns! Oh! Her gowns. . . ." and with that she disappeared through the door as suddenly and without warning as she had entered it, and the little room almost rang with silence.

We prepared for sleep without speaking and lay down together wearily. As I leaned over to blow out the lamp, my eyes met Khadijah's. They were twinkling. "Well, now," she mimicked, "tell me all about yourselves . . . I can hardly wait to hear!" With that the room went black, and we lay in the strange night and giggled a little before we fell asleep.

It was not the light that woke me so much as it was the birds twittering. I rose and dressed, and went to the well for water before I woke Khadijah. I looked down at my sleeping child—a child in my mind only, because she was the youngest and the one whom we had not expected to live. Now, as she and I began our new lives, in this year of 1847, she was a woman of seventeen. Of medium height, with long, dark hair—not unlike my mother's and mine—her face was oval and her eyes dark. Her teeth were straight and perfect, and she moved with an unconscious grace. 'Alí Taqí had been planning a marriage for her before he left, but that was all changed now, and I wondered at the fate of this young woman who lay sleeping, unaware of how truly beautiful she was.

"*When I was your age, I had had three babies, and you were already a year old,*" I thought as I gazed at her, "*and your father was the age I am now when he married me. Time . . . how mysterious is time.*" I stood watching a moment more until the sense of the quickly passing years began to make me feel vulnerable, and then I woke her.

True to her word, Fatima came to fetch us before we had really got ourselves together, and first we took Khadijah to the sewing room where she would learn the skills of weaving and fine dressmaking. Then I was led to the apartment of the Khánum . . . the Lady. We went into her sitting room, and Fatima smiled her toothless smile at me.

"Now, don't be afraid. Are you afraid? Don't be. She is a good lady; it is alright, you'll see, it is really alright," she said in her rapid repetitious manner. I smiled at her, thinking of Khadijah's mimicking the night before, and we stood alone for a moment . . . and then Lady Shaydah came into the room.

Fatima had said she was beautiful and gracious and that her gowns were lovely, but I was not at all prepared for this. True, I had never before been in the presence of a real lady, and I don't know what I had expected—an imperious haughtiness, perhaps, or someone somehow removed from the reality of life by the stature of wealth and position. But Khánum was neither of these.

My first impression was of freshness, like the new morning itself as she came gliding into the room, filling it with life and brightness, and all around was the soft scent of a garden. Her expression was grave and curious, inspecting a new servant, but her eyes of deep rich brown were soft with kindliness. I rather imagine my mouth dropped open like a street urchin's. I know I stared.

"You must be Shirin. I am sorry to hear that you have been widowed, and I pray that Allah will strengthen you. Did you have a good rest last night, and enough to eat . . . you and your daughter?"

She stood waiting politely for my answer while I stood staring at her lovely face above a gown of soft green. Suddenly then, I caught hold of myself. "Yes! Oh, yes, thank you, Khánum," and I dropped my eyes to the floor. "And thank you for the supper last night. We are very grateful . . . we . . ." I trailed off into silence as I couldn't think of anything to say.

She waited to see if I would finish, and when I didn't, she spoke again. "Then I think you can begin to go to work immediately. There are two trunks of clothes in my dressing room that need to be sorted and mended, and then they must be cleaned with a damp rag, brushed, and repacked. Later in the day you will need time to settle your things, so while there will not be time to do all the clothing today, it is alright, we will continue tomorrow.

"Come, I'll show you, and Fatima will help you get started. I'll return presently. Later this afternoon, I shall want to speak with you a little." She started to leave and then turned again. "Ask Fatima whatever you need to know, and if I am near, don't be afraid to ask me." With that her eyes glowed again with the soft warmth, though still she was unsmiling.

She turned and left the room then, and only when I heard myself exhale did I realize I had been holding my breath.

"Didn't I tell you?" said Fatima, and she took me into the dressing room to begin the sorting.

We worked all morning long, almost without glancing up, but all the while, Fatima's voice kept up a sprightly accompaniment to the brush and needle. She told me of my tasks, of the rooms here in Khánum's apartment, then of the men and women of the household, then some bit of news from the bazaar, abruptly returning to me and my work. Listening to her talk reminded me of a child's hopping game, jumping back and forth, left and right, from subject to subject, but it made the time pass quickly. At noon, Fatima stopped me. "Go back to your room," she said, "and start the tea. I will fetch Khadijah and some lunch for you. After lunch, you can stay in your place if you like. I imagine you might want to settle your things a little. Khánum wants to see you later," she said. "I'll . . . I will come tell you when to come. Yes, that will be best. I will come. Go now. I will be there in an eye blink with the food. Tonight I will show you the larder, and after today you can fetch for yourselves."

When the afternoon sun began to lose its midday heat, I sat back on my heels and surveyed the result of our efforts. The room was swept and clean. Our lamp was on the table, and our pallets out of the way in the north corners. Our boxes of clothes and cooking things, arranged in an orderly line along the south wall covered with the three small carpets we had brought with us, made a mandar—a serviceable low divan.

I spoke to Khadijah. "Well, it is home now, eh? What do you think?"

"It will never be home! Not without Hasan and Papa!" she said petulantly. Then in a moment, "I don't know if I like that old seamstress. She's impatient and she yells at me; she must be crotchety with age."

"She's in a hurry for you to learn while she still has eyes to teach you with, don't you think?"

"Perhaps so. She says I should be grateful," she added with a childish pout. "How can I be grateful when it is such hard work?"

"Ha! That is not such hard work, sitting down to do it. Be grateful, indeed, Khadijah, for only Allah knows where you would have ended up without your father to arrange a marriage for you. Now, you can be useful as long as you live. Oh my, yes. Be grateful indeed."

"Aha . . . I see you've made your nest since lunch—made your nest." It was Fatima come to take us back. When she had deposited me with Shaydah

Khánum and gone, and I found myself suddenly alone with the lady, and the fear everyone had been telling me not to feel, and which as yet I had *not* felt, suddenly arrived. I had been wondering what she would want to speak with me about, but now the wondering became an acute worry. What if I made all the wrong answers? What if I could not answer at all?

She began by asking me about myself, where I had been born, how many children I had had, what I enjoyed most. At first I answered in a word or two, but she would tell me a little about herself, in a conversational way, not revealing too much but, informing, explaining, almost as if she were setting an example of how the questions ought to be answered, though I was not aware of that at the time. Rather, the effect was to set me at ease, so that soon, as the questions came, I found myself answering her in an easy, less self-conscious manner, sharing myself and my life in a comfortable flow.

Finally she rose and said, "Now, if you will, I need to dress for the evening meal, and you can help with the gown and hair. Come, I will show you."

That night, I lay for a while after Khadijah had gone to sleep, staring up into the black, wondering about this first afternoon.

The conversation that had been treated almost as if it were a social visit was, of course, a measuring . . . I had been aware of that . . . but lying in the stillness of the night, I realized that her exploration into my thoughts and character had been a most thorough one, much more than was necessary for a lady's handmaid. I wondered why, and so, on that second night in our new home, fell asleep uneasily, wondering if the Lady Shaydah were as lovely and guileless as she seemed.

* * *

We had been a part of the household of Mírzá Abbas for about six months and already were beginning to feel as though we had been there always, when I woke one night to the sound of whispering in my room. I lay rigid with alarm as I listened, but in a moment recognized the unmistakable voice of "Too-Tee."

"Fatima?" I whispered. "What's going on? What do you want?"

"Oh, Shirin . . . I'm sorry to have wakened you," she whispered in return, coming over to where I lay . . . "We've had travelers come through, a sister of one of the women and her husband who is now over with the men. They needed a place to sleep, and I knew there was room in here for another pallet. I hoped you would not even waken. It's just for the night. Is it alright with you?"

"Of course . . . of course it is alright," I scolded her, "but I was frightened, and if I am to have a guest, you should have wakened me."

"Well, I . . . I didn't like to bother . . . and you and Khadijah need your rest . . ."

"I see. Well . . . welcome," I spoke softly into the darkness, "Will you be comfortable?"

"Thank you, I'm fine," came a strange voice softly.

Fatima volunteered, "She's very tired. They've had a long day. We fed them and now she needs to sleep. I'll go along. Again, I'm sorry we woke you."

"No, no, it is alright," I said sleepily and dropped off again, thinking as I did so that I would meet my unexpected guest in the morning and find out all about her journey.

In the morning, however, there was no sign of anyone when I woke, and I was not sure that I had not dreamed the whole thing when I remembered that there had been the sound of soft weeping just as I was falling asleep, and I knew that that had been no dream. I asked Fatima about it later, but she repeated the same thing she had said in the night. I continued to press her, however, for I was curious about the weeping and where they had gone off to before daylight, but Fatima could not answer me, as she suddenly remembered an errand she had to attend to for Khánum, and after that I forgot about it, and we never spoke of it again.

It must have been stored in my mind along with a number of other strange things, although it was a long time before I remembered it. I remember too, being interrupted in the middle of my work for Khánum one morning and sent back to my room "until I send someone to fetch you." I had been dusting a collection of miniature bottles of which Khánum was very fond that morning when suddenly a woman I had seen often in the gardens and whose name I learned later was Fareshteh came into the room. She went immediately to Khánum and spoke in a low tone. Khánum looked at her a moment without responding and then said, "Thank you. I will join you in a few minutes." The woman left then, and Khánum seemed lost in thought. The apartment grew very silent, but it was not so much the silence as the atmosphere that made the moment memorable. I distinctly recall a sense of heaviness invading the room and I felt burdened by what I thought might be sorrow in Khánum. I wanted to offer to help or at least inquire if anything were troubling her but felt too uncomfortable to speak and so remained silent. The only sound in the room was the little "tick" each tiny bottle made as I dusted it and set it back down on the shelf. Into the quiet came Khánum's voice low and strong: "You may leave now, Shirin. Go to your room or make yourself otherwise comfortable until I send someone to fetch you. The work will wait."

After these two events, I sometimes noticed little things: people talking together who suddenly would quiet and then turn away at the approach of a third person. A strange face would appear in the women's quarters for a day or two, only to disappear again. Sometimes there were the sounds of carts and horses in the night. Each incident by itself might have meant nothing, and no one incident seemed important enough to pay much attention to, and so I remained for a long time unaware of the questions that were slowly collecting within me. Besides, I forgot all of it when one day we woke to a sense of muted excitement.

There was an undertone of laughter in the voices of the women, and I learned at the well that this was to be a sort of holiday. All I could get anyone to say was that "Teacher is coming." Most of us gathered in a large shaded grassy area beneath the fruit trees as soon as the morning chores were done. The sight of us all in our working black gathered in a chatty cluster reminded me of a flock of blackbirds. Into the middle of all this came the Lady Shaydah, followed by another slightly smaller woman. And I had thought the Lady Shaydah was beautiful!

This woman walked with an air that made me sit up straighter just to see her. Her manner was bright and forthright, and she carried in her hand two volumes. One, I was to learn later, was a book of her own poetry, and the other, Holy Koran. As the two women approached, the "flock of birds" fell silent. The two moved into our midst, and in a moment after a greeting, the lady seated herself and began to read to us. I had never heard a woman read before. The sound of the familiar words of Koran as they used to flow in the deep tones of my Uncle Firuz, flowing now in the light, strong tones of the woman's voice, was very strange. Strange or not, it was a sweet comfort to hear again the sounds of the words foretelling the joy of the promised Great Day of God. The cadence sang like poetry, flowing over me with the softness of long remembered lullaby:

> . . . There is a Register
> Fully inscribed
> To which bear witness
> Those nearest to God.
> Truly, the Righteous
> Will be in Bliss:
> On Thrones of dignity
> Will they see all things;
> Thou wilt recognize
> In their faces
> The beaming brightness of Bliss
> Their thirst will be slaked
> With the pure Sealed Wine. . . .*

I had just begun to get used to it and had leaned back comfortably against an apricot tree to enjoy it when suddenly she stopped and, smiling, handed the Book to Khánum, who *also* began to read it aloud! One woman reading was a magic exception, but two of them! I could not believe what I was hearing, and then I found myself suddenly propelled into longing . . . aching and determined that somehow I, too, would learn to read! I had heard that morning, of course, that "Teacher" was coming, but what she was to teach us, I had not thought about. I merely supposed that we were to be instructed in some new method of household tasks, or

---

* Koran 83:20–25.

perhaps taught to recite some poetry. Even while she was reading, I failed to make the connection, so startled was I. Moreover, I then thought that the Koran reading *was* the lesson; we were to hear the holy writings. We had that opportunity seldom enough.

Finally my desire to read, awakened by the sight and sound of the women before me, was so overpowering that it drove all other thought from my mind. At last, Khánum closed the Holy Book and returned it to the Teacher. She then began to separate us into small groups, and I found myself in a cluster of five women—Khadijah, Fareshteh, and two others.

We sat chatting for a few moments, or more correctly, the others chatted . . . I sat, lost in the immensity of this idea, until "The Reading Lady" came to us. The power of her presence as she stood among us was such that it silenced us all. As she knelt beside me, I studied her face. Her eyes were dark and piercing and darted quickly from face to face in our group. She had a small mole high on her left cheekbone, and her dark hair shone in the morning sun. She radiated a powerful strength from her person and the delicate perfume of attar of roses from her clothes. She looked directly into my eyes, placed the books in my lap, and smiling, asked, "Do you wish to learn to read?"

"Oh, yes, Khánum," I breathed, then firmly, as I realized she was truly saying those words to me. "Yes. Yes, I do."

"Then you shall. Shaydah Khánum tells me your name is Shirin. Is that correct? I have the right woman?" I nodded dumbly. So, it seemed, they had spoken of me. "She believes you will want to read, and later also to write, and that you will learn quickly. She laughed gently at me then, and I couldn't blame her, for the miracle of not only learning to read, but someday to write also, must have widened my eyes like a child's. I was so astonished I could hardly believe what I was hearing. But it was all true, and she opened the Koran and began to show me the letters and the flow of letters that went together to make words and the soft wash of print that became verses and whole pages of holy writ. At first I could not understand what she was pointing out on the page, but she patiently showed me again, and then again, how the first letter was repeated farther down on the page. "Do you see?" she coaxed, "it is the same mark, so it makes the same sound."

Suddenly, I saw it for myself! I held in my lap this veritable magic carpet, and my hands began to tremble as I found the first letter repeated several times on the page. I was able to pick it out over and over again. So I saw that it was more than a jumble of meaningless marks. It was all arranged in a series of patterns! It could be understood, and I, Shirin, the barefoot orphan-girl of Shiraz, would come to understand it! Not only the words of the Prophet, but poetry, the record of the past, the thoughts of great thinkers, and the journeys I believed I would never make . . . all could be opened to me now. Soon I would be able to gaze through windows now curtained by illiteracy onto vistas of endless distance. Secrets of unimaginable wonder were soon to be mine, and as the realization of this new freedom began to grow in my mind with the unlocking of but a single letter, I turned and looked at my Teacher with the wonder of it in my eyes.

My gratitude for the gift flamed into adoration in a second, and I believe I would have died for her that morning, had she asked me to. She watched me and smiled. Her own eyes changed as they met mine, and her face told me she knew—she knew my longing, my determination, my vision, and my adoration . . . and she understood.

* * *

Suddenly the sháh died, and that weak and somewhat useless king was replaced on the throne by a seventeen-year-old boy. A youth was hardly what we needed to save our government and our economy. After the unsuccessful wars of his youth, Muḥammad Sháh had lived in his palaces to a large degree uninterested in the nation he ruled, in her welfare, in the state of her treasury, or in her people. His interest lay, rather, in his own unhappiness, which followed him like a faithful though mangy dog through the later years of his life. His wives cared nothing for him (nor he for them so far as anybody knew), and his sons loved him little if at all. Why his life was so loveless I never heard, though it was said of him that in an effort to buy the affection of his family and the good offices of his associates, he was genial enough and indulgent. The result was a huge royal household with neither discipline nor much visible order. At least, this was the talk in the bazaars in the days immediately following his death. It could hardly be said that the country suffered much national grief.

Fatima sometimes took me to the bazaars with her, as there was a great deal to do there and as there were often mornings when Khánum had little use for me. Fatima's tasks were also easier when I could share some of them. Further, women did not go to the bazaars alone.

Then, too, we liked each other, and the reading and writing at which Fatima, I had discovered, was rather skilled, gave us much in common. I had learned very rapidly, just as Shaydah Khánum had told the Teacher she thought I might, and Fatima and I loved to spend time together talking about some of the poetry we had read and trying out new ideas upon one another. We were a compatible pair, as I enjoyed listening almost as much as Fatima enjoyed talking, so there was no competition to mar our deepening friendship. I certainly had listened enough to satisfy the most curious ear that first morning following the death of Muḥammad Sháh. Sooner or later in the bazaars, one heard almost everything.

It seems that the one person to whom the sháh felt close was his prime minister, the Hájí Mírzá Áqásí. A clown, a fool, a sly and ingratiating snake of a man, Hájí Mírzá Áqásí used the king's love starvation to feather his political nest. He fawned over the king, and the king in turn not only adored him and spoiled him, he ascribed to him spiritual powers he did not have (believing Áqásí could do miracles). The sháh all but gave him cart blanche in matters of government policy as well as the royal treasury, with the result that the half-crazy old fraud made one foolish, official decision after another, butchering the national budget. When the sháh died, it became apparent immediately that Persia was in political and economic turmoil. Hájí Mírzá Áqásí was terrified from the moment of Muḥammad Sháh's death, knowing full well that he might lose not only his high position but his life as well.

There was a great deal of fuss about the accession of the new sháh, which proved to be not an orderly process. With the large number of wives and concubines, none of whom gave a fig for the sháh himself, the palace was rife with jealousy over the royal chair, each woman believing her son to be the likeliest candidate. It sometimes turned out that whichever youth had the most powerful mother became the ruler. It proved so in this case, although as a matter of fact, young Náṣiri'd-Dín was the rightful heir. His mother was appointed acting president of a council of four regents while the decision was being made.

Hájí Mírzá Áqásí had taken the boy with him to Áqásí's private residence near Oazun. He hoped to ingratiate himself with the lad, but also in effect to hold him hostage on the gamble that, to get the boy back the council would also recall Áqásí himself to the court. Thus, Áqásí thought to protect his future. The action may actually have borne some fruit, for two weeks later when the young sháh's regents made their first decisions and called the youth to rule, Áqásí lost only his job, not his head, and retired in disgrace to that same residence where, some years later, he died, an ugly and embittered old man.

The new sháh had a cruel facet of character that betrayed itself only occasionally in the early years of his reign but erupted in his maturity with a volcanic violence that spewed its hellish effects on whichever hapless subjects were in its path. I think, in retrospect, that he tried to be a good king, and indeed, he is remembered for a number of useful and humanitarian reforms.

However, Náṣiri'd-Dín Sháh had a first regent who later became his prime minister. His name was Mírzá Taqí Khán. To call him evil is no exaggeration and to say of the young sháh that he was ill-advised is to speak the literal truth. Despotic and cruel from the beginning, Khán acted often without consulting the crown. He was rigid and clever but not thoughtful, and, as a result, often moved impetuously, intending expedience but instead creating chaotic situations. It would be months and even years, of course, before all of this became apparent, and all I knew or thought of those first weeks after the sháh's death was the gossip of Muḥammad Sháh's diseased state that finished him, Hájí Mírzá Áqásí's disgrace, and the excitement of intrigue. Of the broader implications of the change in rule, I thought little, for my life, having centered around childbirth, cooking, and carrying water, had aroused in me, as yet, no interest in affairs of state.

The day of Náṣiri'd-Dín Sháh's coronation was a national holiday and a welcome day of picnicking and dancing, and had you asked me that morning what I thought the new sháh might have to do with my life, I might have thought of the opulence of his jewels and his vast power, and, contrasting all that with my simple life with my daughter in our one room, shrugged and said, "Nothing."

It would have been an answer from that childlike innocent self within me that, along with a number of people I held dear, was to perish soon in the bloodbath of the sixties.*

Fatima brought me a visitor one day about noon. He was a strapping young man of about sixteen or seventeen, and when he introduced himself as my nephew, my little sister's son, my eyes filled with tears. We spent a long time catching up on family history, and I was comforted to learn that my sister still lived and was content with her life. Khadijah and her cousin Ḥusayn were introduced, and the three of us talked together all through the lunch hour. . . . We served him sweet treats and, of course, tea. It seemed mysterious, as I look back on it now, that I should have first heard of the Báb through this stranger and relative who was passing through Tehran with a merchant on business. Perhaps I would not have then had I not asked, while lost for a moment in childhood memories, "Is Shiraz as beautiful as I remember?"

He frowned before he answered. "Yes . . . oh, yes, it is still the most beautiful city in the whole world, but . . ."

"But what?"

"It has become an unhappy city since the heretic came and upset everything."

"Heretic? What heretic?"

"You have not heard of that man some are calling the Báb . . . who claims to be (may Allah forgive me), the Qá'im?"**

"No, but surely one mere heretical fool could not . . ."

"Ah!" he interrupted, "but this 'one mere heretical fool' has been teaching his heresies with such persuasion that he has gathered around him hundreds, perhaps thousands, of followers."

---

* 1264–1267 A.H. (1847–1850 A.D.).

** Qá'im (Guy-eem). "He who warns"—a forerunner, or John the Baptist figure.

"Not thousands, surely. Just in Shiraz?"

"No-no, not just in Shiraz . . . all over . . . even here in Tehran there is some talk about him . . . but it all began in Shiraz. He kept a shop there—was a merchant like my employer. Then he just began teaching all his ideas, and . . ."

"What ideas?"

"I don't know . . . heretical ideas, but he is diabolic! The ideas spread like a disease. There are those who claim they've seen his followers spread the disease by a form of sorcery."

"How? Do they use spells, or charms, or what?"

"I don't know. I stay away from all of the talk as much as I can . . . I don't want to be too near them . . . I don't want to catch it, or whatever happens. Anyway, it all ought to die away soon. He's in prison where he belongs, and without him to do the magic, the followers will drift off."

"What if he can wield his sorcery from the prison?" This, from Khadijah.

My nephew shrugged. "He can't. Probably. It's too far away. They say he's way north of here even, near the Russian border. Anyway . . . it surely set Shiraz astir for awhile."

He left not long after, carrying a present for my sister, one of the few treasures I had saved from my little home, a ring with a bright red stone of some kind set in it and two small blue ones, one on either side.

Also there was a packet of tea from Khadijah to the aunt she had never known, and we had wrapped these in a pretty blue and gold silk scarf Khánum had given to me. I rehearsed him over again on the names of my children and what had happened to us, and I made him promise to bring word if ever he got back this way again.

Khadijah and I stood together, watching him walk away, and I thought again of my little sister and of how I had wept that departure morning so long ago. I wished I could go to see them all again: my mother, Uncle Firuz—dead, he had told us, these last three years—and my little sister, for in my mind they were all still there, just as they had always been—my mother especially—and I could see her in my mind's eye, squatting over the pan in the sunlight, her busy big-veined hands sorting the rice. I turned away from the sight of the gate where he had disappeared and said to Khadijah, "May the protection of Allah go with him." Before she turned back toward the logia leading to the work rooms, she asked me, "Mama, do you think he *can* send his sorcery and trap us?"

"What?" I asked her absently, my mind still on my family, "What are you asking?"

"The heretic. From the prison. Do you think . . ."

"Oh, that," I said. "No, I don't think so. I'm sure it's too far away." I smiled at her, and she went off comforted. To myself I added, *"I wonder what his ideas were, anyway."* But I thought it unwise to say that sort of thing aloud.

In the days that followed, I often caught myself thinking about the heretic, still curious to know if the things that drew the minds of men to heresy were sorcery as people said or, as I was beginning to suspect, the ideas themselves that worked a kind of magic of their own. I wished, for the first time in a long time, that I had a husband to ask, or that it would not be unseemly to speak to a mullah about it. "Well, I don't have, and I dare not ask," I lectured myself. "This is just one more trial in being left a widow, so make the best of it." I would forget about it then for a while, but inevitably, while falling asleep or mending for Khánum, I would think of it again. Sometimes while lying in the dark room at night with the soft sounds of Khadijah sleeping nearby, I would stare into the darkness, as if answers might appear on the black expanse of ceiling.

One night, while lying so, it occurred to me that the answers to all of it were probably readily available. The next time the Teacher came, I would ask her if such things were not written down somewhere. Surely, someone must know if there were truly sorcery or not . . . perhaps the Teacher herself knew and could tell me. I resolved to ask her, and the resolution alone made me feel so much better about it all that I put it from my mind almost as if the puzzle were already solved. I fell asleep immediately, and it was some weeks before I thought of it again.

When I did, it was during a walk with Fatima. We had some piles of old rags to carry the full length of the logia, and while we walked, a bird flew over our heads, and his shadow crossed Fatima's face. Quickly, I made a sign to ward off the arimani,* the evil spirits, and as I did so, I was re-

* Arimani are evil spirits or djinn (genie).

minded of this whole business of sorcery. I did not want to ask her about the magic, because she would no doubt think I was crazy, but thinking about it again reminded me of the heretic. "You hear about everything, Fatima," I said. "Have you heard anything about a heretic from Shiraz? My nephew told me about him. He says he claimed to be the Qá'im and so is in prison now and silenced. Have you heard of him?"

"Oh, yes, I've heard a little, just a little . . . what else did your nephew say about him?"

"Not much that I remember, only that they are saying in Shiraz that he put spells on people, and that is why so many people believed him." I halted momentarily and frowned at her. "What do you think about that?" She smiled and shrugged and strode on ahead of me.

"What do I think about what? The spells or his being the Qá'im?"

"About the magic, of course," I said, running to catch up. "If he were the Qá'im, the mullahs would know, and they wouldn't have put him in prison."

"You wouldn't think so. No, you certainly wouldn't think so. I wonder about it though, with thousands of people believing he is . . . maybe . . . "

"Oh, Fatima, he *couldn't* be." I said firmly, dismissing the thought. "I don't think he used magic, exactly, do you? I wonder what his ideas were that he taught, and why he was called 'the Báb' . . . that seems a strange title for a person . . . 'the Gate.'"

"Ah! Now that I do know about," Fatima said. "The promised Qá'im is to warn us just before the Judgment Day. He is the one through whom we are warned of the Qayyúm,* so since He Who is the Word of God is to come through the teachings of the Qá'im. He is called 'the Gate of God.'"

"Is that what he said . . . that the Qayyúm is coming?" My mouth dropped open.

"Well, yes. I'm only telling you what I've heard, now. The Báb says that One is coming Who is greater than he . . . the Lord of Judgment Day, Himself, the Lord of Hosts . . . He Whom God Will Make Manifest."

"The Return?!"

"Yes. That's what he says."

---

* Qayyúm (Guy-oom). "He who arises."

"Well, no wonder they silenced him!" I said with a short laugh. By now we had deposited our bundles and were standing outside in the sun. "Imprisoned him," Fatima corrected me as she moved off. "They imprisoned him, Shirin, but that doesn't mean they silenced him. Not yet."

That night as the sun set, I stood looking through the window and off toward the mountains of Mazindaran in the general direction of Russia. Somewhere up there, tucked in among the hills and hidden deeply within the haze of dusk was that prison, and inside it . . . dark-browed and fierce-looking, I imagined . . . was the heretic himself, conjuring up what kind of magic spells only Allah knew. I shuddered. Fatima's parting statement had frightened me a little. She seemed to think he could continue to influence people from inside the prison. Maybe there *was* some kind of magic that could reach out and capture people's minds. Yet there was still that other thought I had had. . . that ideas worked a magic of their own, but that hardly seemed likely either. Oh! This was confusing! I shook my head to clear it and went to be with Khadijah and the other women for a while. We played with the children, and laughed. Then we ate some sweets until it was time to put the little ones to bed.

Afterwards, there was some gossip about the household, and two of the women began to bicker. Soon most of the group had taken sides, and the rest of the evening was spent in polite talk and little jokes, but all of it was barbed and filled with angry innuendo, so I left early because I was growing more and more uncomfortable listening to it.

Later in bed, I thought of the prison again, and the confusion returned, and the fear. Suddenly it occurred to me that after only one day of thinking about the heretic and discussing him with Fatima, here I lay, confused and frightened. Could that be the effect of the magic? Still . . . ever since that first reading lesson, I had found myself suddenly thinking things I had never thought before, asking questions of the world around me, seeing the most familiar sights differently. Again I thought . . . *"there is something magic in the ideas themselves."* Immediately, I was struck again with the absurdity of the idea, and so back and forth the conflicting thoughts ran in my head, until I almost cried, "Oh! What is happening to my mind?"

Then I remembered my resolve to ask the teacher. I smiled and settled back, expecting sleep to come now, as it had before, but it did not.

Instead, my eyes flew open again with a sudden recognition. Ask the Teacher! It is the Teacher and her reading and all this thinking that is upsetting me! Perhaps the reading *is* wrong! Perhaps it *is* against the will of God. Men have always said that we ought not to tax our minds with education and thought, but I had always felt that I was smart enough to figure out anything, if someone would just tell me the details. Now here I was with details and more confused and frightened than ever in my life. Oh—I *would* try to read and write! Why couldn't I just mind my business and be content with my life as other women did, and not try to be something I wasn't? Look how peaceful and safe the early evening had been (well, before the argument began), when we had all been playing with the children. That, no doubt, is because it was the natural way for women to be. I was never like this when the children were small, when 'Alí Taqí was alive. He wouldn't have allowed it. He would have protected me from this confusion! Now at last I understood why he always used to grow so cross with my unfeminine directness and blunt manner. Why, his very last words to me were that I was too bold for a woman. What would he say of the reading lessons? Oh! He would be angry, and worse, ashamed of me. I could see him in my mind's eye looking down at me from Paradise, but his face was sad with his shame. I did not want him ashamed . . . or Uncle Firuz, either.

Suddenly breaking into my thoughts came the sounds of hoofbeats from out in the road, galloping up the main drive to the biruni and the banging of fists against the door accompanied by the cry of a man's voice, urgent and breaking in the clear cool night. "Abbas! Mírzá Abbas! In the name of Allah! Open the . . . " There was the rumble of men's voices as the house received the visitor, and then all was silent.

I lay with my stomach in a knot until, with a choke, I began to weep. I sat up in the dark, my arms hugging my knees with tears running down my face. Tomorrow, I would ask Khánum to request of Mírzá Abbas that he find for me a husband. Further, I resolved to give up the reading! It was all too much for me. I had had all I wanted of ideas and writing lessons and thinking . . . of questions and heretics and voices in the night! With all my heart, I wanted only to be back in the little house in the south of the city with my babies, tiny Khadijah, the little vanished Fatima who had died before I ever heard her say "Mama," and my bright laughing Hasan. It was the first time in months I had wept, and I fell asleep after a long time, hating myself, hating my widowhood, and hating it because I was alone and afraid.

3

SHIRIN: 1847

The confusion that in the middle of the night I had thought might destroy my reason spent its energy in my storm of grief and by daylight seemed again only interesting questions. When, in the morning, I thought of my vow to give up the reading and writing, I knew that, sinful or not, I would not keep it. As for marrying again . . . no. The sounds of birds chirping their welcome as I went to the well and the cool fresh odors of dawn helped me feel that not only was my world still in order but that I had much to be thankful for.

The cry of the night visitor, however, which I had already relegated to that collection of unexplained mysteries that seemed to be a part of this household, was quite a different matter. A good many of us had heard it, and at the well everyone was talking about it. There was a lot of guesswork and conjecture, but no one claimed to know anything, and the general opinion seemed to be that we would surely get the true story and all the details from the "Parrot" when she arrived on the scene. I was as anxious to question her as anyone but by noon had not yet seen her . . . which seemed a little out of the ordinary, for with that ubiquitous quality she had, she was usually within hailing distance. I assumed, however, that she was at work in another part of the estate and thought surely that Khadijah would have seen her and looked forward to having my daughter fill me in on all of it during lunch. But Khadijah had been as anxiously awaiting the lunch hour as I, thinking to get it all from me. When we joined the others, we found that no one had seen her all morning, and I began to wonder if she were ill. When it became apparent that no one had seen the Khánum either, we all became uneasy. It began to seem likely that Too-Tee's absence, Shaydah Khánum's seclusion, and the event in the middle of the night were connected.

Later that afternoon, Too-Tee appeared. We crowded around her asking if Shaydah Khánum were ill, but she reassured us on that score, saying that she was in with a headache but nothing more serious, and that she and Fareshteh had been in the bazaars all morning doing shopping for the household. She often went to the bazaars for as long as two or three hours, and we should have guessed where she was, but I think it was the eerie quality of the cry in the night that had set us all on edge and so caused us to react to her not at all mysterious absence with an unwarranted alarm. As for the night cry, not only had she not heard it, she said, she had not even heard *of* it, for she was busy with Khánum from dawn until she had left for the bazaars.

Of that outing she had much to say. Just as Fatima loved to gossip, she loved also being the center of attention and so was in her glory that afternoon as she imparted the news of what we came later to call the "Battle of Ṭabarsí."

In the beginning it was not a battle. The heretic, called the Báb, though safely confined in the prison far to the north was nevertheless, as Fatima had said the day before, not yet silenced at all. Two hundred and two of his followers had been set upon by government troops and were barricaded in a shrine miles to the north of Tehran, a shrine they were rapidly turning into a fort. She told us of how they had been marching together through the countryside, on their way to meet some companions, when suddenly a group of angry townsfolk armed with guns accosted them and began to call them ugly names. The Bábís, she said, stood and waited, neither drawing a sword nor responding to the insults, until at last the townsfolk fired upon them. Six of their number died, and still their leader, a young priest named Ḥusayn, cautioned them to wait. Then a number of more shots were fired, and a youthful Bábí was struck in the chest and died.

"Thou knowest that we cherish no other desire than to guide them to the way of Truth and to confer upon them the knowledge of Thy Revelation. Thou has Thyself commanded us to defend our lives against the assaults of the enemy," cried the young mullah, Ḥusayn, addressing the sky. And with that, Mullah Ḥusayn drew his sword, and the Bábís began to defend themselves.[1]

Mullah Ḥusayn, who had never fought before, being a quiet and studious young priest of twenty-five years, nonetheless quickly got the feel of battle and, angry from the pain of grief for the loss of his companions, headed directly for the man who had fired that last fatal shot. The man hid in fear behind a tree. Mullah Ḥusayn, with his sword in his left hand, attacked, and with one mighty sweep clove in two the tree, the man, and the musket![2]

Too-Tee acted out the story as she told it, and I was amused to see her large bulk, still swathed in the black chador she had worn to the bazaars, dancing about as if in battle herself while her skirts flowed gracefully to her body's leaps and turns. Her "sword arm" went sweeping from left to right, her voice rose and she puffed and grunted as she built toward the climax of her story. I dared not chuckle at her, however, for all of the others were listening in rapt attention, but I turned to Khadijah at the account of the cleaving of the tree and whispered, "Do you believe that?"

"No. No one could do that, could he?"

"I should think not."

But Fatima continued, saying that Mírzá Táqí Khán had not believed the account until the leader of the troops brought the evidence in the form of half of the musket. I confess I was impressed then and began to listen more closely. Mírzá Táqí Khán was, it seems, zealous in the name of the boy sháh and alarmed that Muḥammad Sháh and that fool, Áqásí, had allowed so many of the people to become "infected" with the heretical claim of the Báb. He believed it imperative in order to preserve both civil and ecclesiastical order that the Báb's heresies be thoroughly stamped out. Fatima explained to us that when the townsfolk of Barfarush had attacked the Bábís, the regent had dispatched troops—not to aid the luckless Bábís, but to reinforce the attackers. The followers of the Báb had fought when they had to and continued their journey when they could until they came to the Shrine of Shaykh Ṭabarsí, one of our Muslim saints, and there, hoping they might be safe in the shrine, made their stand. Others, hearing of their plight, had joined them until now there were, hidden behind the walls of their crude fortress, 313 students of the heretic.

After the uneasy morning, the gossip and speculation the story had aroused among the women came as a welcome distraction and seemed to relieve everyone's minds. Everyone's, except mine, that is, for the night had been for me too fraught with a number of emotions, and as I noticed this change in them, this quick switch from anxiety to excitement, I glanced toward Fatima and saw that she was watching the women closely. She was standing off to one side, she who loved the center of discussion, and observing the talking, the wondering, the expressions of anger and sympathy both for and against the heretics. She allowed this for a while, and then when it seemed to be at its height, she clapped her hands and called out, "Alright everyone! Enough talk. Enough wasting of time. Let us all return to our tasks. Allah knows our talking will not make one bit of difference to the Bábís *or* to the government. Come, come, back to work." She watched a moment more and then turned and left the yard and disappeared into Khánum's apartment, but not before she had glanced my way, and in that instant following the moment of watching her watching us, I understood that her performance had been just that. The whole thing, the story of the Bábís and their flight to Ṭabarsí and the story of Mullah Ḥusayn and his courageous swordplay, while probably true enough, was nevertheless told to us deliberately to take our minds from the morning's discomfort.

Too-Tee's playacting and her dramatic storytelling had been used by her to avoid telling us about the midnight intrusion just, I also realized, as the questions I had asked about the weeping lady traveler who had shared my room and who was gone by daylight had not been answered, not at all because she had suddenly remembered an errand for Khánum, but because she had not wished to answer. All the night noises, all the strange incidents, all the unanswered questions I had been gathering for months and dismissing as unimportant were not unimportant at all. They were not happenstance; they were not coincidence; they were connected to each other, and Fatima knew their meaning. Now, as she turned before entering Khánum's apartment, her eyes met mine over her drawn black veil, and I could see that she knew I understood all this.

In the light of the deepening friendship between us, I felt almost guilty that I had guessed her secret and for a moment wanted to run to her and reassure her that it was safe with me, but she probably knew that anyway. At any rate, the impulse died as she turned away. So stunned was I by the impact of this realization that I stood rigid until she was gone. It was only after I had come to myself and was walking back along the logia that it occurred to me that I did not know her secret at all, because the secret was not that she said and did things to distract us . . . the secret, of course, was why.

* * *

As the days went by, the stories of the siege continued to come to us, for all of the northern provinces became interested, and the news traveled from local bazaar to local bazaar, by mule-back and on foot through the tales and stories of travelers. Sometimes we would get one account one day, and the opposite the next. But somehow Too-Tee had a way of sifting wheat from chaff, I suppose because she had heard and related enough gossip in her lifetime to know truth from falsehood, the way some people know where water can be found underground or feel the presence of evil upon entering a room.

There was a story from Barfarush. The mullah had stood in his pulpit and roused the townsmen to a pitch of religious fervor and then sent them out to arm themselves and attack the Bábís when they came through and destroy them as "evil destroyers of Islam."

"If they *are* trying to destroy Islam, then they *are* evil, are they not, Mama?" Khadijah asked me that evening at supper.

"Well, yes, of course . . . *if* they are truly trying to destroy Islam. But according to Fatima, they believe themselves to be heralding the Herald of God . . . The Lord of Judgment Day, Himself."

"You don't believe that, do you, Mama?"

No, Khadijah, not for a moment, but *they* believe it and that, I think, makes them not so evil. What do you think?" I confess that my interest in her opinion stemmed from a need to compare my own with someone else's. The reading lessons, the effect of the teacher on my mind, had set me to giving voice to ideas and opinions that in the past, I would have kept to myself, partly because I had learned the hard way not to "have" too many ideas, lest they be poorly received and I be told I was speaking out of turn; partly too, because my ideas these days were coming to me so rapidly it was almost as though some voice spoke them into my head . . . they surprised me so with their sudden appearances, and I wanted to see if others ever agreed with me.

"I suppose they *do* believe that. I suppose that to be wrong if you believe yourself to be right is not the same thing as evil."

"Then," I said, "the townspeople are not evil either, are they?"

"No" she responded, "of course not. They are only obeying the mullah . . . and the mullah would not tell them to do evil."

That, of course, I knew to be true, and so was, again, lost in confusion. "It's all very mixed up, isn't it?" I asked Khadijah. She nodded in agreement, but I could see that she had already lost interest and turned her attention to her own thoughts. *When we are very young,* I thought, *if a danger does not threaten our own selves, it does not really exist.* But I needed someone to discuss it with. I wished the Teacher would hurry and come to us. There was so much I wanted to ask her. I asked Fatima when she thought the Teacher might come, and she said, "Soon, I hope." But that was all I could get out of her about it. We heard also that the Bábís were still in the Fort, and that the prince-regent of the Mazindaran area had led his troops to camp near there, presumably to stay until the Bábís tired of hiding and came out. But as the weeks went by, we all but forgot about it in the soothing stream of dailiness.

For me, the high point of those days was when, at last our teacher came. I learned that she was called Ṭáhirih* and that she was socially prominent and of a wealthy family in Qazvin. Not only was she able to read and to teach us, she was a poetess as well. I had adored her from that first afternoon when she opened to me the gate of learning, but I had then no

---

* The account given here of Shirin's conversation with Ṭáhirih is fictional and based only on what is known of Ṭáhirih's personality.

idea of who she was, or that she was widely renowned for her beauty, intelligence, and poetry throughout Persia. I think I had somehow thought of her as my own . . . much as a child regards his mother as his personal property, though he may be one of eight children. My adoration had confined itself, however, to a mute worship and a burning desire to learn rapidly—for my own sake, yes, but also to make her proud, to vindicate her faith in my ability and make her efforts on my behalf worthwhile.

The "ideas" that had sometimes tortured my thoughts and disturbed my sleep continued their worrisome appearances. Further, the stories of the Bábís and of the mullahs, the perpetration of the heresies of the imprisoned Báb upon the minds of men at every level of society, which I had earlier dismissed as bothersome though curiously exciting nonsense, were beginning to affect the whole population of Tehran, and indeed much of the country. My confusion as to which, if either, faction was guilty of evil, together with my penchant for disturbing contradictions of thought about my learning and reading and writing, finally drove me to approach her one day as we were resting during a break in our lessons.

She sat alone on a small bench placed in the shade, beneath a fruit tree. I walked to within a dozen paces of her and stopped, unsure if I should disturb her rest. Struck, as always, by her loveliness, I stood watching her, frankly staring I suppose, as I attempted to discover the secret of her beauty. She had a lovely flawless complexion, except for the little mole, so much a mark of beauty I know now, that all over Europe women were affecting them. All about the courtyard women chattered, laughing and teasing, their voices blending into a soft buzzing except for a shrill note now and then, or a sound of jealous pique rising for an instant above the feminine chorus. Here in the peace of the shade she sat; serene, dignified and alone . . . yet somehow not alone, for there seemed to emanate from her some indefinable presence of another, as though she carried in her bosom the knowledge and memory of a lover . . . a lover who she knew would never leave her bereft or betray her trust, yet a lover free in his loving, not caught in the imprisoning web of his own hungry and clutching adoration. Still, this was not all of it. There was yet some other quality I could sense but not name. All of this radiated from her, and I was struck again, as I was that first time I saw her with, what in spite of her exquisite femininity, I can only call "power." She looked up and saw me then and smiling, beckoned me over.

I took one more step forward and paused. I think I may have even opened my mouth to speak, but no words came. A shyness overtook me that was greater than my confused mind and driving curiosity, greater than with my first impression of Khánum. My adoration of this woman, who somehow appeared able to do anything and seemed unafraid of kings, overcame me completely, and like a timid child, I shook my head no and moved away.

Later, in bed after Khadijah had fallen asleep, I thought again of my confused emotional state and was angry at myself for my foolish withdrawal. *Why* had I not asked her what I wanted so very much to know? *Why* had I forfeited my only opportunity to learn what my heart needed so desperately to understand? Weeping with annoyance and regret, I fell into a restless sleep.

Sometime in the night, I found myself as though back in the courtyard in the midst of a sunny day. The colors of sky and trees were so brilliant as to be almost iridescent. It seemed someone commanded me to walk, and soon the brilliance faded to a muggy grey, and I found myself walking through a cold and damp mist toward a dim light ahead that barely penetrated the fog. As the light grew plainer, I saw Ṭáhirih seated on the same bench as earlier in the day. With her presence, the light grew bright. I stopped. She smiled. "You must never be afraid to speak your heart, Shirin, least of all to me." With that, my timidity was gone.

"I don't like to intrude on your privacy."

She made a deprecating gesture and asked me to speak my mind.

"It is just my mind I wish to ask about. Since I've been reading the lessons, and Fatima and I talk a good deal with each other . . . so we trade ideas about the verses and the poems . . . sometimes I think . . . well, at night often, I find myself . . . oh, the strangest thoughts, and . . . " I was struggling so, but she was silent and patient, and soon I had unraveled the worst of the tangles and was able to put into words, the gist of the conflicts about good and evil, and the terrible need in me to learn; the curiosity; the yearning for other places that had almost put me in tears over the toys by the door in Shiraz; that had consumed me on the journey to Tehran so many years ago; the need to *know* that had burst forth in the blurted remarks that had so troubled 'Alí Taqí. I began to weep as I told her of my fears in the night; that I knew it was wrong to be so unladylike, to be plagued with this wish . . . and found the courage, at last, to ask about the Báb and his heresies, sheepishly confessing my fears that maybe his magic was behind my new confusion.

She listened to all of it with a grave and kindly look, and in her eyes there burned a warm flame of understanding. "Shirin," she said at last, "you are not mad; you are intelligent. You long to know because you have a mind. And as for your sense of longing—that comes from your soul, it seeks its home and will search through all creation until . . . "

In my agitation I interrupted her, "But we are women! How can we search for our souls' homes if, as the mullahs tell us, we have no souls?"

"Tell me, then: how can you be so fearful of being evil, if you have no soul?" It was as though a prison door had opened. I stood shocked into silence by the obvious.

"Then the mullahs are . . . mistaken?"

She smiled.

"Then what of the Bábís? Are the mullahs mistaken about them, too?"

"Remember, Shirin," she said, "the mullahs are only human beings."

"But he claims to be the Qá'im! . . . the Mahdí!"

"Yes, he does."

"But the mullahs say he is not! If *they* cannot be trusted to tell us who is, and who is not the Qá'im . . . then who can?"

She studied me for a moment and then said quietly, "The Qá'im can. Who else could possibly know?"

At the back of my tongue I felt another question trying to be born, but lost it when she said to me, "Shirin, do not be fearful of your yearnings but go courageously, and when you will have journeyed three long and sorrowful journeys, your soul will find her home."

I awoke in the morning with her words on my lips, and so real seemed that dream that I could not banish it, but heard her voice in my mind throughout that whole long day.

As the days passed and lengthened into weeks, the effect of the dream faded somewhat, but I never once questioned Ṭáhirih's ability to know my future. Where three journeys could possibly lead me, I had no idea, nor any clue, as to where or even why I might ever leave the estate of Mírzá Abbas.

Life was, for me, in the next months, peaceful as I worked and studied Koran and poetry, talked with Khánum, Khadijah, and Fatima. With Fatima especially my comradeship grew. We never mentioned the silent look that had passed between us the day of her playacting, though the subject of the Bábís was on everyone's mind from time to time.

The work kept us all very busy that winter of 1848. It seemed that the home of Mírzá Abbas housed more guests than ever. The biruni was often the center of activity, and I fell asleep often to the sounds of male noises drifting faintly from there in the crisp nights.

* * *

Suddenly, in the early summer of my thirty-fifth year, my world exploded. All the simplicity of my life disappeared. I had always known hardship, and known as well the loss of family and husband . . . the loss of my darling Hasan . . . but even in those griefs, rending my heart with sorrow and coloring my hours with a sense of darkness, I was not at a loss as to what to do. Life went on in its reasonable and predictable way. Though I had often been frightened, I had never felt helpless, for the knowledge that all was in the hands of Allah had given me courage and my love and duty to Khadijah had given me purpose. I had thought that whatever life held for me that, at least, would remain constant.

To begin with . . . Mírzá Abbas, whom I had come to believe was the soul of goodness, did something I had not thought he would do. He bought a slave. The slave came to the estate, and it was through him that we finally learned the full story of the battle of Ṭabarsí, for he had been there! I caught a glimpse of him once or twice. Khadijah and I were very curious to see what a Bábí looked like. I don't know that I expected them to look very different from anyone else, but I was curious all the same. He looked thin and worn from a year of near starvation and the siege. I expected him to be half-mad with sorrow over his lost companions and the humiliation of defeat, but he was not. I longed to speak with him myself, to ask him what the Báb was like and what his heretical ideas were, and how he ever became convinced of their truth . . . but of course, he never came near the women's quarters.

But, as one might expect, somehow Too-Tee got the whole story and told it one night to a small group of us: Fareshteh, Khadijah, me and a couple of others were in my room, seated in a circle on the carpet, gathered around the samovar, drinking tea and nibbling on some fruit. Too-Tee had been sitting quietly, not quite her garrulous self, and I inquired if she were perhaps feeling ill. At first she said, "No," but after she caught me looking at her again when we had all laughed at a remark of Khadijah's—all but she, that is—she admitted that her heart was somewhat heavy, for she had heard that day, she said, the full story of Ṭabarsí.

"You mustn't feel too sorry for the heretics," remarked a woman named Ghazal, "especially if they are enemies of Islam."

"Maybe they're not," interjected Khadijah, "maybe they are merely mistaken in their belief. After all, if the Báb weaves magic spells. . . . "

"I don't think they are spells," I said, "I think they are ideas. Ideas have great power, I find, all by themselves. Maybe the Bábís . . . but never mind. Tell us what happened, Fatima."

"Whether the Bábís are heretical or not," she responded, "when you hear, I think you will feel for them too. Are you sure you want to hear it? It is a very disturbing account."

"Yes. Oh yes," we all chorused, thinking only to while away an evening with a little excitement. We refreshed our tea, took up a fig or an apricot, and settled down to be entertained. Soon, lulled by the sound of Too-Tee's voice, we were carried off to the forest of Mazindaran, where, some on horseback, some on foot, we found ourselves marching through the trees with the Bábís.

But it was instead of a little excitement, a tale of heroism and love, of betrayal and death, that drew upon my heart a picture of both dedication and savagery such as I had not known could live in human breasts.

"Muḥammad, the new slave, "Fatima began, "was there. He was, to begin with, one of only a few of the 313 who hid there, first from the persecutors and later from the prince's troops, who lived. They are nearly all dead now." We sobered at that statement and began to listen in earnest.

* * *

"You remember that day, last year, when I told you of how they had been set upon by the people of Barfarush, and of how the young mullah, Ḥusayn-i-Bushrui, led them, after seven deaths, into battle?" We all nodded.

"I remember," said Khadijah. "You showed us how he chopped in two a man, a musket, and a tree. But I didn't believe you at first."

"That," said Fatima, "is understandable, but it is true. He did. The more amazing part is that most of the Bábís were either young students or old Koranic scholars, and Mullah Ḥusayn himself was a pale, erudite young priest who had never held a sword. According to the slave Muḥammad, his hand trembled as he rode to his first battle.

"After the townspeople had been dispatched, the Bábís rode northeast, where they were attacked again."

"Why?" asked Puran,* a childlike little woman, though I think she was older than I.

"Because they were flying a black standard!"

"A black standard?" Khadijah asked, turning to me.

"A sign of the coming Qá'im," Fatima answered her. "When the Lord of the Age arrives, tradition says He will fly a black standard."

"No wonder they got attacked, then," someone remarked. "Usurping a tradition is a very dangerous business."

"Worse," I agreed, "to be dishonest with the things of God is more than merely dangerous; it is blasphemous. But go on, Fatima," I said, for she had fallen silent and was picking at a loose thread in her shawl. "What happened next?"

"They arrived at a shrine that was named for a Shaykh named Ṭabarsí, who was buried there, and decided to take shelter inside, pray for protec-

* Poor-on.

tion, and wait. As they entered the courtyard, the keeper of the shrine greeted them. Seeing Mullah Ḥusayn, he fell at his feet, for it seemed the very night preceding, he had dreamt that the prince among Martyrs, the Imam Ḥusayn, had arrived at the shrine with a band of followers and remained there throughout a great battle during which they had met martyrs' deaths. In his dream, the long-ago-martyred Imam looked exactly like Mullah Ḥusayn. The caretaker begged to be allowed to join the little band, and so, after explaining to him the claims of the Báb and warning him that all must be prepared to die in the coming days, they welcomed him to their ranks. The date was October 12, 1848.

"Immediately, they commenced to build fortifications outside the shrine, to protect themselves from a surprise attack," Fatima said.

"They built a fort," I said.

"Yes, and it turned out to be a well-taken decision, as that very evening a group of horsemen came from a nearby village and began to taunt the Bábís, announcing that they were there to avenge one of the men who had died in the earlier struggles, and that they would not retreat until all of the Bábís were dead.

"A number of the company drew their swords and, loudly invoking the Lord of the Age, leaped forward on foot to engage the horsemen. The Bábís were so fierce that the horsemen fled. A man named Nauar Khán asked to be allowed to meet their leader, Mullah Ḥusayn. Khán joined the Bábís in their devotions and afterward was introduced to Mullah Ḥusayn. He inquired of the Bábís as to who they were and why they were there, and when he had heard the story of the Báb and the plight of his followers, he accepted the Báb as the Qá'im and hurried back to his village to gather provisions for the group encamped in the shrine."

I thought, as I listened, that it was the courage and courtesy of the heretic's followers that was attracting men to his cause far more than sorcery, though I said nothing but continued to listen as Fatima warmed to her recital.

She resumed, "The building of walls and postern gates and the digging of emergency tunnels proceeded. For days, the little group labored to make their refuge a place of strength and safety, but every few days, they would be again attacked by people of neighboring villages who, at the persistent instigations of the mullahs, marched out and fell upon them. Laying aside their building, the Bábís each time would defend themselves and drive off their attackers, resuming construction when the villagers had been repulsed.

"At last they were finished, and they raised the same black standard that had curled above their heads as they had traveled from Badasht to Barfarush and through the forests of Mazindaran to the Shrine of Ṭabarsí. There it flew for the next eleven months, while beneath its long and fluttering folds, the Bábís prayed and fought, starved, and died.

"Meanwhile, the Sa'ídu'l-'Ulamá' who had been inciting the people to harass the little group was growing concerned. The repeated attempts to drive them from their shelter and interrupt and prevent the completion of the fortress were meeting with little success. Indeed, now and then even a member of the harassing rabble, upon seeing the courage, the spirit, and the joy of the Bábís, would desert his companions and ask to join the growing band. So the number of Bábís swelled until at last there were 313.

"The Sa'ídu'l 'Ulamá' sent word to Náṣiri'd-Dín Sháh that these heretics had every intention of winning as many converts to their cause as possible, that already a number of whole nearby villages had joined them, and that when the heretics' number grew large enough, their intention, he felt sure, was to direct a campaign against the sháh, proclaim themselves independent of his sovereignty, bringing great disgrace upon the hereditary crown. 'The standard of revolt,' he pleaded, 'has been raised by the contemptible sect of the Bábís. . . . what greater triumph could signalize the inauguration of your rule than to extirpate this hateful creed that has dared to conspire against you?'"[3]

"One of the sháh's advisors assured him that a small detachment could completely subjugate the Bábís in two days. The sháh gave his consent, and the long siege began.

"The sháh's troops stationed themselves in the small village of Afra, which commanded a view of the fort, and their first move was to intercept the food that was daily being sent to the fort by their well-wisher, Nauar Khán. Then the fort's water supply was also cut off.

"On the day the fortress had been completed under the leadership of Mullah Ḥusayn, there arrived his dear friend and companion scholar,

Quddús. Immediately upon Quddús's arrival, Mullah Ḥusayn surrendered his leadership of the band, and Quddús assumed the responsibility. When the water supply was gone, Quddús turned to Mullah Ḥusayn at sunset and said, 'The scarcity of water has distressed our companions. God willing, this very night a downpour of rain will overtake our opponents, followed by a heavy snowfall, which will assist us to repulse their contemplated assault.'[4]

"And so it happened. The Bábís set out all they could find as containers and caught the torrential rain that fell in the night, while Ábdu'lláh Khán's troops were surprised in their tents, and most of their ammunition was ruined. The following night, an early snowfall such as was almost never experienced until mid-winter further played havoc with the encamped army.

"Nevertheless, Ábdu'lláh Khán's troops continued their preparations for the attack. As they were ready to launch their first assault, Quddús mounted his horse and, accompanied by Mulla Ḥusayn and three others also on horseback, rode sedately out of the fort followed by the rest of the company on foot. Together they cried, 'Yá Ṣaḥibu'z-Zamán!'* ('Oh Thou Lord of the Age!') and the sound of it, filled with confidence, joy and their willingness to die if God willed it, rang through the morning air, striking fear into the hearts of the sháh's troops. The troops, lying in hiding to surprise the unwary Bábís, leaped up and ran away in every direction. In forty-five minutes, the first battle was over. Ábdu'lláh Khán himself, two of his officers, and some 430 of his men were dead.

"Some of Quddús's men would have gone in pursuit, but he called them back to the fort, saying, 'We have repulsed the assailants; we need not carry further the punishment. Our purpose here is to protect ourselves that we may be able to continue our labors for the regeneration of men. We have no intention whatever of causing unnecessary harm to anyone. What we have already achieved is sufficient testimony to God's invincible power. We, a little band of His followers, have been able, through His sustaining grace, to overcome the organized and trained army of our en-

---

* Ya Sa-heeb-oo-Zha-man!

emies.' Of the Bábís, one man only was badly wounded, and none had died."[4]

"None?' asked Puran in an incredulous tone.

"None," replied Too-Tee. "For the next nineteen days, Muḥammad has told us, the defenders spent the daylight hours digging a moat around the outside of the fort to discourage attempts to scale the walls. Laughing and singing, they worked with the joy of lovers, he said, even then knowing that probably death would be the only end of all this.

"Prince Mihdi Quli, one of Náṣiri'd-Dín Sháh's half-brothers, arrived with an army and camped on a hill nearby. The prince sent a man to the fort to ascertain the purpose of the Bábís.

"Mullah Ḥusayn replied, 'Tell your master that we utterly disclaim any intention either of subverting the foundations of the monarchy or of usurping the authority of Náṣiri'd-Dín Sháh. . . . Let the prince direct the 'ulamás of both Sárí and Bárfurush to betake themselves to his place, and ask us to demonstrate the validity of the Revelation proclaimed by the Báb. Let the Qur'án decide as to who speaks the truth. Let the prince himself judge our case and pronounce the verdict. Let him also decide as to how he should treat us if we fail to establish, by the aid of verses and traditions, the truth of this Cause.'[5]

"The messenger promised that within three days this would be done. Instead, on the morning of the third day, the prince gave the signal to three regiments of infantry and several regiments of cavalry to open fire upon the fort.

"From inside the walls, the voice of Quddús called out, 'Mount your steeds, O heroes of God!' and the gates of the fort swung open.[5] Part of the prince's army had built barricades not far from the fort, and Quddús and a group of men advanced upon those to defend the fort from the attackers. The prince directed his operations from the safety of a nearby village. Riding into their camp, Mullah Ḥusayn and his companions completely surprised the enemy, and when the prince saw what was happening, he jumped out a window and ran off barefooted into the snowy woods."

We all smiled at the picture of the barefooted prince.

"The entire group was put to flight, leaving the village quarters empty of soldiers. In the prince's apartment were chests filled with silver and gold, but they left it all as they had found it and returned to the fort.

"Mullah Ḥusayn rode up just in time to see Quddús bleeding from a wound in the mouth. Quddús tossed his sword to his friend, and with a sword in each hand, the intrepid priest-turned-defender fought on, while Quddús was borne back to the fort by his men.

"So the weeks wore on. The little band had now been under siege for three months."

"Three months!" one of the women said in an awed tone.

"Three months was only the beginning," Fatima responded. "One morning in early February, Mullah Ḥusayn announced to the company that this was the day of his martyrdom; this day he would lay down his life for the cause of God. Performing his ritual ablutions, and wrapping around his head the green turban, the sign of the covenant of Muḥammad given to him by his beloved Master, the Báb, Mullah Ḥusayn went off to a corner of the fort to pray. When he returned, he called for those who might wish to join him for his last battle. Accompanied by a goodly number of companions, he mounted his horse and, armed only with his sword and a dagger, and crying out once again his ringing invocation to the Lord of the Age, he rode out to face the cannon and musketry of the prince's thousands.

"There were seven groups of the prince's men, each behind a wooden barricade, firing guns and cannon at Mullah Ḥusayn and his companions. He charged into first one barricade, then another and then another. With each charge, he dispatched a number of the enemy and routed others, who left their cannons and made off into the forest. Shouting, wheeling, turning, Mullah Ḥusayn rode and slashed, oblivious to the rain of bullets that fell like hailstones around him. Seven separate barricades saw his galloping approach and heard his battle cry as, one after another, he engaged the soldiers of the prince.

"Then suddenly, the moment came. His horse's foot became entangled in a tent rope. In the seconds that passed as he attempted to become free, one of the prince's soldiers took careful aim from where he was hiding in a tree, and shot Mullah Ḥusayn full in the breast. A minute or so later he fell from his horse, exhausted and bleeding. His companions lifted him to his horse and bore him back to the fort. Weeping, they laid him at the feet of Quddús. Quddús asked to be left alone with him, and, believing him to be dead, they withdrew in grief.

"One of the men, however, peeked through a crack in the wall and was surprised to see Mullah Ḥusayn respond to Quddús' call by rising to a sitting position and answering. For two hours the two friends, the thirty-six-year-old dying priest, the first to have accepted the Báb as the Promised One, and the twenty-seven-year-old scholar, the last and most learned of the eighteen original disciples of the Báb, talked together.

"Near the end, Mullah Ḥusayn was heard to cry out, whether to Quddús, or to the spirit of the Báb who lay in the prison to the north, no one knows, 'May my life be a ransom to you! Are you well pleased with me?'[7] A moment later he was dead. Quddús, weeping, kissed him tenderly upon the brow, and invited the others to see the remains of their dead companion. He lay with a smile of contentment on his face and was buried that day with his fallen comrades."

By now, my little room was silent, save for the song of the Parrot as she wove the tale of the beleaguered heretics and, with her storytelling skill, unfolded before us the strange and dramatic events. Beneath our hands the fruit lay untouched, and the only sound other than Fatima's voice was the occasional click of a glass as one of us helped herself to more tea and the soft bubbling of the simmering tea water. Outside the night came to its full darkness, the tiny creatures of evening fell silent, and through the door the rising moon cast a shaft of pale light tracing a path across the storyteller's lap and from there to the samovar, where its reflection in the polished brass made a warm and golden glow in the darkened room. Drawn hypnotically to the dull light, all five of us stared at it as we sat in our silent circle.

Fatima had heard the story through the tales of Muḥammad, the slave. He had told of the eight months yet remaining in the Battle of Ṭabarsí. Eight long months of increasing hardship, of starvation and illness in the cold of winter and of a last final betrayal, all repeated to us that night by Fatima.

"Quddús gathered the pitiful band of Bábís inside the most sheltered room of the shrine. In a mixture of grief for their lost friends and exaltation at the unqualified success of Mullah Ḥusayn's last foray, they listened as he warned them of the future: 'Whoever feels himself strong enough to withstand the calamities that are soon to befall us, let him remain with us in this fort. And whoever perceives in himself the least hesitation and fear, let him betake himself away from this place. Let him leave immediately ere the enemy has again assembled his forces and assailed us. The way will soon be barred before our face; we shall very soon encounter the severest hardship and fall a victim to devastating afflictions.'"[8]

"For forty-five days, during the worst of the mid-winter cold, all was quiet. The prince's army retrenched and shivered in their tents. Even though they made no attempts to harass the Bábís, still they saw to it that the supply lines remained cut.

"When one day the prince heard of the death of Mullah Ḥusayn, he crowed with anticipation; with the lionhearted defender removed, he believed he could finish off the campaign and go home. With two regiments of cavalry and infantry, fifteen hundred troops, he surrounded the fort.

"Quddús called for a mere eighteen men to 'sally out and . . . administer a befitting chastisement upon the aggressor and his host. Let him realize that though Mullah Ḥusayn is no more, God's invincible power still continues to sustain his companions and enable them to triumph over the forces of their enemies.' The eighteen men, crying Mullah Ḥusayn's old cry to the Lord of the Age, raced out of the gates and into the camp of the enemy, dispersing them until they broke up completely and ran off in every direction. Their leader galloped into the village and, leaping in fear from his horse, left one boot dangling in the stirrup, and ran off to safety, limping on one boot and one stocking foot."[9]

There was the sound of muted chuckling in the listening circle.

"There came then, new armies with new leaders. Again a mere eighteen defenders drove them off. Then again thirty-six routed the enemy. The prince's troops constructed towers outside the four corners of the fort and arming them with cannon, fired down into the courtyard. The Bábís attempted to hide in their tunnels, but the rains had flooded them and turned the courtyard to mud, and in the days that followed, their clothes rotted until they were covered with little but filthy rags.

"One of the defenders had brought with him his little ten-year-old son. His name was Aqa Siyyid Ḥusayn, but he came to be called 'the beloved' by all of the Bábís. Bravely, the little fellow was obedient and happy-spirited, and in those unbelievably trying days, did whatever he could to help. His father was shot in the hand, and as the little boy rushed over to attempt to staunch the bleeding, a persecutor's bullet found its mark and he rolled over in the mud and gore, his little limbs quivering in death.

"During the nights, then, the Bábís built the walls higher so that the prince's towers were no longer effective. Burning brands were thrown over the newly-extended walls, and the little shelters built by the unskilled hands of the band of students and scholars burned away.

"The time was growing short. The Bábís were so hungry they were reduced to cooking and eating their saddles, their scabbards, and finally their shoes. When all that was gone, they ate the fresh spring grass growing up just outside the postern gates.

"Still, there were daily attacks by the troops. For eighteen days, there was no rain and little water. Each Bábí took a swallow of water in the morning and lay exhausted with hunger and thirst all day until they were attacked. Then, leaping to their feet, they fought with courage and energy born of their devotion to God, until the attack was repulsed, whereupon they would again lie down.

"Finally, they were reduced to grinding the bones of dead horses, making a kind of flour paste and eating that. Heartbroken, they ate their bone-flour, mixed with the cooked flesh of the disinterred horse of Mullah Ḥusayn's that had died of wounds in the same battle as he, and which they had buried out of their respect for its courage and loyalty.

"At last the prince himself, thoroughly embarrassed at his inability to rout the stubborn and stout-hearted defenders, and disgraced in the eyes of the boy sháh, requested a conference with the Bábís. The date was May 9, 1849. Quddús sent two of his companions to meet with the prince. They arrived at his tent and were courteously received and offered tea.

They declined, saying they could not take refreshment of any kind while their companions lay exhausted with starvation and thirst. The prince picked up his Koran and wrote in the fly leaf:

> 'I swear by this most Holy Book, by the righteousness of God Who has revealed it and the Mission of Him who was inspired with its verses, that I cherish no other purpose than to promote peace and friendliness between us. Come forth from your stronghold, and rest assured that no hand will be stretched forth against you. You, yourself and your companions, I solemnly declare, are under the sheltering protection of the Almighty, of Muḥammad, His Prophet, and of Náṣiri'd-Dín Sháh, our sovereign. I pledge my honor that no man, either in this army or in this neighborhood, will ever attempt to assail you. The malediction of God, the omnipotent Avenger, rest upon me if in my heart, I cherish any other desire than that which I have stated.'[10]

"The prince signed it and affixed his seal. When Quddús received the Koran, he kissed it and called upon God to decide between them with His justice. Then he told his companions it was time to leave, for 'by our response to their invitation,' he told them, 'we shall enable them to demonstrate the sincerity of their intentions.'

"Quddús now prepared himself, as Mulla Ḥusayn had before him, by praying and wrapping about his head the green turban presented to him by the Báb, and leading the 212 survivors of the original 313 who had endured the long months of siege against armies of thousands. He mounted the prince's horse (loaned to him for the occasion), and rode, for the last time, through the gates of Fort Ṭabarsí."

Fatima's voice was growing hoarse after the long hours of talking, and the night was wearing thin. The crescent moon, which earlier had shown through the door in its rising, had crossed the sky and now was beginning to drop its lower horn into my western window, and in the east, the first faint darklessness was brushing the top of Mírzá Abbas's courtyard wall. The flame beneath the samovar had long ago gone out, and I became aware that my feet were numb with cold and my legs chilled to my knees. Fatima coughed to relieve her tired throat, and Khadijah finally broke the silence. "I thought you said that they mostly all died, Fatima."

"I did," Fatima responded. "The prince's promise was not kept; oh no, not kept at all. In less than twenty-four hours, the Bábís were being shot from cannons, tied to trees, and used for target practice by mounted horsemen. Some were sold into slavery, as was Muḥammad here, and some were disembowled to the howling amusement of the soldiers, because when they ripped their bellies open with swords, there fell out small piles of undigested grass."

I felt a roaring anger arising from the very marrow of my being. At the treacherous prince and his savage and heartless soldiers yes, but after all, one grows to expect cruelty from men whose business is killing, but the mullahs, the men of God whose business is virtue—my anger began to settle upon them with a silent vehemence, and especially, I think, upon the Sa'ídu'l-'Ulamá', to the likes of whom we had, all of us for generations, entrusted the eternal well-being of our souls.

From across the circle came Fareshteh's voice broken with emotion, "And Quddús? What was the fate of that noble youth? Do you know, Fatima?"

Fatima was silent a moment and then she said, "Yes, I know. He had grown up in Barfarush, and so the next day he was taken in chains back to his hometown. For three days he was imprisoned, while no less than the Sa'ídu'l-'Ulamá' himself incited the townspeople to a frenzy of hatred with lies and threats, urging them to 'righteous action' against the prisoner. The next day he was marched through the streets, barefooted and bareheaded while the women of the streets were encouraged to spit upon him and torture him. Down the very streets his now dead mother had longed to see him some day parade to claim his bride, he was paraded now in chains. The crowd began to hack at him with knives and daggers, spitting and throwing dung at him. He cried out, 'Would that my mother were with me, and could see with her own eyes the splendor of my nuptials!'

"At these words, the screaming inflamed mob grew yet bolder! First one arm was hacked from him, then another, until he sank in a heap upon the ground, while he gave up his legs to the mob! During his torture, he was heard to whisper, "Forgive, Oh my God, the trespasses of this people. Deal with them in Thy mercy, for they do not yet know what we have discovered and cherish.'"*

"At last the remaining members of his poor mutilated body were thrown into a fire. Sometime during the night, a friend tenderly gathered his severed remains and hid them for a respectful burial."

---

* This account is taken from Nabíl-i-A'ẓam, *The Dawn-Breakers*, pp. 329–413.

4

SHIRIN: 1850

I have said that my world exploded. The first pieces from its shattering fell that night with the tale of Ṭabarsí. My realization, sometime earlier during my dream with Ṭáhirih that the mullahs were—like the rest of us—prone to error, lit the fuse, as it were. But it was this discovery, begun during those troubled and wakeful nights, of a sense of my own self as apart from the circumstances of my life that had enabled that fuse to burn. When I heard the story of betrayal—the foul treatment of that brave and earnest band by the clergy—and realized that men and women all over Persia, not to mention Iraq and Turkey and Arabia, had lived lives of service to the wishes of that same clergy, and that my life and the lives of all other women throughout the world of Islam were determined in more ways than not by the whims of these men, my anger became a great pressure in my head and breast.

I resolved never again to have anything to do with religion. God? Yes, Allah, the Merciful, is good and forever beyond the corruption of His servants, but now that I was learning to study Koran for myself, I knew that beyond the words in its pages, as my prayers gave me to understand them, I wanted no further business with any of it. Heretics or no heretics, I was lost in admiration for the sincerity of the Bábís and pained to my very center for the suffering wrought upon them by the priests and their fanatical followers.

As for the Bábís as individuals, however, had they not gotten themselves caught up in religious fervor, they would have never suffered all this. Though my heart ached for their plight, religion, I concluded, is filled with angry people and evildoing and not to be taken too seriously by those who would live sanely and well. I thanked God for the haven of sanity that was the estate of the learned and noble Mírzá Abbas and his kind and thoughtful lady. I thanked God, too, for my Teacher, intelligent and free, as well as dear, funny Fatima with whom I could discuss anything, even religion, with reason and dispassion.

The rest of that year was uneventful. The story of the Battle of Ṭabarsí lay heavily on my heart. In the spring of 1266 (or 1850 as we reckon time in the West), among the many friends and guests of Mírzá Abbas, several men came often to the house to visit. I had come to recognize the faces and voices of these men, seven of whom were cruelly killed in one afternoon. Mírzá Abbas was a man of courtesy, refinement and learning. His biruni was, as I have said, often the scene of gatherings that lasted sometimes late into the night. We often heard laughter floating from there across the night air, and only very, very occasionally was there the sound of voices raised in contention, for his guests also tended, in the main, to be men like himself, and the gatherings—while friendly and often convivial—were of men coming together to smoke the water-pipe, to trade opinions and knowledge in order to glean wisdom from each other, and to discuss the Koran.

That seven of them would have been Bábís, I would never have imagined in a thousand years. They were, to begin with, too learned to be taken in by the claims of an ignorant heretic (I had long ago discarded any belief in the Báb's so-called charms and spells), and too stable in their wisdom to be party to fanaticism. But one afternoon, the household was plunged into grief by the deaths of these men.

As happenstance would have it, Fatima and I were present. We had gone together to the bazaars with a cart-driver from the household, and suddenly there was a babble of raised voices and a shift of the crowd as the shops were cleared of buyers and shopkeepers alike. One by one, the prisoners were led to their deaths.

The first was Hájí Mírzá Siyyid 'Alí of Shiraz, a retired merchant who had recently undergone a journey into the north country and had been lodging here in our estate for a little while. He was arrested and was begged to recant his belief in the Báb. But he refused. I learned later that he was none other than the Báb's own uncle and had reared him, so I supposed his loyalty was somewhat understandable. Mírzá Abbas, among others, had attempted to buy his release, but to no avail. The government would allow that only if the Hájí recanted, and that he would not do.

"Hear me, oh people!" he called out to the crowd which had gathered about. "I have offered myself up as a willing sacrifice in the path of the Cause of God. . . . For over a thousand years, you have prayed and prayed again that the promised Qá'im be made manifest. . . . And now that He is come, you have driven Him to a hopeless exile in a remote and sequestered corner of Adhirbayjan and have risen to exterminate His companions. . . . With my last breath, I pray that the Almighty may wipe away the stain of your guilt and enable you to awaken from the sleep of heedlessness."

At that, the executioner turned away, claiming that his sword needed sharpening. He attempted to refuse to execute, and we watched while, with much raising of voices and shaking of heads, a brief-argument flared between him and the Amir's guard. At last he returned and did the deed, but he wept as his arms sent the sword downward to its bloody task.

When the head of the Hájí fell, there arose a noise from the crowd such as I had never heard before, the mingled cries of lust and anger and also the sounds of souls repelled by what they were seeing. I could not see over the heads, so I saw only the flash of the sword and heard the roar of the crowd's reaction to the Hájí's death. I saw the tears falling from the executioner's eyes, however, and that sight alone all but brought tears to my own.

I glanced at Fatima, who stood beside me, and through the mesh in the eyepiece of her veil, saw her eyes fill with moisture, and then, behind the unshed tears, grow hard.

They were leading out now the second of the men who were to die that afternoon, Mírzá Qurbán 'Alí, a man well known for his sense of fairness and justice in his business and personal relations. Also, learned and pious, he was well regarded by everyone, and even the Amir who sent him to his death expressed his wonder that such a wise man could believe in the heresies of the Báb. In addition to all of this, he was a man of much political influence, as he was well acquainted with no less than the mother of Náṣiri'd-Dín Sháh, so every possible opportunity was made to enable him to recant, but he refused them all. In fact, he cried out, "He whose name is 'Alí, in whose path I am laying down my life, has from time immemorial inscribed my name, Qurbán-'Alí,* in the scroll of His chosen martyrs. This is indeed the day on which I celebrate the Qurbán festival, the day on which I shall seal with my life-blood my faith in His Cause."

As he walked to the spot of his death, he reached down and gathered into his arms the decapitated body of the Báb's uncle who had just died, and held his own neck still for his execution. The sword flashed, but struck poorly, and only partly severed his head. The blow sent his green turban, the sign of his descent from the bloodline of Prophet Muḥammad, rolling away from him. When he caught sight of it, he cried out a verse from the poet Rumi, while his life bled away as he spoke:

Happy he whom love's intoxication
So hath overcome that scarce he knows
Whether at the feet of the Beloved
It be head or turban which he throws.

He fell dead then, and the crowd began to wail and mourn, they were so touched by his ardor. A few people turned away with sounds of repugnance, and I, too, wanted to leave. I pulled at Fatima's sleeve, but she slowly shook her head no, and continued to stare at the scene before us.

* *Qurbán* means "Sacrifice," and 'Alí was the Báb's name; hence, "Sacrifice for the Báb."

The third was a youth from the city of Qum, who would have been at Fort Ṭabarsí had illness not prevented him from traveling. As he approached, he saw the two bodies on the bloody ground and cried out, "Well done, beloved companions!" Then he cried out, "Accept me, O my God, unworthy though I be" and continued to pray until his head fell and the crowd roared.

The fourth was a man I recognized from his many visits to Mírzá Abbas. He was an extremely learned Islamic scholar, and I could not believe he, too, was a follower of the Báb. Certain there was some mistake, I waited for him to speak up on his own behalf, and sure enough, in a moment his voice rang above the sounds of the gathered people. "Hear me, O followers of Islam! My name is Ḥusayn, and I am a descendent of the Siyyidu'sh-Shuhadá, who also bore that name.* The mastery I have obtained over the intricacies of the Islamic teachings has enabled me to appreciate the value of the Message which the Siyyid-i-Báb has brought. . . . I appeal to every one of you to call upon the 'ulamás and mujtahids** of this city and to convene a gathering, at which I will undertake in their presence to establish the truth of this Cause."

I could not believe my ears! I stood with my mouth agape beneath the veil that covered it, unable to take in this scene of horror before me. One after another, these friends of Mírzá Abbas were proclaiming their faith in the heretic's message, but moreover, they were doing it in the face of certain death and standing before the beheaded corpses of their predecessors. Surely, though, this man would end the bloodshed, for he was casting out a challenge to the assembled crowd to invite the religious leaders of Tehran and call a meeting where he would attempt to explain, and prove by reason, argument, and holy writ, the truth of the Báb's message.

I felt a thrill as I heard this, in spite of the ugliness of the scene, for I had long wanted someone to do just that for me. Somehow, I believed

---

* The Imám Ḥusayn, one of the twelve Imáms in Islam who was martyred for his faith.

** Islamic clerics.

Too-Tee would be able to get an accounting of what would be said there. I was just reaching for her sleeve to tug at it again, just opening my mouth to say, "Good. Then this can all be settled once and for all, and you and I can learn what the Báb teaches . . . " when the guard stepped forward and interrupted the siyyid. "I carry with me your death-warrant signed and sealed by seven of the mujtahids of Tehran, who have in their own handwriting pronounced you an infidel. With that, he drew a dagger and stabbed Siyyid Ḥusayn in the heart! The shock of witnessing the brutal death of that reasonable man affected me so that I became suddenly rigid. The feeling of faintness that had overtaken me at the first decapitation had passed, and now, with this fourth death, I felt lightheaded and dazed. So I stood silently, neither weeping nor gasping, as a fifth, then a sixth, and finally a seventh victim of the swordsman came, one after another to the bloody spot to give away their heads. When the fifth victim caught sight of the bloody scene, he grew angry and called the slayer a wretched and heartless tyrant; nevertheless, he begged him to quickly do his job, "that I might join my beloved friend, Ḥusayn." The sixth, a man we had seen many times at the house of Mírzá Abbas, came next to the spot of martyrdom. Finally, the last of the seven, seeing his two friends before the executioner, ran forward and begged to be first. Someone produced two more swordsmen, and the three of them were beheaded at once, and with that it was over.

The crowd was sounding a long and steady roar of bloodlust and anger, broken with a number of screams from women onlookers, and several hate-crazed peals of laughter. I stood, still silent, with sobs of outrage paralyzed in my throat. Slowly, I became aware of Fatima beside me. At some time during the carnage, we had taken one another by the hand and stood now, like two statues, black-draped and stone-still, as slowly the crowd began to disperse around us. The cart-driver rushed up and found us so, and apologizing profusely for having lost sight of us, led the way back to the cart, and we climbed in among the parcels we had purchased earlier, and all three of us rode silently home.

It was a sad time for us at the estate of Mírzá Abbas. Mírzá Abbas himself took to taking walks alone out through the west gardens at sunset, and often when I stepped to the window to watch the afternoon fade into dusk, I would see him away out there, looking as small and sad as a lost boy, sometimes silhouetted black against the blood-red of the setting sun, and staring north. No doubt, I thought, even he, with all of his wealth and wisdom, must be curious about the Báb imprisoned in those northern hills, for of the seven martyrs of Tehran, five had been close friends and companions of his. I had long thought the Báb was, as I had first pronounced him to my visiting nephew, an ignorant and heretical fool. But if Hájí Siyyid 'Alí was his uncle . . . that made a great deal of difference. The Báb had been well-reared by that same uncle, and was no doubt educated and well-versed in the Holy Writ. I learned, moreover, in the days that followed, that the Báb, as a child, had lived in his uncle's house because his father had died, and the trip north that had brought the siyyid to stay with us had been a journey to the prison to visit his nephew. Then too, the Báb was a descendent of Prophet Muḥammad. Heretic he might be, but he was not ignorant, and if he could win the allegiance of men such as these seven to his cause, whatever, in the end he might prove to be, he was, above all, no fool.

Nevertheless, if even *I* had been shocked to learn of the affiliation of these wise and respected men with the odd sect and that the very uncle of the heretic himself had resided in our house, what effect must it have had on Mírzá Abbas?

We paced through the last days of winter with a stoic patience, believing that the festival of Naw-Rúz would cheer the downcast household. The New Year's celebration, with its merriment, its dancing, the warmth of family and the happiness in the eyes of the children at their delight in the candy, games, and gifts of coins was always a joyful time at Mírzá Abbas's. Once it had done its uplifting work, summer would not be long away, and that surely would cheer us all and perhaps give even the government something else to think about. Perhaps the Bábís could be forgotten, or at least let alone for a while.

But the sorrow was not to be so simply outlived. The troubled days grew more troubled still as we heard news of yet another close friend of the household's. His name was Vaḥíd, and I remembered him as the taller of two men who often came together to the biruni. Like the Báb, Vaḥíd was a siyyid, a descendant of the Prophet Muḥammad, and he wore a green turban as the symbol of his sacred lineage. The other, much shorter, yet far more imposing, was Mírzá Ḥusayn 'Alí Nurí, also a prominent man of Tehran. Vaḥíd had been his guest for most of the winter.

But now Vaḥíd had gone home to Nayriz to celebrate Naw-Rúz with his wife and four sons. Apparently he too was a Bábí and had begun to teach openly the sayings of the imprisoned one to his acquaintances in Nayriz.

The stories drifted back to us that Vaḥíd and about seventy of his friends were under attack in a large building they were now attempting to fortify. It began to look as though there were another "Ṭabarsí" in the making. As the days passed, the interest in the Bábís was no longer just one more object of mild curiosity in a world full of diversions. They and their plight were on everyone's lips. Daily, there was some new story of death, and what became increasingly apparent was that the mullahs were growing more and more uncomfortable at the rapid spread of the sect and putting more and more pressure on the government to put an end to it.

The "government," in this matter at least, was really the prime minister, Mírzá Táqí Khán, the rigid and uncompromising adviser to the sháh. The Bábís, as nearly as I could make out, were mostly all decent, honest, well-meaning, and often learned. They were peaceful at heart and wanted only to tell their story. But, of course, it was just exactly "their story" that the mullahs did not want told.

The spring became warmer, and soon the heat of mid-summer was upon us. Vaḥíd, it seemed, had earlier lost his beautiful mansion. He had possessed an estate not unlike Mírzá Abbas's, and a fierce mob, incited by the local mullah, descended upon it one day, looting and vandalizing. They had destroyed his valuable possessions, burned his house, and killed his livestock, even the horses he rode. So he immediately set off on foot to spread the news of the arrival of the Qá'im and His message—that the Lord of Judgment Day would soon appear. This of course meant that all religions of "the Book" would be affected—Judaism, Christianity, and Islam.

I thought the truth of that unlikely, but realized it was hardly heresy. From town to town he traveled, and in every town, men flocked to hear him and declare themselves followers of the Báb. The local governor threatened to capture the wives, confiscate the property, and take the life of anyone who cast his lot with Vaḥíd, but few paid him any attention. They were falling into line behind Vaḥíd and the Báb's claim by the hundreds! Or so they said. Finally, Vaḥíd and about seventy of his companions were trapped in their "fort." The governor sent over one thousand men to rout them out. A battle raged for days with, as at Ṭabarsí, small parties of seven and fifteen emerging from the fort, making small forays against groups of persecutors many times their number, and driving them off. Again, like the men of Ṭabarsí, Vaḥíd's companions were sent a Koran with words of deceit written inside. Many of the men left their weapons behind, thinking that they would be returning to their homes. Some escaped, some were killed, and some ran, alternately hiding and searching, hoping to find Vaḥíd. He, however, was in the hands of his captors.

When the troops had captured Vaḥíd, they took his green turban, wound it around his throat, and dragged him by it through the streets. The women of the town danced around the dragging corpse, playing cymbals and beating drums. No sooner was the news of his death made known than five thousand men set upon the believers whom he had taught. Captured and chained, they were tortured and killed. Their houses were burned, and their belongings stolen. Their wives and children were taken also and subjected to brutalities so horrendous they were left to the conjecture of those of us in the women's quarters, for the men would not say the words in our hearing.

Too-Tee came to my room and told me of it, weeping all the while. She grieved for Khánum and for Mírzá Abbas who, she said, had shed tears for a day and a half. "I am afraid for them, Shirin!" she said between her sobs, "for Khánum says he does not sleep and eats but little, and she, herself, looks like a ghost."

Dear Fatima: I had to conceal a smile, for in her love for Mírzá Abbas and the lady, she had so lost herself in weeping that her eyes were swollen nearly shut and her chubby face was red and blotchy, and the overall effect was as gently amusing as everything else about her. Even so, I too, was worried about the Lady Shaydah and hoped she would not become ill.

"One by one, their dearest friends," Fatima began and then fell silent. Together we sat, not speaking, and I was thinking that surely this was the nadir of their sorrow, that perhaps from now on things would quiet down and the healing could begin at last. My thinking, however, was wrong, for ten days later, during the first week of July, in the northern city of Tabriz, they executed the Báb.*

* See Foreword, p. xi.

5

SHIRIN: 1850

Oddly enough, in all this time, it had never occurred to me to wonder if Mírzá Abbas were himself a member of the Bábí group. I believe I still had not come to realize that this was something intelligent minds took seriously. In spite of the seven prominent martyrs of Tehran, and Vaḥíd and his hundreds, I had assumed all along that, like myself, Mírzá Abbas (and the Lady Shaydah, of course), were victims of surprise as well as grief when they heard of the fate of their friends.

But when the news reached us that the Báb had died in a hail of bullets from the 750 rifles of the sháh in the city of Tabriz far to the north, Mírzá Abbas called a halt to all of the activities about the estate, and for three days the grounds were quiet with mourning. There was a great deal of gossip, of course, and much talk of miracles, just as I would have suspected there might be. At first I scoffed at all of it—the story that the sháh's riflemen had missed him the first time around. Nonsense. Seven-hundred-fifty skilled riflemen firing at close range, as a firing squad does, do not miss; not all 750. Nor did I pay much attention to the story that a great gale arose the moment following his death and that the skies remained dark all the rest of the afternoon. A noon dark, they called it. But later on, when visitors came who had been there and seen it all, there was no longer any argument about the firing squad. Ten thousand people had witnessed it, and I know now (because I later came to know one of them), that among them were British diplomats, who sent accounts back to England.

As for the gale and the darkness, it was terrible, they said; it was so dark the chickens roosted, and dogs cowered in the doorways whimpering. It was not an eclipse. People were so frightened of it that they shut themselves up in their houses and refused to come out until morning. I had thought it was more rumor of magic and spells, but Khánum assured me it was all true. In a nearby city, an earthquake was felt that same afternoon, so perhaps the "noon dark" was somehow connected to that awful occurrence.

I was touched, I confess, by the Báb's last words and the story of the eighteen-year-old boy who died with him. The lad had begged to be with him wherever he went, and the Báb had promised that he should always be with him. They were led out to the execution post together, and the boy was bound so that his face lay against the Báb's breast. He died smiling. We heard later that he had written his family a letter, assuring them that this was his choice. In it he had also put aside their argument to him that this business of the Báb would have no ending and that he should let it all alone . . . a sensible argument most any father would have advanced, I think. But the youth had countered by pointing out that nothing in life ever really ends, and that as for their fears for his life, of what use were they? "At most we can but be slain for God's sake," he had written, "and, oh, what happiness were this!"[1]

As for the Báb himself, his last words, I confess, troubled me for a long while afterward: "The day will come when you will have recognized Me; that day I shall have ceased to be with you."[2]

During those days of mourning, even Khadijah and I spoke in low tones to each other in our room. I stood by the window watching the sunset one evening. "When he went out there and gazed to the north," I mused, more to myself than to Khadijah, "I believed he must have been curious about this man responsible for the deaths of his friends. I never thought that he, too . . . that his gazing was, well, prayerful." Khadijah made no answer to this. She knew I referred to Mírzá Abbas. Into my mind now, all of the long deferred questions came crowding. This then, was the meaning of the weeping woman; the occasional strange faces, the busy comings and goings in the biruni. This was why Mírzá Abbas had bought the slave, to give him a place among his fellow believers to recover from the ordeal of Ṭabarsí. It was the story of some mistreated, if not killed, fellow believer that had brought, on occasion, the shadow of sadness to the bright brow of my beloved mistress, Lady Shaydah, and the cry of the night visitor that had so disturbed the household had been a message bringing the first reports from Ṭabarsí.

How clever of Lady Shaydah to instruct Fatima to tell us of the battle, without letting us know the household was involved, for I had no doubt that both Mírzá Abbas and his lady trusted Fatima with their secret.

No wonder she always knew so much about all of it; they had kept her aware of all that was occurring throughout Persia, and she used her penchant for gossip to inform them when it would have looked suspicious for them had they appeared too curious. Now I understood why she had insisted on staying to see the seven gory deaths that day at the bazaar; no matter how dreadful for her, she had known Mírzá Abbas would want a full report of it all. He would insist upon knowing who died and how and what his last words had been. Dear loyal Fatima, with her nearly toothless smile and repetitious recitals, would see that she had all the information for him, observing meticulously every heartrending detail. What a true friend she is to the family she serves, and how grateful I am, I thought, that she is my friend as well.

As if the death of their prophet were not enough, there was again news of new upheavals in the province of Zanjan to the west, an area in the mountains where most of the people spoke Turkish. Actually, it had been going on for some time, but in the excitement of the stories of Vaḥíd in Nayriz, the seven martyrs here in Tehran and finally the climax of the execution of the Báb, himself, I had paid but little attention. Now that all the other was over and now, too, that I knew of the family's persuasion, I became alert to the stories coming to us from Zanjan.

It seems that of all the fighting, this involved the most people, the most bloodshed. Here there were women and children involved. A whole section of a city was blocked off and made a kind of "living fortress" for hundreds of families under siege from government troops. Mírzá Táqí

Khán was apparently determined to rid the country of the Báb's followers even if he had to kill every man, woman, and child in Persia to do it. But the women and children, too, fought back. The children ran errands and carried messages. Their mothers supplied powder for the firearms, loaded rifles, and cut their long hair to use as twine to tie down the recoiling cannon. One young woman disguised herself as a man and fought alongside her male companions for five months before she met her death, much as the great Mullah Ḥusayn had met his. Crying "Yá Ṣaḥibu'z-Zamán!" she charged four barricades of the enemy, routing three of them before she fell. She had earlier cried out in contempt to the governor's troops, "Why befoul by your deeds the fair name of Islam? Why flee abjectly from before our face, if you be speakers of truth?"[3]

The besieged area was filled with a desperate and ever diminishing populace of some three thousand people determined to hold out as long as necessary. But in the end, like the men of Ṭabarsí, like the men of Nayriz, they were defeated. The same ugly ruse of sworn promises within the covers of Holy Koran was used to call them from their refuge, and when the eighty-year-old man, whom the Bábís had chosen to be their spokesman, asked the leader of the government's troops if he would indeed honor his vow, that same commander ordered that the old man's beard be pulled out by its roots before putting him to death. When it was all ended, over eighteen hundred men, women, and children had died in Zanjan.[4]

From the chamber of Khánum often came the sounds of weeping in those days, as I moved about her dressing room in silent dusting or sweeping. She wore a pallor that made me afraid for her health, and her eyes grew red-rimmed and dark, though the kindness still glowed through their sadness. My heart nearly broke for her.

Mírzá Abbas was no better. No longer his hearty self, we saw little of him, as he kept busy night and day with what activities I did not know. I can only assume that somehow he was attempting to ease the burdens of the Bábís he knew, though I imagine there was little enough he could do. More than once in the night, when I would have thought him asleep for hours, I would waken and hear, drifting softly through the dark, the sounds of his voice, mournful and sometimes breaking with sorrow, chanting prayers.

As for my dear friend, Fatima, while it would seem that all this sorrow around her would result in a great loss of weight or even make her ill, she remained as efficiently busy and rotund as ever. Indeed, her devotion to Mírzá Abbas and Lady Shaydah seemed to spur her on to even greater energy, as she did as much as she could to spare them any further worry. But her appearance changed drastically. The old familiar grin that had so often split the large sphere of her face in two, the hearty laugh that had rung out across the courtyard from the toothless and cavernous mouth, came very seldom. Instead, the corners of her mouth turned downward, and the bright firm cheeks that had glowed like small melons paled and drooped so that dewlaps hung wobbling above her throat. Her eyes, like the eyes of Khánum's, were dark with sadness in those days of despair.

Yet every once in a while as she might look up from her work, I would notice—in the same way one catches a glimpse of moonlight through the clouds of a midnight storm—that from the depths of her eyes would come an unmistakable flash of joy . . . and I would be mystified.

Suddenly the country was quiet. It seemed that perhaps with this last great defeat, plus the death of the Báb, himself, that Mírzá Táqí Khán had achieved his aim.

It was not long before that uncompromising Amir met his own end in a manner, that while less brutal than the tortures he had meted out to the friends of my master's and the other followers of the young prophet, was no less deceptive and cruel. Because he had lost thousands of government troops in the battles of Ṭabarsí, Nayriz, and Zanjan, presented the government in a poor light, and had *still* failed to put down the ever-growing belief in Bábísm, and further because the young sháh was learning not to trust the people who served him, Mírzá Táqí Khán had earned the sháh's distrust and displeasure. The prime minister knew this and, suspecting his death might be the result, remained within his house for a period of several weeks. Upon hearing a message that he need not fear the sháh's displeasure but should repair to the public bath house where he would be met by a royal messenger who would instruct him of his sovereign's wishes and be given instructions for his future service, he hurried there, eager to enjoy the reassurance of his honor and the pleasure of the steaming joviality of an afternoon with his companions. When the wily Táqí Khán had arrived and was happily settled, he was informed that his majesty's will for him was that his wrists were to be slit. Knowing there was no recourse, he submitted without struggle and watched himself bleed his life into the sewers of Tehran.

I thought, perhaps, that while the heresy had not been stamped out, the terrible loss of over two thousand lives, including that of their prophet, himself, would have left only a few Bábís remaining in the country and that the death of their most powerful antagonist would ease the resistance against them. At first it seemed to. There continued to be deaths here and there in groups of two or five, or the hatred for the followers of the Báb took the form of simple harassment by citizens ever ready to perpetrate brutality upon somebody. They now understood they were free to trouble and torture these believers, and indeed, they were even encouraged by their mullahs and given to believe that stoning a Bábí would earn them a place in Paradise. But the great sieges seemed to be over.

* * *

The second phase of the explosion of my world was of an entirely different nature, and to me, more shattering than the first. It came in the form of a tall Russian, blond and blue-eyed, who visited often at the biruni of Mírzá Abbas. He was the personal secretary to Prince Michael Dolgoruky, the ambassador to Persia; in fact, he himself was a Dolgoruky, Count Nicholas, Prince Michael's nephew.

Shahane and Khadijah had become close friends in spite of the difference in their positions, and Khadijah had told me at night how she and Shahane had peeked at the handsome Russian during the evenings when he walked in the gardens at sunset with friends. "But I think he knew we were looking, Mama," Khadijah told me. So they ran away giggling. As the weeks wore on, Shahane peeked more and giggled less.

That the count's interest was drawn to the daughter of Mírzá Abbas and Shaydah Khánum was soon the common knowledge of us all. Seventeen years old and nearly as lovely in her unfinished womanhood as her mother, Shahane was a maiden any man would find on his mind.

Shahane means "little eagle," and already she bore herself with a strong air, though it was perhaps more a consciousness of wealth and position and a wish to be thought of as her mother's daughter than any true mature strength.

So when the announcement came that there was to be a wedding within a year, I was not surprised.

Indeed, all of us were excited and delighted. It meant, of course, that the months ahead would be spent in preparations and, since she would be moving to Russia to live, great trunks were to be filled with clothes and jewels and other possessions with which she would not wish to part. Also there would be a large dowry, much of which would be in goods of value, all of which would need to be prepared and eventually packed. The wedding of the daughter of a wealthy and prominent merchant would prove to be wonderful and costly. I remembered then the games of "wedding" we had played as children, never dreaming then that I would ever be privileged to actually witness such a grand affair.

As the days passed with much discussion of gowns and patterns, of western dress and Persian dress and of the preparations for the ceremony and celebration, I found my heart growing light with anticipation. It was in that same light spirit that I looked up from where I sat squatted before a kettle, sorting rice one evening, to see Khadijah enter our room with her eyes filled with excitement and pleasure.

"Mama, oh Mama! You will never guess what has happened to me . . . never in a thousand years!" She dropped to her knees in front of me and took me by the shoulders, giving them a little shake in her excitement. "Guess!" she commanded. The look in her eyes filled me with happiness for her.

"Now why should I try to guess," I laughed, "when you have already said I will never be able to? Just tell me. What has happened to you?"

"Shaydah Khánum just called me to her apartment and said that Shahane was weeping at the thought of leaving home and not knowing anyone, or about the Russian customs or language or anything, and is frightened at the strangeness of it all. And she said that since I am about Shahane's age, and because I am already an excellent seamstress, that I . . ."

I was beginning to know what was coming. My ears heard no more, for the realization that my only surviving child was to be taken from me was sending a lance of white hot pain through my heart! I had opened my mouth to say, "No! Absolutely not! You must not leave me!" when I heard the youth and joy in her voice.

"Just think, Mama! Russia! I shall live in St. Petersburg! In the court! I shall be the personal maid of a nobleman's wife and . . . " Then she saw my eyes. Both of her hands flew to her mouth and her own eyes widened and filled with tears. "Oh, Mama! I will have to leave you!" I think she had not even thought of the cost in her youthful excitement. "I can't! Besides, you would be left all alone. I will not go, Mama. I don't have to go. Lady Shaydah only said that I may, if I like; that Count Dolgoruky *agreed* that I might. Surely Shahane should have a companion, but it needn't be me. She can choose another . . ."

I put my fingers against her lips. "Shhh," I said. "I will miss you, only Allah knows how much! We will miss each other, but you must go. It is time you had a life apart from mine, and it will be an opportunity for you to see the world. No," I said, swallowing my grief, though I could not hide the tears. "You must go." Then as I thought of how I had longed to travel like that, and of what might come of it for Khadijah, I put aside my sorrow as best I could. "No," I said again, "you must certainly go." I laughed then to drive away the tears, and Khadijah laughed with me when I said, "Listen to me repeating myself. I am beginning to sound like Too-Tee."

But the anticipated wedding lost its charm for me from that hour. I tried to comfort myself by remembering that Khadijah was young and going off to adventures, perhaps a wonderful future, that she was not dying, like Hasan, but all I heard of those self-directed lectures was that I would be forever alone, that not only my only child but my closest companion was leaving me. I felt as if life were over. I begrudged each day its ending and saw the sunsets from our window now as a great blood-red tolling of a silent knell.

* * *

Then, like a sudden crack of thunder during the lull in a storm, came the electrifying news . . . there had been an attempt on the life of Náṣiri'd-Dín Sháh, and the would-be assassins were Bábís!

Oh why? I could not help but register my extreme disgust to Fatima, and she agreed that while it was hardly surprising that the gentle and harmless sect had finally resorted to a vengeful retort, why now? Why had they not had sense enough to let well enough alone? It seemed that two young men, half-crazed by the deaths of family and friends, had perceived Náṣiri'd-Dín Sháh as their foremost enemy. While the late Mírzá Táqí Khán had been the avowed destroyer and the most enthusiastic in his zeal to stamp out the sect, still, reasoned the youths, the sháh had done nothing to change that or lighten the cruelty with which it was being done. He could have stopped the killing with a word and had not done so.

So taking what they believed to be justice into their own hands, and without the knowledge of any of their Bábí friends, they procured what weapons they could and lay in wait for the sháh as he passed by on his daily ride. It was a pathetic attempt that reflected both their youth and their distraught state of mind, for their pistols were packed with a light shot that would have been hard put to have provided birds for the royal table, let alone put his majesty to death. He was but lightly wounded. They were immediately executed, of course, but the reverberations of that feeble attempt, as if the small charge had been fired into a large pond, spread throughout Persia, gathering momentum as they traveled.

Now the bloodbath began in earnest. The three hundred who had died at Ṭabarsí, the eighteen hundred in Zanjan, came to seem but a dramatic overture to the opera of death that now unfolded in Persia and before the eyes of Europe. The Russians, the French, the British, all of whom kept diplomatic offices in our country, wrote to their homelands accounts of the slaughter. The shock and outrage of the awful happening sent blood trickling daily into the streets of every Persian city. The news of the atrocities oozed like the blood itself into the letters to families at home, flooding them with the anguish of the writers and staining, like a nauseous stickiness, the normally stilted language of diplomatic briefs.

It would be years before we knew this, before all of the details of the repercussions of that act would be known; years before the world would hear of the cruel attempts to destroy thousands of people in the most brutal ways; of how families were killed, the father hacked into minced meat before the eyes of wife and children, the mother then strangled and left lying dead while the children wept and pleaded with her to waken before they too lay beside her, their tiny throats slit; of how families were burned to death in their houses; of how men were tied to the mouths of cannon and blasted to bits; of those who had their feet skinned, soaked in boiling oil and then shod with horseshoes and made to run through the streets to the delight of the howling mobs. One man, who had had holes dug in his skin where candles were then placed (a favorite and popular method of dispatching a Bábí), danced down the street singing and laughing. When the candles burned down to the fat in his shoulders, they burned the fat itself, and when the candles burned out, they were relit. Over and over the persecutors were amazed to hear their victims singing on their way to their deaths, "We all come from God, and to Him shall we return!"

Hundreds died, then thousands, until in the years to come when the score of those days was reckoned, it was found that many thousands had given their lives for the new Faith. And "given" is truly the word; for they were in many instances offered the chance to recant.

My heart nearly broke for Khánum, for in addition to all the blood in our lives, she also was losing her daughter to the tall, golden-haired man from Russia. The only difference was that she had other children to love and foster after Shahane was gone and I did not, though I notice that never has one child been able to take the place of another, no matter how dear, so I believe her sense of approaching loss was not less than mine.

In the winter before he died, I have mentioned that Vaḥíd had been the guest, while in Tehran, of his friend and frequent visitor of Mírzá

Abbas. His friend's name was Mírzá Ḥusayn-'Alí Nurí. The son of one of the wealthiest ministers of the sháh, he stood in line to inherit his father's position. He was descended, I learned much later, from the Sassynian Kings of Persia, and also from the Hebrew Prophet Abraham, through Abraham's third wife, Keturah.*

Though still a young man, maybe thirty or so, he was already well respected by Mírzá Abbas and many others, some a full twice his age. I had seen him a number of times as he arrived or departed our premises on his visits and was always struck with his appearance. I think the secret of it may have been his vitality. Some massive source of energy glowed within him somewhere, like the unapproachable cauldron of a volcano. He was not a large man, either in height or build, and it would seem as if the energy within him should have burned him away. But he contained it somehow, as some men can reduce a wild-eyed lunging stallion to trembling stillness with a look and one soft-spoken word.

There was a dignity in his bearing, his walk, and even in the infrequent sound of his voice that bespoke a wisdom and certainty that, without hauteur, carried an air of regal authority that, it seemed to me, even a sháh would not dare to question.

Yet in spite of what I can only call his majesty, he was as kindly as one could imagine and possessed of a hearty sense of humor. He would stop often in his movements to help someone, a woman with a bundle, a man struggling with a recalcitrant mule, a child who had stumbled and fallen who needed dusting off and setting on his feet. I was told he always carried coins for the needy and, indeed, had become known in Tehran as "the Father of the Poor."

The sight of him had a strange effect upon me. I could not have put it into words in those days, but there was something of that same majesty that seemed to catch hold of me and not let go; something that insinuated an image of the man into my deepest center—an image that in all the long years ahead never left me.

As a matter of fact, it was through him that Prince Michael and Count Nicholas Dolgoruky first came to the house of Mírzá Abbas. Mírzá Ḥusayn-

* See Genesis 25:1–4 & I Chronicles 1:32–33.

'Alí's sister was married to the man who served as the Persian secretary to Prince Michael. His name was Mírzá Majid-i-Ahi. Seeking some social life among men of education and refinement, the prince was introduced to Mírzá Ḥusayn-'Alí by Mírzá Majid and subsequently invited to Mírzá Abbas's for an evening. Soon the prince became a regular visitor and began before long to bring his nephew who, during an early evening visit caught sight of the eyes of the lovely Shahane as she walked in the sunset.

When Mírzá Táqí Khán met his end in the bathhouse, the man appointed to the position of Amir-Nizam in his place was named Mírzá Aqa Khán-i-Nurí. He admired Mírzá Ḥusayn-'Alí and believed him to be the finest and most admirable as well as the most learned of the Bábís. The new prime minister invited Mírzá Ḥusayn-'Alí to visit him, hoping that perhaps together, they could bring an end to the bloodshed. Mírzá Ḥusayn-'Alí Nurí remained the guest of the Amir until summer when he left for Shimiran, a section north of the city where wealthy Tehranis often spent the hottest weeks of the season. He was there at the time when the two youths made their attempt on the life of the sháh, and the Amir Nizam, suspecting there would be an immediate bloodbath, hastily scribbled a message to him to remain there in the foothills and not return to the city.

But Mírzá Ḥusayn-'Alí Nurí believed he could hearten his friends among the Bábís if he came into the city and so rode immediately down into town. The next day he was thrown into the Síyáh-Chál—the Black pit—an old unused cistern, now a place for thieves and murderers. To reach its depths, one had to descend into the dark by a long winding stair with no railing. The dungeon was pitch black and airless and infested with vermin. It stank with filth from the prisoners, who were offered no facilities for cleaning themselves or disposing of their wastes. As soon as he arrived, there were laid across his shoulders two great heavy chains that held the manacles that kept his arms and legs chained together. One of the chains rode his shoulders like an ox-yoke. It was only much later that I learned he had lain in that dark and filthy pesthole for four months and that the chains had torn the flesh of his shoulders to the bone.

We heard, the very afternoon of his imprisonment, a strange story about him. We had all known him to be kind and far beyond us all in a lofty piety we barely understood . . . but how much so we had not known until that evening. As the guards were leading him down the streets of Tehran to his imprisonment, among the rabble throwing stones and spitting at him, one dirty old woman of the streets picked up a stone to throw at "this evil enemy of Islam." Apparently, there was a purity of motive in her act, lacking in the rest of the rabble. The guards, who were in a hurry, brushed her aside. But in that stately and gentle voice that brooked no argument, Mírzá Ḥusayn-'Alí Nurí told the guards to stop and allow the woman to throw her stone at him. She should not be denied, he explained to them, her opportunity to render what she truly believed to be a service meritorious in the sight of God.

On the evening of the third day after the assassination attempt, Khadijah and I were together with several other women in the arjuna eating almonds and the peaches that were just now coming into the peak of their ripe flavor, and talking, when suddenly Fatima stepped into the room, her face a mask of grief. There were tears streaming down her sagging cheeks. In the same way that a violent gust of wind blows over a tent, scattering the cooking fire and destroying that fragile and temporary home in a moment, so she moved into our midst and destroyed our tenuous evening's peace with a single word.

"Ṭáhirih!"

"No!" I shouted back to her, denying what I knew to be true by the appearance of her face before she ever told us. But, of course, it was not to be denied. My adored and beloved Teacher was dead! I clapped my hands over my ears, because I *would not* hear what I knew she would say, but I heard in spite of myself the voices of the others, saying, "No, not our Teacher!" "How?" "Why?" And in my heart I cried out an angry call to Ṭáhirih, "Surely; you too were not a Bábí!"

Already the others were gathering around, and Fatima had begun to tell us of her death. I sobbed, I wept, but I listened. It turned out there was a great deal about my teacher I had not known, though I suppose that is not surprising. Not only was she a Bábí, she was one of the first eighteen people to become a follower of the Báb, and the first and only woman to ever, according to Fatima, be recognized as a disciple of a new religion. About five years ago, just before the beginning of the Battle of Ṭabarsí, a group of Bábís had gone to meet in a place called Badasht. It was north of Tehran, along the way to Ṭabarsí, and the purpose of the meeting was to lay plans for the rescue of the Báb, who was at that time imprisoned in the mountains. Somehow that never happened. Instead, the meeting, which lasted several days, became the moment when the followers of the Báb were forced to choose forever whether they were going to remain Muslims or leave Islam behind and give their full allegiance to the Báb . . . forced to understand that Islam and Bábísm were not the same. Until that moment, they had thought they could believe the Báb to be the promised Qá'im, follow his teachings, and still remain loyal Muslims. But at Badasht, something happened.

I was having difficulty at this point in the story understanding how and why that choice had to be made, and Fatima laughed and said I was certainly not alone. "It happens in new religions always, Shirin," she pointed out. "Perhaps the clearest example of how it happened in a religion of the past was when Jesus told His early followers that to be loyal to Him they must eat His body and drink His blood. If they were not willing to do that, He said, they would have no part, in His message. He was not speaking of cannibalism, of course, but some of his followers did not understand that, nor did many of them take the trouble to figure out what He did mean. Instead, those people whose Holy Book had such strong injunctions against the drinking of any blood and strict laws about the eating of certain kinds of flesh, merely reacted in shocked disgust at his apparent disregard for the laws of Moses, and, the scripture says, "turned away and after that followed him no more."* That was their moment of testing and decision. This moment at Badasht was the testing of the Bábís. Ṭáhirih was part of that test.

"Mírzá Ḥusayn-'Alí Nurí, the wise and gentle Bábí who lay now in the Síyáh-Chál, was there at that conference, as was Quddus, who later led the band at Ṭabarsí. Others were also there. Ṭáhirih and Quddus each had a garden in which to set up camp during the conference, as did Mírzá Ḥusayn-'Alí Nurí, who had arranged for the lodging. On the particular morning in question, Quddus was visiting Mírzá Ḥusayn-'Alí Nurí in

* John 6:66.

his tent when Ṭáhirih sent for Quddus and asked him to visit her, as she had business to discuss with him. He, however, was busy with Mírzá Ḥusayn-'Alí Nurí, and because Mírzá Ḥusayn-'Alí was feeling a little ill, he did not wish to leave him. Quddus sent word back that she should visit him instead. At first she refused, but in the end came striding from her tent into the tent of Mírzá Ḥusayn-'Alí Nurí's, intent on her errand, wearing no veil!"

There was a gasp among us as Fatima disclosed this. I could not believe it. The beautiful and ladylike, poised and learned Ṭáhirih would certainly not commit even the slightest breach of etiquette, let alone break so great a hallowed tradition of Islam as to commit such a shameless act of immodesty! Surely, she would not be the cause of the sins of those men there, who were by her thoughtless act forced to look upon the naked face of a woman! But that is precisely what she did! And, what is more, it was not inadvertent at all. She knew exactly what she was doing . . . she did it on purpose! She seated herself sedately in the group with the eighty men gathered about Mírzá Ḥusayn-'Alí Nurí.

Some of the men leaped up and ran from the tent. Others tried to hide their faces. Still others shouted at her angrily. One, so shocked at the apparent defection of a woman whom he had considered saintly, cut his throat and ran screaming out of the tent. Ṭáhirih, however, looked joyful, and her face was filled with light. "I am the Word which the Qá'im is to utter," she said, "the Word which shall put to flight the chiefs and nobles of the earth."[5]

Quddus was staring at her angrily and had drawn his sword. For a moment it looked as though he might run her through for this act of impiety. While he seemed to be considering it, she looked at him and rebuked him for something that he had not done in Khurusan, which, she said, she believed he should have done. He retorted hotly, "I am free to follow the promptings of my own conscience. I am not subject to the will and pleasure of my fellow-disciples." Having made her point, Ṭáhirih turned her eyes to the assembled group and, with her face radiant with joy, cried, "This day is the day of festivity and universal rejoicing, the day on which the fetters of the past are burst asunder! Let those who have shared in this great achievement arise and embrace each other."[6]

"So it seems," Fatima told us, "that the first act of social change and human difference of the new religion is none other than the shedding of the veil, signifying the casting off of the age-old oppression of women, one-half of the human race—and with it, the oppression of all of the downtrodden peoples of the earth." There was a long silence while we tried to digest this. If this was what the teachings of the Báb were about, I thought, no wonder there was such resistance, and no wonder too, that women were dying for him as well as men. I was amazed, but remembering as I did the sense of power that had radiated from Ṭáhirih whenever I had seen her, I understood suddenly why she had seemed always so sure of herself, why she could say to us the encouraging things she had said, why she seemed to know more than even the mullahs. She knew that she, a woman, was as valuable and loved in the sight of God as any man. She was also responsible to God for her behavior—but only to God. Now I knew why I would have died for her, and even as I came to understand it, it was as though I could see her smile and hear her voice saying, "No, not for me, Shirin, for you too, belong only to God."

I was so moved, I was weeping, but Fatima was still speaking. She went on to tell us that Ṭáhirih had angered the sháh some time ago. Her fame for her beauty, her intelligent mind, and her poetry had made her the most socially sought-after woman in Persia. Her high birth and wealth had made her more desirable still. When she attended a wedding, for instance, the guests would desert the dancing and the musicians and gather around Ṭáhirih to listen to her talk of poetry and the love of God.

The sháh had proposed. Summoning her before him, he had told her to give up her belief in the Báb and his heresies and return to the "true faith." She refused. He had asked her again, saying that she was much too lovely to die, as all of the Bábís eventually would. If she would recant, he said, he would marry her and set her over all of his other wives. She declined, saying that her Beloved (by whom she meant the Báb), awaited her in the next world. It was hard to believe he had not had her killed on the spot.

She had been taken, then, to the house of the mayor of Tehran, where she had been living as guest and prisoner ever since. The mayor's wife had become her friend and confidant in the months that followed.

But following the assassination attempt, the order had gone out to destroy the Báb's followers to the last man and woman, and this very night she had died. Her last request, Fatima said, had been that the mayor's son, who admired her, might go with her to see that she was allowed to wear to her death the wedding gown she had donned as a symbol of her love for God . . . and that her body be buried and covered with stones. She had provided her murderers with her own white silk scarf, with which they strangled her, stuffing it down her mouth and throat.

When the mayor's son had returned to his mother less than an hour before, he had told her he had faithfully carried out Ṭáhirih's requests and lovingly buried her body, neither mutilated nor profaned, in a newly-dug well and covered her grave with stones.

He had also reported her last words. Though Fatima whispered them in a voice hoarse with grief, they rang in my heart like a gong that I knew even then would echo around the world. "You can kill me as soon as you like," Ṭáhirih had cried, "but you cannot stop the emancipation of women."[7]

6

SHIRIN: 1850

I slept fitfully, but I slept. However, before the sun had risen, I felt Fatima shaking my shoulder. "Wake up! Shirin, wake up! You too, Khadijah, waken! I have much to tell you, and you must get your day started, for there is a great deal to do." She told us then that she and the Lady Shaydah and also Mírzá Abbas, along with Mírzá Majid and Count Nicholas, had sat late into the night making plans. If, as we had heard the night before during the account of Ṭáhirih's death, it was true that the order had gone out that every Bábí must die, then Mírzá Abbas and his family were all in imminent danger. Therefore, in order to save the life of his eldest daughter at least, the preparations for her departure would be made this very day, the wedding held quickly this evening, and the first thing tomorrow morning she and Count Nicholas and their party would depart for Russia.

The wedding, which was not to have taken place for many weeks yet, would now be over by tonight, and my daughter would be among that fleeing retinue and would leave me tomorrow morning. Twenty-four hours more, and all that was left of my family would be gone. I faced the rising sun, wanting only to die.

Somehow I got through the day. Fatima and I and several others managed to accomplish in a morning and an afternoon what would have normally taken days. I don't know how we did it, except that the frantic need to save the life of Shahane drove us to our tasks. Khadijah and I worked alongside each other much of the time, mending and brushing, sorting and packing. I thanked God for all there was to do, for had I had the time to reflect upon what we were preparing for and upon how rapidly the hours were passing, I believe I could not have borne it. Then suddenly it was evening, and the wedding was scheduled to begin. There was to be only a brief ceremony of prayers read by Mírzá Abbas himself, assisted by Mírzá Majid (since the mullah had refused now to perform any religious rites for Bábís), and though the count had planned a Christian ceremony to follow the simple rites of the Bábís, now, the Russian rites would be deferred until the arrival in St. Petersburg.

We women waited in the women's quarters for the ceremony among the men in the biruni to be completed, after which Count Nicholas would come in the time-honored tradition to fetch his bride from us, as we called out in a chorus of celebratory chants. After the ceremony, an evening of enjoyment was planned, even though it was to be considerably subdued compared to the original plans, now discarded. Some guests were expected, however, so I was not surprised to hear the sounds of horses and men's voices approaching the house just as the faint strains sounded from the biruni as Mírzá Majid chanted the last prayer.

But Mírzá Abbas suddenly appeared outside the biruni door. His head came sharply to attention and he frowned. In moments then, I realized that these were not guests, as armed horsemen led by a mullah on horseback broke through the gates of the estate screaming, "Death to the Bábí dogs! Death to the infidels . . . enemies of Islam!"

In moments, all was madness. Count Nicholas and Prince Michael hurriedly unsheathed their swords and, invading the arjuna, seized the bride by the arms and removed her from sight. I ran toward our room, dragging Khadijah behind me, and all around were the shouts of men and the screams of women! Children cried, and the sounds of horses' hooves pounded across the yards. Soon the eerie orange of flames rose in the early dark of the summer night, and Khadijah and I alternately ran and then stopped and stood clutching each other, only to start running again. Then suddenly I heard a man's voice shout, and she was yanked from my grasp, and I turned and screamed, "Khadijah!" into the dark, but she had disappeared!

All around the fires roared! The horses and riders were everywhere, and dark figures ran first this way and then that. It was madness, and I, as mad as the next person, found myself running first in one direction, then in another, not knowing how to save myself or how to help . . . wanting to do both, unable to do either. I heard my own voice moaning aloud, "Oh, Allah, the Merciful! Oh, Khadijah! Oh, God help me!"

Dashing down the dark logia, I suddenly tripped over some massive obstacle and fell. Pulling myself to a sitting position, I saw in the eerie light of burning buildings that I had tripped and fallen over the body of Mírzá Abbas. I whimpered, "Oh . . . oh no," but my voice was drowned out even to me, by the noise of the crackling fires and the falling timbers, the screams of the dying and the pounding of hooves. Insanely, I ran to the apartment of Shaydah K͟hánum, I don't know why, to tell her of her husband's death, I suppose, and from the shadow of the logia saw four men emerging from her door. I ran in to find her lying on her pallet, blood spattered about the lovely chamber I had kept for her these last few years, her throat a great bloody grin where it was slashed and a piece of broken sword protruding from her breast. I must have fainted then, for the next thing I remember I was rising from where I had lain across her body, my hands sticky with her blood, and thinking, "Khadijah! I must find Khadijah!" Struggling to my feet, I ran out of the room to the logia.

In the bright light of the fire I saw, in the center of the courtyard, an incredible sight. The great bulk of Fatima, in her chador, dancing that same absurd dance she had danced that day four years ago when she had reenacted for us the swordsmanship of Mullah Ḥusayn, only now her arms bore a real sword and she held at bay three armed horsemen with her wild sweeps and leaping turns, shouting the battle cry of Ṭabarsí: "Yá Ṣaḥibu'z-Zamán! Yá Ṣaḥibu'z-Zamán!"

The horsemen wheeled and pranced about, helpless before the terrible rage of this fat and toothless woman. Then suddenly, I heard myself cry, "Fatima! Behind you!" as a fourth horseman galloped up from the rear and, taking aim as he rode, fired his rifle into her fleshy back. Even as she fell, the four galloped away, across the courtyard and out the gates, and the attack was over . . . the sudden quiet broken now only by the moans of a dying few and the crackling flames.

I rushed out to where she lay on the bloody ground. Throwing myself down beside her, I took her face in my hands. "Oh, Too-Tee," I wept, forgetting that we had never called her that in her presence, but she opened her eyes and looked up at me. "Shirin, dear Shirin," she whispered.

"I will get help!" I said. "We will get you to safety!"

"No, Shirin, stay with me. I have only a moment more. Tell Mírzá Abbas for me . . . " but I shook my head and she understood.

" . . . and Kh́ánum?"

I nodded. "Kh́ánum, too," I said.

"Ah—they have succeeded here, then. They will kill us all if they can."

"But not you, Fatima!" I protested.

"Too-Tee," she corrected with a feeble hint of a smile. My tears flowed at her untimely humor, and a great sob of sorrow and anger tore from my throat.

"They shouldn't have hurt you! You were never a Bábí!" I cried. "You were only the messenger for . . . " but even as I spoke, I realized my mistake and fell silent as I looked into her eyes now filming with death. She looked back at me and saw.

"Don't grieve for me, Shirin. It is good to give one's life for God's cause. Don't you understand that?"

"No!" I cried as I felt her slipping away from me. "I don't! You must live! You must live for . . . "

"For . . . what?" She was laboring now to speak. Then she answered her own question (as she always had, I later remembered wryly), in words similar to the youth who had died on the breast of the Báb. ". . . all life ends . . . in death . . . but to die . . . for *God's* sake . . ."

The tears were raining from my eyes so copiously they fell onto my hands clasped over hers. "Oh, Too-Tee," I wept, "You can't be saying you love God more than your life!"

The filmed eyes closed and then opened once more and looked at me in the diminishing firelight, and before they closed a last time, I saw again in their faded depths that unmistakable flash of joy.

Through the wave of grief that washed over me then, I heard the sounds of running boots and cried out in terror as a man's hand roughly gripped my shoulder. "Get up!" he commanded hoarsely. "Come with me! Come now!" I turned, terrified, to face my assailant and saw that it was the tall blond form of Count Nicholas. "Come now!" he repeated, taking me by the arm and beginning to pull me to my feet and away from where I had knelt, "lest they return! You are to come with us!"

I declined softly, foolish with shock. "Oh no, there is too much work to do here. I must make arrangements for all these burials, and there will be so much food to prepare . . . "

"Come, my dear," he said, explaining carefully in a softer tone, "Your daughter is safe with me and waiting for you, and the caravan is ready to leave. We depart for Russia tonight . . . right now." Dimly, my mind registered the facts. *Khadijah, safe! And I to be with her . . . praise be to Allah!* But aloud, I said, "How can I just leave them?" I turned back once more to Fatima. "She . . . they . . ."

"I am afraid this time," he said gently, "the dead really must bury the dead." All around now the smoke was rising in great clouds directly upward blotting out the stars in the windless night. The fires were dying a little, and the crashing of falling timbers now came only intermittently. Confused, I looked about. The well was profaned by a draped chador that told of a victim lying halfway into its depths, and all around in the eerie light lay the shapeless lumps that were the dead. The fruit trees alone still stood unharmed, patiently holding out peaches and apricots for tomorrow's breakfast. But the great estate of Mírzá Abbas was dead. And those who had made it what it was were dead also. Still dazed, I looked up into the smoke-blackened, sweat-streaked face of Count Nicholas Dolgoruky.

He took my arm, and conferring upon me a title never meant for the orphaned niece of a Shirazi mule-driver, coaxed, "Come with us to Russia, Khánum, there is nothing more here you can do."

BOOK 2

The Sun of Righteousness

"BUT UNTO YOU THAT FEAR MY NAME SHALL THE SUN OF RIGHTEOUSNESS ARISE WITH HEALING IN HIS WINGS."

Malachi 4:2

7

SHIRIN: 1850

Long after the caravan carrying Count Nicholas's party had wound its way through the foothills behind Tehran, a red glow from the dying fires of Mírzá Abbas's estate glowed like a beacon from below. When the hills suddenly became steeper and we knew the journey had begun in earnest, the trail-master called a halt to allow the animals a few minutes rest and to tell us that for the next two hours, until we reached the summit of the ridge, we would be required to walk.

Shahane, Khadijah, and I stood together in the cool night air, looking back down the long way we had come. The red glow was hidden now in the folds of the hills, the only sign of the recent tragedy a column of dark space in the sky, where smoke, still rising from the embers, blotted out the stars that otherwise shone with such lively brilliance in the vast and unfeeling night.

Shahane was weeping, her face twisted with sorrow. Khadijah stood with her arm around her, weeping also. I wept not. My losses in the past had taught me that grief in one form or another is always with us, and that, for me, the time for weeping is when I am alone and at leisure—although when that would be in a traveling community, I had no way of knowing. Then, too, the unexpected good fortune of finding myself a part of the journeying party and the prospect of being with my daughter after the long weeks of believing her to be lost to me forever tempered the shock of this horrendous night.

The count walked back to the howdah to see if we were alright, and taking Shahane aside, whispered words of comfort and love, attempting to ease her burden as much as he could.

The night was chilly in these heights, and Khadijah and I stood shivering but relieved to be out of the lurching howdah for a while and on our feet.

I could not help but remember that other journey so many years ago that had brought me to Tehran to become the bride of ʻAlí Taqí, and then following his death and Ḥusayn's, another with Khadijah that had brought me to the estate of Mírzá Abbas and all those I had come to love as though they were family . . . Shaydah Khánum, a number of the women, Mírzá Abbas himself, our gracious rescuer, and my beloved Fatima—our Too-Tee. My sorrows tonight were, though no greater than those earlier ones, multiple and fresh, and I thought, *"It seems as though I am always fleeing sorrow."* Yet each time, the journeys had led from sorrow, through fear, to a greater and fuller life, albeit within my small orbit. So beneath the grief that had not even yet taken full hold of my spirit, I felt the slightest stirring of anticipation. *"What lies ahead beyond these hills?"* I thought.

Suddenly, I remembered Ṭáhirih and my dream of her prophecy for me. "You will make three long and sorrowful journeys, Shirin. Then your soul will find its home." Those first journeys could not have counted, because they took place before she knew me, nor could they truly be called long, so this undoubtedly was the first of the them. "*But I don't want them!*" I thought, "*Enough of sorrowful journeys!*" not realizing I had said "Enough!" aloud.

"Enough of what, Mama?" Khadijah asked me.

"I was just thinking aloud. I've had enough of tragedy this night to last a lifetime. But we are together, my darling; we are alive and together!" We embraced each other tightly then, in the cold mountain air.

"And," she said, the ring of untried youth in her voice, "we are going to live in Saint Petersburg—in Russia!"

8

SHIRIN: 1850

We had just begun the two-hour walk to rest the animals while climbing deep into the foothills when we heard a horse galloping toward us from the south. Frightened, lest it be the harbinger of further brutality on the part of the sháh's troops, we stood breathless. There was nowhere to hide, and we all looked to the trail master with entreaty, but he merely said, "If it were many horses, I would share your fears, but as it is only one . . ."

Nevertheless, I thought he looked somewhat less confident than he sounded, and I noticed that he placed his hand on his sword hilt. Uneasily we watched, and in a few minutes, the horse arrived, sweating and snorting with breathlessness. Small wonder the poor beast was spent, as it had carried two riders up the steep trail as fast as it could manage. Clinging to the rider was a woman, veiled and (I imagine) rigid with fear. She looked at me and called out with the sound of relief in her voice.

"Fareshteh!" I cried out. "Is it you? You escaped!" We embraced, and tears ran down our faces.

"I hid in Khánum's apartment after I found her there dead. Oh, Shirin, it was terrible! They had slit her throat and driven a sword . . . "

"I know," I interrupted, waving my hands as though I could somehow wave away the memory, "I saw her there as well."

"I thought that since they had already visited her rooms they might not return, so I hid behind a trunk. I squatted there until the rooms began to burn so fiercely that I had to get out of the heat and smoke. I stepped around to the back and saw Ali-Habib on his horse about to leave. He saw me and offered to bring me to you. He thinks if I can ride with you for a few days or so . . . I have a cousin who lives in a small village near Tabriz. He will shelter me, I am sure."

And so it happened. I had always liked Fareshteh but had not known her very well. I had thought her to be bright and clever and noticed that she too, had enjoyed the reading and writing and had worked very diligently at the lessons. In the next days, I came to know her very well, indeed. There is something about being in difficult circumstances with another that wipes away all reticence and unnecessary formality.

I then realized she was a Bábí and remembered then that it had been she who had wept at Too-Tee's story of the battle of Ṭabarsí and had inquired tearfully after the fate of Quddus. We became, in those short days, close and dear friends, and when we bid her good-bye, it was with tears and promises of prayers to be exchanged between us for health and safety and the blessings of Allah.

I gazed back at the point in the trail where she had left us in the company of one of our guides. For a separate fee, Count Nicholas had persuaded the guide to take her to the village of her cousin. Still, she would be on the trail for a good while longer, and I feared for her. Would she be safe in the hands of the local tribal guide to whom Count Nicholas had entrusted her . . . or would he enslave her, or sell her, or kill her? If she survived her trip to the village, what then? Was her cousin a Bábí also, or would he reject her because of her beliefs? And if so, would he report her to those who might subsequently kill her?

I remember thinking, "How I have come to love this woman whom I have hardly known. In just a few short days, she is as dear as a sister, and now as suddenly as we came to know each other, we shall be unknown to one another as long as I live, as with my childhood friend, Maria. I shall never know whatever became of her."

* * *

It was January 30, 1853—by the Western calendar—when we finally arrived in St. Petersburg. The journey had been long and hard and had lasted for over four months. When we left Tehran, we had traveled by mule train, then later north almost the full length of the Caspian Sea by rough barges that rocked and twisted in the autumn winds, and after reaching the western shore, by stage coaches, which were considerably more comfortable than the howdah (except when they rolled over large bumps or bogged down in mud).

These last, long, cold miles had been in sleighs drawn by three horses hitched side by side, and, though we had been bundled in furs and woolens of one sort or another, we three women had never known anything like this kind of cold. I must confess we suffered, even though Count Nicholas had been more than solicitous. However, I must confess likewise that never in my life had I seen anything so beautiful. The long, low, gently rolling hills of white and the meadows, behind which grew great forests of white barked trees that looked, in this season, as though they were made of ice themselves, were strange and beautiful to the point of being unearthly. In the inns at night, we lay on mattresses filled with straw, which were soft (though crackly sounding), and very warm because attendants had placed hot bricks down where our feet lay. Sometimes, when we were near the forests, we could hear wolves howling in the distance. It was frightening at first, but when I grew used to it, seemed comforting, and lulled me to sleep.

We received our first lessons in Western culture the evening we came to St. Petersburg. We had arrived around ten-thirty—well after dark, but because there was a full moon, we were able to travel. Still, we could not see the house well—though there were a few lights glowing from some of the rooms, enough for us to see that the house was very large—and were greeted by a serving man who seemed delighted to see the count and his party. He also was not terribly surprised, and I learned only later that Count Nicholas had sent a messenger the night before, announcing our impending arrival. After greeting us, the servant lit torches and sent several others to the coaches to fetch our things. Then he showed us to our room and helped us to understand (by signs and pointing, for of course we had no language between us), how we could freshen up, and showed us how to ring for him if we needed anything. His name, I was to learn later, was Popov.

The bell rope was a long strand made of silken cords, woven together to make a thick rope with a huge tassel at the end, and I was tempted to play with it to see how it worked. I was amazed to see where we were. Khadijah and I both stared around us like children. Not only was there a sleeping room where we would rest in a huge double bed with, I found later, mattresses stuffed with goose feathers—such softness and warmth I couldn't have imagined—there was also a separate room for sitting and lounging and generally making oneself at home. We were told later that it was a dressing room, but my goodness, one could do far more than merely get dressed in it. There was a toilette beyond that. Popov poured hot water into a basin on a stand in the toilette, and bowing slightly from the waist, left.

Each of the rooms was double the size of our one room at Mírzá Abbas's, and the ceilings were very high. There were lamps set in the walls, and before he had left, the servant had lit them all. Our furniture, and there was a great deal of it—tables and little chairs, lamps stands and small chests of drawers—were all gilded and so graceful. There was even a little writing desk where I could practice my writing, and I wondered if I would ever get a chance to use it. It was all grander than Khánum's apartment, and I was sure that even the sháh had never owned anything finer. What I was *not* sure of was why we were here—perhaps because the hour was late. Tomorrow, we would be shown to the servants' quarters.

We had hardly gotten our faces washed or had a chance to speak much of our surroundings to one another when there came a knock at the door. Count Nicholas's voice called to us, "Are you ready for something to eat? I will take you down to the dining room. Shahane and I are very hungry, how about you two?"

We were very hungry also and beginning, as well, to feel the reaction to the long journey—a bone weariness that made the bed look like the plains of Paradise.

We followed the count back along the hallway and down a wide stairway to the entry. It was also huge. More like a sitting room than merely a place to enter the house and hand over your coat to a servant, it was larger than our whole room at Mírzá Abbas's.

"The family dining room is in here," said the count, opening a door. What he meant by "family dining room" I had no idea, but learned later that it was one of three in the house. There was a long narrow table in the center of the kitchen where the servants both worked and ate, and a formal dining room for parties and guests. The family dining room was grand enough for all the guests one would ever want, in my opinion. It was as gilded as our rooms upstairs, and the walls were covered with green silk damask. There were two large candelabra on the table that made a soft and homey glow as we took our places.

There were cabinets on either end of the room that contained china and crystal. There were paintings on the walls of summer meadows with picnicking friends and of winter vistas deep in snow, with the odd three-harnessed horses drawing sleighs over the hills.

Count Nicholas's mother, named Olga, was there, along with his unmarried sister, Natasha, as well as a young brother named Dimitri, probably in his middle teens. I had not guessed there would be so much family and was surprised further to see that the women were unveiled. Khadijah and I were, of course, still in full purdah (although Shahane had removed her facial covering and was wearing just the chador covering her hair), and were amazed to see men and women not only sitting together at one table in the same room, but the women unveiled! Had it been only the count's family, it would have been understandable, but with male servants coming and going from the kitchen and us, of course, strangers and guests, I was somewhat shocked. I think the count's family were as surprised by our hidden faces and forms as we were surprised by theirs, as, for an awkward moment or two, we all stood staring at one another.

We soon recovered ourselves, and the count's mother bade us be seated and have something to eat. They smiled, trying to penetrate our strangeness hidden by the purdah. As for us, we sat in a daze of unfamiliarity and fatigue. Finally, Natasha said we must eat, and so timidly we removed our facial veils. We did not eat very much . . . or rather I should say *I* did not eat much. Khadijah ate heartily, her head turning at the size and grandeur of the room. She was eagerly noticing everything, already accepting her Western adventure as hungrily as her supper. As for me, even as I ate gratefully but sparingly of the bread and pickle and baked fish, and sipped the tea; all I could think of was lying down in that big bed.

During our supper, young "Dimitri" posed a question to his elder brother, whom, of course, he had not seen for the two years while the count had been on assignment in Persia. The boy's mother immediately seemed agitated, and the count answered quickly and decisively. I could not understand anything they were saying, but I could feel an argument shaping up. Things grew rather heated between the two.

It wouldn't be until the next morning that I understood fully the scene that was unfolding before me, and Shahane would fill us in on what was going on. It seemed that Dimitri who, I learned, was only sixteen, had been badgering his mother to allow him to join the army and go to the Crimea to fight. His mother had said no, of course, and finally quieted him by falling back on "wait until your brother comes home and ask him." So no sooner had we passed the bread than the boy had begun to discuss it. Count Nicholas, of course, said no, that he was far too young to even think of leaving home and especially to go off to war. Dimitri coaxed and argued his reasons until the count grew angry. Dimitri rose from his chair, threw down his napkin and headed for the door. The count shouted at him to sit down, there would be no further discussion. I saw and understood, without help, the count's strong gesture, as he pointed to Dimitri's chair and shouted the one commanding word, "Sit!" Dimitri sat, pouting, but within a few moments his eyes filled, and he rose and stalked out of the room in an attempt to hide his tears. So, however oddly, I was comforted that first evening as I realized that Russian or Persian, Christian or Muslim, families are families the world over, and none of us is ever really very far from home.

After we had returned to our rooms, Khadijah was filled with excited chatter, even while we changed into our night clothes. With a luxurious sigh, I laid my aching body down. No sooner had I closed my eyes than the room began to rock, and it was at least a week before I was no longer plagued with that rocking sensation from the constant swaying of the howdah and lurching water craft. It happened to Khadijah, as well, but it only amused her and did not delay her falling asleep at all.

The next day, I expected we would be moved to the servants' quarters and Khadijah asked Shahane about it. Shahane laughed and asked Khadijah if she had not understood her role as companion. "You will not be a servant here, my darling," Shahane said, "but my own dear sister. I will want you to sew for me, though," she added, "you are so good at it."

I nearly said, "Then that will make me your mother," for I would be happy to be able to relieve her loneliness if I could, but when I remembered her mother had been my beloved Shaydah Khánum, I knew I could never approach such ladylike elegance, so, lest I offend that sweet girl, I held my tongue.

I could not believe I was to actually *live* in the spacious rooms we were occupying, and wondered, too, what I would be doing with my time. Probably, I concluded, they would find tasks for me soon enough, and then perhaps I should be moved to the servants' quarters.

Plans for the Christian wedding proceeded immediately. It was to include guests mostly of the court of the Tsar, many of whom were related either by blood or marriage to the groom. Within a week we were all rested sufficiently to turn our attention to other things, and so began discussions of clothes, guest lists, food, and decorations.

I was excited when I learned that the rites would be held in a large cathedral, for I had not been in a mosque of the Christians before, and we drove over there one day to see the inside. It was rather an exciting outing, as the weather was cold, though the sun shone beautifully, giving at least an illusion of warmth. We were bundled up in our warmest things with fur robes tucked cozily around us, and the servants brought out hot bricks and placed them at our feet.

The cathedral was very large and a little frightening to go into, so hugely empty and gloomy and even ghostly, with small candles burning here and there and statues of various men and women placed about. Of course, knowing as I did that God is not pleased with statues and representations of prophets and other graven images, especially in a place of worship, I was understandably nervous at what I saw. I was therefore, a bit disconcerted when everyone else knelt upon entering the cathedral and genuflected before these idols. I was not sure it was alright to enter this building at all, and had I not remembered from my studies of Holy Koran that the Prophet Muḥammad had counseled His followers to help the "people of the Book"—that is, Jews and Christians—I would not have done so.

Among the various images painted on wood and suspended above us, I recognized Jesus, hanging on His cross, and His honored mother. I didn't know who all the others were, but they all seemed to be holy to the Russians, and I murmured beneath my breath "Il ilaha il Allah"—"there is no God but God"—and felt relieved. The priest came out of his room to greet us and speak with the count. He was a tall man with a dark complexion, and beneath his tall black hat, he had long black hair that came to his shoulders. He wore a bushy black beard. His eyes were dark and piercing, and his deep voice echoed somewhat in the empty sanctuary. If one were to replace the black hat with a turban, he was hardly different from a mullah back home. He was polite but gruff, and I found myself, as with the mullahs, a little afraid of him.

Khadijah was busy, in those days, sewing dresses for the bride and the women who were to attend her, and though I do not sew very well, I could help her by cutting out and arranging pieces and doing some simple preliminary basting.

Already, Khadijah was picking up some words of Russian, while I floundered with the strangeness of the language. But we managed.

I was assured by Shahane that I was to share the spacious rooms with Khadijah and would not be moved to servants' quarters, so it seemed I would be able to try out the little desk after all. I wondered what I would do once the sewing was done, and I supposed I could manage to make myself useful in some way or another. In the meantime, learning to find my way about the huge house and attempting to understand a little of what was being said around me kept me busy enough, and each evening found me very tired.

Before retiring, the entire household gathered in a small chapel for evening prayers, and Khadijah and I were expected to join in, even though we understood not a word of what was being said, except now and then, when the count would take pity on his bride and explain to her. She, in turn, would relay the meaning to us. Although these people were not Muslim and worshipped graven images, it all seemed harmless enough.

I found myself rereading parts of the Koran to see what God had to say about these people and their beliefs and found that He seemed to accept them. So I supposed that the evening prayers could hardly do us any harm; after all, I concluded, prayer is prayer, and I remembered that Prophet Muḥammad said that intentions are always taken into consideration by God. Nevertheless, at the end of the devotions, I always asked forgiveness, lest I be doing something wrong.

About a month into our residence in the house of Count Nicholas Dolgoruky, Shahane told us one day that the count had arranged for a tutor to teach her the language and that Khadijah and I were more than welcome to join in the lessons. I was delighted and could hardly wait for our first session! I was surprised to find that we were to learn French and that it was not Russian spoken in the household at all, except when addressing the servants, who knew only a few words of French. Our teacher was a man named Zhukovsky, and he had been the tutor of the youthful prince, Alexander. He was now fairly old, in his seventies, but he was happy to be at work using his wonderful mind and earning a few kopecs. He had been a somewhat noted poet in his youth, we learned, and a close friend of Pushkin's. All three of us were delighted to find that Zhukovsky spoke both Arabic and Persian, and he told us his mother had been Persian. I asked if we would be taught Russian as well as French, and our tutor laughed at my question. "You are one for learning, are you?" he asked, but his eyes were twinkling, and I felt he was pleased to find me so eager. He assured us that perhaps later we might learn Russian; in the meantime, we should attempt to master one thing at a time.

The wedding day approached. There had been parties and dinners and much visiting back and forth by relatives and friends of the count's, and I was embarrassed and uncomfortable at first to be included as though Khadijah and I were family, but after a while I grew used to it and at last began to enjoy it very much. Conversations at dinner and during the evenings of visiting were stimulating, and I was amazed to hear the women taking part in all of it instead of sitting silently and listening as we had always done at home. It was also somewhat amusing to me that I, who had always "spoken out of turn," was the only silent one. There was much talk about the war currently going on in the Crimea, and to listen to the people speak of it all and discuss their various opinions of this or that battle or strategy set my brain to spinning so much that sometimes I could not sleep, as a result of going over and over the conversations.

At one of the houses where we were entertained, Ivan Petrovitch, the eldest son, had just returned from the Crimea. He had been badly wounded and was almost completely helpless. It seems he had been standing only a short distance from a terrible explosion and so now was missing his right leg below the hip, as well as his right arm. But worse, the right side of his face was horribly disfigured, with most of his jaw having been blown away and his eye and nose destroyed. He tried to be cheerful, though his speech was so garbled only his family could understand a little of what he was saying. They were proud of him and pretended that all would be well, but we all knew otherwise. Young Dimitri, who had continued to pout and agitate about joining the army, turned pale upon seeing him, and after that party there was no more talk of wearing a fine uniform and going off to be a hero.

Of course, I would talk about all of this with Monsieur Zhukovsky, who did his best to clarify my many *many* questions, but who usually ended up shaking his head at me, saying with a chuckle, "Khánum, please; leave the history and politics for another time, let us get to our lesson now."

Along with the wedding finery and other work surrounding the lavish ceremony, Khadijah and I began sewing for ourselves. I had, after all, left Persia with only the clothes on my back. Fortunately, I could wear Khadijah's clothes, and though both Shahane and Natasha had given me a few things, still I needed new clothes of my own. Khadijah, on the other hand, though she had packed on the day we left home, wanted some Western wear. Khadijah and I could wear each other's clothes, but we still needed new things.

Our lives here were vastly different from our lives as serving women at home. We were slowly learning to manage without our veils. It was very difficult at first, and I felt as though I were appearing naked when in mixed company and tried at first to disappear into the woodwork. But of course my own nature, so forward and unmannerly, would allow that for only a little while, and I soon was feeling more and more comfortable in my Western costume.

I had never paid any attention to my hair, covered as it usually had been, and probably would not now either, had Khadijah not become excited about her own, as she and Shahane spent hours fussing with theirs. At last they got me interested as well, and soon the three of us could while away an afternoon changing clothes and dressing one another's hair as though we were children playing at "dress up." Sometimes we three women felt quite lost in this huge house and huge country, so far from everything we had known. During these times when we were alone together and could speak our own tongue, and knowing no one could understand us, would laugh at the Russians and their strange ways as well as at ourselves, until our sides ached and tears ran from our eyes.

Everyone treated me as though I were a "lady," as if the title of "Kh́ánum" were deserved, and I must say I relished it, though it was some time—two years or so—before I stopped feeling as though I were perpetrating some kind of fraud.

9

THE PAPERS OF EDWARD J. H. HILLHOUSE III: 1910

A somewhat stout young man, full-faced and golden-haired, sat opposite a solicitor on a spring afternoon in London. The year was 1910. Between them was an imposing desk, filled with papers in jumbled piles. The solicitor was elderly and wore a pinz nez. His heavy tweed suit, complete with vest, gold watch, and chain had a bulky solidity about it that belied the frailty of the small, thin man inside. He was harumphing and coughing while his trembling fingers searched among the disorder on the desk.

"Yes indeed," he was saying between coughs, "It is right here—just as soon as I—ah! Here it is!" He sat down and drew a thick folder from under the piles of legal sheets and notices on the desk's upper left corner. As though the mere possession of the folder worked some kind of transformation, the old legal gentleman suddenly strengthened and was in total control of the room.

"Well, sir," he said, in a new and hearty tone, smiling at the young man, "you are—as we well know—Edward John Henry Hillhouse the Fourth."

The young man smiled his agreement. "When did you first meet me, Mr. Cooper—when I was four? Five?"

"Um, something like that. You were a little bit of a tadpole. Been a long time, I know that. Your father brought you in here and introduced you. Proud as a peacock of you, he was. 'Meet the fourth E. J. H.,' he said, 'Give Mr. Cooper your hand, Johnny,' and you reached out to shake my hand, just as manly as might be. Yes sir, watched you grow up and go through Cambridge and all. But you didn't follow your father into Her Majesty's Diplomatic Service, did you? S'cuse me, *His* Majesty—still can't believe the Old Girl's been gone since aught one. Why not, John?"

"It's not for me, Mr. Cooper. I like it on 'the place.' Enjoy the English countryside too much to go galivanting about the world, I s'pose."

"A crofter* at heart, eh?" John nodded and smiled, and Mr. Cooper went back to business. "Well, son, I'm sorry your father's estate took so long to settle, but you know how the prime minister is . . . has to have a little bite of everything comes along. Miss him, I expect . . . ah, your father, that is, not the prime minister."

John Hillhouse smiled at old Cooper. "Yes, sir," he replied, "though I have to say that after Father's apoplectic seizure . . . well, it was almost as though he were gone from us already. It made those last two years very difficult for us all. So it seems as if he has been dead four years instead of only a year and a half."

"I s'pose. Well, John, I believe you'll find everything in order here. The will is a simple one. Since you are his only heir, everything goes to you—the lease on the flat here in London and the place up country. After the bills, of course. They're all paid. Weren't many. Some leftover medical expenses, but some of that the Diplomatic Service took care of. Your father was a conscientious man and a meticulous recordkeeper, so he didn't owe much. Oh, there is a little bequest of five hundred pounds to the old man who worked about, for him and your late mother—Robert Edgewood, was it?—but that's the only thing. Your inheritance is not large, John, but

---

* One who farms a small peasant farm.

then you already know that. It should help keep you going, though, if the sheep business hits a flat spot. Have you any questions, then? Oh, hold on, there's this key in an envelope. It's to a bank box—lockbox, of course. But nothing of any commercial value in there, he told me, just old letters, diaries, personal papers from his years in the service, that sort of thing. Mostly sentimental, I rather imagine. We old people do that, y'know. Can't bear to throw things out, so we leave it all to our children and let them do the housecleaning." The lawyer smiled up at John and chuckled.

Young Hillhouse held out his hand to the solicitor and smiled. "Sir, I can't thank you enough for your care of Father, and of Mother, too, while she was alive. I feel somehow as though you . . . "

"Yes, yes," Cooper interrupted with a deprecating gesture, "I know, family friend and all that. Seems to be our portion, actually. If I can be of any service to you—help you out with any of this—don't feel a bit shy about dropping me a line, or even nipping in to see me."

"I won't, sir." John Hillhouse picked up the copy of his late father's will, pocketed the little key in its envelop, and left.

He had intended to take the rail back to the country that evening, but by the time he had gone to the bank and retrieved the bulky envelope from the strong box and done a couple of minor errands for his wife, Carolyn, it was nearly dinner time. He decided to have an early supper and stay the night in the flat. He dropped into a favorite place, enjoyed a small kidney pie and some rice pudding, and then walked up to Edgeware Road to hail a horse cab to take him to Maida Vale. His parents had maintained a small flat there, for just the sort of convenience he now needed. It was particularly handy during the winter.

By the time he had alighted, paid the driver, and walked up the short walkway to the house, it was already dark. He would have liked to have let Carrie know about his day, and that he would not be home until morning, though she was used to his day trips that turned into two or sometimes even three days. He thought to himself that they ought to see about getting a couple of those telephoning gadgets, one for the flat and one for the country place. Opening a bottle of red wine, a nice Burgundy, while in the kitchen, he thought about how he might speak to Carrie through the telephoning machine and say, "I've had a busy and fruitful day, and you mustn't worry; I shall spend the night here and be in on the first train tomorrow." And she, her voice hollow and tinny with distance, would answer back some little trivia about the roses or what the dogs had got into that afternoon. *"Yes, I must get such a machine—though I suppose they're frightfully costly,"* he thought, pouring himself a generous glass of the wine.

The sitting room was small but adequate for the short stays the family needed. There was a small fireplace with a cherry wood mantel on one end of which sat three porcelain Ming dogs. On the other end was his father's humidor. The room was arranged for comfort, centered around the fireplace, and his mother's touch was everywhere. She had liked light blue and rose, and her own easy chair, comfortable and worn with age, was a dusty rose. Between it and his father's chair was a small, three-legged round cherry table with raised scalloped edges that, his mother had often commented, made it handy for keeping things from spilling off but difficult to dust. It contained a small cloisonne box that never had held much except an occasional needle where his mother had been mending, and a few straight pins.

The walls were hung with paintings of gardens and pastoral scenes, cheerful and filled with light. The drapes that helped shut out the noise of the busy city matched the blue of the walls. The only heavy furniture was a medium-sized rose and blue love seat under the windows, and his father's Morris chair, made from a deep wine leather. John set the wooden pin that adjusted the footrest, sat down and opened the envelope that held his father's papers.

"Good thing I decided to stay," he thought. *"This way, if I run across anything needs attending to, I can do it tomorrow before I leave."*

Taking a hefty sip of the wine and resting it on his tongue for a moment before swallowing, he untied the string that held the envelope closed and settled back to what he hoped would be a simple and probably dull task of checking over papers that he had probably seen duplicates of, or heard recounted long before in his father's own voice.

He was, therefore, a little surprised to see a note to him written in his father's familiar hand:

3 May, 1904

"John,

"I think you may find the collection of papers you now hold of some interest. These are notes and some copies of reports and what have you, which I gathered during the years in Russia and Western Europe. You'll see as you read them (if you bother), that all these notes aren't the sort of thing one necessarily passes on to Her Majesty's government.

"You'll also see that they are not at present, nor, do I think, ever will be of any monetary value. But I think things may have moved along in the world to the point where you may find them to be of quite some interest at a personal level. If not, by the time they are several generations old, they may be of some historical value.

"John, there are strange goings-on on this old earth, and the world I knew as a boy, which was, by and large, the same world you entered in 1875, is fast passing away. The events I have set forth in these papers, you will notice, I heard of as they were occurring, and in some cases even lived in the midst of all of it. You will see as you read. I could not help feeling at the time that these kinds of events are those that change the history of the world forever.

"Now, you will be saying; 'Well, of course, all important events change history,' but John, I'm speaking of something larger than movements or wars, more powerful than kings and armies. I am thinking along the lines of the days when our Lord Christ walked this earth, and of how because of the events surrounding that mild-voiced and kindly Man who never got more than forty-five kilometers from His home, the Western calendar dates from His birth, and our history is measured in the balance of His words. But perhaps I am only caught up in the emotionalism of the time of which I have written here, and history will prove the passion and bloodshed of those days to have been spent in vain.

"Perhaps the Cause of which I write has by now passed into the oblivion of those dreams and ideas that know only a brief moment in the light before they are buried forever with the men who dreamed them and who lived and died for them.

"Or perhaps this will have proven, as my instincts tell me, to have been the beginning of something that will propel the world into an age of which you and I will have only the briefest early glimpse. In any case, by the time you read this I will have moved into oblivion m'self and will either have been buried with the dreams, or will, from some loftier plane, celebrate the coming of a new and glorious age!

"Dear John, forgive my emotionalism and just read the papers (if you so choose), and remember your old Da with tolerance and affection.

"I send you my love again while I still can—and remain as ever,

Your Father—"

and then in the familiar and formal script:

Edw. J. H. Hillhouse III

10

SHIRIN:

The wedding of Count Nicholas and Shahane was very grand. Never in my life had I seen such gowns and jewelry, nor did I ever expect to again. Princesses and duchesses were wearing huge diamond or ruby pendants, or jewel studded tiaras. Khadijah was beside herself with envy of such opulence and whispered to me during the ceremony that someday she meant to have such things for herself. I whispered back that I hoped for her sake her wishes could come true, but inwardly, I doubted very much if they would.

Two things impressed me most favorably. One, that the bride and groom stood together before the priest instead of being read to by a mullah in separate rooms, and made promises together in each other's hearing; and two, that while the bride was veiled—as she should be, of course, during the ceremony—since married women were not normally veiled in the West, the groom could raise the veil at the end and look upon his bride, as the priest put it, "before God and this company." I thought that was lovely and fitting and certainly should get the couple off to a fine start as makers of a family.

There were guests there from around the world, as the count, you remember, had been a secretary to his uncle, the Russian ambassador, and so had met many important diplomats. Because the Russians were fighting

England, France, and Turkey in the Crimea, relations were strained with their ambassadors, who had left the country, but in the interest of old friendly partnerships, one of them who had worked in Ambassador Stanton's service came. He was an Englishman, a man named Hillhouse, Edward Hillhouse, of the diplomatic service of Queen Victoria. He had come to know Count Nicholas well, when they were both serving in Persia, and he spoke French fluently, as well as a few words of Persian. I was seated near him at one of the dinner parties. He helped me with my stumbling French, and together we managed to carry on some sort of conversation, however halting, and laughed often at our mutual misunderstandings. He was so courteous! I found him charming. Even after the wedding and its attendant festivities were long over, Mr. Hillhouse was occasionally a guest at the home of Count Nicholas, and he and I often spoke together and became, if I may say so, very good friends.

Because I was so fascinated by languages, and he was fluent in several, we had a sort of game we played together. I had mentioned that I was surprised to find so many similarities between languages. "For instance," I said, "the name 'Eli' in Hebrew is similar to "Ali' in Arabic; and 'Soloman,' in Hebrew, in Arabic is 'Sulleymann;' and our Ibrahim becomes Abraham in Hebrew."

"And 'El' or 'Eli,'" he countered, "an early word for 'God' in Aramaic, which Jesus spoke, becomes 'Allah' in Arabic. Or listen to this," he smiled, "'cold' in English is 'kalt' in German, and 'God' in English is 'Gott' in German. 'John' in English is 'Juan' in Spanish and 'Jan' in Dutch and 'Ian' in Gaelic and 'Jean' in French and . . . what is it in Persian again?"

"Yahya," I answered, and then we had a hearty laugh. Afterwards he explained about the Romance languages and Semitic languages and how they are the "children" of some earlier common tongues. I was amazed. I was also grateful again for the great gift of literacy, given to me by Ṭáhirih, and grateful to God for these opportunities to learn and even to "play" with it.

Meanwhile, once the work of the bridal finery and trousseau was over, I found that the worry of having nothing to do was groundless. Servants took care of our cooking, cleaning up, washing of clothes and all of that, and for the first time in my life, I had none of this to do, and while I felt it somehow slipshod of me for letting someone else care for my needs, I soon came to enjoy the freedom from these household chores. Often, I attempted to engage some of the servants in conversation, especially Popov, who did so much for us, because I felt as though I might feel more at home among them than among the wealthy family of my hosts, and also because I wanted them to know how much I appreciated their labor on our behalf. But it was fruitless; they understood nothing I said and only grew upset because they believed there was something I needed and they could not understand what it was. They would go, then, and get the count or someone to translate, which always embarrassed me, so I soon gave up my attempts to make friends. The count indicated to me that being too friendly with the servants was not quite acceptable anyway.

So I studied—and studied and studied! Old Monsieur Zhukovsky was a dear, and because I enjoyed it all so much, he gave me things to read and helped me to understand. Also, because he was fluent in Persian and Arabic, he could help me with my Koran and answer some of my questions about the differences between Islam and Christianity. The first thing he did was reassure me that the Christians were not really bowing before graven images—at least, that is not how they saw it. They merely used the statues as reminders and aids to their concentration. I was much relieved, as it seemed as though everywhere I turned in the house, there were pictures of the saints and the holy family of Jesus on the walls. Icons, Monsieur called them, and he told me of how they were beautifully executed by artists, and some were very expensive. I came to appreciate them for their beauty and enjoyed especially the one in our room because it was of the virgin mother of Jesus, and of course, we Muslims hold her in the highest regard. Her lovely blue robe set off her sweet face and dark eyes as they were fashioned in the icon.

After our hour of language study each morning, my girls (I had begun to think of both of them as mine), Shahane and Khadijah, would escape gratefully to more youthful and pleasurable pursuits, and leave Monsieur and me to deepen our friendship for an hour or so. We both looked forward to these marathon conversations that sometimes lasted until noon.

Often we left the schoolroom, and as soon as the weather would allow it, walked together in the garden while we talked—or perhaps I should say where the garden would be when summer finally came.

It was laid out beautifully with paths and benches and fountains. There were statues of little naked children wearing tiny wings, which shocked me, until Monsieur explained that they represented the angels in heaven, by which the faithful would be surrounded upon their deaths—much the same, I gathered, as the maids of heaven, by which Muslims will be attended. At any rate, marble or flesh, I shivered for them in the cold during the barren and empty early spring months. At least our walks gave us fresh air and a little exercise. Monsieur needed the exercise, as did I actually, and the count was grateful to me for rendering what he considered a kindness, but of course it was no kindness on my part. The kindness, I felt, came from the count for allowing me these wonderful days, and from Monsieur himself, for putting up with my relentless questioning.

One of the first things I wanted to understand was the war. When I asked him about it, he snorted and said, "Gracious, dear Lady, whoever understood a war?" but then began to explain what it was about.

It seems that Tsar Nicholas was concerned about the well-being of the Christians who lived in the Crimean area (or at least that's what he claimed), because they were threatened by the Muslim Turks who would, if they conquered the Crimea, not allow the Christians to practice their beliefs. I sighed with sadness. It seemed as though, once again, religion was bringing out the worst in men rather than the love and virtues that everyone said it would bring. Though I had my own beliefs and, I realize now, certain superstitions about God and all of it, I was reminded again of my vow not to have too much to do with religion. Here again, were people being sent to their deaths over their beliefs. I said nothing of this to Monsieur, however.

He continued, saying there was a great deal more to it than religious squabbling. These countries had been quarrelsome for some time over a number of issues, and the Tsar, I was given to understand, was not only by right the ruler of the disputed area but was the most powerful ruler in all of Europe.

France resented this. Ever since the defeat of Napoleon, France had been picking at her scab and was hoping to reestablish her reputation as the most feared and respected power in Europe. Napoleon III, attempting to step into his uncle's boots, had joined Britain in this effort not only because he wanted to "protect" the Holy Land but also because he was hoping he would gain some credibility with Britain, which had believed him an imposter. Why the British were involved at all, I was never able to quite get straight. I think they had promised to protect the Turks, who were intent on fighting for the rights of the Muslims in the area (not to mention control of the Middle Eastern route to Jerusalem). Of course, the Russians said this was tantamount to apostasy, to fight on behalf of the Crescent instead of the Cross.

I rather agreed with some Englishman or other who said some years afterward that, as far as he could tell, the British had gotten into it because they were bored by too many years of peace. At any rate, all of it was foolish, in my opinion, and in the opinion of Monsieur as well because he was a poet and hated violence in any form.

Surprisingly, I found myself looking forward to the Russians', or rather I should say the Christians', annual celebration of the birth of Jesus. I would miss our Persian Naw-Rúz celebration at the opening of spring—the gifts for the children, the parties, and the wonderful traditional food. Though I had been aware since childhood that Christians held such celebrations, I learned the customs that first year in St. Petersburg. The infectious holiday delight was similar to our Naw-Rúz. But in addition to food, gifts, and parties, there was another custom I found entrancing.

The children were not allowed into the main parlor for several days before Christmas, and finally right after the midnight prayers, on Christmas Eve (just as the Baby Jesus was being born, their parents told them), the entire group of us crowded together outside the parlor doors, which had been mysteriously shut and locked. When the children were nearly mad with impatience, the doors were unlocked and the count called out, "Alright—come in now," we entered.

The room was dark except for a large fir tree, propped standing in the center of the room, and decorated with little gifts and lovely baubles which shone in the dim light. It was also dotted with hundreds of little candles! They were lit just before the doors opened and the sight was so beautiful.

Not only the children, but Khadijah, Shahane, and I, indeed all of us stood there, struck silent at the stillness and the beauty. Though it was only a pagan symbol, it truly seemed holy, and the smallest children stared up at it with such a look of wonder on their little faces.

Standing back, nearly hidden in the gloom of the room, stood Popov and another servant, Melikov, each holding large pails of water. After the initial silence, the family and their guests (as Melikov accompanied us on a balalika), began to sing songs of joyful celebration and soft hymns commemorating this night. Then, as the candles began to burn down dangerously close to the branches, Count Nicholas and the older boys in the group blew out the candles one by one, filling the room with the perfume of wax, while Popov lit the lamps. There were a few more moments of quiet while all were still lost in the spell of the beauty and the music.

"Well," Count Nicholas would say, "what do you suppose the Baby Jesus has brought for all the good children?" and the silence gave way to a bedlam of squeals and shouts, as the count handed out one gift after another, calling out the children's names in turn.

For the second year in a row I was enchanted by this custom, and so that winter of 1854, I decided to study the Bible. Since childhood, I had been taught that Jesus was one of God's messengers; still, no one at home seemed to like Christians very much. I thought of my little friend Maria, from whom I had been separated so painfully. Had she had a tree like this? Not in Persia, certainly, as trees were not plentiful, but there must have been some custom she cherished. I concluded that it might be a good thing to see just exactly what Jesus had taught that was so different. Whatever it was, it was making Christians and Muslims enemies enough to kill each other, even here in my new land. But, before I could even get around to asking Monsieur if he could find and lend me a French Bible, the Tsar died.

Tsar Nicholas had always been a fanatical militarist. He even slept on a hard cot in the palace because he believed it would discipline him, and he thought of his army and navy as extensions of himself the way some men think of their sons. Like those same fathers, he also had little understanding or even interest in the feelings of his men. Further, he had labored to build a great fleet, and now in Crimea, all was being lost. His very good friend and commander of the army, General Menshikov, was a poor tactician, and the Tsar, angry at what he considered no less than betrayal, replaced him near the end of the war. General Gorchakov was a much better choice but came too late to the scene, and before he had even taken command, Nicholas was dead.

Fine moral talk of religions and the Holy Land notwithstanding, the war had been mostly about Savastapol and the command of the Black Sea. The Russians lost. Even had they, in the end, won the right to rule the Black Sea with their navy, they no longer had a navy to rule it with—and the army, Nicholas's beloved plaything of over 300,000 men, was effectively destroyed in the field.

Monsieur said that while tragic, it was predictable. The Tsar had also effectively destroyed his entire empire through neglect because his only love was his armies. There was some talk that in his despair, he had courted his death. It would certainly appear so. He attended a wedding on February 12th in his horse guard uniform—lightweight clothing, hardly fit for a Russian winter—and immediately came down with a cold that same evening. He insisted, however, upon keeping a supper engagement with a friend who was himself ill with the flu and had asked to be excused. The Tsar would not hear of it. The next day he attended a review at the riding school and that night developed influenza himself, and by the 14th of February 1855, at the age of fifty-nine, was dead.

The war in Crimea was to last another full year. Perhaps, after all, the rumors that the Tsar had courted his death were true. Dying as he did, when the war was lost but not over, meant the most powerful ruler in Europe never had to face his humiliating defeat.

When Alexander II acceded to the throne at thirty-seven years of age, Monsieur was very excited about it. The new Tsar would be, he felt, the hope of Russia. Our talks, now, were taken up by his reminiscences of the Tsar's childhood and youth.

What a sweet boy Alexander had been! Monsieur Zhukovsky's face shone when he related the stories, and I realized he loved him as though he were his own child. He had entered the Tsarevitch's life when he was born, for he had earlier been the tutor of the Tsarina Marie, who was of Germanic descent, from Hesse-Darmstadt, I believe. He had schooled her into her new environment, even as he was schooling us. She liked him very much and immediately engaged him to tutor her son. One of the first stories he told me was of an incident that had occurred when young Sasha, as the family had called the little prince, was only just seven.

It had been the day of his father's coronation in December. An attempt had been made upon Nicholas's life by a group of three hundred disgruntled soldiers, supported by a goodly crowd of civilians, who later came to be called "The Decembrists." They had believed his elder brother, Constantine, who was properly in line for the throne, should be their new Tsar. Constantine had abdicated some years before, but this was not known except to his father, Alexander I, who had announced the switch in his will. It was the soldiers' belief that Constantine would make a better, less heavy-handed Tsar than Nicholas, who already showed little interest in much besides his lovely wife, whom he adored, and his army.

The new Tsar had been mounted on horseback and was riding in the parade grounds near the Winter Palace when suddenly a crowd of soldiers and others began shooting—mostly into the air to frighten the crowds and make known their displeasure with their new ruler. Then it began to escalate. Tsar Nicholas did not want to fire back, even though he himself was the target of some of the shots. He felt it would not do to have bloodshed on the first day of his reign. One of the best loved and most respected generals in all of Russia, a much decorated hero of the war of 1812 against Napoleon, and popular with the Russian people, rode out to the crowd to ask them to desist. The crowd shouted at him to return to the royal ranks, and when he did, as he turned his horse around and exposed his back to the Decembrists, someone shot him in cold blood.

A second general tried to coax them into quiet, and he was shot in the back also. Then it was that the three large cannon which had been brought up and aimed at the crowd, hoping to intimidate them into silence, were fired. How many died that day, no one knows. The crowd ran to the frozen surface of the Neva River, hoping to escape the Tsar's cannon, but they were followed, and there was a great deal of bloodshed on the Tsar's first day after all. The bodies were pushed into holes in the river that night, in the hope of keeping most of the general populace ignorant of the facts. Later, many of the mutinous Decembrists were publicly executed, and several of the leaders, notably one Alexander Herzen, were exiled to Siberia.

Monsieur was a friend of a good number of the leaders of the Decembrists, and while loyal to the royal house, was understandably nervous as to what that might mean for his future. He went to the nursery where the Tsarina was watching over her little ones to express his sorrow and his loyalty. Knowing she thought highly of him and trusted him to be honest with her, he believed she could well make the difference between him and underserved punishment. The little boy had been in the nursery during the uprising and had heard all the frightening arms fire and shouting. He knew only that his father was in danger and might be killed. Everyone kept telling him it was nothing and that everything would be alright, but little Alexander knew better, for he was a sensitive youngster and bright, and it was obvious that his grown-ups were lying to make him feel better, as they, themselves, were very obviously frightened. His youthful soul, Monsieur told me, was wounded by the event, and, as it all turned out, that day colored the entire life of Alexander II.

Not only was Monsieur Zhukovsky not punished, but ultimately put in charge of all the little Tsarevitch's education and the formation of his character.

"But," Monsieur told me, smiling wryly, "had the Tsarina not thought so highly of me, I should never have been allowed near Sasha because the Tsar neither trusted me (because I had friends among the Decembrists), nor liked me very much (since I am a poet and not at all interested in armies)." But the royal family was young; Nicholas was still thoroughly captivated by his pretty wife, and she could and did frequently influence him—often for the better.

Alex's father would have made him into a copy of his own self, and soon had the little boy sleeping on a hard cot and going with him to watch the army on parade. Understandably, Alexander loved the parades and hated the cot.

There was a second incident concerning the ill-fated Decembrists that Monsieur related to me. Remember that Zhukovsky was a poet and when he told stories, he told them with all the literary embellishments. It was an experience to listen to him.

"When Alexander was fourteen," Monsieur began, "the court had been gathered for a dinner party, and suddenly, Tsar Nicholas of Russia was roaring at his son.

"'You would have WHAT?' and where a moment before the great dining hall of the winter palace had been filled with the warmly undulant sounds of party conversation that January evening, rocking the royal family and guests in a sensuous cradle of wood smoke, candlelight, and wine (enriched now and then with the bright grace notes of silver striking against china), now there was a stunned silence. Tsar Nicholas glared at the boy, his normally protruberant eyeballs fairly popping from his head, and his face dark red. All fifty pairs of eyes turned first to their sovereign, and then to the object of his anger. The Heir Apparent watched his father's face a moment more, turned his gaze quickly toward his mother, seeking protection, and noting there only shock and surprise, dropped his eyes to his plate in moral route. He was fourteen and the future Tsar, and therefore felt too old to cry, but his chin trembled a moment before he mumbled his answer.

"Unfortunately, I was seated 'below the salt,' as they say, and could not help him out by so much as a look."

"What is that—below the salt?"

"What? Oh, it's an expression meaning at the lower end of the table farthest from the guests of honor—I suppose because the salt dish was always near the head of the table."

"Thank you."

"You are quite welcome. May I continue now?" he asked politely, but with a slight edge to his voice, and I realized suddenly that he was a bit of an actor as well as a poet and hated being distracted during a "performance." I resolved not to interrupt his storytelling anymore.

"I'm sorry, Monsieur, yes, please do go on."

"The lad was thoroughly uncomfortable, so he said very uncertainly, almost mumbling, 'I said . . . Sir . . . I would have freed them.'

"The Tsar looked at his guests, and in a theatrical gesture slammed his two hands down on the table. 'Good God!' Taking a deep breath, as if faced with an almost unconquerable obstacle in the density of the boy, he explained with exaggerated patience. 'The Tsar of all the Russias, in whose hands rests the safety and well-being of one hundred million souls, does not *free* would-be assassins! My God, boy, if you care nothing for your own life, (and laid against the well-being of Russia you had best not),' he had interjected with an unctuous humility, 'you might at least care about the future of all those people out there . . . . and these people here.' He finished with a sweeping gesture of his left arm. With his right, I noticed, he reached for another piece of bread.

"Chewing and swallowing, he began to talk again, and slowly the assembled company drifted back to their desultory conversations, especially down at our end of the table, for the Tsar was well-known for his lectures, holding forth for long periods as the mood struck him on subjects that interested few. He was not insistent upon the undivided attention of the whole company if the group were large, although he liked it better that way and warmed to his subject best when he had captured the whole group. Still, as long as he felt he was captivating those gathered immediately about him, he was content. He was content now. He had, first of all, managed to intimidate the young man sitting on his right, who had only a few moments before shocked the entire company by his answer to the royal question. He had, further, given the lad to understand that he, Tsar Nicholas the First, the Little Father of Russia, was deeply involved with the good of his people, and that this devotion to an ungrateful populace motivated his every official act. Having embarrassed the youth before the very men and women who would someday be his subjects, the man felt avenged for the personal blow to his paternal pride administered by the boy's answer, and now spoke more softly.

"'Alright, you say you would have freed the Decembrists, but don't you see how wrong you would have been? Those soldiers had defended Ukrainia clear to Moscow and come to know Napoleon's troops. They had picked up from them some dangerously libertine ideas—"Free Thought" and "Nationalism" and "atheism" and other such nonsense. When your grandfather died, they had expected that Constantine would come to power, because he was next in line to Alexander I. What they did not know, in fact what I myself did not know, was that Constantine had abdicated some years before. My father had so noted it in his will.

"'This . . . ahhh . . . surprise, somehow gave these insurrectionists the idea that what they *expected* to happen was therefore what *should* happen, and they thereupon used their newfound erroneous philosophy to move from there to the insane idea of assassinating their true Tsar on the very day of my coronation! Such a thing was certainly not to be tolerated! Men have no right to take the will of God into their own hands!'

"The Tsarevitch told me later," Monsieur said, "that it seemed to him that the substitution of his father on the throne for his uncle Constantine was less the will of God than the will of Constantine, but naturally he would not have dared to say so. Instead, he sighed, and smiled weakly at his father, who was obviously warming to his subject.

"You must remember that the boy had heard the story of the Decembrists' Revolt hashed and rehashed, since the day it had happened, and he remembered it all clearly enough anyway. He recalled, with a knot in his stomach, the terror and the sounds of shots and the screams of the women. For years afterward, he had had nightmares of it all, and remembered well, the hushed voices in the nursery, but above all he remembered the speculation of the consequences, and his own overriding fear that his father might die.

"But the Tsar had not died; not that day nor any other, so here Alex sat at table listening to the interminable tirade against 'free thinkers' that had begun when someone had remarked to the Tsar that he had heard this morning of the banishment of Alexander Herzen and his friend Professor Ogarov to an even farther outlying province. At first there had been a general discussion and murmured congratulations offered to Nicholas for his wisdom and decisive action against these two free thinkers, and then someone had remarked that all free thinkers would ultimately come to such an end, and that the very idea of such a usurpation of the divine rights of the Tsar—coming from the University of Moscow through the mental machinations of Herzen and Ogarov and others—was what came of atheism. Indeed, remarked another, Herzen had introduced these dangerous concepts to our impressionable youth etc., etc., etc . . . until the boy thought he might fall asleep, and it was right then that his father had turned to him and asked him . . . 'What do you think of all this, Sasha?'

"'I can't see very much morally wrong about wanting to think what you can't help thinking in the first place,' the boy had replied soberly, 'I think freedom to think and to act as seems right to a man ought to be allowed him. After all, if God gave us minds and wills, He must intend us to use them for something,' he added, hoping that by bringing God into it to be on safer ground with his father. Then his father had said, 'That's nonsense, don't you see? If we allow people license to do as they please, they will become uncontrollable. Look at the Decembrists who tried to assassinate me—they were acting as they believed to be right, they said. What choice had I but to hang the leaders and banish the poor dupes who followed them?'

"'Well, *punish* the leaders, perhaps,' said Sasha, frowning as he grappled not very successfully with the ambiguity of the arguments racing around his ears like flies in a stable, 'but the followers, I . . .'

"'Listen here, Alexander Tsarevitch. Put yourself in my boots . . . as someday you will be . . . and think! What would you have done to the Decembrists?'

"The boy had thought a moment, waded through the inconsistencies of all the discussions he had heard on it over the years, and finally in confusion, had fallen back on his feelings. 'I would have freed them, Sir,' he said firmly, and in the moment of silence before his father's roar, the entire company saw the heart of Alexander II."

Zhukovsky continued, "The Romanov line began with Michael Romanov in 1725, and I will tell you that so far, Alexander II is the most sensitive and intelligent of them all. Oh, yes, Khánum, I have great hopes for Alexander and, through him, for Russia."

"Do you believe, then, that freeing the Decembrists would have been the right thing to do?"

"No, Madam, I do not. But neither do I think that putting them to death or banishing them to the frozen wastelands was the right thing either, and my point about His Majesty, is that he is of a gentle heart and so would have, I am sure, found a way to handle it better than Nicholas had."

"So, if I understand you correctly, you believe that, unlike his father, he has the good of his people at heart."

"Yes, I do. But it will not be easy for him. His father labored long and ceaselessly, attempting to create Alexander in his own image and instilling in him the need for ruthless autocracy. His mother and I were hard put to undo it as much as we could. It was entirely her influence and admiration for me—and later Sasha's and my mutual love for each other—that kept me on as his tutor for his entire youth.

"When he was nineteen, Nicholas wanted him to travel throughout much of Russia and see the country and the people for himself. I was fifty-six by then and not in the best of health, and, as the Tsar had never quite approved of me anyway, he chose a man named Kavelin to accompany him. The Tsarina, however, insisted that I be allowed to go also—and Sasha insisted as well. Fortunately the Tsar gave in to the pressure of his wife and son, and while the journey was very hard on me and I was nearly a year recovering after our return, I would not have refused even if it had meant my life.

"What a journey!" he said, with a force and enthusiasm in his voice, usually beyond his elderly manner. He turned to me, as we paused to sip some tea, and his face was bright and glowing.

"We traveled first by railroad to Moscow, then by stagecoach, by troika, and even, in some places, by oxcart. Alexander saw so much of Russia! There had been drawn up a carefully planned itinerary, but Alex said it was foolish to stick to it, because of course, where they knew he was coming, all would be cleaned up and a nice face put upon people and villages, with the squares swept and the best food in the village sacrificed for us and the towns' committees. There was a great deal of that, of course, but suddenly, without warning, Alex would demand that we halt in some little flea-infested village, and he would insist upon meeting the people himself, and even going into their houses to speak with them.

"The serfs, my dear Madam, in the event that you do not know, are not merely servants; they are the property of the landowners. They can be, and often are, rented out or even sold and *always* sent to fight in the wars. They are not trained soldiers but merely starving men in uniform. I am always amazed that they fight as well as they do, defending the land that is not only their home but also their prison.

"Their houses are thrown together with whatever materials they can find lying about, as their owners do not build them houses and they must scavenge what they can. The miserable things leak (we seldom saw even one which had a complete roof), and in the winter, often the serfs freeze to death. Their little shelters have no chimneys and so are filled with smoke, which can escape only through the doors. The doors themselves are . . . well, disgraceful.

"Their lives are so wretched that they seek escape in cheap spirits and stay drunk, and even comatose, as often and for as long as possible."

I wanted to interrupt his recital and ask if our servants, in Count Nicholas's house, lived in huts like that, but didn't want to risk displeasing him in the middle of a story again, so I did not. However, I learned later that such was not the case. Our people were house servants, and several of them, having rooms off the kitchen, were kept well, and fed well, and often thought of as nearly family.

Monsieur Zhukovsky continued. "The women have baby after baby until they die of exhaustion, and the babies die also, more often than not. They are filthy dirty, and they and their houses stink like pig styes. My boy would go in and sit down and drink whatever little warmed tea they could offer him, to be hospitable, but refuse any food on the grounds that he had eaten too much the meal before, for he knew the sacrifice they were making. At first Kavelin and I went in with him, and I continued to—but after about two visits, Kavelin stayed outside—too filthy and smelly, he said. The Tsarevitch would talk with them and promise them that when he came to power, he would do his best to help them have better lives. They seemed pleased by that, but I am not at all sure they had any idea of what a better life consisted.

"At first, when we had returned to our conveyance, he would weep. 'How is it, Zhuie, that nothing has ever been done about this? How did it get to be like this in the first place?' By the end of the journey, he had stopped weeping, but said a number of times, striking his knee with his fist, 'By God! When I am Tsar, this will be ended. I will free these people from this misery! Zhukovsky, I swear I will!'

"'I am overjoyed to hear this,' I said, 'but how will you do it? Your grandfather, Tsar Alexander I, had a similar idea, but when it came down to it, it couldn't be done. In a small province, where he tried it out, the landowners revolted at the loss of so much of their property and source of revenue. The freed serfs themselves became gangs of criminals, living off what they could steal, rather than work the little acreages they had been given. They are so ignorant, my boy. Their lives are so mean.'

"'I know, Zhukovsky,' he had said thoughtfully, 'but there is a way—there must be—and I will find it.'"

11

THE CONFESSIONS OF PADRE VITTORIO:

JMJ*

Inasmuch as this account of my life is quite properly labeled a "confession," though in this case not in the sense of asking for absolution, but rather "to acknowledge," as in the literary sense, even so, I believe I ought to begin in the usual manner of confession.

"Forgive me Father, for I have sinned."

Because, of course I have, many times and in a number of ways. Yet, as long as I can remember, I have loved Holy Mother Church. I first determined to spend my life in her service when I was very small, seven years old. I remember because I had recently made my first communion, on Easter of my seventh year. That would have been 1844.

I remember the morning very clearly. We were at Mass, and my mother was radiant with devotion as she knelt to receive the Host. We children were not so much radiant as watchful, for my father was keeping his eyes on each of us in turn, the warning in them a message that if there were even the slightest misbehavior, we would be severely punished when we reached home. What constituted misbehavior in our father's eyes was not

* JMJ = Jesus, Mary, and Joseph. A mark often employed by Catholic priests when writing, as a sign of respect.

always easy to determine. It could be as small a thing as a sneeze that interrupted the quiet hum of the service, or an itch that demanded scratching just as Padre Giuseppe reached us with the wafer. But there was never any question about what the punishment would be. We would be beaten. He always said that he was not "sparing the rod, lest he spoil the child," and my four brothers and our little sister believed that. I never could. I believed then, and I believe now, that he simply enjoyed beating us.

He was tall, my father—tall and thin and dark haired, with long limbs and ropy muscles—and his face was long too, with a pointed nose and chin. Unfortunately, I look like him. There was a distinct gleam of fanatic purpose in his dark eyes as he wielded the stout birch rod he kept for our frequent punishments. At least three times a week, one or two of us would find ourselves on the business end of that rod while he applied it to the business end of our anatomy. But, for me, the most convincing moment in this frequent ritual was the first time he took my two-year-old baby sister by the hand and began to lay her face down on the table in our dark little kitchen. My mother, who was quiet and sweet tempered, cried out to him in a voice I had never heard from her before.

"No! You will not touch her! If you must beat someone, beat me—but I swear before God, I will *kill* you before I let you lay a hand on her!"

For a moment he stared at her incredulously, as my mother did not speak up to him ever, and, strangely, he capitulated. Then he beat me instead.

I hated my father.

On that certain morning during Mass, when I knew I would serve God always, we were kneeling at the communion rail and I had just received the Host. Even as it melted against my tongue, I heard a voice in my head as clearly as though it were from my brother who knelt beside me. It said, "Vittorio, sleep not."

I thought at first my brother had spoken, and I whispered to him, "What did you say?"

"Nothing," he whispered back, his eye on our father whose tongue was just now reaching for the wafer. "I didn't say anything."

As I frowned in puzzlement, I heard it again. "Sleep not."

I concluded that it was the voice of God Himself, though what He intended by this, I had no idea. I guessed since God never spoke to ordinary people that it must mean I was going to be a saint. I knew I had a long way to go to become saintly, but, like most children, though I knew I was terribly bad, I also believed I would somehow magically reach perfection when I became grown up, and so it didn't seem such an outrageous thought after all.

In the meantime, I would be as obedient as I possibly could. If I could not please my earthly father, perhaps I could please my heavenly One, and so my life changed that morning.

Not for the better, I assure you. Trying not to sleep was very difficult, and over and over, I failed. What sleep I did manage was often accompanied by a dream of myself at the communion rail, and again that strong voice, repeating, "Vittorio, sleep not," and I would jerk awake in a guilty sweat. Night after night I would pray fervently before retiring that He would help me to "sleep not," but night after night, sometime before dawn, I would drop into a peaceful world of delicious blackness and wake to the tortures of guilt at having failed again.

Waking at dawn to do chores was growing increasingly difficult, and my work suffered. We lived on a small farm in the northeastern part of what is now Italy, a little south of Bologna, in what was then in the Papal State of Romagna. Though there were six of us children, as well as Father and Mother to do the work, it seemed there was always another chore urgently waiting.

We had two pigs that, in the good years, gave us more. We could not afford a cow, but there were two goats that needed constant care, feeding and milking, and a tired old donkey to help with the field work. Then too, we had a large garden where we raised most of our food and a small field where we grew feed for the animals. We tried from time to time to use part of the field for a money crop—something we could sell in the village—strawberries or cabbages. But more often than not, either from weather, lack of demand, or the prices plunging downward, it turned out badly.

The more tired I became, the more my work suffered, and the more my work suffered, the more acquainted I became with Father's infernal rod. This attempt to stay awake at night went on for I don't remember how long. It seems, to a small boy's memory, like months, but perhaps it was only a few weeks. I begged God in my prayers to speak again to me and tell me He knew of my suffering on His account, but there was no heavenly voice, and I sometimes wondered if I had made it all up.

As you might imagine, my attempts at saintliness faded away as the presence of daily life pushed aside the clarity of that rarified moment at the communion rail. But my overall intention remained, and I always knew I had a vocation.

Part of what kept me firm in my conviction was a sensation I sometimes enjoyed during my prayers. Once in a great while, the dutiful obedience of daily prayer would move into a bliss that came with the opening of my heart. I would be praying, and suddenly my heart would seem to burst open with a small, almost audible, "pop," and the sweetness of the ensuing bliss would spread from my heart throughout my entire body. I could then not stop my prayers, and would go on and on, telling our blessed Jesus over and over of my love for His Church, and begging Him to allow me to remain always one of His beloved and to be allowed to serve Him all my life. I would believe then that God loved me in spite of my obvious shortcomings, and I would smile in my bliss and sometimes weep for the joy I was feeling.

My father was not pleased when I mentioned at the supper table one night in my thirteenth year that I was going to be a priest when I grew up. He ranted for five minutes about wasting my life and doing useless work and not being there to provide for him in his old age and on and on.

Mother *was* pleased and surreptitiously slipped an extra piece of meat into my stew, accompanied by one of her tender smiles of understanding. I'm sure Father would have prevented my ambition, but our good Padre Giuseppe colluded with my mother to get me into a boy's seminary.

So the years went by, and I grew toward manhood. I was fifteen the day I left home for the school where I would receive my earliest studies toward holy orders, and my mother cried as though her heart would break, her worn and tired face paler than ever. When my father pointed out that I was the cause of this pain, that I ought to be ashamed and that it was not too late to change my mind, she stopped him. "No," she said, "God wants him, and we should be grateful." Then she added, "but I will miss you." I knew I would miss her too—miss her thoughtfulness and her feeble attempts to make up for my father's cruelty by the kindly little things she did for us. It went unspoken among us children, but we knew that though our mother loved us, she was helpless to protect us from his rage. Her eyes often told us how sorry she was for our lot, and we answered back with our own smiles and attempts to make her daily work load easier.

Though the discipline in the school was rigid and sometimes harsh, and we boys a little cruel to one another, as boys—even student priest boys—always are, it was an easier life than at home. I had a roommate named Mario (at ordination, he took the name of Francis Mario), who was tow-headed, slight of build, and endowed with the most infectious giggling laugh. Further, he was not very faithful about obeying the rules and often got into scrapes, from which it usually fell to me to extricate him. Worse, he sometimes seduced me into the scrapes with him; then we were both in trouble, which more often than not resulted in a quarrel between us. Yet, in spite of numerous quarrels and misunderstandings over the years, he and I became as close as brothers, and I love him still today. He served at the Vatican as one of the many Papal secretaries. His particular talent is literary, and he worked among the books and tablets of the Vatican Library. It is dusty, silent and lonely work; I have not envied him his tasks.

I mentioned at the beginning of these confessions that I have sinned in many ways . . . as do we all. Most men have what is known as a besetting sin, but I, Christ have mercy, have not one but two. Poverty, chastity, obedience; all these were easy enough. Poverty and obedience I certainly learned well at home. I had a struggle with chastity in my youth, but it came in time, and I have not been over troubled with it in my middle years. I recognized early enough that my two besetting sins were these: my hatred of my father, which, try as I may, I cannot overcome. I have somewhat forgiven him for his treatment of me, but of my brothers, sister, and my saintly mother, I could not. I have hated him all my life.

The other is my ambition. I think that, too, is related to my father, because he told me over and over that I was of no account and would never amount to anything; that my choice of the priesthood was because

I was lazy and afraid of real work. It is not true. I have worked as hard as any man alive and have, as a result, risen in the hierarchy of the Church. When I am not living in Rome and serving there, I am sent out of the country to various assignments. Of late I have been stationed in France and Austria.

I think there was a time when I thought that if I worked well and served with some distinction, my father would finally see the value of my vocation and be pleased with me at last, but it never happened. He died a few years ago, still not reconciled to my choice, and if nothing else, I learned that seeking the approbation of men, even of one's own father, was of no value in the eternal scheme of things, and a waste of time. "We ought to obey God rather than men," St. Paul said, and I know now that that applies as well to attempting to please others. It has taken me nearly forty years to learn that.

After the long years of study and discipline, we came at last to our ordination day—in 1858. We were twenty-one.

Naively believing that adventures and struggles and difficulties with rules were finally behind us, Father Francis Mario and Father Giuseppe Vittorio were suddenly priests of our Lord Jesus Christ. Like comrades in arms with the combat behind us, we bid each other a heartfelt "Addio and Buona Fortuna!"* not knowing if or when we would ever meet again, and went off to save the world.

I was assigned to a small, poor parish only a day and a half's journey from where I had grown up, so sometimes I could get home to see my family. That part was good.

I soon found I was not overly fond of parish work. The heartbreak, the constant round of baptisms and burials and the neverending debilitating poverty, so much like that suffered by my own family, often depressed me. I saw, in the early marriages of expedience and the yearly birthings that stole the health and beauty from the eyes of the young girls, my mother's past and my sister's future, and I longed to be elsewhere.

**Addio*: good-bye; *Buona fortuna*: good luck.

Then too, my homilies were too intellectual for the simple folk I served. I was twice told that I must simplify them or be given prewritten sermons to deliver. I couldn't seem to do it, however, so before long found myself delivering shallow thoughts in words written by some other priest and sent to me from the bishop, and of course, this made it even more difficult, not to mention humiliating.

But I was conscientious and did my very best. Looking back on it now, I see that—though I cared about my parishioners, though my heart bled for their sorrows, and though I tried with whatever means at my disposal to do what I could for them—to my everlasting shame, I see also that a secret eye in my heart was always on Rome and the earning of position and honor.

12

HILLHOUSE PAPERS:

The wine was comforting in the loneliness of the London flat so lately emptied of the presence of John's parents, and he settled back into his father's chair, preparing to delve into the reading that lay ahead of him. His father's letter had quite taken him aback, and he was, to say the least, intrigued. He took another sip and, setting the wine glass carefully on the cherry table to his left, began to read the first of the papers entitled "notes":

1866—Paris:

"For the last three years I have been stationed here in Paris, and, I must say, it is the best of duties. The city is always lovely, and the life here is surely to the liking of one such as myself, who is not encumbered with family (at least not yet) and is free to enjoy all the city's amenities. Even better, unlike those early years of my employ in Persia, I can get home for holidays and it is an easy journey. Even in winter, it is better. Ah, beautiful Paris.

"This Christmas I shall go home not only to celebrate the holiday with my parents but to be married. Margaret is a nice woman and of good family, and both her parents and mine approve wholeheartedly. I think it will be a good thing to be settled down and possibly even raise a family. (Can't have the name of Hillhouse dying out, can we? Pity I have only my two sisters.) In any event, Margaret is thrilled to be moving with me to Paris. Of course, if I were still assigned to Persia I wouldn't think of taking her along. Don't know what I shall do about that if I draw some arduous and difficult duty in a year or so, such as the year I spent in Persia.

"Never have I seen such bestiality among the populace! To speak of blood running in the streets and soaking the fields; I actually saw it on an occasion or two! Well, three times, actually. The first time I saw a mob cutting off peoples ears and forcing them to eat them, I was nauseated and ill on the spot, and until I left for England, there were nights when, hearing the commotion in the streets outside the embassy windows, I could not sleep. I could not ever expose Margaret to that!

"Ah well, time will answer all those questions, won't it? In the meantime, I feel quite lucky to have found this woman, whom I deeply admire, and will be quite content, I think, to be shackled to domesticity at last."

John stopped reading and took another sip of wine. He had known his father was not verbally demonstrative, but to read in his own words the understated declaration of love for his mother quite surprised John. He would have thought his father would have been more eloquent about his feelings in private notes, such as these, which almost seemed to be in the style of a journal. Further, he couldn't help but be amused at his father's slight reluctance about giving up his bachelorhood. He himself had had similar feelings when he had finally secured Carrie's promise to marry him, and the headiness of pursuit and submission had given way to the stark realization that he was taking upon himself the full responsibility of manhood and that of a householder. But he knew, too, that his parents had been devoted to one another.

He imagined it had been similar for his father as at the moment when his own reluctance had given way—at the first sight of Carrie in her white gown and veil, emerging from the narthex on her father's arm. An absolutely weak-kneed devotion had seized him, and his eyes had followed her every step down the interminable aisle until she was safely at his side and the Vicar had pronounced her his own. He thought of her again, waiting now for him at home up-country, her blonde hair hanging in soft waves to her shoulders and her slight form warm and welcoming in her blue woolen robe, hazel eyes smiling while he smiled back.

Turning his attention back to the task at hand, he again raised the papers and continued reading:

> "Yet, it has been, for all its pleasures, a difficult time for the world and for France. But it is a time of hope as well. The European scene is changing. When I remember that it has been only fifty years since the death of Napoleon and the end of the wars he so brutally foisted upon Europe, sacrificing to his ambition, an entire generation of young Frenchmen (not to mention the lives of those who were forced to defend their homelands from his invasions), I am amazed at the sheer amount of change. After all, it was only thirty more years—1848—until Europe was rent by revolution, and all this has wrought such change that the world of Europe seems almost to be a different world.
>
> "Of course, the lines of monarchy continue unabated as always, though almost all of the monarchies are now constitutional. Even Náṣiri'd-Dín Sháh of Persia has consented to a constitution, although in his case, I fear it means little. But it will come, I feel sure, as the concept of personal freedom and the right to a voice in the government is taking hold in almost every European country. That is good, no question about that.
>
> "Fortunately, our beloved Queen has been serious about the constitutional rights of *our* people, but of course, England has always led the way throughout the world as we all move from enslavement into freedom, hasn't it? After all, it all began with the Magna Carta in England's own meadow. Aside from France, our dear Victoria has brought much of the change *and* the stability into being quite by herself unaided, except for the Prince Consort. (That was not meant to be a facetious remark, referring, as it might do, to her numerous progeny.)

"Of course the American colonies have come up with their odd ideas about getting rid of monarchy, but they are only playing at government, having been reared for the most part in the bush, or what they refer to as the frontier, and among savages. Admittedly, George III was a bit hard on them, and I s'pose they feel they are getting even, but surely they will come round in time, and see the need for a throne, or be taken over by some conqueror or another. Granted, their system has worked for them for nearly a hundred years, but that is hardly enough time to swat a fly, as it were. As we all know, democracy has been tried before and always failed, containing, as it does, the seeds of its own destruction—the fall of both Greece and of Rome was demonstration enough of that. And monarchy is, after all, the natural order of things, having existed throughout all recorded history in every land and tribe.

"But here, I have noticed, is the strange part. Since 1848, not only Europe but the *entire world* has changed drastically.

"In China in 1850, the Taiping rebellion destroyed the old imperial policies. She had never wanted to lose her isolation from the rest of the world, but that is no longer possible since the rebellion.

"At the same time, Japan seemed to awaken from her ancient enslavement to the rigid policies of the shoguns and their caste system. That began in 1854, when Japan opened her ports to a very limited foreign trade.

"Then, of course, there was India. Her Majesty's government faced a terrible time during the mutiny of India in 1857 and '58. But from then on, India could no longer regard us as just one more conqueror to be endured and eventually overcome by patience. India began to discard many of her traditional customs. Of course we English had outlawed 'suttee,' that barbaric custom of burning widows on the funeral pyres of their dead husbands, but they seemed to take it well, and I suspect, many (no doubt mostly women), with relief. That seemed only the beginning, however, as the Indian people began to cast off one after another of their ancient traditions.

"Finally, of course, there was the Crimean War. Interestingly enough, even though with the help of France, Austria, and ourselves the Ottoman Turks won their war, they lost in the winning. The empire of Sultan 'Abdu'l-Azíz has not even begun to recover from the wounds of that war. Because we built for them railroads and other public amenities, they owe a huge debt to us and our allies, which they have not been able to repay. Further, part of our agreement to help them was to insist that they extend equal liberties to all Ottomans, not just the sultan's own Muslim subjects. H'mm, I do seem to be digressing a little, but my point is this—

"Around the whole world, the old ways, which have endured through disease, starvation, territorial warfare, and the other ravages of time, for at least two thousand years, and in the case of the Far East, even longer, are effectively gone.

"So it is that within the last *fifteen* years, the four great sections of the world, that is—Christian Europe, the Buddhist Far East, the Muslim Mid-East and the Indian sub-continent—have effectively become a single unit. It puzzles me. When I have pointed this out to my colleagues, they shrug and say, 'Well, it's the railroads and the telegraph isn't it?' They don't seem to think beyond the confines of British expansion. Or they tell me I am making too much of it, so I am learning to keep some of these thoughts to myself. After all, I am only a junior ambassador, and I don't wish to have my superiors thinking I am going dotty already. But at least I can record them here in the hope that one day I shall be vindicated.

"I cannot agree with them. It is not enough to say that it is because of the railroads and telegraph and a few other industrial experiments; the changes are too huge and too rapid . . . and too widespread. How *could* it be due to those things? The telegraph was only invented in 1844 and is not yet practical. That is a mere *twenty-two* years ago, and I am speaking of millions and millions of people whom the influence of railroads and the telegraph have not yet reached, nor will they, I rather imagine, for generations to come."

Finishing his glass and pouring a bit more wine, John sat thinking about what his father had written. He thought to himself that since then, Africa and the United States had become a large part of that single unit.

"Father, you appear to have been quite on the money," he said aloud. The telegraph didn't become practical until 1870 or so, and the United Statees has seen its own revolution, with its people divided over slavery and almost split into two nations. Yet, British expansion *has* been responsible for a large part of it. After all, had we not needed coaling stations all over the world for our steamships, Africa might still be lost in isolation and steaming in mystery.

After a few moments more of thoughtful silence, he pulled himself from his reverie to read the one final line in that section: "Something momentous is happening!"

13

CONFESSIONS:

JMJ

Fortunately for me, the years of parish work did not last very long, although it seemed at the time as though they would never end. Because I showed an aptitude for language and detail, I began to be tapped by the bishop for errands that demanded these particular skills. At first they were mostly written work and, very rarely, some that required research visits to the Vatican itself. That was, to my still boyish heart, a treat beyond measure.

It is difficult to convey in mere words the feelings that seized my spirit when those visits took place. The moment the horses' hooves sounded their first clattering entrance into the city, my breast would fill with joy and my heart begin to beat faster. Rome! The aptly named "eternal city," once the domain of the Caesars' mighty empire that had ruled the known world, was, until lately, the center of the papal lands and states, which of course included all of Italy, Piedmont, Tuscany, Lombardy, and Venetia. Now, still, it is the seat of our glorious Church. The visible sign of Christ's kingdom that had inherited the seven hills and the ancient sites exuded now, like summer's heat from the stone of her streets, unmistakable waves of papal power. And I was part of it!

As the years went by, I was more and more needed for the work I loved and—because I loved it—executed with such care. After about seven years, I could barely believe my good fortune when, in 1866, I was invited to make my permanent residence in Rome.

Assigned to a small apartment near the offices I served, it was only a short walk to the library and the vast files for research that became available to me. When I was not working, I spent hours and sometimes whole days wandering about the city visiting ancient sites. When I caught sight of one of the princes of the Church strolling along the street, I wondered if I would ever wear the red hat of a cardinal. In my heart I was determined that I would, but in the meantime, I knew, many years of hard service must pass before that could come about.

When the weather was inclement, I loved to read many of the world's classics from the lending portion of the library.

It was in the library one rainy afternoon as I poked about the stacks, searching for something to occupy my upcoming evening's leisure, that I turned a corner, and who should be suddenly there before me but my best friend and old roommate, Father Francis Mario. He was standing with his hands clasped behind him and his legs splayed from beneath the skirt of his cassock, making him look not unlike a large letter "A." He was grinning widely. He had recognized me as I rounded the end of the stack and was waiting for me to see him. When I did, it was almost more than I could manage to contain the shouts of delight that raced up from my belly and pushed against my throat. We embraced each other as best we could. (His small stature and my long legs had me looking down at the top of his head.) We managed to express our joy in whispered tones.

"What are you doing here?' I asked him.

"I work here, now. I live here . . . you?"

"The same! I've been here about seven or eight months . . . and for you?"

"Over a year," he whispered, "why haven't we met up with each other before this?"

"I work for the legates' offices and am gone a great deal of the time. Often I get sent on errands to the north—the areas of Piedmont and Tuscany, mostly."

We made plans to meet that evening at a small *Caffe* we could afford, and there we ate supper together. His tow-colored hair had turned a light brown over the years, and the boyish giggle had given way to a rich deep laugh. But the twinkling blue eyes that had led him (and sometimes me) into such mischievous pranks in seminary still sparkled with his same humor and love of life.

After an hour or so, we still had not begun to exhaust the wealth of things we had to say to each other, so we wandered back to his quarters, laughing and talking all the way.

I was astounded when I walked in. Compared to my spare and colorless two small rooms, it seemed more than spacious. I expressed my wonder, "Mother of God! You should see *my* pitiful lodgings, Mario. Who are you, anyway, the Holy Father's first cousin?"

"No," he laughed, "this apartment is near the library and archives, where I spend most of my time. Also I had a suite mate, but he was moved out of Rome, so until they find another for me, I have all this to myself."

"You say they will be assigning you another suite mate?"

I needn't tell you that we looked at each other then, both thinking the same thing, and began grinning from ear to ear.

We sat up most of the night, reliving the deviltry we had got into in seminary, and catching up on the years that had passed since the day we had bid one another good-bye, and I wandered home to my little place, sometime before dawn, in a happy daze that was only slightly intensified by wine.

In about six weeks, our request to share his apartment was granted, and I moved in. I had to leave the next day, on an assignment in Piedmont, and did not return for two months, but upon my return, we settled happily into our respective routines.

So after that, when I was in Rome, we shared that set of rooms in the Vatican far from the papal apartments. It overlooked the city rather than St. Peter's Square, and the rooms were richly furnished with heavily carved furniture and deep piled chairs and sofas. The walls were painted a dusty yellow and hung with paintings of the Italian countryside, scenes from the Holy Land and the life of Christ. One wall was entirely covered with a huge bookcase, and what with the interests of my librarian friend and my own, was full to overflowing with books, some lying untidily sideways atop the others in the row, with still more overflow piled on fireplace mantel and tables. We even had small stacks on the floor beside our beds. Often in the evenings, we sat before a fire, while through the window stars shone down on the city. Sometimes we read, sometimes we caught up on backed up work or perhaps shared a bottle of wine and talked long into the night.

In another eighteen months or so, I was made first secretary to a papal legate (my second promotion since moving to Rome), and frequently given assignments in Austria. Several times when I had returned, I was allowed to report to Pope Pius IX himself. It was an honor to meet him face-to-face and to converse with him, however formally. I could not help but feel, at the Holy Father's infrequent words of praise, a sense of what I perceived to be my growing importance.

Though my father had died by this time, even so I hoped somewhere in my heart, with the same mixed needs of the peasant child I had once been, that he would finally be proud of his eldest son, and at the same time, reveled in smug triumph over my memories of his scorn.

I admired Pius. In the earliest days of his papacy everyone admired Pius. The meanest peasants loved him. He had been, they say, though reared in a once wealthy family with a long pedigree, a loveable child, a bright student, and always devout from his earliest youth. His background was a matter of some pride to him, descended from some royal line or another, and he had often commented that this was a gift from God to him, for that though our Blessed Lord had been born in a stall, He nevertheless was descended from kings.

Pius was sickly as a boy, given to seizures, melancholy, and even periods of an almost incoherent confusion, but by the time he was ordained in 1829 at the age of twenty-seven, all that had improved so much as to seldom trouble him. Now, he was a man of great kindness, with a round and open, friendly face and a saintly manner. He was a shining example to us all as a devoted servant of the Mother of God—and our Holy Mother Church. These were, indeed, times that cried out for devotion in her service.

Pius had been elevated to the papacy in 1846 and astounded Europe with his liberalism. He allied himself immediately with the liberal nationalism, which was within two years to explode in revolution all over Europe, so of course the people loved him immediately. He introduced a number of reforms within the church. He allowed, for instance, other news organs beside the official "Diario di Roma," encouraging a forum of ideas and actually allowed a box to be placed in the Vatican so the people could make suggestions and register complaints. He called upon the various heads of the provinces to provide public work projects, hoping thereby to minimize unemployment, which, he hoped, would also reduce crime. No wonder the peoples' loyalty grew rapidly.

Back in the days of Napoleon Bonaparte, that butcher had nearly succeeded in stealing the power and wealth of the Church, but fortunately Bonaparte was gone by 1815. In their love for Pius, the poorest people would bring their pitiful collections of pennies to him cupped in their hands, calling "Vive Pio Nono! Vive! Vive!" In fact, they came with torches and instruments, singing and shouting praises for "Pio Nono," parading through the streets at night and throwing flowers before his carriage in the day when he went out among them. His popularity was greater than any pope had enjoyed for many, many years.

I marvel still to think that the entire Christian world—not only we Catholics, but the Protestants and Eastern Orthodox Christians—spent their own money to recover some of the wealth and lands of the Roman Catholic Church, though, as we all knew, much of those lands and wealth were never recovered from the losses of Napoleon's day.

Pius loved his popularity. He seemed to need the people's love, and he worked very hard at deserving their adoration.

But within two years of his accession, the revolution that swept across Europe in 1848, changed the pope. Pius declared the entire concept of personal liberty anathema, though I believed by the time I moved to Rome in '66 that, given his own leanings toward liberalism, he would eventually come to be reconciled with this new concept of liberty and find a workable compromise. Alas, he never did, but more about that later.

Meanwhile, he feared for the power and wealth of the church, and for the souls of the people, so in 1864, he issued the Syllabus of Errors. It listed some eighty separate heresies against the Church. He hoped it would tame and subdue the loosening passions of the faithful, but I soon found in contacts with my people, in what was then my parish work, that no one paid very much attention to the Syllabus. Even we priests found it irrelevant to the daily sins and sorrows in the simple lives of the people we served. It was more for the guidance of bishops than for laymen, so it was then—as it is now—largely ignored.

As for the faithful, they found the Syllabus cold and repressive (especially the ten items that had to do with marriage), and it seemed to them very unlike the voice of their warm and kindly Holy Father. They came to believe that the Syllabus was the result of undue influence upon him by conservative and repressive bishops. Now they marched through the streets crying "Long live Pio Nono—alone!" and singing of him: "As beautiful as hope / Strong as a lion / Gentle as a lamb / As just as God!"

And Pius, caught up in the myth of his own heroism and somewhat inebriated by it, said, "We will cede as long as our conscience permits us, but arriving at the limit we have already pre-established, we will not—with the help of God—go beyond it one step, even if they tear us to pieces!"[1]

"What ingrates!" he cried somewhat later, "I have given them amnesty and reforms!" He was shocked that he could never quite satisfy his subjects, who wanted more concessions of papal strictures, and then more, and who had not afforded him the gratitude he felt he deserved.[2]

All this was in the past, of course, but it affected our lives in those years, and Mario and I spent long hours in the evenings discussing the effects of all of it, and of the growing impatience among the populace with the strictures imposed by the Church. Even Mario and I had our complaints, and as I have said, I carried some rather strong opinions. We felt free to discuss them with one another, but only by ourselves and never with anyone else.

Having been reared in poverty, I understood the people's complaints about the annual crop tax we were required to pay the Church. I have said over and over that I hated my father, and certainly there was much about him to hate. But still and all, he worked like a slave, and worked all of us in the family like slaves, trying to make crops enough to see us through the winter. In the fall, no sooner would the grain be cut and the hay made to feed the donkeys, the little pigs weaned and beginning to fatten, the grapes made into jellies and wine, and the apples and pears, beans and peas, dried and stored for the winter, than the church's tax collectors would come for their tithe. As our family grew, my parents soon saw that the supplies left after the priests had taken their share (and eaten one, if not two or three, sumptuous meals my mother prepared for them from our meager supplies), there could not possibly be enough left to keep us through the winter, to use as seed the next spring and feed us until the following harvest. So my father would bury almost half his crop in straw near the woods and take the small pigs and the goats well back into the timber when he heard the priests were coming. It was the only way we could live without starving.

My mother was deeply concerned at the sin of their lying, but she went along, for she understood that without this dishonesty, we would surely starve, as we went hungry enough before spring as it was. We children—when we were very little—did not know what they were doing, but by the time we had grown old enough to question the annual hiding, we were told not to mention it to anyone, on pain of a beating such as we had not known before. It was the only time, I noticed, that my mother countenanced my fathers threats.

As I grew older, I realized that all the neighbors did the same thing. I thought my parents and the neighbors clever to so outwit the collectors, and whether Father Giuseppe knew or not I have no idea, but I know that when I became a priest and found my parishioners were doing the same, I conveniently did not see, nor did I inform the priestly collectors of what I knew.

Mario understood and sympathized with my anger about this, but having grown up with a certain amount of means, he had other complaints that troubled him more. He grew incensed at the idea of priestly confession. "Why should the people have to confess before another man," he sometimes railed, "after all, we priests sin our own sins, and apostolic ordination or not, who are we to forgive? Why can we not just take our sins to God and trust Him to forgive us? I think people's sins are nobody's business but theirs and God's."

"But Mario," I would counter, "whether we are sinners or not, we have been given the power to forgive sins by the laying on of apostolic hands at our ordination. Besides, how do we know the faithful will remember to confess, if we don't hear their confession. It is part of our function as priests."

"Maybe," he would answer, "but I notice that when our blessed Lord was among us, He never required anyone to confess directly to Him, nor did He assign penance to even the woman taken in adultery. He seemed to trust us to move through our lives in faith, and by faith to find our way to God.

"I sometimes think," he mumbled almost inaudibly one evening after one of our discussions, as though he were ashamed to admit his own thought, "that our Lord was not nearly so preoccupied with our sins as Holy Mother Church."

I had to concede that he had a point.

There came an evening when I noticed a change in Mario. He seemed either to have no interest in discussion and, pleading fatigue, retired early, wishing me a cordial "Buono Notte," or else he would leap into discussion as eagerly as ever, become heated almost to the point of anger—which was not like him—and then as it seemed he was about to blurt our something of importance, retreat into silence before suddenly rising from his chair and going to bed. I asked him if anything were troubling him and inquired after his health, but he assured me it was nothing. I asked if I had done something to cause him annoyance, but he put his hand on my shoulder and reassured me that I seldom annoyed him and, that the next time I did, he would certainly not stand short on saying so. But Father Francis Mario was troubled, and it puzzled me that given our long close friendship, he would hide it from me.

14

SHIRIN:

In 1856, when the war ended and Alexander II became Tsar, I was forty-two, and the next ten years were busy and fruitful. As one might imagine, St. Petersburg became comfortable (though never like home), and Count Nicholas's family very, very close.

Olga, the count's mother, was terribly dependent upon him. Some years earlier, her husband had died as the result of a hunting accident. He received a bullet in his head and unfortunately lingered for several days. Until Nicholas grew up to become the head of the household, Prince Michael cared for the family. She was in her mid-fifties when I came to St. Petersburg and seemed to be in poor health. Before I had been there very long, Prince Michael himself died, and this only exacerbated her condition. Later I came to understand that her illnesses were more in her mind than in her body. Her constitution, I finally realized, was as iron strong as my own, but her lonely helplessness had begun with her husband's death. She had been pregnant with Dimitri at the time, and the shock and fear it all engendered resulted in a massive melancholia and a breakdown from which she never entirely recovered. Given to sick headaches, spells of the vapors, and other feminine complaints that I have never understood, she would often take to her bed for days at a time.

The family fussed over her and had, in fact, set aside a small room with a chaise and all the accoutrements she might need, just off the library, where we most often congregated. Instead of being shut away alone upstairs, she could retire and yet be within hearing distance of any activity and often, I noticed, would join us. For a while, I thought the family didn't understand that she was not truly ill, but one day Natasha explained that they all knew her condition was in her mind but loved her and tried to help her in the only way they felt they could. I realized then that "Mama's resting room" had been placed where it was intentionally, hoping it would lure her into the evening's activities. Sometimes it did.

I liked Olga. She was pleasant always, her round face usually wearing a slight smile, even on her worst days. Reared with wealth and well-trained in all the social graces, she tried not to complain and was thoughtful of the needs of family and guests. Although I remained grateful for her kindness to us, I found her interests—needlepoint and knitting, flower arranging and medicaments—so mundane they tired me, so we never became close. It is probably a good thing we didn't, as I think eventually I might have spoken up in my customarily direct way and asked her why she didn't just take hold of herself. I came at last to see that there was a certain wisdom in her family's pampering. It gave her a sense of being loved and needed; she knew they cared, and it held her melancholia at bay. In short, it kept her sane.

As for young Dimitri, he never quite outgrew his fascination with the army (Ivan's disfigurement notwithstanding) and finally joined the cavalry, and within the next ten years rose rapidly in the ranks. The army became his life's work, so we did not see much of him.

However, he soon married and had a boy and two girls in quick succession, whom we saw twice a year, at Christmas and for two weeks in the summer. I never saw anyone grow so fast. In spite of the fact that they turned our quiet ordered household into a palace of pandemonium during these visits, they were a tonic for Olga. She fussed over them and spoiled them shamefully, and almost never had a sick headache while they were with us.

Natasha truly became a friend to me. For a while, I wondered why she had never married. She was attractive enough—tall, blonde, and slim, like her brother, and well-versed in domestic arts—but I found that she, not unlike her mother, had so worshipped her father that no man could measure up in her eyes to the godlike ghost who had left her when she was eight. As a young woman, she had had one serious suitor whom she truly cared about, but in the end, Shahane confided to me, he had chosen another, and the two "desertions" left her with a protective shell no one ever could penetrate, least of all herself. She was much younger than I, sober and bookish, and her tastes in literature were far removed from my own. She read for entertainment and to give herself a life through the stories, and while I was often entertained as well, I read primarily for information. She was as thoughtful and sweet-tempered as her mother, but, thank God, without the frailty. She did, however, open to me the world of Western culture—opera, ballet, theater and symphony—and she and I could spend hours discussing the merits of plays and the grace of the ballet.

How I loved the glittering excitement of a night at the ballet or the theater! That moment when the curtain rose as the overture ended would set off something in me that made my breath come shorter and my heart pump with the fine measured beat of a runner. The dim house-lights and the first sight of the set before the story began, the sound of the actors' voices reaching up toward the last rows of the gallery, the playgoers in their finery—and even the intermission with its glass of champagne—seemed to be another life, and I sometimes felt as though I belonged there and need never go home. Khadijah loved it all, too, though she seemed to enjoy the dazzling clothing and jewels of the women and the power to bestow them that radiated from the men more than the performance itself. I was often reminded of her statement at Shahane's wedding; that someday she would have those things for herself.

I had a difficult time learning to appreciate Western music, but with Natasha's capable help came to understand it and have loved it all my life since.

In the final say, my guide and teacher, Monsieur Zhukovsky, became my closest friend. We spent hours at a time with each other, and, to the profound pleasure of both of us, he became my true mentor. Further, we were of like minds in many ways. He understood my driving curiosity and my "Persianness," and so we never needed to explain ourselves to one another.

There was a month one summer when Mr. Hillhouse had come from France to visit the count. He chose to spend his holiday with us instead of going to England. Perhaps I should say "to spend his holiday with his friend the count," rather than "with us." Yet somehow when he came, I always felt he was visiting me. I suppose it was just because we were so . . . how shall I say it? . . . compatible. He loved theatre also, and so on several evenings our whole entourage trooped off to see some play or other currently running in St. Petersburg. Often it would be based on something Pushkin had written (whose poetry I was coming to enjoy), but of course there were others.

Having come so far from my old life in Persia, you can imagine my surprise when, one evening, a group of us—Mr. Hillhouse, the count and Shahane, Khadijah and a Mr. Vasily Lipilinov, one of several gentlemen who seemed anxious to squire my daughter about these days, and Natasha and I (who found ourselves courteously attended by Mr. Hillhouse, himself)—walked into the theatre to find that the play that evening was about none other than the Báb.

The Báb! I was not sure I wanted to see it. That heretic and the chaos he engendered had taken from me all whom I'd loved and left my daughter and me bereft and literally standing in ashes! Had it not been for the kindness of the count, we would be only God knows where—starving or somehow otherwise victimized, if not dead—this very night.

I did not want to make a scene among the others who were so looking forward to an interesting story and an evening's entertainment, so instead of protesting, I set my teeth and prepared to endure the production. I was surprised before it was over to find myself thoroughly engrossed in the plot and, further, learning some things I had not known about those days.

Shahane and Khadijah also learned a great deal that evening. They had lived through it all, but as children and very young girls, and only during the play did much of the actual history of those years come together for them. Several times I was amused to hear one or the other whisper to each other, "Oh, is *that* why that was happening?"

After we had returned to the house, over cake and fruit brandy in the library, we had a lively discussion. You may be sure I was able to add quite a little to the evening's remarks. The count also had much to add, and I found that Mr. Hillhouse's sojourn in Persia was during part of that time, though he said he had been very young. It seemed strange to me to think that while he was in Persia, perhaps even becoming one of the "British diplomats who wrote home of the horrendous tortures and the Báb's death," I was sitting in our little room at Mírzá Abbas's, as Too-Tee told us of it.

I was able to tell them of Mírzá Abbas and the Lady Shaydah, and only with some difficulty was I able to keep my feelings in check. Shahane wept openly several times.

Olga, her eyes filling, said, "Oh, my dears, I had no idea of how terrible it must have been for you!" She had stayed home that evening with a slight case of dyspepsia but had joined us for our refreshment, and ever the consummate hostess, tried for our sakes to turn the subject to something more cheerful. But that couldn't seem to last. Very soon one or another of us, still in the spell of the evening's drama, would bring it up again. Then too, sorrow or no sorrow, I was caught up in the memory of those eventful days. I was surprised to learn that the life of the Báb was being discussed throughout Europe and especially among ambassadors and the court circles.

"If it weren't for the play, I don't think I could believe that to be true," I said. I was watching Count Nicholas poke at the fire and search out another small log. "Why would Westerners be interested in an obscure Islamic heretic who is already dead?"

Mr. Hillhouse answered me. "He is not so obscure, Khánum. As a matter of fact, two books are being written about him and his life. One is by a Frenchman named Count De Gobineau; the other, by a countryman of mine, Sir Edward Granville Browne, a rather noted individual—a distinguished student of all things Oriental. May I have a little more brandy, Nicholas?"

"Until tonight, I had no idea he would have captured the attention of the West," I said.

"I should say he has," the count said, offering more brandy to each of us in turn, "and by the way, Khánum, I am not at all sure he is truly a heretic. It appears that his teachings are being accepted by thousands in Persia, even in spite of the persecutions, and even more in Baghdad and its environs."

"Just because people believe him, doesn't mean he isn't heretical . . . "

"Obviously, that is quite correct," he said, seating himself and retrieving his cake plate, "but it appears that he has begun a reformation of Islam that can—and may—bring her into the modern age."

I wanted to point out that Islam is younger than Christianity by nearly a thousand years and was hugely instrumental in awakening Christendom from the dark ages, introducing to Europe algebra, Arabic numerals, and table etiquette, not to mention soap. Through its centuries in Spain, Islam was indirectly responsible for the Renaissance. So why, I wanted to ask, is it Islam that needs modernizing? But I felt it would not be polite and would surely cause ill-feeling.

Besides, there was no denying that the West was more modern in the sense of inventions and political thought than the East, but I couldn't see that Christianity had much to do with that.

What I *could* do was enlighten the company on the Battle of Ṭabarsí, inadequately covered in the play, and both the count and Mr. Hillhouse were able to tell us much about the persecutions, some of which they had witnessed with their own eyes. I found myself thinking again of how mysterious it was that Mr. Hillhouse should have been in Persia in those same days I was picking apricots in Mírzá Abbas's gardens, hardly knowing England existed, and that now this Englishman and I should know each other so well in Russia.

Count Nicholas set down his empty plate and swallowing the last bite, said, "Speaking of Baghdad, my late uncle, Prince Michael (may he rest in peace), was able to effect the release of a prominent Bábí from the Síyáh-Chál who subsequently became their leader. He was sent into exile and I believe ended up in Baghdad. Mírzá Ḥusayn-'Alí Nurí, his name was, if I remember correctly. We offered him asylum here in Russia, but he declined. He felt his fellow Bábís needed him, I think."

"Mírzá Ḥusayn-'Alí Nurí!" I said, startled, "Are you sure?"

"Yes, dear Khánum, I am almost positive."

"I *met* him! Or rather I've seen him! He used to visit Mírzá Abbas rather often." I told them of the effect he had had on me and how impressed I had been with his regal demeanor and cheerful kindliness. I tried to explain how beyond the normal meaning of those words he was—but was unable to. I couldn't find a way to express it.

"Indeed," the count said. "That's interesting. My late uncle was also much impressed by him, and when I asked him in what way, he could not explain it either."

"Oh drat!" Khadijah's friend, Mr. Lipilinov, called out, scrubbing at his trouser lap with his napkin, "I've spilt my brandy!" We all sympathized, and Olga offered to ring for someone to bring water and a sponge, but he said it was time he was getting home anyway, and with that the evening ended.

Later, still in the throes of my memories and the emotional evening, I lay unable to sleep, listening to Khadijah breathe softly beside me. I went over all the evening's discussion again. Thinking of the nobleman whom I had glimpsed for such a brief moment nearly ten years ago, I was surprised to realize I had seen him in my mind's eye many times—in fact, almost every time I had thought back on the years at Mírzá Abbas's there he would be, walking across the courtyard in his majestic manner, or stopping to help someone with his exquisite courtesy. I was sorry he had been imprisoned and tortured, and grateful that he had received only exile instead of death. I had known he too was a Bábí, though I had not thought much about that. It was his regal demeanor, his impressive wisdom, and that restrained powerful energy that had so captured me.

Perhaps Count Nicholas's opinion was to be considered—that the Báb's message was not true heresy. I remembered the seven prominent and respected men whose deaths Too-Tee and I had witnessed that day in Tehran; Mírzá Abbas and my Lady Shaydah; Ṭáhirih, my beloved teacher; and Mírzá Ḥusayn 'Alí Nurí. All of them were people whose character and reputations I had most respected, and I realized they had all followed the Báb. Surely they could not *all* have been misled—could they?

At twenty-eight, Khadijah was not yet married, and I had come to believe she never would be. We had had so much to adjust to and so much new to master—just learning how to behave in a Christian society with its intimidating personal freedoms had been a challenge, and coming to understand and speak the language was enough to keep us occupied. She had escorts to balls and concerts and the theater, however, and seemed to enjoy herself. No one had seemed to strike her fancy though, and while she had had several proposals of marriage, she had turned them down.

Now, suddenly, here he was. His name was Rubin Mikailovitch Dubinski. He was descended from a prominent Polish Jewish family, who had become Christians. He was—like his uncles, father, and grandfather—a financier and extremely wealthy.

Khadijah came into our rooms one evening breathless with excitement, her cheeks spots of red from her own feelings and the cold outside. I was in bed, drowsy but not yet asleep, and her excitement and the freshness of the cold air that clung to her clothing roused me from my sleepiness.

"Look, Mama," she cried, "look at what Monsieur Dubinski gave me! He wants me to marry him!" She was dancing around the room, swinging her skirt with one hand and, with the other, holding out to me a large emerald brooch. The stone itself must have been about fifteen millimeters long.

"Well, hold still, for heaven's sake, so I can get a look at it! Oh my, it's beautiful and so—so—imposing!" Of oval cut, the stone was framed in delicate gold filigree. She disappeared into the dressing room.

"I presume you have accepted," I called out to her. "You would hardly have allowed him to give you a gift of this measure had you not."

"Well, of course I accepted," she called back, standing before the mirror and trying the brooch against her dress in several different ways. "Wouldn't you?"

"I? My darling, I hardly know him. I hadn't realized you were so serious about him."

"Oh—well—I haven't been, up until lately." Coming into the bedroom she said, "But now I am! It *is* alright with you if I marry him, isn't it, Mama?"

"Yes, I think so. He seems gentlemanly enough and is pleasant company. But we know nothing of his character. In the end we shall have to seek the count's opinion and, of course, defer to his judgment."

She made no answer to that. Instead she said, holding the brooch out before her, "Won't this be absolutely stunning with my pale green silk?" and left again.

"Aren't you coming to bed?" I yawned.

"Not yet, I'm too excited. I think I'll write in my journal awhile. Besides," she said, reaching for the bell pull and ringing for Popov, "I'm hungry. I want some warm milk and a slice of bread and butter. Do you want something?" But I was too sleepy to answer her beyond a muffled "umm" that I hoped would pass for "No."

That she had said nothing of her feelings for him, I had not really noticed. After all, I had married in a time and place where my feelings were not taken into consideration, and my only concern beyond whether or not he could keep her in some comfort—which judging from the brooch and his reputation, he would be more than able to do—was whether or not he would be kind to her and considerate of her welfare. That, I knew Count Nicholas could help determine, as he had known the man for a long while. My last thought before I fell asleep was, "I wonder if he will require that she become a Christian" which, I was to find, would be the very least of my worries.

One day, not long after, Popov knocked at my door. "There is a rather travel-weary looking man from the east at the door, Khánum. He has a package for you and will entrust it to no one else. I am sorry to trouble you, but would you come down and receive it from him?"

"Of course," I answered and began to follow him down the hallway. I stopped. "Did you say from the East; could he be Persian, do you think?" Popov merely looked confused at my question, so saying no more I returned to my room and threw a shawl around my head and shoulders, covering my lower face as I approached the front door. Sure enough, a tired traveler stood there holding a small package wrapped in cloth. "Are you the woman called Shirin?" he asked in Farsi. "Is this the house of Count Nicholas Dolgoruky?" I assured him of both instances, and he handed me the package. "This comes to you from Baghdad—from the cousin of my employer, 'Abdu'l-'Alí. She is called Fareshteh. I am to tell you she knew you from her days at Mírzá Abbas's in Tehran and that the count befriended her on the night of the fire."

I spoke with the man for a few moments more, asking questions about Fareshteh, but he was not only unable to answer them very well, he seemed reluctant to converse at length with me. He would say only that he was in St. Petersburg on business for his employer, that he would be here for a week or so, and that he would call again before leaving for Baghdad to see if I wished him to take anything with him in return. He seemed most anxious to be on his way. Reluctantly, I let him go.

I ran across the entry hall and up the stairs to my room, sat down, and looked at the little package. Fingers trembling with excitement, I opened it. Wrapped in a little scarf was a gift of two cones of sugar, a not unusual gift. But—what a surprise to me—there was also a letter! I had enjoyed my reading and writing and had made the best possible use of it, speaking as I now did two languages and a few words of Russian as well. Still, it had never occurred to me for even one second that I could write to a friend in Persia or that someone would write to me. The task of getting it there and delivered to the recipient seemed far too monumental. Yet, here I sat, holding the miracle in my hands. I settled down to read.

April 1863 in Baghdad

> "Oh, my dear Shirin! How I hope this reaches you. How I hope you are sitting somewhere now in a shady spot, a cooling grape arbor perhaps, reading these words I pen to you."

I had to smile because she would have no way of knowing that I sat near a fire and bundled against the cold, as we were in the middle of a winter season.

> "How long has it been since that terrifying night when Hamid and I caught up with you in the foothills of the Elburz mountains, the odor of smoke still clinging to our clothes, and the ugly pictures of death in our eyes? Over ten years? How I long to know what has become of you all. Are you well? And Shahane Khánum, and Khadijah? Perhaps, if all has gone well, Shahane Khánum and the count have children. I long so for children of my own, but it appears

that it will never be. I have been married for two years now to a very nice man named ʻAlí-Muḥammad. My cousin arranged it for me, and I am most content. At any rate, I think of you so often and am so grateful that for me, at least, everything has turned out as it has.

"My cousin, ʻAbdu'l-ʻAlí, who also shares my beliefs, as does my husband ʻAlí, has a business and is sending this missive to you via one of his traveling employees who goes sometimes to Russia, and now for the first time, to St. Petersburg. (Oh, I do so hope this finds you!)

"Not only because I long to 'speak' with you via this missive, but also because I want you to learn of something that has happened. You will remember, of course, Mírzá Ḥusayn-ʻAlí Nurí, as no one who sees him ever forgets him. You will remember too, perhaps, that he was released from the terrible Black Pit of Tehran by the largesse of your count's uncle, prince Michael Dolgoruky. He lay in that terrible place for three months, and no one can even describe the awful filth of it. The muck of years of prison filth formed their only floor (spilled food, vomitus and, since there are no other arrangements for the prisoners' personal needs, you can only imagine what else), and the stink and foul air bore disease to the prisoners, and the constant darkness created by the prison walls surrounded them at all times. How they survived for even weeks, let alone months, chained together as they were, I cannot imagine.

"In addition to being chained by the ankles to the other prisoners, Mírzá Ḥusayn-ʻAlí was singled out (I suppose because he seemed a natural leader) and made to wear around his shoulders a huge chain, so heavy it bent him over when he tried to walk in the prison yard, and in those several months, cut the flesh of his shoulders clean to the bone. It is said that the scars are still there over the deep pits in his flesh and that he cannot use his arms without pain.

"Several days after 'our fire,' he and his wife and three little children were told they must leave Persia. The littlest child was so young they feared for his life if he attempted to travel during the winter season through the mountains, so he remained in Persia with an aunt, to be sent for when he was older. The others were given no time at all to prepare for their departure. So the little family—Mírzá Ḥusayn-'Alí; his wife and the two children, Abbas, of eight years; and his younger sister, six or seven—set out with only what few possessions they could gather in a few days and left Persia for Baghdad.

"I tell you this not only because I thought you would want to know whatever became of him, but because my cousin moved his household to Baghdad as well. So I have been living in Baghdad, and it was here where I have been married. It is a lovely city, and the great river Tigris flows through it, dividing it into sections.

"But my cousin and husband have often gone to gatherings of the believers, and Mírzá Ḥusayn-'Alí has often spoken at these gatherings. He teaches, and the wisdom of this man is phenomenal! 'Alí-Muḥammad says no matter how long he speaks, no one ever interrupts him. The place is silent with spellbound listeners.

"Most of the young believers are so poor, Shirin, they have nothing to wear and practically nothing to eat, but they live together and share what little they have—a handful of dates, perhaps—or they borrow one another's shoes. They sleep on the bare floor because they do not have even the simplest furnishings.

"Mírzá Ḥusayn-'Alí himself is nearly as poor as his followers. Every day, he goes among the poor of the city and gives them a few coins to help them through the day. Yet he himself lives very frugally, and as a matter of fact, owns—my cousin tells me—only one shirt. Every night it is washed so he can wear it again the next day. This is the same man who, when he was married, was so very wealthy—and his bride also, who brought so large a dowry with her that it took a train of mules, to deliver it. They shared so liberally with everyone that Mírzá Ḥusayn-'Alí became known as 'the Father of the Poor.' Yet, even though, when he was in prison, the authorities stole it all from him, he remains as generous as ever with what little he has.

"Of course, my dear 'Alí and my cousin always related all they heard to me, but the most remarkable part is the joy of these young believers. Some of the older men would come here sometimes afterwards and discuss even more what they learned, and they, too, were always so happy! I wish I could convey to you our joy when we are here together! I know you would love to be a part of it all, and I often think of you when we are talking."

I could not help but feel as though I were back in our little room at Mírzá Abbas's, gathered around my samovar, Too-Tee telling us of the Bábís and how they fared.

"But oh, Shirin! The most exciting thing has occurred! I know you would remember that the Báb kept speaking of the coming Teacher; one whom he called, 'He Whom God Will Make Manifest' . . . I *know* you remember.

"Well, He is here! He has come! And you will never guess Who He is! On second thought, perhaps you will, because although I never suspected, when I heard what has happened it was as though somehow I had known it all the time.

"He is Mírzá Ḥusayn-'Alí Nurí!"

I could understand what she meant. While I was not sure that he was the Promised One, or if indeed there even IS a Promised One, still, if anyone could be, it would surely be he . . . that wonderful, kindly, stately man, so courteous and yet so strong in mind and heart. It saddened me to learn how horribly he was being treated by the mullahs and the government, but at the same time, I was comforted to know that he had survived the awful bloodbath that had overtaken so many others. Fareshteh continued:

"After He had been here in Baghdad for almost ten years, he was suddenly told by the Ottoman government that he would have to leave. I understand that one of the officials said, 'If we don't get him out of here, he will convert the whole world.' At any rate, they sent him news that he must leave Iraq and go northwestward to Constantinople, where he would remain a prisoner and be farther from home than ever. Twelve days before that, he told his followers that He was the Promised One of All Ages and Religions—'He Whom God Will Make Manifest'! Then, within a day or so, He left Baghdad by mule train, although He Himself rode a beautiful red roan stallion that some of the followers purchased for Him. When He left Baghdad, people wept and cried that 'our Father is leaving us!' and begged Him not to leave. Some of the people threw themselves in the path of His horse, hoping either to stop Him that way or die rather than be parted from Him. Muslims, Christians, Jews, and who knows who else all grieved at His departure.

"Here is another wonderful thing. About seventy people were allowed to go with Him . . . and 'Abdu'l-'Alí, and 'Alí-Muḥammad and I are among them! I have no idea where beyond Constantinople we will go, or whether or not we will even survive the journey, but none of that matters, for whatever our fate, we will be with our Beloved Lord!

"In any case, I expect you will not hear from me again. Oh, how I would so love to know if you are well and if your life is satisfactory. Just know that whether or no, I send you the blessings of Allah, and commend you to His care. I will be your friend forever.

Fareshteh"

I resolved to write her a letter immediately, telling her of our journey and of our life in Russia, and send it along with the messenger when he came. But for now, I was happy to just read the letter once more, and then to share it with Khadijah and Shahane.

15

Dubinski seemed to be truly enamored of Khadijah and showered her with gifts even before the wedding took place. He was not a handsome man, being neither tall nor possessed of classic features, but he had a beautiful smile that lit up his dark eyes and a head of thick, black, curly hair that was very becoming. That, along with his good nature and thoughtful manner, immediately endeared him to everyone as soon as they met him. The count had only the best things to say of him.

Khadijah was in a whirl of delight, designing and making her wedding gown and the gowns for the bridesmaids and clothing for the days following the wedding, a suit for traveling, and ensembles for the first day and the second and so forth to last the entire first week.

Her ceremony was to be fit, it seemed to me, for the Tsarina herself, and I cautioned her about the expense. She assured me that Rubin had said to go ahead and plan it as she desired and that he would cover all the costs. I was not comfortable with this and was even more uncomfortable when the count told me he and Olga would like to give the couple a gala party following the wedding. My objections were cheerfully overruled by both Rubin and Count Nicholas. I was always conscious of our being the count's permanent guests and living on his charity. It seemed to be of concern to no one but me. I confided this to Zhukovsky one morning, and he responded by saying, "Shirin, my dear friend, between Dubinski and the count, they have all the money in the world. Relax and enjoy your good fortune. Besides, what would Shahane have done without Khadijah when she first arrived? You have more than earned your way."

"Perhaps Khadijah has earned her way, but I haven't. I have done nothing to aid this family, I . . ."

"You have given *me* a reason to go on living in my old age; you are like a daughter to me, and though I live on their largesse as well, that is worth something. Anyway, have you no idea how much they all love you? Your constant enthusiasm often puts heart in Olga, and Nastasha has someone with whom to share her love of the arts. Just you, yourself, are a great gift to them all."

I was somewhat comforted but still felt very much in debt and hoped someday to find a way to repay them.

The wedding was wonderful. Khadijah, who still, even at twenty-eight, had a tendency to pout when things were not quite going her way, pouted fairly regularly during the days of preparation, but they were short stints, over as soon as the problem of the week was resolved, and she was otherwise the happiest I had ever seen her. Mr. Dubinski, as I suspected he might, asked her to become a Christian, and you may be sure she pouted at that—but not at changing religions, as she had never been even slightly knowledgeable about Islam, but merely at the necessity for classes in instructions. I was a little troubled about it myself, but I had come to see that Christians were not so different from everybody else and so supposed it could do her no real harm. Then, too, I recalled the verse from Holy Koran, in which God had told Muḥammad, *"Truly those who believe and those who are Jews, and the Christians and the Sabeans—those who believe in God and the last day and do righteous deeds, they have their reward from their Lord and no fear shall be upon them . . . ."**

After all, in spite of my curiosity about all things religious (and certain superstitions about it, which made me smile at my own foolishness), I had, you remember, little use for it myself. In addition, Dubinski told me that it was far better for his business and for making his way as a Jew in

* Koran 2:62.

an Orthodox society for them both to be Christians. While I thought that the wrong reason to embrace a religion, I could understand his reasoning. Khadijah was willing, at least at this point in her life, to do anything to please him, so she took her instructions and was baptized in due course. I requested that I might be able to take them along with her, and I did. It satisfied some of my curiosity about it all, but Zhukovsky was better at explaining my questions than the priest who was our teacher.

The ceremony went off without a single problem, and the couple enjoyed their party immensely. Khadijah was having such a good time that she didn't want to leave, but her eager bridegroom, over her laughing objections, whisked her off at last, and they departed merrily in a whirl of good wishes.

I am happy to say that within two years, Khadijah made me a grandmother. She bore a little girl, her only child, whom they named Katherine Shaydah. Catherine had been a common name in Russia since the time of Catherine the Great, and Shaydah, of course, came from our dear Khánum, whom the three of us held in such loving memory.

Both she and Rubin were insane over their child and began at once to spoil her horribly. As a matter of fact, Rubin spoiled both his child and his wife, and I had to smile when I realized that Khadijah's wish that someday she would have glamorous gowns, precious jewelry, and a social position for herself had certainly come true. Her life became a round of parties and balls and entertaining. We seldom saw her, she was so busy with her many activities. Fortunately, Shahane had long since found her way and no longer needed Khadijah, though they remained friends and met from time to time and of course traveled in the same social circle. I was so happy for her and doted on my little "Katrushka." I think I had never been happier, and the idea that life could ever be sad again seemed as remote as the top of the sky.

I was not the only one reacting to her child in those days. Zhukovsky was watching "his boy" and alternated between beaming with pride and frowning with worry.

Alexander II's reign seemed to be taking hold. It appeared that Zhukovsky had been correct. Here was a Tsar who truly seemed to care about his people and his responsibilities to them. By 1861, he had realized his first ambition, and announced the Emancipation Act. The serfs—all forty-eight million of them, three-quarters of the Russian people—were free.

"I can see your pride radiating from your face, dear friend," I said one morning over coffee and rolls.

"Yes, I am proud, Kh͟ánum. I am beginning to feel that my life's work, which I once thought was my early success in literature, has, in reality, been the education of this man." His face clouded. "I only hope . . . " He paused and brought his cup to his lips.

"Yes?" I prodded.

"Alexander is given to knuckling under to stronger minds than his own, just as he did with his father. Already it is showing up in this matter. Freeing the serfs was a wonderful thing to do, and he gave each of them acreage to farm along with their freedom, but their former owners did not like that."

"That's certainly understandable," I said, breaking my roll and buttering a piece of it, "after all, to lose both their human property and then acreage besides must strike something of a blow to their revenue each year."

"No one would expect them to like it, but I am sure a more equitable arrangement could have been made. While their loss in real property was considerable, their loss in income will work them little hardship. But the landowners complained bitterly and muttered among themselves about injustice and that they should be paid for their loss. So, Alexander ruled that the serfs must pay their former owners for the land over a series of years in annual fees."

"That hardly seems unjust," I said.

"Had the fees been less per year, it would not have been, but as it stands, these fees take almost everything the serfs can earn. Kh͟ánum," he said leaning across the little table toward me, "they are not much better off than they were before." He leaned back again and stared at the floor. "I fear his action was more appeasement than justice . . . and the emancipation itself premature."

"Premature? I would have thought you, of all people . . . "

" . . . would believe it long overdue?"

"Yes."

"In one sense, yes, but perhaps he might have done something about training them in agriculture first, getting them ready for their new lives. That they have no idea how to manage for themselves hasn't seemed to occur to the Tsar, wrapped warmly in his palaces as he is, and immersed in his personal life. He expects them to find their own way. But Khánum, they can't."

"Why not? They have always farmed, Zhukovsky—for generations, you told me."

"Yes. But in spite of having spent decades in agriculture, they know very little about it. They have merely followed orders in the past and stayed as drunk as possible when they were not toiling, so their harvests, which have always been poor, are already showing every indication of becoming even worse."

Zhukovsky's worst fears were to materialize in the years to come. The serfs did not do well at all. Moreover, there had always been frequent droughts over the vast plains, and in those years, as they always had, the serfs starved and died by the hundreds.

Even in our own household, we could see the problem. While most of our servants, knowing their living quarters were better here than they could hope to make for themselves, stayed with us and earned a few kopecs now for their services, there were those who without thinking had left the moment they heard the news of the emancipation, stealing beans and rice and a ham or bacon on their way out the door, as it were.

Yet the Tsar, with his idealistic dreams of a fair and prosperous reign magnanimously bestowed by himself, and enforced by the divine right of kingship, was, within his limited experience with self-government, doing what he thought best, not to mention expedient. By now, after almost a century, the influence of the American and French revolutions, as well as the European revolutions of 1848, was slowly infiltrating the thinking of the upper classes, and setting them to agitating for a greater voice in government. I didn't understand that then, of course, but I would in later years. Tsar Alexander began to discuss with his aides and nobles the idea of forming some kind of parliament. Yet, recalling his father's constant lectures in his boyhood, he remembered that Nicholas had believed with every drop of blood in his body that the only way to safely and effectively rule was with total autocracy.

Alexander was humane but, having been reared by an autocrat, had little concept of justice. He was steadfast in his intentions but had no personal backbone to see his decisions through. In short, he was divided into two parts and found it very difficult, in fact almost impossible, to reconcile them.

But reconciled or not, the serfs were free, and Russia was reaching for her future. It was Alexander's task to help her find it.

16

HILLHOUSE PAPERS: 1910

John put his father's papers back in the large envelope and stood up. Stretching and yawning, he decided he had had enough to think about for one evening. He banked the fire, and taking the last sip of the wine to finish the glass, returned the bottle to the kitchen, corked it, and went to bed.

The next morning, he boarded the railway early. The train headed northwest, and before noon he was seeing the familiar soft hills of the midlands—cattle country—and home.

He loved the Hereford country, with its undulating horizon of green, the white-faced cattle grazing peacefully and, occasionally, sheep dotting the hills like small clouds against the sky. Grateful to be returning to the clean and quiet countryside after the noise and choking soot of London, he sat leaning dreamily against the window, thinking of his family as the train moved smoothly along.

John's family consisted not of a group of children but of his wife, Carolyn, and their three Collies, which helped with the sheep. Both of them loved the dogs—Maggie and McClure (called Mac), and one of their male pups, Hamish—as though they were the children it appeared now they would never have.

Once, John's family had been serious sheep men, in the days of John's great-great-grandfather Henry Hillhouse. The "place," as John always referred to it, was located not far from the Welsh border, near a gurgling stream that Carolyn had dubbed (for rather obvious reasons) Buttercup Rill. It wound picturesquely through the hillsides, emptying into the River Wye, and the house itself was built on the top of one of the hills—hence the family name.

When his ancestors had first come to the farm to scratch a living from the windswept land, along with what game they could hunt, they had built a sod house with a thatched roof. In an area so given to cold weather and biting winds, most people built in the lee of a sheltering hill, but not John's ancestor. John had once asked his father why, and his father had told him that the question was as old as their name itself, and nobody knew the answer. Over the generations, the family prospered. They had built a larger house attached to the original, and the old sod house had become a shelter for the animals—a cow and several pigs in those days. At last they had become people of substance. His great-grandfather, the first Edward John Henry Hillhouse, had served King George III with distinction in the 1760s, and he had been awarded a medal and a sizable sum of money, but no title . . . which was better, the family often joked, than some who were granted titles, but no money.

So began the serious sheep business. Success followed, and a still larger house was built of stone, with parquet floors, walls of bird's eye maple, mullioned windows, and fireplaces in almost every room. The outer walls were enhanced nowadays with ivy.

All that was left of the original building were three shallow troughs where walls had once stood, overgrown now with grass. The Hillhouse days of affluence had faded as the cattle business took over the area, and most of the sheep now being raised in England were in the north, near the Scottish border. The Hillhouse sheep business now was one of experimental breeding only, but the fine old house still stood, and John and Carrie lived there, however frugally, with their roses and their dogs. It was no longer cold and forbidding on top of the hill but sheltered by fine old oaks. The windows looked out across the creek to the sheep fields with only the sky and the Malvern Hills on the eastern horizon, and John thought it was paradise.

"Halloo!" he called out, blowing into the house like a sudden gust of wind.

"Back here," Carrie answered, from the kitchen, where she was making soup. "What's this Halloo? Are you fox hunting?"

"Yes! I am!" he said gathering her up in his arms, "and you, my pretty," he said, lifting his eyebrows and pretending to twist a moustache, "are the poor fox, now at my mercy. H'mmm, soup," he said dropping his arms and turning toward the stove, "What kind?"

"Chicken—with vegetables and rice. You stayed overnight. Was your meeting with Mr. Cooper a long one? Did everything go alright? Did you remember my thread and the material?"

"No, yes and yes." John moved to the scullery and began washing his hands. "It became late, and I had some papers of Father's to read, so I stayed. Took your broken platter round to the china shop. It can be repaired, but there may be a slight crack showing, he said. It should take about three weeks. Everything alright here?"

"Fine," she said absently, dishing out bowls. "Hungry?"

"With soup for luncheon? Old Girl—need you ask?"

Late in the night, after they had both been asleep for an hour or so, he woke to hear Carolyn weeping. "Oh, Darling," he said turning over and taking her in his arms, "again?"

"I'm so sorry, John. I've been trying not to wake you."

"That never matters. What brought it on this time?"

"I don't know for sure. Your homecoming perhaps. I am always so happy to see you when you've been gone, and I just so wish I could greet you with happy news—the happiest news. And this time, I really thought maybe . . . "

"Shhh," he coaxed, smoothing her hair and kissing the warm bony spot behind her ear. He began to mouthe the comforting things he had said so many times before, knowing they were meaningless. "Remember, my mother didn't have me until they had been married seven or eight years. We've two to go, still." He didn't mention that his mother had lost three before she successfully carried him to term. Carolyn had never even conceived. She pretended, for his sake, to believe his reasoning, and finally nestled against him, stopped weeping, and slept.

By that time, John was wide awake, and after Carrie dozed off, he rose, put on a dressing gown and went downstairs to the library, a comfortable room in dark green and oak. Oaken bookcases lined two of the walls; the remaining two were covered in a deep green, gold-flecked paper above maple wainscoting. Large windows overlooked the sheep barns and Carrie's greenhouse. He stirred up the banked fire and stood, leaning arm-on-forehead against the mantel and holding the poker, searching the depths of the flames as though he might find an answer in there as to why they could not have children. He was the last of Hillhouses. He hated to think that one day his own gravestone, standing next to Carrie's in the family plot just over the hill, like those of his parents, glistening and bright, the carving clean and crisply legible, would be the last ones in the sizable group, now mostly green with moss and leaning against the weather. The place would belong to some other family then, probably cattle growers. But more, he would have loved to have had a son to walk the hills with him. He could imagine himself teaching the boy about the sheep and the intricacies of breeding techniques, sharing with him the excitement of the spring when the ewes were lambing, the pride at the annual fair in a prize winning ram, such as Hill Boy had been. He put up the poker and slumped in his favorite chair. His own disappointment seemed minor compared to Carrie's grief. "*She would make such a wonderful mother*, he thought, *and she longs for a baby so. Dear God, if there were only something I could do!*"

Sighing, he picked up the copy of Thackery he had been rereading of late, but he couldn't put his mind to it. He still wasn't sleepy, so he wandered out to the kitchen, heated a cup of milk, and returned to the library. He retrieved the big envelope he had brought from the city and took up his father's papers.

"Something momentous is happening!" his father had closed his first notes, back in 1866.

"*Apparently,*" John thought. "*I hadn't ever looked at history quite that way; neither had any of my history teachers. But Father was right as rain. The world has changed a great deal in those mere fifty-odd years, and it seems to have shrunken even more since Father wrote that.*" John smiled to himself as he remembered that his father had often been "right as rain," but then, he thought, a man doesn't rise in her Majesty's service to an ambassadorship without an astute wit.

Turning to the next page, he continued reading:

"November 1868:

"So I am off to be married the week after Christmas. Now that I have decided to do it, I can hardly wait. Margaret is a wonderful woman, intelligent, and sensitive. She comes from a fine family, and although she is no longer young, neither am I. At thirty-nine years, while that is hardly old for a man to marry, I find I could not be less interested in the young pretty flibberty-jibbits I meet here in Paris, nor the ones I meet at the 'drawing-room pony auctions' at home where all the mothers parade their daughters out at Christmas balls and what have you. I believed for a long while that I should never marry at all. Why would I imprison myself with a lovely jailer, who would spend her time wanting things and demanding my time, when she knew well enough at the start that I am gone most of the time and cannot be there to satisfy her every whim?

"I have, however, thought often of 'S' who lives in St. Petersburg and of whom I have come to be very fond. Her mind is quick and astute; she has a delightful manner, as life seems to fascinate her. It is as though she is always waiting for the next moment to arrive so that she can learn something new or go off on another adventure. God knows she has had adventures enough, though never of her own choosing! Her life has been far from easy, and while she is of a thoughtful mind, she has nevertheless retained the most delightful sense of humour.

"She is quick to enjoy, slow to anger, and her ability to forgive seems uncanny. She would make a wonderful companion and, I confess, her dark loveliness entrances me every time I am with her."

"*Well, Father,*" John thought, smiling to himself a little crookedly, "*who would have thought this of you . . . a secret yearning, eh? You old fox, you!*" He kept reading.

"Alas there are things that make it all impossible. First of all, she is a Muslim Persian, and while I might be forgiven for marrying a non-English woman, to marry outside the Faith is not acceptable—not to me (though I am certainly not terribly devout), and certainly not to Her Majesty's government. Further, she is past childbearing age, and I do so want to insure the family line. At my age, I could be forgiven a marriage with a woman a year or two older than I (we could always fudge a little about our ages), but the difference here is considerable and would be out of the question.

"So there's an end to it!"

"*Aha,*" John thought, smiling wryly, "*met a Persian woman did you, Father? And you never so much as mentioned her once in all the years since.*"

"I am fortunate to find a woman with Margaret's fine mind, kind heart, and her exceptional good sense. She is in her early thirties and has told me that she also feared she would never marry, not because she had not had opportunities but because she felt the proposals came from callow young men more interested in her family background than in her. 'After all, Edward,' she told me, 'I *am* of a rather serious temperament. Nor do I deceive myself about my appearance. I am not beautiful.'

"In truth, she is not, but she *is* rather handsome, I think, with a marvelous English face, strong and ruddy with well-chiseled features. More, she carries herself with a dignity that attracted me the first hour I met her. She writes that she also can hardly wait for our marriage, and especially to come to Paris to live. She has not been here since her first visit during her early girlhood. I hope and believe she will be happy here. Since Napoleon III became President in 1848, the old city of Paris, so distraught during her revolution, followed by the grief of the losses suffered under Napoleon Bonaparte, has become a delightful place to be.

"He has widened the streets of Paris until they are now lovely boulevardes and has begun to enlarge the Louvre. And, of course, there is the new opera house he commissioned a few years ago.

"Napoleon III is a bit of a genius, I imagine, and understands this century as do few of the statesmen of our time. More, he is a good man at heart, I believe. He is a devout Christian (even if Roman Catholic), modest, unassuming, and democratic; he truly cares about the common folk and the poor.

"He, along with Alexander I of Russia, was the first King ever to propose general disarmament among the European nations. During the Crimean war, he sent three times as many troops into the fray as did we British. Those qualities, combined with his shrewd political sense, have put him in a position to be the finest European ruler of our generation. In fact, already he has earned for himself the unofficial title of 'the Arbiter of Europe.'

"In spite of these admirable qualities, his decisions tend to be self-seeking. Made president of France following the revolution of 1848, in only three years he had 'stolen' the revolution. In 1851, President Louis Napoleon proclaimed himself Napoleon III, Emperor of France, and in spite of my belief in monarchy, this is not the way to achieve it. I find that dangerous. It bespeaks an ambition of which I am honestly afraid. So often it precedes a move toward tyranny, unless such an eventuality is prevented by removal or assassination.

"Further, he has a mighty desire for France herself.

"Four years ago he sent troops to Mexico, drove out Juarez, and placed the Archduke Maximilian on the throne of Mexico. The United States has just concluded her civil war this last year and, you may be sure, is not happy with Emperor Louis's meddling in the affairs of the new world. She has forcefully reminded him of the Monroe Doctrine, 'America for Americans.' I am afraid this Mexican business bids fair to become something of a fiasco.

"It seems fairly obvious to many of us that he wishes to vindicate his late relative, Bonaparte, in the eyes of France and the world, and further, has intentions of placing his son on the throne when he dies. I suspect that is most of what this "emperor" conceit is about. The man admired his uncle and wishes to found a dynasty, a Napoleonic line. Well, why not? The French revolution accomplished some useful things, but in the end, it failed, didn't it? And here they are back to an Emperor again.

"If he wishes to create a dynasty, at least it appears he wishes it to be a benevolent one for France and sincerely has the good of his country at heart.

"His mother, Hortense, they say, spoiled him as a boy and never let him doubt that his fate was to be King of France. So beneath his surface modesty lurks a colossal self-love, and that is not in his best interests at all—either for himself or for France. It is his one great failing."

17

CONFESSIONS:

JMJ

Along about the same time I noticed Mario's odd moods, I was sent to Austria, where I had several conferences with the Emperor Franz Josef himself. "Now there is an interesting man," I said one evening after I had returned, "I felt sorry for him from the moment I met him, and if I have ever envied royalty, Franz Josef alone, has rearranged my thinking about that."

"Indeed? Why so?"

"Because he is essentially a simple man who loves hunting and a quiet life for the most part. But from the moment he took the throne, he has had barely a quiet moment. He acceded, as you know, because his Uncle Ferdinand abdicated."

"I was never clear about why Ferdinand abdicated, Vittorio. How much do you know about that?"

"Not much. Only that it was because he was feeble minded . . . an extremely lovable man, they say, but unable to rule."

"Yes, of course we had always heard he was feeble-minded, but was he really . . . you know . . . truly stupid?"

"I really don't know much about it, but there is a story that while riding in his carriage one day in a public parade, he shouted to the coachman . . . 'I want dumplings! I am the Emperor, and I want dumplings!' I understand the entire crowd laughed and waved to him, and he waved back and laughed with them. Stupid or not, his subjects loved him. Speaking of dumplings, I'm hungry. Have we any little cakes or anything?"

"No, but there is some peanut brittle."

"Not left over from Christmas, I hope," I called out to Mario as he went to fetch it.

He laughed as he returned. "No, I did a research task for one of the fathers last week, and he brought it to me to say thank you."

"It's good," I said, biting into a piece, "even though it may be left over from *his* Christmas. At any rate, poor Franz Josef was barely nineteen years old. Mother of God, Mario, nineteen! The Crimean War was brewing, and all he wanted was to reign over a peaceful empire and honeymoon with his little bride. Instead, he had to begin his reign fighting a war; more, he was forced to make a huge decision.

"Decision about . . . ?"

"Whom to fight. Should he ally himself with the Russians who, in their search for a warm water port, were threatening his lands from the north, or would he be wiser to side with the Western Allies—that is, France, and also England—who was simply showing up everywhere because she needs those famous coaling ports for her vast navy? He was not in favor of helping England in her imperialism, but she could protect him from Russia."

"Why would he ally with Russia, then? Where's the decision in that?"

"Well, Russia had offered him spoils from the Ottoman Empire, now weakened and called . . . "

Mario interrupted, grinning, "Oh, yes, 'the sick man of Europe.'"

"Just so. And Russia planned to defeat the sick man. It was tempting for Franz Josef, but he truly believed that nothing would be gained by making war over lands and power, and of course he was right. In the end, he did very little and cast his lot, however weakly, with the Western Allies. Tsar Alexander II resented the daylights out of it and hated him from then on.

"And as if that weren't enough, Mario, his marriage was a disaster, although he adored his bride."

"Elizabeth. What is it they call her?"

"Sissy."

"Yes, Sissy."

"She was sixteen years old. She worshiped him as only young girls can do when they first feel love, but even though she adored him, she was in no position to become the Habsburg Empress. Her mother-in-law, Sophie, tried in every way she knew how to teach the girl and bring her to some kind of maturity, but only succeeded in alienating her, and before long the two were mortal enemies.

"From the beginning of the marriage, Sissy rode horses almost all day, every day, and spent the rest of the time in her bedroom talking with her pet parrots. This way she didn't have to face either members of the court or her dreaded mother-in-law. The poor child slept very little and ate so little as to become thin as a stick, and everyone worried about her health. But she's a stubborn one. She clung to her habits beyond all reasonable attempts to change her.

"Franz Josef would have liked to have seen her happy, but he worked long days, and often well into the night, so he had very little time to spend with her. I have to say that she hardly tried to please him or anyone else and was as self-absorbed as it is possible to be.

"Now recently, the emperor has lost his brother, Maximilian, whom Napoleon had made king of Mexico, and of course, we all know how much the Mexicans liked *that* idea."

"Yes," Mario amended, "They solved the problem though—with a firing squad. Oh, you should have been here, Vittorio! Maximilian's wife came home to France and begged Napoleon to do something to save her husband, but he wouldn't help. He had already advised Maximilian to abdicate, if things were so bad, but Maximilian refused. Charlotte yelled and screamed at Napoleon and literally went mad in his presence, throwing herself onto the floor and tearing out her hair. Then she came here and demanded to see the Holy Father."

"Yes, I heard about that. It was quite a horrible scene, I've been told."

"Oh, Vittorio, I wasn't in the audience room, but it's common knowledge that she screamed and shouted and had to be led away to a hospital. They shot Maximilian anyway, and she's as mad as can be, locked away in Belgium."

"It seems as though the royals have their troubles, just as the common folk do. But of course that is my point of all this. That same year, the Archduke What's-his-name (Franz Josef's uncle or a cousin or something), renounced his title."

"So that leaves Archduke Frances Ferdinand as His only heir to the throne."

"Unless Franz Josef has sons."

'He might, Vittorio. He's young."

"But even so, they wouldn't be able to rule for years."

"And the Austrians, I understand, don't approve of the archduke's wife."

"Well, no, she's a commoner . . . and God forbid," I said smiling, "that one of us lowlifes should ever get within snatching distance of a crown."

"Especially the Habsburg Crown. Haven't they ruled more or less forever?"

I reached for my fifth piece of the peanut brittle, "For God's sake, hide this stuff before I eat the whole tin! Since 1477. In fact—well, as we all know, the history of the huge Habsburg holdings has been the history of Europe, and he is terrified of losing it for his heirs. My God, what will happen to Europe if the Habsburgs fall?"

"What happened when Greece fell, Vittorio? What happened when Rome fell? Somebody else just took it all over. Besides how could it really fall? His domain is a part of the Holy Empire of Christ and is, after all, in God's hands."

"Well, yes, you're correct, of course, but look at how much power the church has lost since the '48 revolutions. Anyway, he has been attempting to hold his empire together, which has been constantly under threat since those revolutionary days, and the only way he knows how to get things done is through what he terms 'order and discipline.'"

"So I've heard," Mario said, "He's very . . . what? Imperial!"

"He is. Rigid and cold and aloof, but I came to know him a little, and beneath all that royal posturing is a friendly, if somewhat shy, good-natured man. I spoke with his confessor, Father Sebastian, and he agrees. He told me that all Franz Josef wants of life are two things: to live with his wife and family with happiness, and to preserve his empire in peace to bequeath to his heirs. This, he feels, is his sacred duty—much, I suppose, as the Holy Father believes it is *his* duty to hold together the papal states for whoever succeeds him."

"H'mm, I suppose," Mario said yawning, and I could see he was rapidly losing interest in the Emperor of Austria. So we ended the discussion, but not before I had commented that while I had been there, Franz Josef had asked me about Rome and the Holy Land and announced his intention to make his pilgrimage to both places in the near future. Of course, I encouraged him.

By now, the emperor had abrogated a good many of the rights granted the people under the new national constitution, among them the schools which had been nationalized. But now they were once again in control of the Church, thank God, and he also restored the rights of the bishops to communicate with Rome. It had been an uncertain time, but it appeared that all would come right, at least as far as Austria and the Church were concerned, and I felt I had done well in my sojourn there.

By the time I had returned to Rome, I had all but forgotten Mario's troubling behavior but found within a week that whatever seemed to be bothering him was still bubbling, and his discomfort on my third or fourth night home was all but palpable. There was a tension that pervaded the atmosphere of our rooms, and I finally questioned him seriously about it.

"Something is troubling you, my brother," I said, "and I want to help you with it. For heaven's sake, open up and let me into this . . . fear . . . or whatever it is. I am your *friend*, Mario, or have you forgotten?"

"No, Vittorio, of course I haven't forgotten. And yes, something *is* troubling me, and I would give anything to tell you about it, but I can't."

"Have you done something? If so, would you like me to hear your confession, instead of going to your regular confessor? That way, no one would know beside me and you know that I . . ."

He laughed. "No, Padre Giuseppe Vittorio, I have not sinned any exotic sins, but thank you for your offer. No, this concerns my work, and must remain within my own private mind. But you are correct . . . it troubles me. Oh, how I wish I could share it with you! I just cannot."

I think that much helped him to feel better and, for a while, he was again his old self, and I, at least, forgot about it. After all, as priests, we were all in possession of knowledge we could not mention to others.

One evening, maybe a month later, we were sitting, as on so many evenings, both silent and reading, and the only sounds in the room were the snaps of ancient plaster from the fire's heat and the crack of burning logs. Suddenly Mario laid aside his book almost angrily and rose from his chair.

"Vittorio, I cannot keep this inside any longer! I must tell *someone*, and you are elected!" I had been deeply engrossed in what I was reading, but snapped the book shut sharply and sat bolt upright on the couch, as I realized my friend was finally going to confide to me what had been so long on his mind.

"Tell me? Yes! What have you to tell me?"

"A few weeks ago, I was handed a sheaf of papers that had been brought from the pope's offices to file—letters, mostly, and other communications—the same sorts as usual. Now, you know that I am not encouraged to read what I file, other than to get enough of a gist to know where to enter it. "

I nodded.

"But when I glanced down at one certain letter, I caught myself reading it thoroughly, as though it were a letter addressed to me. I was captivated and read it not once but twice all the way through. I filed it immediately, of course, but as the days have passed, I have found myself taking it out from time to time and rereading it. Vittorio, I don't know what to think! I have puzzled and puzzled over it. I have even prayed about it!"

"About what, Mario? What did the letter say? Who was it from?"

"From a political prisoner. A Muslim—at least I think he is a Muslim. He's from Persia or Baghdad or someplace, though now he is imprisoned in a Turkish prison in Palestine, and he claims to be some kind of Messenger from God and instructs . . . *instructs,* mind you, the Holy Father, himself!"

"Oh, Mario," I said in a deprecating tone, "The Holy Father must get letters from madmen all the time. Men who think they are Jesus, women who claim they are to bear the new Jesus and request the pope to father the child. Besides, he's a Muslim! Surely, you are not deceived by . . . "

"I know that, of course, but this was not like that. This writer seemed eminently sane and cautioned the pope about the dangers to the world, and . . . oh, I can't remember all of it. It is quite lengthy and has a tone that . . . I got a sense of . . . I can't explain, Vittorio, you need to see it."

"I don't need to see it, Mario. You need to forget it. I'm telling you, it can't be anything important. Surely, of all people, the Holy Father would be the best judge of its source and its meaning . . . and of the spiritual state of the writer. Don't you agree?"

"I suppose you are correct," he said, somewhat doubtfully, "and I am making too much of it. Yes. Yes, I am sure you are right." Then, sighing deeply, he retreated into his shell again.

Soon, we bid each other good night and went to bed. I felt, as I lay falling asleep after my prayers, that I had not helped Mario very much; that it seemed to me he had capitulated to my reasonable argument merely because he couldn't convince me and did not want to pursue the point further. I was sorry I couldn't do a better job of comforting him, but knew that without the letter, itself, I could hardly make a convincing argument, and there was no chance of my seeing it. Only the librarians and certain clerks, such as Father Francis Mario, were allowed into those sections of the library, and to remove something from the library would result—if caught—in his immediate disgrace and summary dismissal. He would end up saying Mass for ignorant peasants somewhere in the muddy countryside a thousand miles from Rome and his beloved library. Besides, Mario was a man of honor, and such a thing would not enter his mind.

I yawned and stretched and thought about several letters of my own that I needed to write tomorrow and soon fell asleep.

Inexplicably, then, for the first time since those long ago days when I had lain as a little boy on my straw pallet, I had the dream. I had long before consigned it to my childish imagination and not even thought of it for many years, but this night it came again as clearly as it had so long ago. A voice, authoritative but kindly, spoke in my dream.

"Vittorio," said the voice, "sleep not."

18

HILLHOUSE PAPERS:

Carrie and John had been to a party. Sometimes, on Saturday evenings, the neighbors from the small area around the village of Carter-upon-Wye gathered together to exchange the local gossip. They came with dishes from home and sat about on whatever tables were provided. Some of the houses, such as John's and Carrie's, huge old places built generations ago, had tables that sat ten or more. In other smaller houses, the neighbors sat wherever they could find room. But either way, the evenings were convivial, and, invariably, they all ate too much and talked without stopping from the moment they arrived until the moment when they stood outside the door calling good-byes.

Usually the talk was about sheep and cattle-breeding and the markets, or whatever news someone had brought up from London or Oxford. The news was only part of their purpose for gathering of course, and the evenings tended to be long, with a little more ale than was really good for them, and noisy with merriment. The men usually gathered in the parlor after the meal and exchanged hunting stories, while the women cleaned up out in the kitchen. That was when the gossip was shared about whose children were seeing whom and when there might be a wedding, or when a new baby was expected.

It was after such an evening that John and Carrie had walked home, laughing and retelling some of the evening's stories, arriving late and a little chilly from the evening air.

Carrie deliberately did not mention that the wife of young Mortimer Freeman, who ran the feed and grain mill, was expecting in April or May, lest John think she was fretting that she, herself, was not. "*But,*" she thought to herself, *"they were only married in June of last year, and there is to be a baby already. Why does it seem, for other people, to be so easy? Whatever is wrong with me?"*

When they arrived home, Carrie went into the house, while John detoured off to the barn to check on an ewe that had been ill. "Oh, John!" she called out to him, running back to the front door, "Maggie's having her puppies!" John quickly looked, saw that the ewe seemed much better, and ran to the house. "Not already!" he said brushing past Carrie and hurrying into the scullery where, at delivery time, the whelping box was always set up. "She's not due for at least two weeks yet!"

Maggie looked up at him with soft and worried eyes. She was lying on a pile of dirty clothes that Carrie had gathered to wash in a day or two, and apparently, from the tone of his voice, her master was not pleased about it. Still, necessity had forced her to her usual birthing spot, and box or no box, these clothes were what seemed to have been provided.

The collie was licking two tiny, wet, rat-like creatures, which were squealing and trying to make their way to her belly to nurse. "It's alright, Girl," John said, kneeling and rubbing the dog gently behind her ears, "we'll get your box set up first thing in the morning." Meanwhile, Carrie had run to the barn and brought back the soft old blankets that always lined Maggie's whelping box.

"Here, Sweetheart," she said, "let's get you fixed up more comfortably for the night anyway, alright? John, you lift her up while I slide the clothes out from under her and put the blankets down."

John struggled with the puppies and the heavy dog, trying to be as gentle as he could. Carrie struggled with the pile of clothes and blankets, while Maggie struggled with labor pains—nervously watching the puppies already born. In a minute or so, all was settled. Carrie made a pot of strong tea, and she and John settled in for a night's watch. Maggie went back to work.

Sometime before dawn, she appeared to have finished, and seven somewhat undersized puppies were digging into the cozy warmth of her soft, milk-damp fur. After giving her a dish of water mixed with a little warm milk, John and Carrie went gratefully off to bed.

The next morning, the couple was red-eyed and yawning in church. Later, after checking on all the animals, followed by a light lunch, they settled in to read but soon were dozing in their chairs. Monday morning, John left for two days in London.

Later in the day, when Carrie went in to see how Maggie was doing, she found her licking one of the puppies and nudging it with her nose. She whined softly to Carrie when she entered the scullery. "What's the trouble, Girl? Oh-oh, let me see that pup." Carrie picked up the puppy. It was dead.

All during the long afternoon, Carrie periodically visited the scullery to make sure the puppies were alright. Everything seemed to be going along smoothly, when suddenly, after supper, another puppy showed signs of extreme weakness and was refusing to nurse. Maggie was visibly upset.

Carrie warmed a square of flannel in the oven and wrapped the pup in it, keeping it near the stove. Later she heated a little watered sheep milk and attempted to bottle-feed the pup, but it refused to take anything. Helpless, Carrie held the tiny baby collie and watched it die. Then, as the evening progressed into night, and night into the early hours of morning, Carrie worked with one puppy after another, trying to save each one from whatever mysterious malady was carrying them off. By dawn, all seven were lost.

Maggie was beside herself with puzzled sadness. Where were her puppies? Why wouldn't they nurse? Why were they dying? She turned and turned in her box, searching for her babies. She sat up and looked at Carrie with sad, almost frightened eyes.

"Poor Maggie," Carrie said, petting the collie along her soft nose and jaw, "I'm so sorry, darlin'. I tried everything I know how to do, and so did you." Tears of sympathy ran down her cheeks, and dark circles underlined her blue eyes. "Oh Maggie, my sweet Maggie," Carrie wept, cradling the collie's face in her two hands and looking deep into the brown eyes, now as puzzled at Carrie's sorrow as at her own loss, "I guess we're just not very good mothers, are we?" Maggie sat up and licked Carrie's tears away. Then Carolyn hugged the dog and wept as though her heart would break.

Never mind that Maggie had successfully produced two litters in the past and was an excellent breeder; never mind that nature had known something was amiss and delivered the puppies almost three weeks early. Carrie could see only the death she had battled all night long—the failure, so like her own, as month after hopeful month lengthened into years going by with hopes dashed.

The lack of sleep for two nights this week, the loneliness of fighting and losing one battle after another through the long night with John off in London, and the years of disappointment in her own hopes suddenly combined in Carrie's mind to convince her she was worthless—unable to help Maggie, unable to give John a son, and unable to help herself. Worthless.

It seemed as though at that moment, a black helmet descended upon her from above her head, and her vision dimmed. The rising sun seemed without warmth, and the blue sky with its white puffs of cloud looking down on the soft green of the landscape seemed somehow almost colorless. The only thing she could see clearly was that she would never conceive, never be of any use to herself or to John. The puppies were dead and . . . oh, what of the sick ewe? In the emergency, she had completely forgotten to look in on her. Panicked, she ran to the barn to see how the ewe was doing, and found that its eyes were again filled with matter and that it was lying down in the straw breathing with some difficulty. She was not even able to keep the place running efficiently while John was off on business. Worthless, forever worthless.

Exhausted from the night's unsuccessful labors, her sadness, and from this depression now possessing her like a demon's curse, she walked listlessly back to the house, climbed the stairs one slow step at a time, and fell into bed expecting the comfort of oblivion. Instead, she found that her eyes would not close. She lay, tearless, staring hopelessly at the wooden ceiling.

* * *

In London, John was in the flat for the last time. The purpose of his journey had been to close out the lease, as he and Carrie felt they could not afford to keep it up. He had eaten a light supper at the local pub and was now resting on the little love seat, which had been sold along with most of the other furnishings in the flat. The place looked bleak. But at least the comfortable old Morris chair, along with some paintings—his mother's Ming dogs and his father's humidor—were in storage, waiting for an available conveyance to move them up to the place in the country. His briefcase beside the love seat contained the business of the day, waiting to be looked over once more before bed, and John reached down into it. He glanced at the notes he had made earlier, replaced them, and then retrieved his father's papers.

1869, Paris:

"It has been nearly a year since Margaret and I married, and we are very happy here in Paris. As I predicted, she loves it!

"We are great diners, she and I, and there are such wonderful restaurants here. She also enjoys the plays, the theater, the opera and the concerts, as of course do I. We spend nearly every Sunday afternoon in the Louvre. I must say, ours is a busy life.

"My own life in the diplomatic service remains busy as well. Of late, Her Majesty's government is somewhat concerned about the French emperor. He remains a lovable man, but his health has been, I can only say, most inclement. It seems he has a huge stone in his kidneys and is often in bed and unable to work. Doctor after doctor has been called in, and their advice varies from 'do nothing' to 'cut him open and remove the stone,' but this second option would risk his life. Then the attacks pass, and within a day he seems in the best of health. One would never suspect he seemed near death and writhing in exquisite pain just a day or so before.

"In fact, a colleague of mine has written to Lord Stanley at the home office, saying, 'The emperor is depressed. It is even asserted that he is weary of the whole thing, disappointed at the contrast between the brilliancy at the beginning of his reign and the present gloom—and inclined to retire into private life. This is no doubt an exaggeration, but if he is really feeling unequal to governing with energy, the dynasty and the country are in great danger.'[1] Alas, I feel it is no exaggeration at all.

"His life remains that of the spoiled little boy he has always been. He goes from one mistress to another, and each one, at first, fills his mind and his whole world. She is perfect! She is sublime! She is a woman above all others! Then she will do some little thing that displeases him, and his love is crushed like a rose in the hands of a willful child. But, as with the kidney attacks, he recovers quickly and soon finds another mistress, and again, she is perfect, sublime, above all others.

"Thank God for the empress! For years Eugenie has tolerated his infidelities, more easily now, perhaps, since gossip has it that though as passionate as ever, his affairs are more emotion than action these days. He still tries to be discreet, however, sneaking out in the middle of the night to visit his latest paramour. Eugenie still looks the other way, still cares for his failing health, and still grooms their young son, Louis, for the day he will inherit his father's throne. She even once suggested to the emperor that he abdicate in favor of young Louis with herself as regent. He refused, but personally I think it an excellent idea. She is remarkably politically astute, for a woman. The gossip is that she and his ministers all but run the country as it is, inasmuch as his illnesses and self-indulgence take most of his time and energy. (I hear that Baron Von Bismarck of Germany has described Eugenie as 'the only man in Napoleon's government.')[2]

"It seems that Napoleon III is, in every way, not the man he once was.

"Once so truly concerned for the poor, doing one kindly act after another, now he seems to be concerned only with his own interests. His temper grows shorter, and his sense of self-importance greater with each passing year. I suspect his health is responsible for a good bit of his peevishness; that and the frustration that he is failing to bring France to her former greatness, as when she was under his uncle.

"I was impressed not long ago by an incident I was privileged to hear of, almost firsthand. Some years ago, when I served in Persia—during the days when the Báb was teaching the people that the world was soon to receive a new Prophet of God, and the streets were filled with the blood of his victimized followers—I never thought the thing would make its way to the civilized west and modern Europe. But after the Báb had been put to death, one of his followers, a certain Mírzá Ḥusayn-'Alí Nurí, inherited the leadership of the sect. He is currently a prisoner of the Ottoman Turks in the Citadel of Acca, in Palestine. (It appears that "S" in St. Petersburg has actually met this man. He is, she stated, as kind as the Báb himself is said to have been.)

John thought, smiling ruefully *"Ah, there she is again, that woman father had rather a yen for,"* and shaking his head he continued reading.

"At any rate, the prisoner had written, it seems, individual letters that he had delivered to all the kings and Rulers of the Western world, including the rulers of the American republics, not to mention the Sháh of Persia and the Sultan of the Ottomans. Our own queen, may God keep her, also received a copy of the letter, and, I understand, wrote him back, wishing him well.

"Apparently, the emperor, upon reading the letter, tossed it back over his shoulder, harumphed and remarked disdainfully, 'If this man is a god, I am two gods!'[3]

"The prisoner wrote him a second letter. This one is very specific and to the point and has addressed the very things that I have been saying about Napoleon.

"I was not in the audience room when Napoleon was given the second letter. I am fairly certain of much of what it said, however, for one of his secretaries, a man named Gramont, with whom I have become quite friendly, had dinner with me that evening, and over oyster cocktail, told me about the contents of the letter.

"'It is strange, Monsieur,' he told me. 'There is no possible way that this prisoner could have known about His Majesty's contemptuous gesture, yet he spoke to that very gesture.'

"'How so?'" I enquired.

"'He said in the letter, "*O King! We heard the words thou didst utter in answer to the Tsar of Russia concerning the decision made regarding the war.* * The Lord knoweth; is informed of all. Thou didst say: 'I lay asleep on my couch, when the cry of the oppressed who were drowned in the Black Sea, wakened me.'*"'

"'What did you do—memorize his whole letter? How do you know it by heart like that?'"

"'Because of what came next, Monsieur. The prisoner went on to write: *"This is what we heard thee say."*'

"He stopped speaking while the waiter removed our oyster dishes and replaced them with plates of soup. When he was again out of earshot, I asked Gramont, 'How could he hear him say anything if he is imprisoned in Palestine?'

"'Precisely. Yet he continued: "*Hadst thou been sincere in thy words, thou wouldst have not cast behind thy back the Book of God, when it was sent unto thee.*"'[4]

"'In the letter? He said that in the letter?'

"'That and more. Much more. He said that because of Napoleon's earlier justice and fairness to his people, which had brought hope to a great many souls, he had destined for His Majesty such greatness as a ruler as he could never have imagined.'

"'*He* had destined?'

"'Yes, *He.* He claims to be speaking for God, so he is saying, I presume, that God has destined it. But, he went on to say that unless His Majesty repented of his actions and turned to God, soon his kingdom would pass from his hands. That could be a good thing. I tell you, Hillhouse, I am tired of kings and their machinations at our expense! Louis Napoleon was elected to be president of a French Republic! He was *never* to have been a king in the first place!'

* Crimean War.

"'Apparently, his true reason for fighting the Tsar in the Crimea was not because of the oppressed but to avenge Russia for Napoleon Bonaparte's defeat in Moscow. For that we had to lose even more men! It is not enough that Bonaparte sacrificed an entire generation of young Frenchmen; this self-appointed emperor has decided to add to that fiasco a whole second act!' My dinner companion threw down his napkin in disgust.

"As I am not a Frenchman, I felt it not my place to comment. I thought then of the Báb, and of what I had seen in Persia and the promise of the Báb's, that He Whom God Will Make Manifest would appear. It had never occurred to me for one instant that that promised prophet would write letters to the kings and rulers of the world, calling them to account. All I said aloud, however, was 'Amazing is it not?'

"I tried to catch the waiter's eye, as, being engrossed in our conversation, I had let my soup get cold.

"'Amazing, indeed,'" responded Gramont. "'But now listen to this. He also told Napoleon that he could heal him of all his health problems, if he would but ask. As if anyone could really do that,'" he added.

"'Is His Majesty as ill as we have heard, then?'"

"'Yes, Monsieur. His kidneys grow worse by the day. We try to downplay his health, though, but I have confided in you, Edward. You will, of course, not say you heard this from me. It would not do for Bismarck to get wind of it.'

"'I should say not. And I will say nothing. I appreciate your confidence in me, by the way.' I did not add that I suspected Bismarck already knew nearly as much about Napoleon's health as did we British.

"Between the Chancellor of Germany and that Prisoner in Acca, I wondered what the future held for Napoleon III."

19

SHIRIN: 1869

I have said that what with my joy in my little granddaughter, I felt as though I would never be unhappy again. I knew by then how life works, but I was so delighted with Khadijah's cheerful busyness and our delight in Katherine that I forgot the everlasting pattern.

Right before Christmas, Edward Hillhouse went to England for the holiday to be married in the first weeks of 1868. He had been for an extended visit, knowing that he would not be back for a long time—years at best, and, more than likely—never.

It seemed that whenever he came to visit, life felt richer and more enjoyable. He was courteous from his very heart, it seemed to me, not just "mannerly" because society requires it. He was a cheerful man, and his own sense of amusement matched my own. I counted myself very lucky to know him. His eyes sparkled with much the same delight as I felt when I saw him after a long absence. Invariably, we took each other's hands when we met and laughed aloud with one another—our perennial greeting.

Because he was leaving us, and so that all his well-wishers in St. Petersburg might congratulate him upon his upcoming nuptials, the count had given an early Christmas ball in his honor.

The ballroom in the count's house was truly beautiful. It took up the whole third floor and had a long balcony that overlooked the grounds. Furnished with stone benches and potted trees and flowers, the balcony seemed almost as though it were a garden.

The ballroom itself had a very high ceiling—gilded, and with murals, in the French fashion. All around the room at intervals were tall candlesticks, maybe seven or eight feet tall, each one holding five candles arranged in a circle. Hung from the ceiling on long chains were three chandeliers, carrying their own circles of perhaps twenty-five or thirty candles on each chandelier. There was a dais on one end of the ballroom where the musicians sat, and along the beautiful walls covered in pale yellow watered silk were chairs of a cream-colored material, arranged in little groups of five or seven, for resting between dances and chatting. The servants moved about, carrying trays of refreshing drinks—fruit punches and a great deal of vodka, of which the gentlemen, I fear, partook liberally.

It seemed like a palace to me. And well it might, for not only were some of the guests the same friends and relatives from the court of the Tsar who had attended Shahane's wedding but, I had learned, the whole decor was copied from the style at Versailles.

On the night of Edward's party, everything was so beautiful. The excitement and conviviality of the gentlemen and the glittering shimmer of the women's jewels fastened in their hair or sewn into some of the gowns was intoxicating. Khadijah was all but feverish as she truly basked in her element, and even I, who had never developed a great taste for opulence, was, nevertheless, entranced. Moreover, the music was splendid, and the spritely melodies from the violins rang through the air, infusing everyone's spirits with gaity.

I had learned ballroom dancing during these years in Russia, and, while I was very reticent at first about having men I hardly knew placing their hand on my waist and holding my hand during the steps, I learned after a bit to lay aside my embarrassment. While the intimacy of it still made me slightly uncomfortable, I eventually came to enjoy it. The movement and the music won out over whatever seemed improper.

In Persia, we loved dancing, and often it was spirited and free, even to the point of being erotic, but *never* did men and women touch each other, or even, except in intimate family situations, dance in one another's presence. Rubin Mikaelovitch and I spoke together of these customs at a party once, resting together over punch. He said that in the stricter Jewish communities, the dancing was like our Persian style, men and women separate, and we agreed with each other that along with the freedoms bestowed by Christian teachings came also strong temptations to an easy familiarity that was not always in everyone's best interests. "*Perhaps,*" I remember thinking, "*freedom beyond a certain limit can become a burden.*"

I was soon to see the vindication of that thought in a number of ways and learn the weight of that burden.

On the night of Edward's party, well into the evening when the room had grown warm from so much activity, he and I were dancing together. "I am terribly warm," Edward said.

"Yes," I agreed, "it is becoming close, isn't it?"

"Surprising," he commented, "for so large a room. Would you like a breath of air?"

I agreed, and we stepped out of the ballroom through the large doors that led to the balcony. The night was surprisingly mild for early November. Edward had brought two cups of the fruit punch and handed one to me. Warm and flushed from the excitement and the effort of dancing, we found it refreshing and drank along with it great breaths of the fresh air.

Standing at the rail of the balcony, we gazed out at the lights of St. Petersburg. They were entrancing. The light from thousands of candles and lamps, yellow and warm, gleamed up at us from the city, and though there was only a sliver of moonlight, it was enough to shed a glow over the darker sections of town. The bridge over the Neva stood ghostly and beautiful in the crisp night, the light reflected from the moving river below it soft and undulant, the great fortress of Saints Peter and Paul looming dark and solid beyond. After the noisy party chatter, we were hushed at the beauty and the sudden quiet, accompanied only by the muted strains of the waltz from indoors.

Then Edward remarked, "I love St. Petersburg. I shall miss it so. I shall miss everything about it. Especially," he said, looking directly into my eyes, "this family and the friends I have made here."

Surprised at the intensity of my own response, I answered him. "We shall miss you too, Edward. We will miss you very much!"

He turned fully toward me then and took my hands in his. "Shall you miss me, Shirin?"

"I just told you so," I said.

"No, you said 'we'; you said 'we' should miss me. I am asking if *you* will miss me. Will you?"

Suddenly off balance, I hardly knew how to respond. "Of course . . . " I began awkwardly, but he interrupted me then. Reaching up and moving a strand of hair out of my face, with his finger, he whispered, "Dear God, you are so lovely. Oh, my dear, so lovely!"

I didn't know what to say or how to respond, so I laughed a little and said, "Lovely? I am in my fifties, Edward."

"I know. That is part of your miracle. You have lived this long and been through so much; yet it seems only to have made you more beautiful. Never mind the shallow prettiness of a girl; you have a spirit that shines from inside you, a spirit that . . ."

There was a look of intensity burning in his eyes that I had not seen since the first months of my marriage to 'Alí Taqí, and I suddenly understood what was happening.

I was not prepared for anything like this and so was overtaken by a strange fear. Yet, also bubbling up from my deepest center was a foreign joy such as I had not known before.

He reached for my face again and laid his hand against my cheek. The touch of his palm, warm in the chilly air, was a soft, sweet burning. As I stared at him in wonder, he closed his eyes and groaned softly, "Oh, how shall I leave you?" and before I could register what was happening, his arms were around me and he was kissing me.

So rapidly—it seemed almost as if it happened all at once—I was first surprised, then angry that he, who was about to be married, would take such a liberty; then I was overwhelmed at my own response. Sensations I had all but forgotten rose from where they had lain neglected for years and burst in a moment into an explosion of desire for this man, whom I had come, over time, to regard with such friendship and eager delight.

There was also a moment of shame that I should harbor such feelings for one whom I respected so much.

Then, with a sound in my soul somewhere that felt like the collision of ships in a turbulent sea, the two sensations, trusted friendship and desire, joined together, and I knew what I would never have guessed. Amazed at the sound of bliss in my own voice, I heard myself whisper, "Oh, Edward! I love you!"

Completely forgotten was any sense of right or wrong, or what could happen to any of the people we loved; his Margaret, his duty to his Queen and country, the good name of my family and little granddaughter, my debt to the generosity of the count and his household. I believed only that this was the total meaning of my life, that I would ask nothing of God or my future except to be forever with Edward, to spend the rest of my days smiling up at his dear face.

He looked at me and could read all this in my eyes. Suddenly he looked stricken. He dropped his arms and stepped back into a shadowed spot and all but fell to a sitting position on one of the stone benches. He covered his face with his hands and shook his head. "Oh, gracious God, what have I done?" There was a long silence while he regained himself, and I, in turn, began to know what had truly happened to me.

He looked up at me then, with pleading in his eyes and said, "I am not . . . what do they say? . . . 'toying with your affections!' You mean so *much* to me Shirin! I love . . . ! You are so precious to me! I would never intentionally hurt you! You *must* believe me!" He groaned again and said, "I have wanted you for so long. I never intended for you to know, but tonight I am overwhelmed by how much I hate to leave you. In fact, I feel as though I never can."

"But, my dear, at this point there is no choice in the matter."

"But there is. We do have a choice." He rose from where he sat and took me by the shoulders. "We could stay here together. I could leave the service and remain here with you, and . . . " He looked away from my eyes and into the distance.

"*He wants to mean what he is saying,*" I thought, *"but he can't. He is speaking from the force of his desire."*

"Edward, you would be happy here and away from England? You would be happy without your career in the service?"

"I could be happy if I had you beside me always! Shirin, I could!"

"And without the son you so long for? How are we to build happiness on the ashes of betrayal—of your promise to Margaret and your duty to your family and queen—and of the count's hospitality to us all? And I—how could I live, knowing myself complicit with all of it?"

He turned away from me then, so I shouldn't see his tears, and looked again out at the lights of the city below. My own silent tears were a mix of sorrow, the joy of my discovery—and the knowledge that he loved me in return.

After a silence, he said, "Oh, my darling! Do you think you might ever be able to forgive me?"

"There is nothing to forgive, Love," I said. "You ask what you have done. What you have done is give me a part of myself I did not know existed. I know we can never be together. But I know, too, that I shall love you as long as I live. And I know you love me! My darling, you have given me a great gift!"

"Only to snatch it away again!" he said, striking the balcony rail with his fist. His voice was hoarse with intensity. "My God, I should be drawn and quartered!"

"Oh, my dearest one, no. Kiss me again, Edward."

"After what has just happened to you—how do I dare?" Then gathering me again in his arms, he murmured, "Oh, but how can I not?" As he drew me toward him, I inhaled the smell of him, grown familiar from the years of our friendship, and in a voice I had never heard before, heard myself murmuring, "Sweet man. Oh, sweet, *sweet* man!" His kiss was devouring, and I grew weak as my hunger for him grew. It was a hunger I knew would never be eased beyond this kiss of parting. Dizzy with desire, I stumbled as we pulled reluctantly apart. For a moment, we stood silently looking at each other with lost and desperate eyes.

In the end, there was nothing to do but go back to the party. For the rest of the evening we hardly dared glance in one another's direction. At some late hour, as the guests were leaving, the room was filled with polite expressions of thanks and congratulations to the bridegroom. As I left to join Rubin and Khadijah, I offered Edward my hand. He brushed it with a polite kiss that inflamed my entire being. He looked up, and our eyes met. I have never forgotten the pain I saw there. "Sleep well," I said, willing him to hear, not my words, but what my heart was saying, "and have a safe journey to England." He nodded in acknowledgment and murmured a barely audible "Thank you."

Still immersed in the wondrous miracle of my loving, I knew my life had changed forever. It was only later, alone in my room, as I caressed my own cheek with the back of that hand that still burned from our final good-bye, that I began to understand what had truly happened. I realized that this joyous stranger I had met in me tonight, this woman, had been waiting all my life to be born.

Alas, I saw, too, that the love for Edward that had so filled me with joy was already turning to pain. More, I knew the pain was a burden I would carry as long as I lived.

20

SHIRIN:

Early in 1870, one morning some six or eight weeks later, as Natasha, Olga, and I lingered over breakfast tea, Rubin Dubinsky came in, shaking snowflakes from his coat and asking to speak with me about "something important." I poured tea for him and, stifling my curiosity, made a production of offering him sugar and cream. He refused and, after a moment's silence, asked if we could withdraw to where we could be alone.

Taking our tea, we went up to my rooms and sat together at a small table. "Now, Rubin," I said, feeling more like his mother than I ever had, "what is this 'something important' you wish to discuss?"

He drew a deep breath and said, "Khánum, how would you feel about moving to Paris?"

"Paris, France?" I responded somewhat inanely.

"Yes—Paris, France. I have business connections there, as well as family, and if Khadijah and Katherine and I were to go there to live, naturally, we would want you to come with us. I'm thinking very seriously about it."

"Well," I said—because taken aback as I was, I couldn't think of anything else to say—"at least I speak the language" (which made Rubin smile). "I have thought you are very successful here, Rubin, why would you want to move such a long way away?"

Sighing a rather weary sigh, he reached for my free hand and took it in both of his. "Khánum, I could pretend it is only business and that there is no other reason for my leaving St. Petersburg, but sooner or later you would see the obvious. I may as well be honest with you. Khadijah and I are not doing well together."

"Not doing well? She seems very happy to me, Rubin, and you both love your little girl so much. Whatever is the matter?"

Rubin stared at the floor for a long time before he answered me. "She has a . . . that is, you know she has always enjoyed the attentions of gentlemen, and now, it seems, she . . . there is a certain man, a Mr. . . . "

"Desyatovsky!" I interrupted, remembering that often she danced and chatted with him at parties and dinners. Sometimes, if the men did not retire alone to drink and smoke, she sat next to him in the drawing room after dinner. I had thought nothing of it, but now, with my own reawakening of desire, what Rubin was trying to tell me seemed obvious, and I wondered that I had not noticed it before.

Rubin pinched his lips together and looked at me with sad eyes. He nodded silently.

"Oh, Rubin, my dear son, is this true? Surely it is no more than a mild flirtation. Surely she would not . . ."

"I wish I could reassure you, Khánum, but I finally faced her with it last evening after we had returned from a dinner engagement with the Desyatovskys and the Stolypins. She has confirmed my ugliest suspicions. She insists she loves me still, and when I suggested that we go away—to Paris—she begged me to stay here and has promised me to end the attachment."

"But you do not believe her? You want to go to Paris anyway?"

"I believe she means to. I am just not sure she can do it that easily. Your daughter, Madam," he said with a wry smile, "is extremely headstrong."

"And self-centered," I added. "I am well aware of it, Rubin."

"So I have agreed to give her time to prove her intentions, but if I find she cannot break it off as I hope, we will go. I wanted you to be warned that it might come to this."

We talked for a long while together, and several times Rubin nearly wept. I thought it strange that Khadijah could not be happy with this man who had given her all she had ever wanted, loved her with his whole heart, and shared with her our darling little Katherine. After he left, I paced my room for a long time, growing angrier and angrier with Khadijah. At home, a husband would not have been so tolerant, and she would have lost her whole existence—her home, husband, daughter, and, in some families, even her life. I planned to take her sternly to task.

* * *

I did not approach Khadijah with my disapproval after all. I decided it was best to say nothing unless she chose to tell me about it. She did not. Besides, Rubin was handling it, and it was up to him how best to do so.

I was having difficulty enough with my own forbidden feelings; the long nights when I lay unable to sleep recalling the night on the balcony, the years of happy friendship and spirited talks we had had, punctuated with humor and laughter, the awful need to see him, to hear his voice, to hold him again, and finally, the terrible realization that I never would.

During the days, I kept as busy as I could, to keep it all from my mind and tire myself so I could fall asleep. Sometimes that was effective, and I would fall into a deep sleep the moment I lay down, only to be tortured through the night with dreams of him. Sometimes the dreams involved Margaret with him where I would rather be, and I would awake in a state of jealous anger, and only after several minutes of stern self-lecture could I get it all into perspective. Sometimes there were brief moments when I felt intense anger at Edward himself for arousing these feelings in me, but I knew that was not truly fair, and these moments never lasted. It would seem, after all the losses of my life, I would be able to handle this one more gracefully, which, after all, had not been through his death. Sometimes I was even momentarily comforted that he was alive and happily living in England and perhaps even having a child to enjoy, much as I was enjoying our little Katherine.

But the worst moments were the mornings. I would awaken each morning to the brightness of a fresh new day, and my first conscious thought was of Edward, followed immediately by the realization that I would never see him again. Each morning, my aching heart would cloud over the brightness, and each morning I would weep until I had cleansed my heart for that day. Then and then only could I arise and take up my life.

The intensity of struggling with these two blows at least brought its own insight, and as I fought each morning to go on living with my pain, I came to understand it better. Death nullifies all contracts and promises nothing; it leaves us surprised, insulted, and empty-handed. We grieve, then continue living. But love, with its fantasy of impossible perfection, promises everything, and its unkept promise can become a torture by day and by night.

Nor does it matter so much whom or even what one loves. I came to see also that Khadijah, who loved clothes, jewelry, and the gay life of wealth and social position, was tortured also, because that love could not deliver the happiness she had believed it would. Poor Rubin, who loved her nearly to distraction, could not keep the promise she had seen in him the night he proposed. As for him, he wanted a woman to care deeply for him, and Khadijah hadn't the faintest inkling how. She had no idea how miserably she was failing him. All three of us loved with our whole hearts. All three of us were suffering.

This insight helped somewhat. It helped relieve both my anger at my daughter and my own pain. Still, the place in my heart that had often sung with the joy of living had turned to a hard little black walnut, and I sometimes wondered if I would ever again hear that singing.

Zhukovsky was growing feeble. Now, almost eighty, he had great difficulty walking and was nearly deaf. He used an ear trumpet in order to hear, and between keeping track of that and the cane he needed to get about, he barely had a hand for himself. It annoyed him no end, and he was becoming difficult. He did not complain openly about his troubles, but he was angry with his developing helplessness, and I often heard the anger in his voice as he spoke of the general state of the world. Part of the "state of the world" was the current situation with the Tsar.

Some years before, Count Nicholas's uncle, Prince Michael Dolgoruky, the erstwhile ambassador to Persia who had brought the count into our lives, had, quite frankly, died of too much vodka, leaving colossal debts and two small daughters. Dolgoruky had been close to the Tsar, so Alexander had become the guardian and foster father of Prince Michael's daughters. He sent them to Smolny, the celebrated convent school for the daughters of the nobility.

The eldest was named Catherine. She was a beautiful little girl, with long golden ringlets, delicate features, and intense, very dark eyes. I had seen her several times at the parties held for the young people during the holidays. She was one of those children who seemed to have been born grown-up, and her unlikely maturity, coupled with her outstanding beauty and a self-contained, grave manner, made of her a fascinating enigma.

The winter of 1869–70 was especially severe. No one ventured out unless it was absolutely necessary, and the deaths of the old and the poor were shocking in their rising numbers. As for us, we stayed by the fire as often as possible, reading, sewing and telling one another stories and gossip. One morning in late February, Olga had remained in bed with a cold, and Natasha was busy with household affairs. Zhukovsky and I were by ourselves, drinking cocoa before the fire and talking.

I had confided to him about Khadijah and Rubin's "trouble." I wanted to see if he had any nuggets of wisdom to impart. Alas, he did not. He countered with a sad tale of his own, again about love and the misery that seems almost an integral part of it.

The Tsar's eldest son and heir to the throne, young Prince Nicholas, had contracted meningitis right after becoming engaged to young Princess Dagmar of Denmark. He was adored by his entire family, including his younger brother, Alexander III. Just as it seemed that the lovely princess and the heir apparent were set to secure the next generation of Russian rulers, the prince died. This was in 1865. It was in every way a great sorrow to the family and the friends of the royal house.

The Tsar was not only devastated, he was lost. Long ago, his marriage had grown stale, but he had not the self-discipline to turn a once passionate attachment into a settled and comfortable friendship. He had had a good many mistresses, which the Tsarina had tolerated with good grace, as royal wives tend to do, but they were merely diversions. Alexander needed to be worshipped. With Prince Nicholas's death, he felt as though he were wandering lost in a forest. His life consisted of his days at his work and his nights spent on a hard cot in a sleeping cell, much as his father had lived before him. The Tsar, at age forty-five, was miserable.

It was just about that time that young Catherine Dolgoruka turned fifteen. The Tsar was not immune to her mystery and began to develop a fascination for his elder ward. I had known about the two girls, of course, and also had felt my own share of sadness at the death of Nicholas Tsarevitch but had not heard more than that.

On this cold morning, after confiding in Zhukovsky about my puzzlement and unhappiness with Khadijah's situation, he confided to me that he too was suffering—from disappointment in his beloved former student.

"It is not so much that he has taken another mistress; he has always done that. It is that he has done it so publicly. He maintains that she is his wife "in the sight of God," and he has all but deserted the Tsarina!"

"But she is a mere child, is she not? She was fifteen when the Tsarevitch died, so she is what . . . twenty now?"

"Exactly, though she is not so terribly young now, but he has been seeing her since she was fifteen, and they already have a child, whom he is now openly acknowledging. Dear Heaven, Khánum, he is nearly thirty years older than she!"

"I've not heard of kings acknowledging their illegitimate children before."

"That is precisely my point. I fear for his future, and that of the nation."

"The nation? How could yet another mistress affect the nation?"

"This one could. All his life, Alexander has been trying to put together the two separate parts of himself—the tender, loving, compassionate man and the unyielding autocrat whom his father taught him to be. Trying and failing."

"Yes, I know. I remember the story you told me soon after the emancipation of the serfs. Of how a group of the great landowners came to him and offered to help out the financial problems created by the emancipation and the loss of property. You told me they said that since the serfs could not pay the taxes on their land, perhaps they could help out by paying taxes. I remember being so impressed that the nobility would actually offer to pay taxes!"

I rose and tucked Zhukovsky's shawl around his shoulders, from where it had slipped down his back. "Thank you, my dear, you are so thoughtful of me," he said, reaching up and patting my hand as it moved across his shoulder. ". . . and you also remember that the Tsar's reaction was to grow livid with them and shout that the organization of the national finances was the business of the Tsar and of the Tsar only!"

"I should say I do remember. I was *shocked* when you said that he then had them all thrown into prison for interfering with the government. I still find it hard to believe."

"Indeed. Well, *now* what is happening is that he is becoming more and more autocratic with the people, and gives all his tender compassion to Catherine and their children. He is becoming more divided than ever. Khánum, a loving union is a wonderful thing—for kings as well as private citizens. But on no account can a king ignore his people's needs, much less those of his family, for his own personal happiness."

Because my thoughts were never far from my own longing, I forgot, for an instant, the Tsar's infidelity to his wife and asked, "But surely, Monsieur, a king has as much need for happiness as any common citizen, has he not?"

"Only if it does not interfere with his duty. If kings rule by divine right, then their duties are to God and that trust, not to their private desires."

"But do kings truly rule by divine right—or is that a justification of power?"

"Here in Christendom, we believe they rule by divine right. Our scripture says, 'Let every soul be subject unto the higher powers, for there is no power but God, and the powers that be are appointed of God.'[1] No, his duty must always come first, Khánum. He is the king!"

I thought then of Khadijah and her duty to Rubin and our Katherine, and of Edward and his duty to his Margaret and his family, and thought that perhaps it is not always so different for private citizens after all, where an initial happiness would be purchased at the price of someone's betrayal.

After a moment's silence, broken only by the click of his cup being set in its saucer as he finished his cocoa, I asked him, "Monsieur, do you believe there is anything to astrology?"

"I don't know that I have a great deal of use for it, but I am forced to admit that sometimes it seems to be uncannily correct in some of its pronouncements. Why do you ask?"

"Only because—with the intensity of the affair of the Tsar, and the situation with Rubin and Khadijah, it almost seems these days as though the skies are raining down love upon people who perhaps ought not be entertaining such feelings. I just wonder if the stars could have anything to do with that."

Zhukovsky answered, "Possibly. But I think it is more likely coincidence. After all, the astrologers say, when these things happen in groups like this, it is because some planet or other moves forward, then backward—retrograde, they call it—and then forward again. That is why, they tell me, similar events often occur in threes. And after all," he smiled, "you have named only two."

I said nothing.

21

CONFESSIONS:

JMJ

Pius was worried. The revolutionary thinking that had troubled Europe now, for two decades, was still spreading its poisonous libertinism everywhere, and again the nations were in a state of unrest. The Kaiser of Germany had given over tremendous power to his chancellor, Otto Von Bismarck, who was insistent upon uniting the Germanic peoples—the Austrian Habsburgs under Franz Josef and the Kaiser's Germans—into one country. It looked as though there might be war again.

Napoleon III, who had championed the pope to the point of requesting that his holiness come and personally baptize his infant son, Louis, was at odds with Bismarck.

"But the Holy Father didn't go," Mario said to me late one afternoon while we were discussing the current situation. We were walking along the edge of the Tiber, watching the ducks follow the boat traffic in the hope of treats from the sailors. "I can't imagine that Napoleon would actually believe Pius could spare the time to travel to Paris to baptize an infant."

"You wouldn't think so," I responded, blowing on my hands to warm them. The setting sun was taking the day's warmth with it. "But, after all, Napoleon has defended the pope's interests for his entire reign . . . maybe he thought he had something coming from His Holiness."

"Maybe. What is Pius going to do? His influence over the faithful diminishes every day, and now he has issued this new statement, similar to the Syllabus of Errors. He's becoming more and more strict," Mario said, "and he used to be so openhearted."

"Well, he is confused. I understand that he said to Cardinal Antonelli that if God did not have mercy on him, and guide him, he would feel forced to abdicate."

Mario stopped in midstride and stared intently at me. "Did he really say that?"

"Yes, why? What are you . . . ?"

"Oh, nothing," Mario almost mumbled, and withdrew into his own thoughts.

We stopped at the same small *caffe* where we had eaten that first night after we had met in the library and had a light supper. During our meal, we again fell into discussion of the state of Europe and the difficulties the church was having, and I mentioned again Pius's fear that he might abdicate. I said, "I understand he still believes his prayers are unanswered. He doesn't know where to turn. Responsible, as he is, for the people's spiritual welfare, he is terribly worried about the separated brethren in the English church and now the Lutherans and other Protestant groups growing in strength. Add to this that the wealth and lands of the Church are diminishing all the time. He believes he is failing his trust. I don't wonder at how he feels so much at sea."

Mario said "hmm" and withdrew again. During a short silence, while I wondered what was going on with him, it was so quiet I could hear myself chewing. Suddenly he looked up from his plate and, in a decisive voice said, "Finish your supper, Vittorio. Let's go home now. I have something to show you."

The minute we entered our rooms, I stirred up the fire, and Mario went into his bedroom. He returned almost immediately with several sheets of thin paper dangling from his hand. As he handed them to me, they fluttered a little in the radiations of heat from the fireplace. I took the papers and began to read, while he sat, alternately watching me and staring into the fire. It was in his own handwriting, and I realized he had copied the letter that so disturbed him, in order to bring it back to our rooms. I read:

"O Pope! Rend the veils asunder! He Who is Lord of Lords is come overshadowed with clouds and the decree hath been fulfilled by God, the Almighty, the unrestrained! . . .

"Thus hath the Pen of the Most High commanded thee at the behest of thy Lord, the Almighty, the All-Compelling. He, verily, hath again come down from Heaven even as He came down from it the first time. Beware that thou dispute not with Him even as the Pharisees disputed with Him without a clear token or proof. On His right hand flow the living waters of grace, and on His left the choice wine of justice . . . ."[1]

I thought immediately, "*Just as I thought. This man thinks he is Jesus . . . how could Mario be taken in by this?*", but I continued reading.

The letter was long and filled with descriptive adjectives and flowery metaphors and images, in the Middle Eastern fashion, as Arabic and Persian always are, and further it bore from time to time references that could be understood best, if at all, only if one were somewhat schooled in Islamic thought. But its purport was unmistakable, and the writer spoke with a certainty of purpose.

At least, his writing was consistent with Christian doctrine, which is practically unheard of among the writers of letters such as these. Normally, they fancy themselves all-powerful and threaten destruction if you do not follow their twisted thinking. Of course, there was some suggestion of a sense of all-powerful delusion here, I reasoned, as he dares to warn the pope to beware of disputing with him. Warn the Holy Father? The Vicar of Christ, Shepherd of the souls of all men is told by this prisoner to beware?

Who is he, anyway? A man in chains locked in a filthy prison in Palestine, the Devil's Island of the Turkish world, and he dares to warn him who defends the name of God in Christ to *beware*! Hardly anyone has ever heard of him. What does he call himself? And as if speaking directly to my thoughts the letter said:

"Beware lest any name debar thee from God, the Creator of earth and heaven. Leave thou the world behind thee, and turn towards thy Lord, through Whom the whole earth hath been illumined . . .

"Dwellest thou in palaces whilst He Who is the King of Revelation liveth in the most desolate of abodes? Leave them to such as desire them, and set thy face with joy and delight toward the Kingdom."[2]

Well, at least he agreed with Mario and me, who often said that in spite of the Church's power and her need for a great deal of office space, that with so much poverty in the world, perhaps she ought to be less worldly. In spite of her losses, she still owned great stores of treasure. We sometimes spoke of how many people the proceeds from their sale could feed, but we always fell back on the obvious. There would still be millions it could not feed, with more being born every day. As our Lord Himself had said, "The poor ye have always with you."[3]

"Beware lest human learning debar thee from Him Who is the supreme object of all knowledge, or let the world deter thee from the One Who created it and set it on its course. Arise in the Name of thy Lord, the God of Mercy, amidst the peoples of the earth, and seize thou the Cup of Life with the hands of confidence. First drink thou therefrom, and proffer it then to such as turn towards it amongst the peoples of all faiths. . . .

"Call thou to remembrance Him Who was the Spirit [Jesus], Who, when He came, the most learned of His age pronounced judgment against Him in His own country, whilst he who was only a fisherman believed in Him. . . . Thou, in truth, art one of the suns of the heaven of His Names. Guard thyself, lest darkness spread its veils over thee, and fold thee away from His light."[4]

"He seems," I remarked to Mario, "not hate-driven, as most of these letter writers are. Rather he seems compassionate and as though he cares what becomes of the Holy Father."

"Still your pens, O concourse of divines . . ."[5]

I started a little at that. It appears that he is writing not only to the pontiff, but to all of us who serve God's church.

> "the Hour that was concealed within the knowledge of God hath struck . . . ."[6]

What is it Our Lord had said? "No one knoweth what day or hour your Lord cometh, no not even the Son, but the Father only, He knows." And "I have many things to tell you, howebeit, ye cannot bear them now, but when He Who is the Spirit of Truth comes . . ."[7]

I continued reading.

> "Hasten unto Him, O peoples of the earth, with humble and contrite hearts . . .
>
> "If ye deny this Revelation, by what proof have ye believed in God? Produce it then. . . .
>
> "O followers of all religions! We behold you wandering distraught in the wilderness of error. Ye are the fish of this Ocean, wherefore do ye withhold yourselves from that which sustaineth you? . . . Hasten unto it from every clime. This is the day whereon the Rock* crieth out and shouteth, and celebrateth the praise of its Lord, the All-Possessing, the Most High, saying: 'Lo! The Father is come, and that which ye were promised in the Kingdom is fulfilled!'
>
> "My body hath borne imprisonment that your souls may be released from bondage, and We have consented to be abased that ye may be exalted.
>
> "The people of the Qur'án have risen against Us, and tormented us with such a torment that the Holy Spirit lamented, and the thunder roared out, and the clouds wept over Us. Among the faithless is he who hath imagined that calamities can deter Bahá from fulfilling that which God, the Creator of all things, hath purposed.

---

* St. Peter.

> "Say: O peoples of all Faiths! . . . The Ancient Beauty is come in His Most Great Name, and He wisheth to admit all mankind into His most Holy Kingdom. . . .
>
> "Say: This is the Day of Bounty! Bestir yourselves that I may make you monarchs in the realms of My Kingdom. If ye follow Me, you shall behold that which ye were promised, and I will make you My companions. . . . If ye rebel against me. . . ."

("Oh-oh," I thought, "here it comes. The inevitable threat of destruction, as ever with these people." But then I kept reading.)

> "I will in my clemency endure it patiently that haply ye may awaken and rise up from the couch of heedlessness. Verily, the day of the ingathering is come."[8]

I laid it down on the small table beside me and said to Mario, "What did His Holiness say?"

"About the letter?"

"Of course about the letter; what does he think?"

"Mother of God, Vittorio—the Holy Father does not tell me what he thinks!"

"I know that, but I thought perhaps you had heard something."

"No, it just came to my hand with a group of communications, none of which was of any import. I was merely to file them, as usual."

"I should think, then, that the Holy Office considers it also of no import. It is probably one of thousands of letters received from madmen who fancy themselves in communication with God. Surely you know how that is, Mario. Surely you have seen such things before."

"Yes, of course. But this struck me especially. I couldn't sleep that first night. Besides, never mind what the Holy Office thinks, Vittorio, I want to know what *you* think."

"H'mmm." I was silent a moment thinking of how to answer Mario. "I believe, my friend, that I may have already said what I think: that it is the work of an unhinged mind and, like the rest of the letters handed to you at the same time, 'of no import.'"

He looked almost disappointed and then brightened. "Perhaps you are right, and I have been making something of nothing. Perhaps I should just forget about it." But I noticed that, rather than consigning the contraband copy to the fire, he returned it to his room. Poor Mario—the letter had kept him from sleeping, he said. I could not understand why; I certainly had no trouble falling asleep.

Sometime before morning, however, I had the dream again, with the voice as clear, as authoritative, and as kindly as ever. But this time it added a quote from the letter: "Vittorio, sleep not . . . awaken and rise up from your couch of heedlessness, for verily, the Day of the ingathering hath come!"

22

HILLHOUSE PAPERS:

"I find it difficult to believe all that has occurred in the four years since Margaret and I married. In January of '69, following our wedding, we honeymooned in Paris and spent a great deal of time locating a place to live and getting ourselves settled. We found an apartment on the second floor of a lovely building in Neuilly-sur-Seine, with a view that included the Arc de Triomphe in the distance. The apartment was furnished in last century's style, with gilded furniture and very high ceilings. The floors were marble and covered with oriental rugs. Gas lanterns set in sconces and placed along the walls at intervals afforded a good light in the evenings. Between them we hung paintings from the small collection of art we were building; we had purchased pieces we especially liked while strolling through Montmart.

"The walls of the bedroom suite were covered in silk, a dark green cloth printed with roses, but it was old and had developed fabric runs in places. In the dressing room, where we bathed, was even a place where the silk had torn away from the wall, leaving a rather ugly flaw in the décor. You may be sure we tried to cover that with a small painting as soon as we could. We found a pen-and-ink sketch of a cathedral, which fit almost perfectly, although it didn't really belong in a bathing room. We joked about it a good deal and promised ourselves to replace it as soon as we could find something more appropriate. Margaret said she thought perhaps a sketch of Sara Bernhardt playing her famous role as a courtesan might just do perfectly.

"Across the street from the bedroom and dressing rooms was a lovely park with a carousel for children, a delightful fish pond, and a small orchestra gazebo, where there were often concerts on summer evenings. Margaret and I so enjoyed listening to them after we retired. Often they lulled us to asleep.

"As I have mentioned, we did a lot of theatre going and dining and what not. It was not such an adventure for me because I had come to know Paris well in my bachelor days, and so it was, as they say, a bit of an old hat, but at least I could show Margaret my favorite places. I could not help but enjoy watching her come to love the 'city of light.'

"It was not very long before she was expecting our first child, and, of course, we were thrilled. Unfortunately, before three months had passed, she had lost the child, and the loss took away from her a great deal of that first delight of living abroad. That, however, was only our personal lives. What was happening to Paris itself and indeed all of France was the 'almost unbelievable part' I've already mentioned.

"Napoleon was no longer as popular among the citizens as he had been formerly, but he was too caught up in his personal problems and challenges to notice. His health, his problems with Bismarck, his ambitions for France—not to mention his ubiquitous if impotent 'affairs de l'amour' took all his attention.

"Meanwhile, Bismarck was moving with all possible speed in his attempt to change the German Confederation into a German Empire, with our Queen's grandson, Kaiser Wilhelm, at its head. Napoleon was in favor of putting Queen Victoria's uncle, Leopold Hohenzollern, on the Spanish throne, but the French legislature talked him out of it. Meanwhile, Bismarck, anxious for a war in which he hoped to destroy France, continued to keep the Spanish throne affair alive. Napoleon continued to push for Leopold. He couldn't leave well enough alone.

"It was his last of so many great mistakes.

"By 1871, he still believed in his own popularity so thoroughly that one day in July he had taken young Louis (who was fourteen by then) in his arms and told him: "My son, your coronation is assured! More than ever we can look forward to the future without fear."[1]

"Nevertheless, in two more months it would all be gone!

"By that August, Napoleon was so ill that Eugenie took Prince Louis and went to Corsica without the emperor. There had been a great celebration planned to commemorate the hundredth anniversary of Napoleon Bonaparte's birth, and his nephew had looked forward to it with much expectation and pleasure, but, alas, could only stay home with his throbbing kidney and watch the empress and his heir go off without him.

"Bismarck had sent to him his infamous Ems Telegram, insulting him and suggesting that he keep his royal nose out of Prussian affairs. Let it be said that Napoleon tried with all his waning strength to make peace, but the French legislature was bound to be rid of Bismarck. Napoleon was, as the Prisoner of Acca had indicated in his letter, powerless to resist his fate.

"The legislature asked Napoleon if the army were in shape to go to war. Napoleon assured them in his customary self-confident style that 'We are indeed ready. The army is well supplied, even down to the last gaitor button.' It wasn't. He believed he had European allies. He didn't. Nevertheless, formally and joyfully, the French legislature declared war on Prussia.

"Margaret and I went home to England for what we thought would be a protracted war period. On the journey home she was extremely seasick due to a second pregnancy and, sadly, lost the child before we docked.

"On September 1st, the battle of the little town of Sedan began. I hear that the night before, the Prussian General Moltke said, 'We have them in a mousetrap! Tomorrow we attack!' But one of Napoleon's generals wrote home, considerably more colorfully, I thought, saying, 'We are at the bottom of a night pot and we are about to be shat upon.'[2]

"Napoleon was so sick he could barely stay astride his horse. Nevertheless, he rode off at the head of his troops. He led his horse out into the heat of the firing lines and rode back and forth, hoping to be honorably killed, rather than face the humiliation of defeat. For five full hours, he struggled to stay in his saddle, and several times had to dismount and throw his arms around a tree to remain upright—he was in such pain—yet he sustained not so much as a scratch. In less than six weeks of war, he was roundly defeated by the end of that day in Sedan. Effectively, it was over. France had lost Alsace-Lorraine to the Germans, and while Paris held out for four more months, the people nearly starved.

"Yet, ever the showman and lover of pomp, and in spite of his professed sensitivity for the poor, he rode to surrender in full carriage and horse equipage, while his soldiers stood watching without food, ammunition, or shoes.

"When Eugenie heard that France was lost, she escaped to England. Napoleon and young Louis joined her there. Our queen had always liked him and found him charming (as did most women), and so, when he asked for asylum, made him welcome.

"He was a sad spectacle. The queen wrote, 'I went to the door with Louise, and embraced the Emperor. It was a moving moment, when I thought of the last time he came in '55, in triumph, dearest Albert bringing him from Dover, the whole country mad to receive him, and Now! He seemed much depressed and had tears in his eyes. But he controlled himself and said, "It is a long time since I have seen Your Majesty." He has grown very stout and grey, and his moustaches are no longer curled or waxed, but otherwise there is the same pleasing, gentle and gracious manner. I gave the Empress Eugenie a nosegay of violets and primroses which seemed to please her. Left then, feeling very tired and sad.'[3]

"I understand that Eugenie had written him during the war, saying that all she wanted of life was a little cottage in England, to share with him and Louis (whom she called Lou-Lou); a little cottage with bow windows and creepers. As was more often than not with Eugenie, she got what she wanted, and her 'little cottage in England' ended up having twenty-five rooms.

"Louis lived there in exile for two more years, a very sad man. Now that he had nothing left, in his private moments he worked to invent a stove that the poor could afford. As a brother monarch, however deposed, he was welcome at all social events. He attended them, now that it was too late, attempting to get the attention of the others, as he held forth about the importance of peace and disarmament, and an international council, but with all his charm and diplomatic skill could not bring anything approaching it about. Who would listen to such ideas at a party between canapés and balancing glasses of champagne?

"Broken and disheartened, by 1873 his kidney stone had grown, they say, almost as large as a small orange. Further there were now stones in his bladder. At last they tried surgery, but it was too late; their skill was not up to the challenge. On January 9th, Napoleon III died.

"In '72, I had returned to my foreign duties, leaving Margaret in England for her health's sake, and, from the windows of Paris, watched that all but destroyed country struggle to recover from her recent tragedy. When I thought back on the creation of the new 'Second Republic' and the promise that had resided within Napoleon III, I could not help wondering what had happened to send it all floating away in his uncle's famous sewers.

"Searching for an answer, neither could I help remembering the Prisoner's Letter to the Kings advising them to care for their poor, to cease living in pomp and luxury while their people went hungry, and to disarm and make peace among themselves. Napoleon had long believed that an international council was the way to peace in Europe, but he had never done anything about it. A long way ahead of his time, actually.

"That thought reminded me of the Prisoner's second letter to Napoleon, which Gramont had told me about, telling the emperor that God could heal his illness and that if he would follow his advice he would be a great king and the hope of Europe for years to come, but that if he chose not to follow that advice, his kingdom would soon fall from his hands. In my mind's eye, I could see the suffering and dispirited emperor riding back and forth through the hail of bullets and smoke of battle, begging fate to kill him, as I remembered that the Prisoner had also written that Napoleon would be without power to resist his fate, and more, come to recognize his own impotence."

* * *

John laid down the papers and thought about what his father had written. Remembering the opening letter included with the papers, and how his father had been so impressed by the history of the Báb in Persia, and later had almost come to feel that Napoleon's fall was actually foretold by the Prisoner and not coincidence at all, John's curiosity was piqued. He truly wanted to go on reading, but the hour was late, and he was tired.

He needed to be up early in the morning because tomorrow he would go home . . . . home to his Carrie and his beloved place up country. He thought about the sick ewe, believing she was probably well by now. He wondered how Maggie was doing with her puppies. Whatever was going on at home, John knew that Carrie was able to take good care of everything. She was not only capable, she loved the place as much as he. He fell asleep with pictures of soft green hills dotted with sheep that turned into white puffy clouds against a pale green sky. Then running toward him in greeting were Mac, Hamish, and Maggie with her seven pups. The pups were a tangle of flopping little tongues and ears as they ran yapping, tripping, and falling over one another. John smiled in his sleep.

The place seemed quiet, almost to the point of desertion, when John alighted from the cart that had brought him from the station, and his eagerness turned to an uneasy sense of foreboding. What was wrong? Maggie would be with her puppies, of course, but where were Mac and Hamish? He moved quickly into the house and called Carrie's name. There was no answer. Mac came running to him, whining. He moved through the rooms looking for her, Mac at his heels, still whining. "Where is she, Mac?

Has she gone to the neighbors to visit?" It hardly seemed likely; as she knew what time he was due in from London. His discomfort growing, he made his way upstairs, carrying his overnight case, and entered their bedroom.

Carrie lay on the bed, her right arm hanging down. Blood pooled beneath her hand on the floor. Her face was white and her body still. Fallen on the floor half immersed in the black puddle was his blood stained razor. Hamish and Maggie were guarding her, lying on the floor near the bed, and sat up as John entered, worry in their eyes. John registered the entire scene in a second and cried out "Noooo!" as he fell over her body. "Oh God, Carrie! No! What have you done? Why would you . . . ?"

She moaned a little and her mouth moved slightly. "Oh God, you're alive? You're alive!" He laid his ear against her chest and heard a beat, rapid, faint and thready. He ripped a piece of the pillow case and wrapped the arm, noticing that the bleeding had stopped some time ago and her arm was already scabbing over. He bandaged it anyway. Lifting her from the bed and moving toward the stairs, he slipped on the puddle of blood and fell against the doorjamb. The wall held him upright while he regained his balance. Carefully, then, oblivious to the pain in his left arm from where he had struck the door, he carried her down the stairs and into the barn as rapidly as he dared. Teeth chattering and fingers fumbling, he hitched up the horse and cart and set out for the doctor's house, some three miles away, urging the horse to move fast and ever faster. All the way, he talked to Carrie. "Don't die, darling! I'm here now. You're going to be fine. Everything will be fine. I promise! Just don't die!"

The horse cantered into the yard of Dr. Miller's house, and the old man himself, tall and lanky, his work coat flapping with his long strides, ran out and helped John move Carolyn through the side door where he had his office.

"I don't know, John," he said, listening to her faint pulse. "She may or may not make it through this. She's strong and young, and the wound did close by itself. But she lost a great deal of blood before it did. Luckily, she didn't know how to cut it properly. You see, to succeed at this, the wrist should be slit lengthwise, not across. Still, she's lost so much blood. Let's not move her into hospital; it will only weaken her more, and they can't do anything I can't do. Leave her here with me for a day, and we'll see how this goes."

"I can't imagine why she would do this! Doctor, why? What was she thinking?" He and the doctor were lifting the woman from the examining table to the next room, where there was a cot made up.

"I don't know why people do these things, John. You and she seem happy to me. You *are* happy, aren't you?"

"*I* thought so," John said, his voice breaking in his agony. "Though she's been sad lately, since she can't seem to . . . Dr. Miller, she wants a child so much . . . but surely that wouldn't . . . it *couldn't* . . . account for this. Could it?"

"I'm afraid it could, old son. She's spoken with me about her disappointment, y'know. Women need to bear children, John. When they can't, they sometimes feel they are defective in some way."

"But that's nonsense, Doctor. My own mother lost three before I arrived, and she never seemed to feel defective."

"You didn't know her before you arrived, John; you can't know how she felt. Besides, she conceived, you see. There's a difference."

"Still, Carolyn knows how much she means to me and how much I count on her to help me with . . . My God, I was just thinking last night about how capable she is."

"I didn't say it is rational, John. It isn't. It has to do with the way women are made. Their entire systems are built around the children . . . their wombs to house the growing babe, their glands to feed the newborns, their monthly cycles. It's nature's doing. They need to mother—if there are no children, they will mother their husbands, God help us."

"I know," John smiled briefly, "She mother's the lambs, the kittens and the puppies . . . not to mention her roses." He stood holding Carrie's hand and looked up at the doctor, eyes pleading, "When will we know?"

"By late this afternoon or tomorrow morning at the latest, I should think. Remember she's already building new blood, even as we watch her. There's a chair and you're welcome to stay in here as long as you like. If you'll take my advice, though, you'll go home and tend to your place after a bit. I'll get word to you if there is any change one way or another."

"If you are sure I won't be in the way, I had rather just sit here."

And so he sat—still and frightened—whispering, along with passages from the Book of Common Prayer, "all shall be well, and all manner of things be well." He kissed her hand from time to time, begging her to survive. Sometime in the afternoon, Mrs. Miller brought a cup of broth and two biscuits to him. He drank part of the broth, mostly to please her. By nightfall, Dr. Miller pronounced her almost surely out of danger and sent John home. "Come in the morning and take her home, he said, "In the meantime get some sleep."

There was no sleep. He cleaned up the blood from the bedroom floor, began to clean the razor then, cursing at it, threw it away instead. He checked on Maggie's pups, found nothing in the scullery and recognized what must have happened. Bruised arm throbbing from where he had slammed against the door frame, he disposed of the ewe which he found lying dead in the stall. He buried it out behind the barn where all the farm's dead animals were buried. He noticed a freshly dug spot. No doubt Carrie had interred the puppies there.

He fixed himself a light supper and found he couldn't eat it. Finally, he lay down and tried to sleep; gave it up and tried to read; gave that up. Lying with eyes open trying to understand what was in Carrie's mind, wondering if he had hurt her someway, asking over and over how she had come to this, John watched the stars gleaming through the window, then saw the sky grow less dark in the east and finally the dawn creep slowly toward another day. With all his might, he willed the sun to rise above the elms on the far hill. When it had, he rose, washed and changed. He drank a glass of milk and hitched up the cart. With a heart full of love and sorrow he went to fetch Carrie, wondering how they would cope with this in the coming days.

23

CONFESSIONS:

JMJ

I had read a treatise, which the author had entitled "The Communist Manifesto," and could not help but admire his humane intentions; he truly cared for the sufferings of the poor. He was a defrocked priest in Germany and wrote the book in 1868. In fact, his compassion may even be why he became a priest in the first place, but his sorrow and unending exposure to their hopelessness had given way to this growing anger in him that led his pen to call for revolution. I could understand his point of view. I, myself, you remember, had found my priestly services to the poor close to unbearable in the never-ending hardship I saw around me day after day, year after year.

Truly, the book was more like a pamphlet, but it had a huge impact for such a small work. Angry because he could not force the Church to conform to his ideas, and further seeing in the Church some very real errors, among them the one about which I had myself complained—the taxing of the poor practically to the point of their starvation—he declared religion in general to be a drug administered by the priestly powers to keep the simple folk oppressed. He labeled it "The Opium of the People," and called upon the poor to rise up, overthrow the Church and the wealthy classes, and establish what he named a worker's paradise. His name was

Karl Marx, and though Communism as an idea was not new, Marx put it into an understandable form, and the theory was absolutely beautiful.

His dream was that all wealth should be held in common by the people and shared equally among them. A lovely idea, I grant you, but one I felt human nature would soon twist into destruction.

"His ideas appeal to a great many people," I said to Mario, "and are beginning to influence the thinking of hundreds."

"I know," Mario responded. "I overhear so many people discussing it."

"The fathers here?" We were walking back to our rooms after early Mass before reporting for work.

"No, not so many here, but on the streets." Mario and I felt that if Marx's ideas were to catch on, it could be very destructive, not only to the Church but to all of society.

"His ideas are not centered around God," I said, "but around man, and that is bound to fail sooner or later."

"More than that, Vittorio, if you look closely at it, they are not even really centered around man but around wealth, and that can only lead to a sickness of materialism. I suspect that the much disliked Syllabus of Errors and the "Aeterni Patris" I spoke of earlier may have touched off a lot of the excitement over Marx's theories."

Mario and I were not the only ones to feel uneasy over the threat of Marx's ideas. Pius's chief advisor and Secretary of State, Cardinal Antonelli, had read the book and was extremely perturbed. He had the Holy Father read it, and Pius, in turn, grew greatly agitated and fearful for the Church. Again he complained that God did not seem to be hearing his prayers.

Things that are supposed to be private and secret have a way of getting out, and it quickly became common knowledge among those of us somewhat closer to the pope's inner circle that Antonelli had told Pius, "There is only one way to resolve this dilemma. The only way for you to save the Church and your spiritual sovereignty is to have your pronouncements proclaimed infallible."[1] Once the pope was known as infallible, Antonelli pointed out to him, he could pronounce communism's ideas as anathema, and the faithful would disobey him only to face the fires of hell. There were a good many other matters that had long needed resolution, so the obvious solution was to call a general council of the Church.

Those of us who worked in Rome were pressed into service to get everything ready. This was the first general council to be held since the Council of Trent in the 1500s.

Mario and I, as well as a good many others, were released from some of our regular duties in order to help make the arrangements for the council, and it was, indeed, a very exciting, not to mention exhausting time.

Everything had to be not only cleaned but repainted and re-gilded. Statues and artwork were cleaned, seat cushions in chapels and sanctuaries were brushed and mended, and even the city of Rome herself was shined up. The fountains were drained and polished, and ancient landmarks were swept of detritus left by tourists and made as new-looking as possible for the expected hordes of people who would flood into the city to watch from the squares. Places to house the many bishops and all the other fathers of the church were procured and made ready. The nuns were kept busy mending and cleaning the cardinals' red robes.

The city's *ristarauntes* and *kaffes* stocked large amounts of extra food and wines, and the Vatican cooks worked night and day hoarding cakes, cookies, and other treats and pastries. Even large numbers of the communion wafers had to be procured and stored for the huge attendance at the Masses that would be said.

Part of my job was to prepare for foreign guests and see to it that they would not be inconvenienced during their stay in the eternal city. I haggled with cleaning crews and innkeepers, with cab-men, carters, and messenger services. Mario, on the other hand, was occupied with providing guide pamphlets, schedule lists, and other written materials, not to mention finding and making quickly available tomes of Church law and precedent. We delegated whatever we could, but as always, some things are never accomplished very well without personal oversight. Added to that, much of the early part of the preparations were done during Lent, so what with fasting and extra prayers, by nightfall, we were so exhausted that we fell into bed without much discussion of anything beyond a quick "good night" and "God keep you."

There were two separate committees to which all questions facing the council had to be brought for approval before they could be placed on the agenda for voting. Both committees were made up of people appointed by the pope, and there were a good many at the council who were distressed that the pope was playing so active a part in the council's affairs. Some went so far as to suggest that the whole matter of infallibility was being rigged by the pope and Cardinal Antonelli.

The bishops of France, Germany, Austria-Hungary, and the United States, who constituted about one-fifth of the entire council, openly opposed the resolution. The pope was overtly petulant at their protests.

"The Council appears to have been convoked for the special purpose of defining the Papal Infallibility, and enacting the positions of the Syllabus as general laws of the Church," wrote Peter Richard Kenrick, Archbishop of St. Louis in the United States. "Both objects are deemed by a minority, of which I am one, inexpedient and dangerous and are sure to meet with serious resistance."[2]

It looked as though the Definition of the Infallibility of the Pontiff would not pass, as nearly one hundred of the fathers were threatening to leave the council and return home rather than feel coerced to vote for it. In the end, several did leave, and two, refusing to feel coerced, voted openly against it in session. But it passed.

On July 18th, a huge crowd of the faithful filled St. Peter's for the final vote, and as the people clapped and waved, shouting, "Long live the infallible pope!" and "Long live the triumph of the Catholics!" a huge storm arose with violent thunder and lightning and such copious hard rain as to shatter one of the windows in the Basilica.

The two who had voted against the Definition knelt before the pope and said, "Credo, Holy Father."* Mario and I wondered if they had truly changed their minds or if the storm had frightened them into "believing."

"Maybe," I suggested facetiously to Mario that evening, "God was letting them know they had best come around and see things the pope's way."

"Or perhaps," Mario responded rather more seriously than I, "God is letting the whole council, *including* the pope, know the whole thing is a big mistake."

---

* "Credo" is Latin for "I believe."

"What do you really think, Mario?"

"I think the whole thing is a big mistake. I think the day will come when the Church will regret this move."

"I rather agree, but," I said with a resigned sigh, "I am a loyal son of the Church and will be obedient to the new doctrine; I will continue to serve her as best I can."

"I suppose I will, too," Mario said, "but . . . "

"But?" I waited.

He mumbled, as though he were speaking to himself. I could barely hear him and knew he felt ashamed of his disloyalty. "I had rather serve just my Lord Christ than an organization that makes up its own rules."

* * *

One of the cardinals, who, in spite of his feelings, accepted the outcome in the end, wrote that the promoters had behaved "cruelly, tyrannically, and deceitfully."[3] The Dogma, defined and declared to be divinely revealed, was announced. It was done.

It seemed as though the great storm was a harbinger of things to come, because the fourth session ended in anticipation of a fifth to open in November, but the next day the Franco-Prussian War erupted, and we all know what happened as a result of that. There were, to say the least, far-reaching consequences for the Papal States, and indeed for the pope himself. Napoleon III had been a loyal protector of the pope and the Church, and now he was gone.

As the new Germany began to take shape, her leaders, though Catholic, were one and all disapproving of the decree of infallibility. Cardinal Hohener had written to his brother, "Stupidity and fanaticism hold hands here, and dance the tarantella, making the music of cats."[4]

Bismarck launched a full-scale attack on the traditionalism of the Church, and non-German Jesuits were banned from the empire, which virtually eliminated the Jesuits from Germany. The Sisters of the Sacred Heart were banned because they were too close to the Jesuits.

In Italy, the papacy was being criticized for being an enemy of nationalism and the unified states, and, conversely, was attacked in Prussia as an essentially Italian power, based upon a college of cardinals containing an increasing number of Italians. By 1876, all the Prussian bishops had been imprisoned or forced to take refuge abroad, and one third of the Catholic parishes were without priests. The editor of "The Catholic Center Party" faced confiscation, and its chief editor was arrested and jailed. Over one hundred other Catholic editors joined him behind bars. In Germany, it was not forbidden to be married in the Church, of course, but it became mandatory to have a civil marriage as well.

The pope was alone. He grew angrier and angrier. He had battled Italy for the residual Papal States and lost. What is now called Vatican City—that is, the Vatican and the surrounding streets and buildings; a narrow strip of land running down to the Adriatic; and, of course, Castle Gondolfo, the popes' summer residence—became all that remained of our once great and extended Holy Roman Empire.

Mario told me our friend, Father Arturo, present when Pius heard the terms of his defeat, said that the Pontiff spat out, "A beggar's remnant? A salaried servant of the State? They would make of the pope a penurious campesino* and strip us of our dignity and sovereignty? Never!"[5]

In the end, he capitulated to signing the agreement. Angry and bitter, he remained much to himself and threw colossal temper tantrums, or so we heard from those who were in his presence. How different he was from the man who took the papal throne in 1846, and whom I had once admired so much.

There were even those who said he had gone mad, but I never believed that, because the mad have no sense of humor. Pius retained his. When someone asked him when he thought the troubles would end, I overheard him reply, "How would I know? I am the Vicar of Christ, not His secretary." So I think the rumor of his madness was a result of being present during one of his convulsions. Though this childhood affliction had been minimal during his middle years, it now returned. At times he was incoherent. He never left the Vatican again, becoming a self-imposed

* "Campesino"; a dirt farmer.

prisoner. Mario said it was interesting; now there were apparently *two* holy prisoners, one in Rome and the other in Palestine.

Half joking, I commented, "You really believe in that letter-writer, don't you? Be careful you don't become an apostate." Actually, I was disappointed; I had hoped he had forgotten about it during the excitement of the preparations for the Council and the gathering itself.

"I don't know for certain, but you must admit, Vittorio, that he has put all this in perspective."

"What do you mean, 'I must admit'? I need do no such thing."

"Think again, Vittorio. First of all, I understand that he warned the kings of Europe and the Middle East as well, and Old Louie Napoleon is gone."

"Well, that's one king out of how many?" I said. "After all, kings do tend to rise and fall with revolutions and wars and what not. You're making too much of this, Mario."

"I don't think so. Look here." He rose and went into his room and retrieved his copy of the letter.

"I've already read it," I said with disgust, flopping down on the couch. "Remember?"

"I know, but things have changed. Read some of this again."

I sighed and, because he is my friend, complied. I read, "Leave thou the world behind thee, and turn towards thy Lord, through Whom the whole earth hath been illumined . . . "[6]

Mario said, "It's as though Pius has been forced to choose between his role as Shepherd of the Faithful and his role as political ruler of the Catholic world. He appears to have chosen the world, Vittorio, don't you think?"

"I don't know. But if he has truly chosen," I agreed, "he's made a mistake, because he has lost the world anyway."

I read on: "Arise . . . and seize thou the Cup of Life with the hands of confidence. First drink thou therefrom, and proffer it then to such as turn towards it amongst the peoples of all faiths."[7]

Then I said, "It almost sounds as if this prisoner is saying that if His Holiness were to accept his counsel, the separated brethren among the

Lutherans and other Protestants would be reconciled, and return to the fold, doesn't it?"

"Oh, wouldn't that make the Holy Father happy?" Mario looked up at me with true joy in his face. "You know, I hadn't even noticed that part. This thing contains so much one can hardly take it all in with only one reading. Remember, Vittorio, when the Holy Father was complaining that God no longer seemed to be answering his prayers, and that he had no guidance? Well, here, look at this!" Mario took the paper from me and pointed to a passage. He was getting excited now.

I followed Mario's finger and read, "Thou art one of the suns in the heaven of His names. Guard thyself, lest darkness spread its veils over thee, and fold thee away from His light."[8]

As much as I hated to admit it, Mario was correct; this letter did take more than one reading. I began to pay closer attention to the voice in the letter.

"It appears that he bears the Holy Father no ill-will," I said, "but what does he mean by 'the heaven of His Names?' I wish he were a little clearer about things."

"Well, look over here, Vittorio, where he writes, 'Oh followers of all religions . . . This is the day whereon the Rock* crieth out and shouteth, and celebrateth the praise of its Lord, the All-Possessing, the Most High, saying: "Lo! The Father is come!"'"[9]

"I think he means that God's Messengers have been called by many names: Jesus, Moses, Muḥammad, Buddha, for example. But the Father Himself—well, that can only mean the Father of *all* humanity. Maybe, he means that he is a new Messenger from God for all the people in the world at once."

"Oh, Mario, no. Not the Muḥammadans, surely; after all, we've always been taught that they are followers of an evil prophet. God couldn't possibly mean that."

"Why not? Muḥammad's followers are only people like us, Vittorio. How many times have we said we could never agree that you have to be Catholic to be saved?"

---

* Peter.

"Well, yes, but . . . "

"Alright. If God can love and accept all Christians, why can't he accept all those who are not but who worship him sincerely . . . even if they are not quite correct in how they go about it? After all, they think they are correct; they, like us, are only following what they 'have always been taught.' Our Lord has said he has sheep in many pastures, and the Prisoner writes that . . . ."

Remembering my dream, I interrupted and finished for him, "Verily, the day of the ingathering has come!"

We sat and stared silently at one another for quite some time. The implications of possibilities such as these were vast and unnerving. So, we didn't talk about it anymore that night.

24

SHIRIN: 1876

Edward was gone from my life, and though after a while, I did not think of him all the time as I had at first and the pain was less exquisite, I never stopped missing him. Finally, that too died away as the years went by, though he was never far from my mind. I realized that not only could I not lose what I never had, neither, as long as we lived, could I lose what I did have. I concluded that our love for each other was a little like my foot or my hand. I did not need to think about it every day to know it was there.

My lessons in Christianity were coming along nicely. I had read most of the Old Testament (which is not Christian, of course, but Jewish), as well as all four of the Gospels and the book of Acts. I learned several things I had long wondered about. Rubin helped me understand things about the Old Testament that I could never have understood properly through Christian teaching. Though Rubin was nominally a Christian, he secretly honored the Sabbath in his own home. We said the prayers and lit the candles on Sabbath Eve, and even Khadijah began to enjoy the little weekly ritual as we sang together and blessed the wine and the challah*

* Challah or Hallah, the Sabbath Bread.

while the sun sank. I thought the ritual not so very different from the Holy Communion, oh, not the way it is administered in the Church, but as the last Passover Supper is described in the Book of Mathew, and again was struck by the similarities of teachings and customs.

To begin with, I loved Jesus (Peace be upon Him); He was so compassionate, so filled with kindly justice. It was easy to understand why Muḥammad had referred to Jesus as "The Spirit of God, Himself," and directed His followers to aid the Christians in building and maintaining their churches, and even to fight for them, if need be.[1]

In fact, the sweetness of Jesus reminded me of Muḥammad, in the story they tell of Him and the cat. The one where the Prophet was sitting on a bench one day and a man came and asked Him to come to see something. As He rose to go, He noticed that a cat had fallen asleep on the skirt of His robe, and in order to rise from His chair, He would have to disturb the cat's sleep. Instead, He took His sword and cut away His robe.

But the other thing I learned was not so pleasant. All the family and the many friends we had in St. Petersburg were delighted to hear I was studying Christianity, and of course when Khadijah was baptized, they congratulated me on her conversion, and a good many of them asked me when I would be joining the church. I put them off by saying I had only begun to learn a little about it and so was able not to have to tell my feelings about that. For if I were to "join the Church," as they put it, which one should I join?

Of course, I suppose it would be the Russian Church, because we lived there, but what of the other churches? There was Edward's Church of England, and there was the Roman Church, and I understood there were others—a German Church, and a Church of Greece, and on and on. I could understand each nation having its own organization, but they didn't believe the same things, and each maintained that the others were quite wrong about their beliefs. Apparently, even the English did not agree on what their church teaches, because a large group of English went to the New World one hundred or so years ago and founded the United States of America. That, I was told, was because they wished to worship differently. Further, the differences in the religions seemed so small and unimportant.

Besides, all I had learned of kindliness, charity for the poor, love for one's neighbor, mercy, truth, faith in the goodness of God, life after death, and so on—all these things I learned of first by reading Holy Koran. Only afterward had I found that the teachings of both Judaism and Jesus were not so different from my childhood training and the ideas I was learning now.

Our friend, Vasily Lipilinov, asked me one day if I did not think it sacrilegious that Muḥammad had so many wives. I explained to him that when Muḥammad came to us, women were kept in herds, not unlike cattle, and traded for horses and given away to pay gambling debts; that baby girls were buried alive; and while this custom was considered a sacrifice to appease the gods, still, baby boys were never sacrificed.

A woman without a husband to protect her was at the mercy of any man's lusts. Muḥammad Himself had only one wife, His beloved Khadijah, for over twenty years until she died, and after that married the widows of the tribal leaders who died in battle in order to give them safety. He taught his followers that to keep women in herds was wrong, and forbade them more than four, and they were cautioned to treat them all equally.

"Perhaps. But there is still another point," Lipilinov went on to say. "The Muslims spread their religion by means of the sword. They were so warlike."

"They weren't supposed to," I said somewhat lamely, "Muḥammad says, '*Let there be no compulsion in religion. What! Wilt thou compel men to become believers? No soul can believe but by the permission of God . . .*'"[2]

Fortunately Rubin Dubinski came to my rescue at that point, asking Lipilinov if he had forgotten about the Crusades, during which the Christians killed almost anybody they could find, not only Muslims, but thousands of Jews, and Christians as well, if they did not approve of their form of belief. "And don't forget," he said, "the famous saying of Constantine, 'In this sign shalt thou conquer,' as he went to war for Christianity, until he had 'converted' most of Europe."

"Well," Lipilinov said, turning away, "that was a long time ago."

"The spread of Islam was a long time ago, too, Lipilinov," Rubin countered, but Lipilinov had left us for greener conversational pastures.

Apart from having heard of the Crusades, I hardly knew what they were talking about, but I knew that the War in Crimea and several others were partly over religion, and often among Christians themselves. I would not have asked him who was the more warlike, for that would have been rude, and besides, these things made me sad, rather than argumentative. Somewhere inside of me, I grieved for the enmity between religions. Still, I was grateful to Rubin for helping me out.

Rubin and I had become very close. What with my sympathy for him over Khadijah's adultery, we talked often, and I did as much as I could for him—little thoughtful gestures, such as bringing him tea, or fetching him lap robes when it was cold—the things Khadijah would normally have been doing for him, had her mind and emotions not been elsewhere.

Together, too, we shared such a love for Katherine, and because her mother was often busy, Katherine, Rubin and I were together a lot.

In Khadijah's defense, I must say that she did at first attempt to let go of her paramour but, as Rubin had feared, was unable to. So, toward the end of 1871, we removed to Paris.

The count's family begged us to put off our move until spring, saying that not only would the travel be less uncomfortable but that Paris was still in the throes of recovery from the Franco-Prussian war, and it might be difficult for us to establish ourselves there. Rubin's mind was made up, however, and he assured them that his uncle had a job waiting for him and even had found him a house, if he were interested in buying right away. As I had long ago noticed, the rich are often not terribly inconvenienced by the vicissitudes of political life. Having been reared with nothing, I sometimes felt guilty that I was now so comfortable, but, I confess, not guilty enough to refuse the comforts.

Leaving the home of Count Nicholas, where I had spent so many happy and contented years, leaving Shahane, Natasha, Olga, and Olga's grandchildren—who, nearly grown now, seemed almost like grandchildren of my own—was, as you might imagine, very painful not only for me but for all of them as well. I told Count Nicholas that I had no idea how I could ever repay him for his kindness, but if I ever could find a way, I should certainly do so. He scoffed at the whole idea and assured me (as he had so many times in the past), that he regarded us as our gift to them, rather than the other way around.

I had put together some simple gifts for Popov, Melikov, and some of the kitchen servants who had made our lives so pleasant, and they were so surprised as to be rendered without reply. Popov managed a deep bow and a smile, so I pretended not to see the moisture in his eyes, and the evening before we left, Melikov came into the parlor and insisted upon playing his balalaika for us all.

It was difficult, too, to leave the palatial house where I had spent so many magical hours with Edward, and that last week I seemed to see him wherever I went—in the house or even looking out the windows at the October garden already covered with snow. As we laughed at table, I heard his laughter; as we spoke of spring, I smelled again the nosegay of violets he had once picked for me as we strolled in the garden.

But I think almost equally painful was leaving Zhukovsky, who was to me teacher, father, and friend. He was growing frailer by the day. When I bade him my final good-bye, both he and I knew we could not hope ever to see one another again. I tried for his sake not to weep but could not control the silent tears that rolled down my cheeks. He wept as well. We embraced over and over. These days the old man slept late, and I was relieved early that next morning when we stepped into the carriage that would take us to the railroad for Moscow that he was not at the entrance veranda with the others to see us off.

As the train moved south through the Ukrainian countryside, I sat staring out the soot-covered window at dark gray skies, thinking that this was the second of the "three sorrowful journeys" that Ṭáhirih had promised must take place before my soul would "find its home." I couldn't help comparing it with that earlier journey that had introduced me to Russia—bundled in the troika, cutting through the clean snow with the iced forests in the distance—with this noisy experience, dirty and sooty, racing along at a frightening speed of almost twenty-five kilometres an hour.

Even though the night we had fled Tehran for our lives, when I was grieving all I had ever known, still, through my shock, I could not help wondering what lay ahead. But in St. Petersburg, I had found—though not a home, truly—so much stimulation and happiness I would have been content to remain forever. Also, I felt somehow as though I were leaving Edward behind, and my sadness at leaving was too great to allow for much curiosity for the future.

The idea, by now become almost a belief, that there was yet one more sorrowful journey ahead, was so frightening I couldn't make myself think about it, so I rationalized that now that I was nearly fifty-eight, I would probably not live much longer, and such an unlikely thing would never happen.

Khadijah was civil but mostly silent, spending most of her travel staring out the window, and I knew she was struggling with two separate sets of feelings. She hated to leave her life in St. Petersburg and her lover, and she blamed Rubin. But always the truest love in Khadijah's heart was pleasure, so she was already eager to experience life in Paris, the very center of gaiety and style.

The grayness of the day outside, the stuffiness of the train car, and Khadijah's pout—not to mention my own sense of loss—made it a gloomy journey indeed. I tried for Rubin's and Katherine's sakes to keep a cheerful air, but had it not been for that little girl, who was wild with the excitement of her first travel, keeping us all playing counting games with the horses she saw as we moved through the countryside, answering questions about the scenes framed in the train window, and about the train itself, I wonder how I should ever have borne it.

Our train arrived in Paris after dark, and we were met by a well-dressed and portly man with thick grey mustaches, mutton chops, and positively overwhelming eyebrows.

"Uncle!" cried Rubin going into his outstretched arms, and returning the kisses on either cheek. He introduced us to his Uncle Samuel, and we were not allowed to call him Monsieur Dubinski for even a moment. He was *our* Uncle Samuel, too, he said. Visibly impressed with Khadijah's dark beauty, he raised the bushy eyebrows at Rubin as he acknowledged his introductions. He took charge of our baggage, bundled us into a carriage, and took us to his house to eat a late supper, explaining that we would be staying with him and Aunt Martha until we were well-settled.

Rubin's aunt Martha was equally portly and equally well-dressed, wearing two diamond rings and a small diamond pendant at her throat, but warm and motherly, bustling about and fussing at her servants, as she made us comfortable. "You should see your faces!" she laughed, "They are covered with soot." We knew our hands and clothes were sooty, of course, but when she led us to a mirror, we laughed aloud at ourselves, we were so dirty. Train travel may be faster than travel by coach or troika, but it exacts a price in dirt. After she had helped us find towels and soap to wash up and sent a servant to brush some of the train filth from our clothes, she served us a good late evening supper. There were slabs of thick bread and butter and a good Russian beet borsht because, she said, she wanted us to feel at home. They both adored Katherine immediately, and the attraction was quite mutual. Katherine, like most children, warmed to attention and intuitively knew that here were people to spoil her.

The next day was warm for October and, after we had rested all morning, we went out in the afternoon to see the city. Even with the recent war and troubles, Paris was lovely and had an air about it that I have always heard mentioned but never adequately described—somehow filled with promise. Then, too, it was "Edward's city" that I had heard him speak of so often. I was entranced by several scenes he had described, knowing he had walked these very streets, and there were moments when I felt as though I might just catch sight of him rounding a corner.

Uncle Samuel directed his driver past the house he had found for us, and though we could see only the outside, it was enough to impress us as desirable and make us want to see inside as soon as possible. It was a large house on the Rue Galilee in the center of a block of buildings, private houses interspersed with shops. There was a butcher nearby, a flower shop just down the street a few doors, next to a tobacconist's and a small café around the corner where, Aunt Martha said, we would be able to get coffees and ices and other lovely treats.

Katherine wanted to go in right that minute, and although her father said that it would be better to put that off for another time, she pleaded, and Uncle Samuel said of course, we should go. So we were soon being treated to hot chocolate and little biscuits. Katherine tried to be very grown-up and ladylike, but Uncle Samuel ruined it by dunking his biscuit in her hot chocolate and winking at her, while wiggling his magnificent eyebrows. Surprised and delighted, she startled the other patrons with loud squeals of little girl laughter. Pretending to be stern, Rubin said to her, "Young lady, I see we shall have to have behavior lessons for both you *and* your Great Uncle."

"What a grand idea!" Aunt Martha said, laughing aloud, "I wish you every success."

The house itself was tall and narrow. It had four stories, with only four rooms on each story, Uncle Samuel explained—one front and one back—on either side of a central stairway. The roof was rather steeply pitched, so I imagined the fourth floor was somewhat cramped. It gave the house a rather quaint look, I thought, with its tall, narrow shape, peaked roof, and windows shining and sparkling in the afternoon sun. Rubin said, "What did they do? Float this on a barge from Amsterdam?" Beneath each window was a flower box, empty now in late autumn.

We saw the interior the next week and loved the house inside and out. So we bought it, or rather, Rubin bought it. Khadijah was soon in her element, decorating and planning, shopping and ordering workmen about. She had turned the two small front rooms on the fourth floor into a playroom for Katherine and a sewing room for herself, which I thought were perfect uses for them. I began to hope that perhaps she could really begin to be happy here after all, and was starting to believe this move had been a good idea on Rubin's part. He, himself, was equally pleased with his new position in his uncle's establishment and left for work each morning whistling his way out the door.

It took three months, all told, for the house to be ready for us. We moved in right near the end of January of '72, and, I must say, not a moment too soon, as Katherine was already running her great aunt and uncle's household with an iron fist in her charming little velvet glove.

As summer came to Paris, so much earlier than we were used to in St. Petersburg, we began to watch the city come alive with tourists from all over Europe and even some from the United States, and a busy social season for those of us who live here. Khadijah was soon sending and receiving invitations for the couple, as always.

In mid-July, Rubin took us all to Cobourg for a week's holiday. We spent every day at the seashore dressed in our bathing costumes, although neither Khadijah nor I were interested in entering the water. Katherine learned to swim, but it was enough for me to see the ocean, as I had, of course, heard of it all my life. It was huge! It stretched as far as the eye could see in three directions and could be smooth and tranquil one day and wild and ferocious the next. When the sun was out, it was as blue as the sky itself, and when the clouds came, it was grey and forbidding-looking. I could not get enough of looking at it and loved to walk along the sand and pick up the shells deposited by the waves at night.

I asked Rubin about them. "They have been alive," he said, "but now the animal inside has died. This is what is left."

"How could a dead thing be so beautiful?"

"Well, of course the shell was never alive. It is more like a little house or a nest for the animal, and when he no longer needs it, it washes ashore. The one you are holding is called a Chambered Nautilus."

"It is so lovely; such a creamy white and these amber striations look almost like the sand does in the morning after a wind. There seem to be so many similarities in the world, Rubin—a oneness, that in spite of all the world's richness and variety, binds it all together." I gazed out at the sea, stretching forever. "The world is so full of lovely mysteries, and the ocean must have wonderful secrets in her bosom."

"Yes," Rubin said looking thoughtful. Then suddenly he took my by the hand. "Come, Grand-Mere, come into the water and experience some of its wonder for yourself."

"Oh, no," I protested. "I couldn't. I might drown."

"Surely, you don't think I would let you drown." He smiled and pulled me gently to the water's edge, and I stepped into it. The day was overcast, with a bit of a breeze, and the waves were gently swelling as they reached toward the shore. They fell against the beach with quiet sighs, and as we walked deeper and deeper into the sea, it seemed to beckon and embrace me with its warmth.

"Oh, Rubin, this is far enough!" I said, as the crest of the next wave reached almost to my chin. "Just another step or two," he coaxed, tugging on my arm. Suddenly we were at a depth where, when the waves crested, we could no longer touch the bottom, and I was truly frightened.

'You're fine!" Rubin said, "I have your hands. I'll not let anything happen to you." Khadijah called out to him, "Rubin, don't take Mama out so deep; she's too old for that!"

"What about it?" Rubin asked, with a devilish grin, "Are you too old for this?"

"Maybe," I said nervously, "it *is* awfully deep."

Suddenly we were caught between two waves and all I could see was water on either side of me and the gray sky up above. I thought the waves would cover my head, and just as I was sure I would be washed away in the sea, we floated up with the crest itself, and I could see the shore and Katherine and her mother watching for us. Then down we went into the trough between the next two waves, and I felt frightened again. It is like life, I thought. Just when you think you can see ahead clearly, along comes a new "wave" and you can see nothing but your momentary place, never sure that it will not overwhelm you. No wonder we frighten so easily! After a few cycles, I understood it was safe enough, that I would not be swallowed up by the ocean after all, so began to laugh and call out to Katherine between my "sinkings."

What a marvelous thing to have happen to me! I came out onto the sand dripping water from every inch of my clothing and my bathing slippers squishing in the sand..

Khadijah was scolding Rubin. "You shouldn't have done that; she could have drowned! Remember we've never been near the ocean before."

"Drown Grand Mere?" he said winking at me, "My dear wife, if I had to wager on either your mother or the ocean, I'd put my money on Grand Mere anytime."

"Don't be cross with him, Khadijah, I was perfectly safe the entire time."

"Do you see what I mean?" he laughed.

"Thank you, Rubin!" I said. "What a wonderful day this has been!"

I took the Chambered Nautilus home with me, and it is here on my bureau even now.

In August, I received a long letter from Natasha, and included in the same envelope was a letter from Zhukovsky. He had written in a thin spidery script, and I could visualize his hand shaking from weakness as he leaned close to the desk to see, with failing vision, what he was writing. It was a difficult scene to witness, even in my imagination, how this once vital poet and teacher was losing even the means to put his art on paper. It was of necessity, therefore, brief but filled with love. I found it difficult to make out many of the words, but after several rereadings, finally understood it all.

"My dearest 'daughter,'

"I miss you very much, and whenever you hear from Natasha or Olga, please know that when they write at the end, 'Zhukovsky sends his love,' that I have truly said that aloud to the writer. I hope you are enjoying Paris, and if I know my eager student, you are sampling a bit of everything that lovely city has to offer.

"Alex continues his failures, as he is too occupied with his child mistress to properly govern. The gossip is all over St. Petersburg, so I expect Natasha will relate the shameful details to you when she writes. I cannot bring myself to tell it, Khánum. Such behavior for a Tsar! He had such promise! It is breaking my heart, so I will say no more about that.

"I miss our 'cocoa mornings,' the hot mug warming our hands and the drink, thick and smooth and bittersweet on our tongues, but mostly, of course, the sound of your dear voice, plaguing me with your everlasting questions. I expect that when spring comes, I shall miss our long walks in the garden, as well.

"With my love to you and all your family, I remain

Ever your devoted friend,

V. A. Zhukovsky"

Natasha had much to say about the family and many of our friends. Dimitri had been promoted again—to lieutenant general! Needless to say, the family was very proud of him. Olga was still as she had always been, alternating between good times and bad but, Natasha said, more bad than good these days, with her health beginning to truly fail now. The count was fine and still active in the diplomatic corps, though closer to home than the old years in Persia, so they did not have to do without him very often. "Shahane is well," she wrote, "and sends her love to you all, and says she will write when she can."

She continued:

"Zhukovsky wants me to tell you about the Tsar. He says he can't bring himself to even speak of it. I shouldn't wonder, Shirin, his behavior is disgraceful! It is not enough that he has taken a mistress, publicly, and thirty years his junior, but he had, as you know, two children by her which he has publicly acknowledged. Now there is a third!

"But the worst part is what he has most recently done. He has moved that girl right into the palace, itself! The public humiliation has killed the Tsarina, and I mean precisely that! She contracted tuberculosis some time ago and now cannot live more than a few weeks longer. The court and those of us close to the royal family are thoroughly disgusted with him. His remaining son, Tsarevitch Alexander, is furious at him for what he has done to his mother, and to the reputation of the throne. As you know, no one has very much respect for the heir because young Nicholas was so loved and bright like his father, while Alexander III, who is doltish and slow, has really not much to recommend him. Still, we are all with him on this matter.

"Whatever could have happened to our Tsar? He began his reign so well, and we all anticipated that he would lead Russia forward into a glorious future. You know it has long been our belief that Russia would lead the world, but I am sure it will not happen now; at least not during the reign of Alexander II. It is so sad for Zhukovsky.

"Speaking of Zhukovsky, you will find enclosed with this letter a short note from him. Oh, Shirin, he labored so to write it! It meant so much to him to pen it with his own hand. I must tell you however that it will probably be the last he will be able to write, as his strength is noticeably failing almost daily. He knows it, and so made that comment about sending his love via the family from now on. It is his way of telling you he cannot manage anymore. He misses you so! As do we all.

"I hope all of you are well, and do kiss the little one for us; we miss her very much, too. With all our best wishes for all of you, we remain your "Russian family," and I sign myself with much love,

Natasha Dolgoruka"

"A quick post scriptum: I nearly forgot to mention two things. We had a letter not long ago from Edward Hillhouse. Margaret has lost a third child, but they still hope for a son one of these days. He serves in England most of the time now. He said to be sure to give you his best regards—not knowing, of course, that you had left Russia. The other is that Dimitri's oldest has joined the army, so apparently he will follow in his father's footsteps."

I read the post scriptum over and over. My heart sang with joy knowing Edward was thinking of me, and I could all but hear his voice as he "spoke" to me through his letter. Then I hid myself away upstairs in my room and wept for a while, until I had got my world back in balance.

We had been in Paris for about a year, and I was in bed one evening reading when I heard loud voices from downstairs. I hardly paid attention at first because sometimes Khadijah and Rubin had angry words, but this grew in intensity, and I began to fear they would wake Katherine. I shut my book and went to the door of her room, to make sure it was closed. Still standing in the hallway, I saw Rubin take the stairs three at a time and rush to their bedroom. Moments later he came out carrying a valise, his cravat untied and his hair disheveled. He saw me and stopped.

"I am so sorry, Khánum," he said, looking intently at me. Then his eyes moved all around the hallway, as if trying to find a way to escape. "It has happened again! I cannot . . . I *will* not live with this! He ran his fingers through his hair. "I have to go away and think! I have to decide what to do! I have to . . ." He looked at me and the anger in his eyes softened and he said again, "I am so sorry. God, I am so sorry!" Then he went down the stairs, and a moment later I heard the door slam.

It was several days before he returned, and when he did, he seemed calm and settled. He spent several hours with Katherine, and he and I had a good talk. He was leaving for good, he said. He would be in and out to see Katherine and assured me that she and I would want for nothing. "Khadijah wants me to tell no one I have left, and I will honor that. I am not anxious for people to think ill of us, either. But I will make my life elsewhere. Oh, Grand-Mere, I had so hoped we could begin again and that it would come right this time." His eyes filled, and I embraced him. There was nothing for me to say, and so I smiled at him and watched him leave.

That evening, the house was nearly silent. I helped Katherine with her studies, and Khadijah spent the entire evening upstairs by herself. After I had put Katherine to bed, I knocked on Khadijah's door, but she said, "Please, Mama, I don't want to talk about it. Not tonight."

I said nothing more than "Alright" and went to bed, though not to sleep very well.

Our lives moved along in this awkward way for nearly a year. Rubin came at least three times a week to be with his daughter, and he and I remained on good terms. He was kindly to us all, even Khadijah, and saw to it that we lacked nothing. He spent the entire week of Christmas with us, bringing far too many presents, and Katherine was in heaven.

Not long into the new year, an evening came when he announced that he was divorcing Khadijah, as he was making new plans for his life. "I will deed the house over to you and your mother," he told her, "and I will see that you receive a reasonable stipend to provide for Katherine's needs. When she is older and ready to marry, I will see that she lacks nothing."

"But as for you, Madam," he continued to his wife, "you will need to provide for yourself."

Khadijah screamed at him. "Provide for myself! How can I provide for myself? Do you expect me to scrub floors for a living?"

"I really don't know. You will no longer be my responsibility. Perhaps you can persuade your married lover to keep you. He is wealthy, is he not?"

Khadijah moved toward him with her arm raised as though to strike him, but, at the look in his eye, held herself in check.

When he had gone, she turned on me in her anger and shouted, her face red and her veins swollen with rage, "How can he do this? He can't do this! My God! We will have to live like peasants!"

I had had enough of her tantrums and screaming at a turn of fate she had earned for herself. I left the room and began to climb the stairs. "You seem to have forgotten, my dear," I said. "We *are* peasants."

After trying to get along on the amount Rubin sent for us, it finally dawned on Khadijah that she would have to find a way to earn some money if she were going to have any of the many little extras she craved.

Back in 1853, the first of Europe's department stores had opened in Paris. It was called "Au Bon Marche," and had become a famous place for women of style. The well-known British couturier, Charles Frederick Worth, now supplied the store with designs. Khadijah went to work as a seamstress's helper at Au Bon Marche.

It was not long before her skill was noticed, and she became one of the head seamstresses. Twice a year, when Mr. Worth came from England to oversee the creation of his latest designs, he noticed Khadijah's ability and encouraged her.

She had always liked sewing—working with the materials and improving on the designs she saw—and so was slowly adjusting to her new industrious life. No longer able to move among the social circles she had known for so long, she became more and more involved in what she was doing. Her days were too busy to allow for old habits, anyway.

Often she would tell me how much she admired Mr. Worth and how he often praised her work. One day, she came home filled with excitement. "Mama, I asked Mr. Worth today what he would think if we changed the drape line on a little dress he was designing, and he stopped and just stared at me. At first I thought I had made him angry. But it wasn't that at all! He was pleased with my suggestion, and said—listen to this,

Mama—'Madame Dubinski, you not only sew beautifully, you have, as well, an eye for design.' What do you think about *that*?"

I smiled and said, "I think we have known that about you since Shahane invited you to Russia, and I am glad Mr. Worth not only has an eye for design himself, but an eye for talent, as well."

"Perhaps I shall get a rise in salary."

But she didn't.

One day, in the fall of 1875, our Katherine, who was now almost thirteen years old, stayed home from her classes with a fever. By nightfall, she was feeling even worse, and in the morning, it was obvious she was really becoming very ill. We sent for the doctor. He said to us, "She has whooping cough, and I am very concerned. It is going around in the schools, and I've a number of little girls from her class who are down with it." He left us medicine and told us not to hesitate to send for him again, if she got worse.

For a day or so, it looked as if the medicine were going to help her, and she was, though still feverish, feeling somewhat better. Then suddenly, in the late afternoon, she became very ill. Of course we sent for the doctor, and he came soon.

He listened to her coughing, felt for her fever, and shook his head. "I think," he said, "tonight may a crucial time. I believe I will stay here with her, if you don't mind." Mind! We were relieved that he would be here with us, and I immediately fixed another plate for supper.

It was one of the longest nights of our lives. Khadijah and I waited and walked the floor, dropping into her room from time to time to ask how it was coming. Dr. DuPont tried to say things to her mother that sounded hopeful, but to me he simply shook his head.

Khadijah retired to her room, and I heard her praying and weeping. In the small hours, I went in to see her. I tried to comfort her, but I could remember all too well how I had felt as a young mother when I lost Hasan and my little one; how it was when Khadijah, herself, was small, and we despaired of her life.

She turned to me with a tear-streaked face, her hair wild and disarranged, and began to tell me how sorry and ashamed she was for the life she had been leading.

"I told God," she said, "that if He will let her live, I will never again disobey His laws or be unkind to anyone or miss Mass, and that I shall give more money to the Church and that . . ."

"Shhh, Darling," I said, "Rest now and don't make promises just yet." I was thinking that these were all the wrong promises and that if I were God, I could not accept such desperate bribes. Still, this was more concern for God—or for anyone beside herself, for that matter—than I had ever known Khadijah to show. If the child survived, I doubted Khadijah would change very much, but if she learned only to be grateful for each day of her daughter's life, she would have come a long way.

At last, I fell asleep holding Khadijah's hand as she cried herself to sleep. Then I woke and went into Katherine's room to stay in a chair beside her bed, and soon fell asleep there, as well. But that blessed Doctor DuPont stayed awake throughout the entire night, and sometime shortly before morning, tapped lightly on my shoulder. He smiled a tired smile and said, "Wake her mother. She is going to be alright."

Khadijah wept with relief. Dr. DuPont asked for his coat and made ready to leave, but I prevailed upon him to lie down and sleep awhile. In a small reading room off the main salon where there is a comfortable couch, he lay down with a grateful sigh, and I watched him fall asleep before I could even spread a coverlet over him. I left the little study and went back to Katherine's room to take my place in the chair where I had spent the night.

Khadijah was sitting in the doctor's chair already asleep. As I laid my head back with a prayer of thanks on my lips, I noticed that Khadijah's face was fully relaxed for the first time since Rubin had left. I glanced out the window and saw, like the tip of a tongue on the lip of the horizon, the first sight of the morning sun. Katherine sighed in her sleep and smiled, and I dropped away, certain that these things were harbingers of better days to come.

25

CONFESSIONS: 1881

JMJ

Mario and I were especially busy following the Vatican General Council. It had made a number of important changes in everyone's schedules, not least of all mine, who traveled so often. Immediately at the end of the council, as I may already have mentioned, the Franco-Prussian war erupted. Napoleon III went to England in exile, and three or four months later, Paris fell.

The Church was deeply involved, because every hospital, convent, and monastery near Paris was overwhelmed with people without homes, wounded from the war, and ill civilians who had no other way to find help. About three hundred thousand civilians were killed or injured in the war—and that was *before* they starved. Out of an army of five hundred thousand men, only sixty-six thousand survived the battles without injury or death. Of course, the schools, too, were in chaos.

For months, we labored to help bring balance back into the lives of the French people, and I was all but living in Paris in those days. Thank God for the Church and the hundreds of nuns and priests who spent day and night doing what they could.

I returned to Rome in '71, because no matter how bad things were in the nearby nations, the celebration of Pius's Twenty-Five-Year Jubilee must not be overlooked. The citizens turned out in droves for the ritual blessings from the pope, either as he stood in the balcony above St. Peter's square or was paraded around the perimeter carried on his litter. But truth to tell, except for a few, he was no longer their beloved Pio Nono. He was regarded, rather, either as a would-be tyrant or, at best, the victim of the machinations of Antonelli and others.

Due to the pope's capricious health and frequent tantrums, between the convulsions and bouts of incoherence and days when he was completely indisposed, Antonelli was practically running the papacy. There were those among us who claimed that was nothing new, that Pius had always been dependent on Antonelli for every thought. Others of us remained loyal to His Holiness, whether from love or opportunity it was difficult to tell, but the Church, both in the world outside and within the Vatican, was angrily divided, and the political maneuvering was more open than I had ever seen it.

I know that I had certainly seen the opportunities for elevation for myself, as I pursued my daily occupations. We all wondered how long Pius could continue to reign in such a condition, and we were attempting to remain in the good graces of all the cardinals who came to the Vatican, with the knowledge that one of these fine days one of them would be our spiritual father, the Supreme Pontiff and the one who could further or completely crush our ambitions.

In '76, Antonelli died. It was a black day for Pius. Antonelli had been his closest friend and companion all his life and his secretary of state for twenty-seven years. There were those who said that, without Antonelli to cover his mistakes and speak for him during his periodic bouts of depression, the pope would not be able to hide his inability to function.

Mario asked me one evening, when I returned from a meeting that had included Pius himself, "Do you think he is mad, Vittorio?"

"No, but I think the Holy Father is seriously depressed, and after all, one can hardly blame him, when you consider what he has suffered constantly for over twenty years—not only the loss of the lands and wealth of the entire Church, but the loss of the loyalty of the people, the return of his childhood illness, and now, the loss of his best and almost only close friend."

"His definition as infallible has only lowered his esteem in the eyes of the faithful, and it seems to have been useless, as I believe the influence of Karl Marx is growing anyway," Mario responded.

"I know. It will probably be better for the Church when he . . . ah . . . in the future. She certainly is filled with gloom these days—not only here, but throughout the entire world."

"He *did* get "folded away from the light," didn't he?"

"He got what?"

"Um, what the prisoner said . . . he should have listened to the prisoner," Mario mumbled.

"What did you say?!" I asked, hoping I had not heard him correctly.

" . . . that he should have . . . "

"Never mind, that's what I thought you said. Mario, I am afraid the pope is not the only one around here who may have lost his mind. You really need to forget about this prisoner and his literary ramblings."

"But you said, the last time we discussed it, that he had said some powerful things."

"No, I merely said that you couldn't understand it all with one reading. That doesn't mean . . . "

"But you agreed that perhaps he had a point that the pope had a choice to make between the world and spiritual welfare of the . . . "

Suddenly filled with disgust at Mario's preoccupation with his stolen letter, I shouted at him angrily, "I agreed with nothing! And if anyone is insane, it is your precious prisoner! I'm telling you one last time, Mario, you either forget him and his letter or . . . or . . . just stop it! I never want to hear about this again!"

Mario turned and stared at me, open-mouthed. I realized I was ranting and was shocked at myself. This was unlike me. But I *was* tired of all this. The Church seemed nearly in her death throes, my future position was hanging by a thread, and all my best friend could think about was some incarcerated Muslim's crazy ideas.

He said, quietly, "I'm sorry if I made you angry, Vittorio. Do forgive me."

"No, no," I mumbled, "it's my fault. I shouldn't have . . . I don't know why I . . . oh, I *am* sorry. God bless you, Mario, and sleep well."

"Good night, old friend," he said, but he looked sad as he went to his room.

I know now that I had hurt him far more than I had thought.

* * *

Il Papa e morto! The pope is dead! The ancient words of sorrow rang like a doomsday gong through Vatican City, to Rome, and thence to the world. The faithful seemed to fall into a deep mourning that could never be assuaged.

But in the labyrinthine corridors and cells of the holy hive, we worker bees were busier than ever—and God knows we had been busy enough for some time. First, there was the funeral for Cardinal Antonelli, who had served the Church for so long. He deserved a burial with a certain amount of pomp, and Pius saw that he got it. Then the following year, in '77 the pope celebrated the fiftieth anniversary of his elevation to bishop. And now it was 1878, and Pius IX, the longest reigning pope in history, was dead.

Not since the General Council had the Vatican been so industrious. This pope had reigned for thirty-two years, so many of us had no idea how a conclave was to be run, but the protocol was well established, and having just been through the council eight years before, the preparation procedures went smoothly.

At the end of the conclave, when the white smoke and the cheering of the faithful informed us that "we have a pope," the man elected took the name of Pope Leo XIII. I hoped with all my heart that I might be allowed to not only keep my job but to continue to rise in the hierarchy of the Church.

It was my good fortune that I did. In about three years, in 1881, I was elevated from my position of First Secretary to the Legate's Office to the position of Papal Legate to France. Pope Leo made me a bishop. Was the position of archbishop in my future? Though I would never have said so aloud—in fact, hardly admitted to it privately—in my mind, I could hear myself being addressed as "Monseigneur," and I liked the sound of that.

In that same year, it was decided that the remains of Pius IX, which had been lying in St. Peter's, were to be moved to their final resting place in the Basilica of San Lorenzo. Mario and I were among the many priests and nuns who followed the carriage containing his coffin. Suddenly, as we rounded a corner of the street, we heard loud shouts and threatening voices. There was a great deal of confusion, then the procession came to a halt. In moments, the Swiss Guards were battling a group of rowdy citizens up ahead. The attackers pushed toward the coffin and attempted to dislodge it from its bier.

Much of the crowd, who had gathered around to watch the procession, dispersed and fled. Some attempted to get closer to the fracas.

Finally, the Guards managed to disperse the angry group, but not without a nasty scuffle that entailed some broken bones and cracked heads. We soon learned that the group was attempting to steal the coffin and throw it into the Tiber River.

On the way home afterwards, when order had been restored and the coffin had resumed its march toward San Lorenzo, Mario and I listened to the talk that raged around us. "Three years after his death," some woman commented, "they still hate him that much? It seems unbelievable."

"He and his doctrines have brought about the separation of church and state throughout Europe, and that is a very divisive issue," her companion responded.

After we returned to our flat, we discussed it. The separation, not to mention the definition of infallibility, was, we said to each other, a divisive issue indeed. "I don't know, Mario," I confessed, "When I think of his whole life . . . and of how hard he tried and how much he suffered. Was he such a bad pope?"

"No, Vittorio, not really. In many ways he was a good pope . . . he was just not good enough."

I wondered if the reputation of Pius could or would ever be restored.

"Not in our lifetime, I'm guessing," Mario said.

"I suspect not. And if it ever is," I said, "it will be because the Church will have labored to reeducate the faithful about Pius' life."

"Reeducate?" Mario asked me with a wry smile, "by leaving a great deal out of the official biographies?"

"Something like that. It's been done before."

"I know."

"After all, old friend, sometimes it is necessary for the good of the Church . . . and the spiritual health of the people."

After a long silence, Mario took a deep breath. He turned and looked directly into my face. "Why do we so often hear that?"

"Hear what?"

"'. . . for the good of the Church.' Over and over, whenever something the least bit questionable is done, whether it is altering some little bit of history, 'updating' the interpretation of a verse of scripture, or defining the pope as infallible, the reason is always and ever 'for the good of the Church.'"

"If you had listened, Mario," I said, a little testily, "you would have heard me say 'and for the spiritual health of the people.'"

"Oh, I listened, Vittorio. And I heard it . . . the inevitable official afterthought."

Suddenly, we were into a most uncomfortable silence. I couldn't help wondering if my recent elevation had touched off some latent jealousy in Mario, who was, after all these years, still only a priest. It didn't seem like him, but what else could have elicited such a bitter comment from my otherwise gentle friend?

I had gone to Paris for a long sojourn on Papal business, and from there to spend Christmas with my sister and her family. When I returned to Paris after the holidays, I found a letter from Mario.

He wrote:

The Vatican, Rome
January 14th, 1882

"My dearest friend,

"I am writing to you, instead of telling you in person when you return, because it is entirely possible that by the time you return, I shall no longer be in Rome. I know this will make you angry and sad. The part that is sure to anger you concerns the letter from the Prisoner, which you have forbidden me to mention in your presence.

"I would honor your wish in that matter, even in this letter, but unfortunately it is a large part of why I am writing, and so—forgive me, but I must mention it.

"As we have already discussed, the Prisoner has written that He has come to bring about the unity of the human race, and long-awaited Peace of the world. He has said that all the religions are from the same source and that the Founders of those religions are all speaking with the same voice, that Voice of God with which He Himself speaks in this age. You will remember that I have never been in favor of confession of one's sins before a priest, and He has declared that this practice is outmoded.

"Further, He has written that we who are monks and priests need no longer live a celibate life. He intimates that while God appreciates our sacrifice, one of the purposes of marriage is to bring forth those who will worship God.

"Those of us who have dedicated our lives to Him can hardly do that if we do not marry. He goes on to say that the purpose of chastity is to demonstrate faithfulness, not forbid marriage.

"I know you think I have obsessed over this missal of His for so long that I am no longer in possession of my full reason, but I assure you that I have never felt more sure of myself and of my mind than at the present. Over and over, I have read the letter and compared its tone with the political atmosphere of the Vatican and have decided that if the Church chooses to follow the example set by our late pope, putting the "good of the Church" above the "spiritual health of the people," as we discussed briefly before you left, then I have no moral recourse, as a man of God, than to forsake the world and its institution, and cleave to the vow I made the day I left home to study for the priesthood. I promised that morning to love the Lord, my God, with all my heart and mind and soul, and to serve Him all the days of my life. While I did not specifically say so, I always intended that that vow should not be moved by any discomfort or human loss, any torture or loss of position, any worldly honor or even any friendship.

"While it never occurred to me that the Christ to whom we gave our lives might return during our lifetime, it seems that that is precisely what He has done—come in a new name, as He promised in Revelations 2:17 and 3:12—and I have come to believe this and cast my heart and soul at His feet.

"It is my sincerest prayer that this will not entail the loss of our friendship, which I know we both have treasured over the years we have known one another.

"But if it does, Vittorio, know it is a price I am willing to pay, though with a breaking heart.

"I have submitted my resignation to the Vatican Library and announced my intention to leave the service of the Church. I shall be excommunicated, I know, but that is a small matter to me now, and I have further written the Prisoner in Acca to ask Him if he will accept me among his devoted servants.

"I will pray for you always, dear brother, and sign this, no longer as Father Frances, but as

Mario Paulo Santini"

I sat in my chair for a long time, the letter dangling from my hands between my knees. Anger would come later—anger, and the question of Mario's sanity. For now, there was only sorrow and a feeling of abandonment such as I had never known.

26

SHIRIN: 1870

Khadijah was working night and day—literally night and day—and I had never seen her happier. Charles Frederick Worth had taken her under his wing, as it were, and helped her with her ideas for designs. Later, he came to rely on her a great deal. In fact, when he was in England, she was literally in charge of the Paris branch of his business. There came a day when she asked him if he thought she could succeed at opening her own house of design.

"Absolutely!" he returned with enthusiasm, then added in a more subdued tone, "I've been expecting to hear something like this from you."

"You wouldn't mind?"

"Of course I will mind! I will be so sorry to lose you, *Mon Cheri*, but I am certain that Paris can use more than one designer, and I am equally certain that my business will survive—and that you will do well." He smiled.

So with a loan from Rubin—who, if only for his daughter's sake, was happy to see Khadijah blooming—we turned the two downstairs rooms on the right into a shoppe; the showroom was in the front, and workroom and fitting room in the back. We three women lived in the kitchen and the left-hand front room, which had been the dining room. It was now our little parlor. Of course, we still had the whole upstairs.

I had been mistaken about Khadijah, thinking she neither would nor could change very much.

Forever grateful for the life of her daughter, she named the shop in her honor *"La Maison de Catrine."* *

Her excitement at her venture, and her determination to succeed, made all the difference; no challenge was too extreme. At last, her willful nature had found an acceptable outlet. And *how* acceptable! Her designs became popular almost immediately, and before two years had gone by, we found ourselves swamped with business.

I say "we," as though I had something to do with it all. My job at first was to care for Katherine (who by now was nearly grown and so immersed in her schooling and her study of the flute she hardly needed any looking after), and—with Katherine's help—to keep our house up. Soon, however, I was pressed into duties in the shoppe. I loved having something to do that was of some use in the world, and for the first time since I had left Persia, felt I was earning my own keep. I was certainly not much of a seamstress, but I could do preliminary basting and help out in the front with our clients.

It was in the front of the shoppe one day, just as I was saying "*Au revoir*" to one of Khadijah's wealthy buyers, that I noticed a tall, thin priest walk in and look tentatively around. He appeared to be about forty or forty-five and was very dark. He had dark eyes and, except for a few streaks of grey at the temples, black hair. His face was sharp-featured with a pointed nose and chin. He had such a severe mien that I immediately thought, "*Oh my, he's going to be very unpleasant,*" but when I asked him if I could be of service, he smiled, and his large mouth took over his face, which suddenly exploded into a hundred tiny wrinkles.

"Oui, Madame," he said in French, heavily accented with Italian. "I am looking for a present for my sister. I do not have a great deal to spend. Can I find something, do you think?"

Together, we looked over some of the general stock, and he found a blouse that he felt able to afford and thought might fit her. When Khad-

* The House of Catherine.

ijah suddenly appeared from the back room, he broke into one of his wide grins again. "Aha," he said, "you must be mother and daughter. You look so much alike."

We began to chat then, and before very long had found ourselves immersed in one another. He was Italian, he said, and a papal legate for Pope Leo XIII. He lived in Rome, he told us, but was in France for a while on work for the Vatican. He was called Bishop Giuseppe Vittorio. He had thought perhaps we were also Italian because of our darker complexions and black hair (though mine is heavily streaked with grey now), but when we told him we were Persian, he was fascinated. He was going home for the Christmas holidays, he said, but would return after the first of the year and would come in to see us again, if that might be acceptable to us. Of course we told him he would be more than welcome.

"And," I said as he went out the door, "if the blouse will not do, bring it back, and we shall find something else for her." He smiled that wonderful smile again, wished us a "Joyeux Noel," and disappeared.

The business continued to flourish. It was not long before Khadijah's name was known among all the wealthy women in Paris. She had to hire seamstresses because, in the spring, women from London and, very rarely, from New York City in America came on buying trips to Paris and visited, among other places, *La Maison de Catrine.*

Katherine herself—like her namesake—continued to flourish. In '81, she had turned eighteen, and during the holidays at a party given by her father had met a young man named Marcel DuBois. He was of a good family and, though not wealthy, of reasonable means. He worked as a clerk in Rubin's family banking establishment. He was a nice-looking young man, blond with curly hair and a sweet manner, not very tall. They quickly grew very fond of one another. Rubin knew his family well and approved of the match, and so in 1880, they were married. Needless to say, her mother designed for her one of the most beautiful wedding gowns I have ever seen.

Not long after the marriage, I received a letter from Natasha. It mentioned little about the family, except to say that all was well with them and that they had, after a long silence, heard from Edward. In 1875, he had finally been blessed with a son, Edward John Henry Hillhouse IV. I was, of course, delighted for him. Having a son had meant so much to Edward, and I could see him planning for the baby's future at Cambridge already. The little boy would be six by now, and my mind's picture of him with golden curls and Edward's face, tagging along after his father on chubby legs, made me smile.

Alas, Natasha wrote that the primary reason for her letter at this time was to inform us of Zhukovsky's death at the age of ninety-eight. She said that toward the end, during the last year or eighteen months, he could barely move. He no longer seemed to know who or where he was, seldom spoke, and needed constant care, even having to be fed. Popov, she said (who was none too young himself), had taken wonderful care of him. I wept for a good while that afternoon, and that evening alone in my bed, I thought of how much I had loved that old man. It was as though he were the father I had never known, and I knew I would miss him for the rest of my days. But he was, after all, very old, and had lived a busy and useful life during an interesting era. He had contributed to the literature of his age and served his nation by educating her Tsar, so, I felt, one could surely not ask for more.

27

SHIRIN: 1882

Khadijah was becoming truly contented with her life. I asked her one evening if she envied the wealth and position of the women who were her clients, but she said she did not. "Oh, at first I did a little, because some of them had been in our social circle when we first came to Paris, but then I realized that it is the clothes and the jewels that I enjoy so much, so I am happy designing. I discovered that I don't need to own them. Further, I remembered that they are not nearly so happy as they appear with all their money and busy social calendars. If anyone should know, I certainly should. The busyness attempts to fill a great emptiness inside them." She turned to me and said with an earnest look, "The rich life will not fill that emptiness, Mama."

"No," I said simply, not wanting to comment, but I thought to myself that my daughter had learned what for her was a huge lesson. I wondered, too, what made people so different. Why had she needed to learn this by walking such a difficult path, when I had been just as poor to begin with but had seemed always to have known that simple truth? Why did the learning of this lesson have to make others so unhappy along the way: Rubin, who had all but adored her; Katherine, in her early childhood years feeling so often as though her mother were out of reach?

Still, because of it (tempered by Rubin's and my love), Katherine had developed a marvelous self-sufficiency and was happy now with her Marcel. Also Rubin had so filled his own life that he was able to move in and out of ours without discomfort and cheer at Khadijah's success without the least bit of bitter ash.

But it was not only the lives of my family that puzzled me. Of late, I had noticed that many—I almost wanted to say most—people did not have a very strong sense of their own value. Until Khadijah was left alone and forced to develop, she had tied her belief in herself to her husband and what he possessed. As Rubin gave her gifts she felt reassured of her value. Later the gifts would no longer suffice; only the attention of gentlemen reassured her.

* * *

The priest we had met before Christmas, Bishop Giuseppe Vittorio, came by often, and he and I became fast friends very quickly. Sometimes in the evening when he was in the shoppe at closing time, we would prevail upon him to take supper with us, and he seemed happy to oblige. In fact, I think he rather looked forward to our invitations, as he began to make a practice of dropping in late in the afternoon. I know now that he was lonely in those days.

He was so interested in Persia and asked me about Islam. We had long conversations about religion. I envied him his belief. It seemed so firm, while mine was always one of questions and doubts.

Thinking about Khadijah and the changes in her, I said to him one evening, "Bishop, do you think you could help me to understand something?"

"I shall certainly do my best."

"In my early life, I knew myself only as Uncle Firuz's niece or 'Alí Taqí's wife. Eventually, I believed this to have been the result of being a woman under the shadow of men, but of late I have come to see that it is not only women who have difficulty understanding who they are. While we've felt ourselves to be like carriages hitched behind steeds, who are, of course, our menfolk, I have realized that men do the same thing. They just find different steeds, as it were."

"Oh? How so?" he asked.

"Men know themselves by what they do for a living, or whether they are well-born, whether they are rich, or whom they serve . . . even the simplest household help. We had a wonderful old servant in St. Petersburg, named Popov. He was a man of much pride, but it all seemed to hinge on the fact that he was not just any servant, but the personal man of Count Nicholas Dolgoruky, a family very close to the throne."

"Was he a Christian?" he asked.

"Yes, of course. Nearly all Western Russians are Christians."

"Then what more could he need?" the bishop asked, "If his soul belongs to Christ, then surely he ought to be proud of whatever he is . . . even if he were still a serf, as we are all slaves of our Lord, according to St. Paul. But then," he added with a puzzled frown, "the Russian Church is not the true Church of Christ, so perhaps the problem lies there."

His answer left me uncomfortable. It was as though he had missed the meaning of my question entirely.

"I thought we are all God's children, and He our Father," I said.

"Yes, that is true, we are."

"I don't understand. Why would a loving father enslave his own children?"

"Come, come," the bishop said softly, "do you in Islam not believe you must submit yourselves to the Will of God?"

"Yes, of course."

"How is that different?"

I felt that it *was* different, but I did not know how to explain, so I merely mumbled that I did not know.

He said, "My daughter, I wish you could find true faith in Christ. After all, He died for you. The slavery I speak of is not so bad as all that. After all, our Lord has said that not even a sparrow can fall without God's notice, and this has led to a beautiful personal love between God and man."

"Yes, I know," I said, "Jesus is so beautiful! Not only did He come to once again announce the eventual arrival of the Kingdom of God on earth, but then He said, 'I am come that ye may have life, and have it abundantly!'"[1]

"Exactly, my child!"

"But, Father," I protested gently, "this same personal caring between God and man seems somehow to have been twisted into a terrible preoccupation with sin and salvation."

The bishop looked pensive and a little sad. "You remind me of my old roommate," he said. "He often said he felt that we concentrate on sin too much."

A little timidly, I asked, "Could he have been correct, sir? So much concern for one's own sins and salvation, it seems to me, would foster an awesome self-interest. Further, that kind of selfishness ignores the needs and sufferings of the 'collective,' to use one of Marx's terms. In fact, might that not account for some of the popular appeal of Communism among Christian nations these days?"

"Nonsense!" the bishop said vehemently. "Communism is of the devil!" The natural sternness of his sharp features made him appear somewhat intimidating.

So, since I did not want him to become upset, I said, "No doubt you are correct, Bishop." Then I laughed and added, "On the other hand, since Mr. Marx has said that religion is like opium, perhaps most of the people are asleep."

"Asleep," he said, looking thoughtful. "Most of the people asleep . . . yes." He laughed, a little nervously I thought, and then abruptly blessing me with the sign of the cross, said, "Speaking of sleep, it is well past my bedtime, my daughter. I must get on toward home. Good night. I shall see you soon."

I sat at the same table in our kitchen where we had had our discussion and drank another cup of tea, although the hour was late. But I was puzzled by the evening's discussion and not finished thinking about it.

"Had Christians developed that sense of abundant aliveness as Christ intended?" I thought. "Instead of frightening one another with threats of hell, perhaps they could have shared this feeling of being alive with Islam as it was developing, and met as friends—as Saladin and St. Frances did—and those dreadful bloody Crusades need never have happened."

I sat with my chin in my left hand, picking and eating cookie crumbs from the otherwise empty plate.

I thought, *"The Holy Koran says Muslims are to revere Jesus, but mostly we don't; and why won't Christians try to understand Muḥammad? The Nation of Islam reaches beyond one's personal patriotism, and Muḥammad indicated that eventually, its fulfillment would somehow lead us toward a full nationhood of the world. But without that mutual respect and friendship, I don't believe Islam can reach the fulfillment of its promise, either.*

"Until we have come to the development of our own selves (without carriages and steeds and what have you), the submission to the will of God that He urged upon us cannot be accomplished. Aha! I thought. That is the difference between being slaves of God and submission. Submission is wholly voluntary. The Holy Koran says, 'Our God and your God is one, and to Him are we self-surrendered.'[2] *We do not fully develop ourselves to become slaves—'to be purchased with a price,' as the Christians say—rather, we develop ourselves in order to submit. After all, how can you offer to God what you do not have?"*

I stood and cleared away the teacups and cookie plate and began to wash them up before retiring. I sighed and thought to myself, *"Christians and Muslims could teach each other so much. I wish they could shake hands, as it were, and begin to do so. But here is exactly the problem, isn't it? We think we must have special names for ourselves. I am a Christian, a Muslim; a Persian, a Russian; the wife of a Dubinski, the servant of a count. And if what I am should somehow be lost, or prove mistaken, would I then feel I am no one at all? So to prove to ourselves we are real, we fight one another. And the pity of it is—it is all to protect something that doesn't exist. Because, if I am anyone, I am a child of God, with no title beyond that, and until we all come to see that, the brotherhood of man and the peace of the world will never be realized."*

I hung the dish towel on the rack and started up the stairs to bed, left as always with my same old problem about religion—that what is meant to unite us, divides us.

"Gracious God!" I thought with a heavy sigh, *"There must be an answer somewhere!"*

28

SHIRIN:

Ever since the European world had begun the practice of posting letters through a system, I had kept up a lively correspondence with Natasha, and had become quite used to hearing from her. But it was so soon after her last letter that I was truly puzzled to receive a small package from her, until I opened it. The package contained a lovely scarf, which she had sewn and embroidered for me herself. It was of a pastoral scene, two troikas pulling sleighs through a snowy countryside. It appeared to be two Russian men racing one another, their whips waving in the air and one losing his fur hat in the excitement. I was delighted with it. She wrote a short letter mentioning the marriage of the granddaughter of a mutual friend, the death of another, and complaining that the government's troubles seem worse than ever.

But also enclosed was a letter from Fareshteh, and my, what a letter it was!

I read:

Acca, Palestine—1879

"Oh, Shirin! It is with all my heart that I hope this finds you still alive and well, although we are both growing old rather rapidly, it seems. When I last wrote, we were leaving Baghdad for Constantinople, where we lived for a few months. Following that, we were taken to Adrianople in Eastern Europe, where we lived for five years. Our journey was in the middle of the winter, and several among our party were so ill upon our arrival that we thought they would not recover. Even the dear daughter of our Lord (who was then a very young woman), was made so ill by that journey that she is still, all these years later, suffering from delicate health. In '68, our beloved Bahá'u'lláh was again moved; this time to the horrible city of Acca, in Palestine. It is a very ancient city, Shirin, and not a very pleasant one either. It is hot and dirty and ugly, and the people there are not at all hospitable. It is so filthy there is a saying about Acca: that even the air is so foul that a bird flying overhead dies. I don't suppose there is any truth to that, but it would hardly surprise me.

"They did not even know who the Blessed Beauty (whom you knew as Mírzá Ḥusayn-'Alí Nurí), is. They knew nothing of His goodness, His wisdom or His holiness; all they had heard was that He was a Prisoner of the Ottoman Government. Therefore He was, to them, an evil person. It was a terrible journey from Gallipoli, where we took ship for Palestine. We were heartened as we reached Acca, as our long sea journey was over, but as we went ashore through the sea gate leading to the city, the townspeople jeered and shouted at us and spit on our Beloved!

"If they had only known how much He suffered day and night, perhaps they would not have treated Him so. He was not well after His enemies tried to poison Him in Adrianople. He was always in pain.

"They put us in a filthy prison after our long journey on the ship and gave us neither food nor anything to drink. The smell of the prison was so foul that some of the women fainted. Dear Bahiyyih Khánum, His daughter, fainted, partly from thirst, and someone moistened her lips from some waste water from a puddle on the floor. She swallowed a few drops, but it was so foul she regurgitated it.

"Later many of us had diphtheria, and several died. Among others, I fell ill with it and was so ill I do not remember very much except that His son, 'Abdu'l-Bahá, whom we all call the Master, came by and nursed me with his own hands, putting cool water on my brow and giving me little swallows of water. Our life was very hard here in Acca, and had I known how dreadful it was to be, I might not have fought so hard to survive. Still, all of that seems unimportant in the face of our subsequent years and our joy at being near our beloved Bahá'u'lláh. It hardly seems possible that it all took place nearly twenty years ago. How everything has changed since then!

"One day, while Bahá'u'lláh's younger son, Mírzá Mihdí, was praying on the roof of the citadel, he stumbled and fell through a skylight and landed on a broken plank of lumber that pierced his body. He died, and his poor mother grieved so terribly! We all did; he was such a sweet and loving young man.

"We were in that horrible place for two years and two months! The Holy Family was finally taken from the prison because Turkish soldiers required the use of the barracks, so the Family was moved into a local house. The rest of us found lodgings in the city, though they are terribly dirty and impossible to keep clean.

"The new house of our Lord is somewhat better than the citadel, but it is still cramped and difficult. It is barely a stone's throw from the sea, which means that there is almost always a breeze during the hottest hours, but the city garbage and other wastes are thrown into the sea, just across the road from the house, and the stench is borne in whenever the windows are open. So it seems He and his family must either swelter and choke in the hot, airless rooms, or open the windows and choke on the smell of the garbage. It seems He never has a moment that is without pain or extreme discomfort of one kind or another. Due to the early beatings, over and over from the mullahs; the effects of His imprisonments; the poisoning and other attempts on His life; the hardships of His various journeys; not to mention the effects of the loss of His son; at fifty-some years of age, He is no longer well. It seems as though every day there is some new indignity or accusation visited upon Him. How I weep for Him, Shirin.

"The Master has taken on most of His Father's public duties, to relieve Him, and Bahá'u'lláh now has time to write. He writes tablets to believers in Persia, Baghdad, and Arabia; and among other things, beginning back in Adrianople, He has written to the kings and rulers of the entire known world—not to mention the ministers and priests of the Christians, the Pope in Rome, the Caliph of Islam, and even the rulers of the republics of the Americas, across the Atlantic Ocean.

"Here follows just a tiny sample of what He has said to them all:

O Kings of the earth! He Who is the sovereign Lord of all is come. The Kingdom is God's . . .

Ye are but vassals, O Kings of the earth! He Who is the King of Kings hath appeared . . . and is summoning you unto Himself, the Help in Peril, the Self-Subsisting. Arise, and serve Him Who is the Desire of all nations, Who hath created you through a word from Him, and ordained you to be, for all time, the emblems of His sovereignty.

By the righteousness of God! It is not Our wish to lay hands on your kingdoms. Our mission is to seize and possess the hearts of men.

Fear God, O concourse of kings! . . .

Know ye that the poor are the trust of God in your midst . . . betray not His trust.

O kings of the earth! We see you increasing every year your expenditures, and laying the burden thereof on your subjects.

Your people are your treasures. . . . By them ye rule, by their means ye subsist, by their aid ye conquer. Yet, how disdainfully ye look upon them! How strange, how very strange!

O rulers of the earth! Be reconciled among yourselves, that ye may need no more armaments. . . . Beware lest ye disregard the counsel of the All-Knowing, the Faithful.

Be united, O kings of the earth, for thereby will the tempest of discord be stilled amongst you, and your people find rest, if ye be of them that comprehend. Should any one among you take up arms against another, rise ye all against him, for this is naught but manifest justice.

If ye pay no heed unto the counsels which, in peerless and unequivocal language, We have revealed in this Tablet, Divine chastisement shall assail you from every direction, and the sentence of His justice shall be pronounced against you.

On that day ye shall have no power to resist Him, and shall recognize your own impotence.[1]

"There was, of course, a great deal more, but I have only heard about these particular statements. Oh, Shirin! I wish you could be here with me and experience the wonder of the presence of our Beloved. If the world could only know Him, all would love Him and turn to Him at once, and the great day of Peace promised in all the scriptures of the world, would arrive!

"Again, I can only pray this finds you well, and then you will know how much I still love you and think of you. I hope too, that someday you will hear more of our Beloved Lord, and embrace His message, as all of us here have. You cannot know, until you experience it for yourself, the joy He brings to our hearts.

Forever your friend,

Fareshteh"

29

SHIRIN: 1881

On the first day of the year in 1881 (which we all thought a lucky omen), Katherine and Marcel had a baby—a little boy, whom they named Maurice. Our little Maurice was a strong healthy baby, with his mother's dark hair and eyes and the round face and cheery disposition of his father. We all adored him immediately! What a lucky boy to come into a family who welcomed him so! I was especially excited because he made me a great-grandmother.

Two weeks after Maurice's birth, while busy in the shoppe one afternoon trying to put into order the tangle of papers and scissors, tapes, and fabric swatches that seemed always to accumulate beneath the counter, I heard the bell ring as someone entered. I glanced up to see an older, grey-haired couple come in and begin to look around. It did not appear as though they wanted to do more than browse just yet, so I returned to my task. After a while, the woman approached the counter, holding a gown, and asking if we had a fitting room.

"Yes, of course," I responded, "it is just through that door. Come, I'll show . . ." I looked up then to her husband and found him staring at me. My breath caught in my throat as I realized I was looking into the blue eyes of Edward Hillhouse!

He blurted without preamble, "Is it you?"

"Yes, Edward, it is!" I found my whole self growing alive and filled with joy and a wonderful energy. "What are you doing here?" A rather inane question, I realized later. It seemed that he and Margaret were on holiday in Paris and that she was doing some shopping, but, of course, if my mind had not suddenly deserted me, I might have deduced that.

He introduced me to Margaret at once. She was tall and hearty looking, with wide shoulders, wide cheekbones, and large teeth. She used a pinz-nez, which dangled now from a gold chain about her neck and had left deep pink depressions on either side of her nose. But she had, all in all, a pleasant look about her and was gracious and friendly. He explained to her that I was among the friends he had known in Russia. She looked at me intently for a moment, smiled, and said, "Ah. It is indeed good to meet you, Mrs. Kh́ánum."

I let her error pass with a smile and a nod. Further, I realized immediately that, in the way of women, she had known for a long time that Edward cared for me.

I called Khadijah, and she came in, thrilled to see him again. The four of us talked the small talk of people who have not seen each other for years. Soon, however, we were all laughing and sharing with Margaret amusing memories of our times with the Dolgoruky family.

After a few minutes, Khadijah took Margaret to the fitting room, and Edward and I stood looking at one another. He was shorter than I remembered, perhaps due to a slight stoop of aging, but his eyes were as young as ever. His face was lined more deeply than in the past, of course, but it was still the same wonderful face I had carried in my mind for so long.

At last he spoke. "There are no words to say how deeply happy I am to see you! You look well. The count wrote, mentioning that you had moved to Paris. I think of you always when I come here, but, I say! I never expected to actually see you!"

"Do you indeed think of me?" I asked, my heart swelling with joy.

"Oh yes, my dear, I do—and not just in Paris, either, but often . . . and everywhere."

"Are you happy, Edward? Have you been happy?" I was struck by a certain hoarse intensity in my voice.

"Yes. Life has been good to me. I have a son, you know—a son and two daughters."

"Natasha told me. She always mentions your news when she writes."

"Oh, then that's good, isn't it? And you? How have you fared—well? You appear to be thriving. And Khadijah—she sews here?"

"This is Khadijah's shoppe. She designs."

"You mean Khadijah is 'Catrine, the coutourier'?"

I nodded.

"You must be very proud of her."

"I am."

"But why 'Catrine'?"

"She named the shoppe after her daughter, Katherine Shaydah."

"Ah, your little Katrushka! How is she?"

"Married—and with a brand new son."

"Married!" We stood looking at one another and smiling. He shook his head. "Time . . ." he said, "how it races along . . . and makes us old."

"Yes." Then I said, "Oh, Edward, I . . . It is so good to see you! . . . I can't . . ."

"I know." He reached and took my hand in both of his. I was amazed to notice that even in my seventies I felt—not so much the old thrill of his touch—but a warm sense of inner settling, as though I had come home. He traced my fingers with his, outlining each knuckle, and turning a ring I wear. We stood looking down at the age in both our hands, the arthritic swelling of the joints, the heavy veins.

He spoke, "If I could turn back the clock to those days with you in St. Petersburg, Shirin, I would. I've often thought that perhaps we should have done it differently. Perhaps I should have put aside my ambitions and my concern for custom. Those things have not the importance I once thought."

"And your need for a son? And your duty to your queen? No, Edward, you . . . we both . . . did the right thing. I've also often thought of what might have been, but it wouldn't have done. There was a time when we first came here to Paris, when Katherine and Khadijah could have hardly gotten on without me. Our lives have had different purposes, don't you think?"

"You believe our lives have purpose, then?"

"I don't know, but I sometimes think so."

"I imagine they may," he conceded. "Yet, I often worry that I left you with nothing, while I have had all that I ever . . . "

"My darling, no!" I said, reaching up and silencing his lips with my free hand. "You mustn't forget I once had a husband and children, and now am so rich with family and love. But oh, Edward, you have been the secret jewel of my life, locked away in my heart, glowing through my darkest days. Granted, it has been, sometimes, more dream than real, but neither has it been marred by all those 'slings and arrows.' But my *love* has been no dream; it has been very genuine—and very true."

His eyes answered with everything I needed to know.

Khadijah and Margaret emerged then from the back room, so Edward formally kissed my hand, let it go, and said, "What a gift this day has been!"

"For me as well."

Margaret bought the dress. It needed only a slight alteration. Khadijah promised to have it finished and delivered to their hotel the next day, as they were headed home to England. We all said good-bye, and Edward, smiling and looking directly into my eyes, said, "Perhaps we shall all meet again, who knows?"

"Yes," I said brightly, "who knows?" Then I watched him walk out the door with Margaret on his arm, his head tipped slightly sideways toward her to better hear her happy chatter. I stood for some time, watching through the window where he had disappeared into the shade of the chestnut trees, reliving the touch of his hands, tracing my fingers as he had, outlining each knuckle and turning the ring I wear.

* * *

At the end of February, the Paris paper contained an account of the assassination of Tsar Alexander II! Shortly after, we received a letter from Natasha. It had little family news, other than to assure us that all were well, except for Olga's chronic illnesses, which seemed to threaten her eighty-three-year old body very little as she continued to live on and enjoy a good appetite. It mentioned, as well, that Dimitri had risen to the rank of general in the cavalry. The purpose for the letter, Natasha said, was to send the included clipping from a newspaper that had told the story. It was hardly different from the account in the Paris paper. Her letter, however, contained information the papers could not have had.

Sometime earlier, the Tsarina had died of humiliation and a broken heart, she wrote. The tuberculosis that had climaxed so suddenly after the disgrace of moving Catherine Dolgoruka and their two children into the palace as the acknowledged mistress of the Tsar had taken its toll, and she died without undue lingering.

> "Less than four months later," Natasha wrote, "Alex had married Catherine, with our poor Tsarina barely at rest in her grave! Have you ever heard of anything so scandalous?
>
> "The Heir, Alexander III, has been livid at his father, and whatever respect and friendliness ever existed between them has never been regained.
>
> "Alex's latest caprice was to announce that he was planning to have Catherine crowned as Empress of all the Russias! Even the poorest peasants were shocked. The people's interests lay with the creation of a parliament and a constitutional government, but the Tsar apparently couldn't be bothered. The more the country cried for representation, the more autocratic he became. The people demanded, and the Tsar ignored them, hiding away in the cozy little nest of his child bride and family. Even the gentry, or perhaps I should say, especially the gentry, were shocked and disgusted with him.
>
> "Strangely, however, his courage in the face of a number of attempts to assassinate him was remarkable. I think perhaps it may have been that he believed in his divine right so thoroughly it never occurred to him that an assassin could possibly succeed. On the day of the assassination, Alex was on an errand, riding in his carriage. Suddenly from somewhere in the crowd of observers, someone threw a bomb. It missed its target and exploded beneath the rear axel and killed a butcher's boy in the crowd, and wounded one of the Cossack guards. But of course, you have seen all that in the papers."

We had. It seemed his advisers had suggested that he take another carriage and leave immediately with all speed. But his natural compassion wouldn't allow it. He leaped from the carriage and surveyed the damage. He faced his would-be assassin who had been apprehended and then examined the body of the boy. On his way to comfort the wounded guard, and see about his removal to hospital, a second enemy rushed from the crowd and threw a bomb directly into his face. He was rushed back to the palace and died two hours later. Ironically, while preparing him for burial, his attendants found in his coat pocket an unfinished draft for the longed for constitution.

> "But it was too late!" wrote Natasha, "Oh, my dears, too late! So now we shall have Alexander III for our Tsar, and all is indeed lost for Russia! He will be more autocratic than his father! Nor has he the intelligence to rule well. Oh, Shirin, you know how we had hoped that Alex would awaken this beloved land of ours and lead us into the coming 20th century! Instead he alienated the people, the gentry, the intellectuals, and European society. And now this."

I thought, "*I am grateful that dear Zhukovsky is not alive to see what became of his 'boy.'*"

"Whatever will become of Russia?" Nastasha wrote in closing. "Pray for us, dear friends! Do, please, pray for us!"

30

HILLHOUSE PAPERS: 1911

John's days were difficult. His beloved Carolyn went from week to week, making all the right gestures, saying all the right things, and laughing at John's attempts to amuse her, but the laughter, for all her attempts, was forced. It was like living with a ghost of the vivacious girl he had married. Further, he lived in a constant state of anxiety, wondering each day when he returned from the fields, the veterinarian's, or the feed mill whether or not he might find her in a pool of blood again, or even dead this time. The neighbors always asked kindly about her health, and he always responded cheerily, "Oh, she's coming along just right—right as can be."

"Oh, isn't that fine," they responded, noticing his tone was just a little too hearty. They were genuinely concerned for Carrie and often went out of their way to drop in on her or bring the couple gifts of pots of stew or a meat pie. Outwardly, no one mentioned what had happened.

The weather that summer was beautiful, and the rest of life seemed to be trying to make up to them for their personal sorrows. Several of the sheep produced young that had great promise for the fair in the fall, and, with luck, this could mean prizes, and in their wake, business and sales.

Moreover, from Maggie's earlier litter one pup, a year-old male named Rob Roy, seemed to live for the herding. He needed only to hear the back door open, and he was at the heels of whoever was there. He followed

Carrie to the henhouse and John to the barn for the simplest errands. They would say to him, "No, Robbie, we're not going to work now," but with tail wagging and ears alert, he invariably did his little dance of hope, crestfallen when they finally reentered the house. Both Carrie and John worked him with the sheep in the nearby low hills as often and as long as they could, and he never grew tired. His hope seemed contagious, and the couple soon came to believe that things might improve for them financially. To speed that end, John went into London and closed up the old flat. He begged Carrie to come with him, but she said she would much rather stay at home. There were "things that need looking after," she said.

"Carrie, you need to get out and see people and do things. You're too cooped up here."

"John, I don't need to 'do things.' I've enough to do right here on the place, especially when you're gone. As for seeing people, Amanda Miller stops by from time to time, and so does the Edgewood girl. And I'm certainly not cooped up. I'm either in the roses or in the field almost every day. The dogs and I take long walks."

"But I miss you when I'm gone, and I want . . . "

"No, you're afraid for me. You needn't be. I will not do anything that . . . that . . . you wouldn't want me to do while you're gone. I shouldn't want ever to worry you like that again, my darling. Now go on to London and stop fussing. Maggie and Hamish, Mac and Rob and I will be here to greet you when you return . . . I promise!" And so, reluctantly, he went, and thought again about how much better he would feel if they owned a telephone.

The landlord was sorry to have them give up the flat, but the money saved on the annual rent would be welcome. He saved his father's old Morris chair and humidor, the rose chair and settee, his mother's Ming dogs and the little cherry table. The rest he let go. These things, they had decided, would work well in their summer room at home.

He had not had time to read his father's papers of late. He stayed too busy watching over Carrie. He took hardly any time for himself or to read much of anything. But the last evening in the flat, he lay in bed, as most of the furniture was gone off to the carter whose dray he had hired to carry it up country, and took up the papers before he slept.

1875

"At last I am a father!" Edward had written, "and Margaret and I are both so thrilled to have a son. Of course, after three failed attempts, we would have been happy with a girl, actually, any child at all, alive and well, but this is just a great pleasure. Edward John Henry Hillhouse IV. We have decided to call him John, so as to avoid the confusion of two Edwards, and I've already notified Pembroke College that he'll be coming along one of these fine days. It went out in our class's annual news review, and we've received congratulatory notices from at least a dozen of my old classmates, not to mention a present or two.

"Margaret is all but living in the nursery, in spite of a full-time nanny, as she is so happy with her little one. I must say, he is a beautiful boy! And so strong and intelligent-looking."

John smiled at his father's description of him and thought how often as a youth he would have appreciated a little more of that kind of admiration.

"I say—I do look forward to walking the fields with him and teaching him how to shoot," his father had finished before moving on. Again John smiled remembering those walks and his first awkward attempts at shooting.

"I've had a letter from Count Nicholas today, and he is much concerned about the activities of Tsar Alexander. It seems he has lost control of himself and consequently of his reign, all due to his infatuation for the daughter of Prince Michael Dolgoruky. You will remember that the Tsar had appointed him as guardian at Prince Michael's death. I barely knew the girl, but I do recall that, even as a child, she was uncommonly beautiful. Also he writes that the Tsar is becoming more and more autocratic, after having begun his reign with such openly liberating intentions.

"Then Nicholas went on to remind me of our time together in the Middle East, saying,

You will recall when we were in Persia together and saw the awful tragedy of the slaughter of the Bábís, and how we wondered what, if anything, would ever come of all that innocent bloodshed.

While putting in order some papers I have had in my possession since those days, I ran across something I have never mentioned before to anyone, not even to my dear wife, Shahane, and as a result had almost forgotten about it. My uncle, Prince Michael, had a copy of a letter sent by the Prisoner of Acca, Ḥusayn-'Alí Nurí (whom you will recall, they now refer to as Bahá'u'lláh), to the Tsar.

How Uncle got it I am not altogether sure, but being a near relative of the Tsar's and his chief diplomat to Persia, it is not especially unlikely. I found it soon after his death among his personal papers, which—what with my having been his Russian secretary—had been entrusted to me. I have saved it among my Persian notes. I will not include all of it, for it is too long, and my English, while adequate, is not scholarly enough to warrant my translating the entire document. I truly wish to share this with you but beg you to show it to no one.

Now because of the way things are going with the Tsar and his foolishness, I find it amazing that the prisoner understood him so thoroughly. I truly wish to share this with you, but beg you to show it to no one. Some salient points follow:

"O Czar of Russia! Incline thine ear unto the voice of God, the King, the Holy. . . . Beware lest thy desire deter thee from turning towards the face of thy Lord, the Compassionate, the Most Merciful. We, verily, have heard the thing for which thou didst supplicate thy Lord, whilst secretly communing with Him. Wherefore . . . We answered thee in truth. Thy Lord, verily, is the All-Knowing, the All-Wise."[1]

Edward, the prisoner did not say what the Tsar had petitioned God for, but it is interesting, is it not, that he claims to have granted the Tsar's request? The prisoner further wrote, "Whilst I lay chained and fettered in the prison, one of thy ministers extended Me his aid."[2]

That, of course, would have been Prince Michael, and I am sure you will remember how we were able to get the prisoner released from the Siyyah Chal in those days. At any rate he continues: "Wherefore hath God ordained for thee a station which the knowledge of none can comprehend except His knowledge. Beware lest thou barter away this sublime station."[3]

Then he writes:

"Beware lest thy sovereignty withhold thee from Him Who is the Supreme Sovereign. He, verily, is come with His Kingdom, and all the atoms cry aloud: 'Lo! The Lord is come in His great majesty!' He Who is the Father is come, and the Son, in the holy vale, crieth out: 'Here am I, here am I, O Lord, My God!,' whilst Sinai circleth round the House, and the Burning Bush calleth aloud: 'The All-Bounteous is come mounted upon the clouds. Blessed is he that draweth nigh unto Him, and woe betide them that are far away.'

"Arise thou amongst men in the name of this all-compelling Cause, and summon, then, the nations unto God, the Exalted, the Great. Be thou not of them who called upon God by one of His names, but who, when He Who is the Object of all names appeared, denied Him and turned aside . . ."[4]

There is a good deal more than I have quoted for you, Hillhouse, but I cannot help commenting at this juncture that whoever the prisoner is or was, I needn't remind you that we who actually saw him know that he was no ordinary man, nor was he some fanciful fanatic. It seems that he, in the strongest terms, uncannily addressed the two conditions to which Tsar Alexander II has, of late, fallen victim: his inordinate desire for a young girl, which has been so destructive both to his family and his nation (you will note that warning in the Prisoner's first paragraph), and the way he clings to his own sovereignty, which has not only overruled his better nature but is making the people more and more discontented. If the prisoner warned the Tsar lest he "barter away his sublime station," one wonders what that station might have been. And would it have had anything to do with the hope that we all held for him when he first came to power?

You may recall that the Tsar has always had trouble bringing the two parts of himself into balance—the stern autocrat and the compassionate father of his people. Now, it seems, that rather than complete that personal discipline, he has taken the easy way and allowed the separation of these two parts of himself to govern his life, ruling his people entirely with his autocracy and saving his sweet compassion for his new family.

Had the Tsar fulfilled the promise in him, then with the sheer size of all the Russias, the serfs freed and the intelligentsia developing, what might he not have accomplished in the way of leading Europe into the future?! Whatever it might have been, it appears to me that he has "bartered it away" indeed. What a dreadful shame it has turned out this way! The price is the growing discontent of his subjects, and it becomes increasingly acute with each passing year."

John read and reread the excerpts from the Prisoner's letter to the Tsar and thought to himself, *"I begin to see how Father must have felt, when he wrote at the beginning of this journal, that 'something momentous is happening.' For since the death of the Tsar and the even more autocratic rule of Alexander III, the well-meaning but weak Nicholas II has been able to do nothing to quell the unrest among the Russian people, which only continues to grow stronger. As for Bahá'u'lláh and his letters and teachings—I wonder what has become of all of it. Will we hear of him again, or, as Father feared, has it all died away?"*

31

SHIRIN: 1893

One day, I was overjoyed to see that I had again received a letter from Fareshteh. I opened it with fingers trembling with excitement because not only did I invariably enjoy her tales of her own life, but by now, as well, I was eagerly looking forward to the latest about Bahá'u'lláh—His teachings and His life. Finding a quiet corner where I would not be disturbed, I sat down to read:

Acca in Palestine

12 June 1892

"Dearest Sister of my Heart,

"I have horrendous news, and it is with two minds that I write this to you, dear friend. Oh, how do I begin? With the most exquisite sorrow, I begin by telling you of our heartbreak. Our Beloved has returned to the world of the spirit whence He came to us. It happened on the 28th of May.

"None of us had had any inkling that this was about to occur. He seemed the same as always. And though we did not have the great blessing of being in His presence often; still, in those infrequent times, we noticed nothing. Then too, we were always so caught up in our joy at just being allowed to see Him and listening raptly to the simplest words that fell from His lips that we were, I fear, not thinking of His well-being but merely of our own. Even though the great Teachers are always taken from us—Moses, Jesus, Muḥammad—still who, among us, would remember that this Mighty Being, through Whom flowed the Words of God, Himself, could ever suffer from that great silence?

"We had heard a day or so earlier that He had developed a slight fever. But there was little reason to be concerned, for He was, after all, He Whom God Will Make Manifest, so to what harm could He possibly come? But finally, we understood that His illness would take Him from us, and we began to gather outside His home at Bahji, waiting for any word. We walked around and around the house, speaking to one another in low tones and waiting, hoping for some kind of miracle.

"Dear Shirin, how strange it was to see all the people of the area filling the road, as they arrived at the blessed house to weep and pray and cry aloud. Many of them were the poor and desolate, whom He had helped so many times with words of kindness, or gifts of food or money. People came down from the hills of Galilee, from Naẓareth, from Tiberius, from Acca and Haifa—Christians, Jews, Muslims, and Zoroastrians—gathering in sorrowful groups, moaning aloud their grief, and calling 'Our Father is being taken from us!'

"But also a good many were the very ones who had worked upon Him such heinous acts of cruelty over the years—people of power and influence in the area. Now they, too, were arriving—distressed, repentant, and weeping aloud.

"We stood outside the house all night long waiting. Perhaps you would not know this, Shirin, but here in Palestine, the rainy season begins in November and ends in late March or very early April, and then it is dry all the rest of the year. But on this night late in May, it rained all night long and all the next day. People said, 'It is as though Heaven, itself, is weeping for our great loss.' But I thought to myself, 'Or perhaps, it is one more gift He bestows upon us—a parting gift of the blessed rain these sere and arid fields always so desperately need.' I found that idea rather more to my liking than the other, though I, too, wept with a grief that I thought could never be assuaged.

"When it was finally over, the Master, 'Abdu'l-Bahá, sent a cable to the Sultan of Turkey—that terrible man who had imprisoned Our Lord so long ago and kept Him a Prisoner for forty years—saying merely, 'The Sun of Bahá has set.'

"Were it not for the Master, I think none of us could have borne this! But praise God, he comforts us and cares for us as he always has, and has assured us that the great Cause of God can never die and will never fail, that from age to age, from dispensation to dispensation, God will continue to keep us and send us His Messengers, that Bahá'u'lláh Himself will be watching over us from His place in Paradise. We are to tell the world, the Master says, and keep faith that all of his blessed Father's promises will be kept.

"As the sun of His earthly light set along the shores of the Mediterranean Sea, the world would appear to have been plunged into darkness. Yet I find myself comforted after all, for we know that the light of the power of the eternal Cause of God is rising like a new dawn and already beginning to fill the earth with the promise of a new day, when 'these fruitless strifes, these ruinous wars shall cease and the "Most Great Peace" shall come.' We know that at last, the ancient scriptural promise is being fulfilled, as already 'the knowledge of the Glory of God' has begun to 'cover the earth as the waters cover the sea.'[1]

"And I smile to myself, Shirin, even as I weep in thanksgiving to Him for His life of exquisite sacrifice, and remember that, finally, after forty years of unrelenting suffering, the Prisoner of Acca is free."

BOOK 3

THE BEGINNING OF SORROWS

"FOR NATION SHALL RISE AGAINST NATION
AND KINGDOM AGAINST KINGDOM:
AND THERE SHALL BE FAMINES AND PESTILENCES,
AND EARTHQUAKES IN DIVERS PLACES.
ALL THESE ARE THE BEGINNING OF SORROWS."

Mathew 24: 7–8

32

CONFESSIONS: 1909

JMJ

The other night, I again spent the evening with Shirin Khánum and her daughter the couturier. They are both such delightful women, and I have become fond of them both, especially Khánum. She is most intelligent for a woman and has such an inquiring mind; it is a delight to spend time with her. I fear I take advantage of their hospitality from time to time, for evenings with them somehow relieve some of the loneliness that has been following me—echoing like footsteps behind me on a dark empty street—ever since Mario left the Church.

At first I was so angry with him—to think he would desert his vows and leave the service of Holy Mother Church—I wanted nothing more to do with him, and so I never responded to his letter. By the time I had returned to Rome, he was gone without a trace, and I do not know how to find him now.

I know he has been excommunicated and, according to the Church, will burn in Hell when he dies, and it grieves me when I remember how often we laughed and made up lighthearted fantasies about how we would manage in the next world, with him forever getting into heavenly scrapes and I forever getting him out. But my sorrow does not erase the joy we knew together as boys or our years in service together as priests. My anger at him has cooled, but my concern for him has not, and I find I wonder all the time how he is managing with this biggest scrape of all.

I worry too, lest he has found no way to make a living. If I could, I think I might write to him and hope to repair our friendship. Perhaps I could find a way to lead him back to the Church and repair the damage to his soul. After all, being a bishop ought to be good for something.

But that evening, Khánum made a remark that has troubled me a great deal. We were discussing something she had on her mind about people not recognizing their own worth—I couldn't quite take in what she was saying—when she suddenly said something like, "Since Karl Marx has called religion the opium of the people, perhaps everyone is asleep." I think she meant it as a joke, but all I could hear was that voice in my soul that has said to me over and over, "Sleep not," and, I confess, it was unnerving. I began to have trouble catching my breath—so much so that I left and came home.

But there was more. Earlier when she was talking about "knowing our own value," I thought of Mario, though I was not sure why. I thought of what we had said to each other about the Prisoner and of how I grew so angry when he pointed out that the pope had failed to listen to the Prisoner's advice and subsequently lost not only his temporal power but his serenity as a person and the respect of the people—and certainly his effectiveness as a man of God. I thought of our final words to each other about this subject when I left for Paris, of how things are done "for the good of the Church" first, while "the spiritual health of the people" takes second place. What was it Mario had said—as "an inevitable afterthought"? I was very angry with him when he said that. I wonder if I would have been so put out had I known I might never see him again.

And to think I had blamed it on envy of me. I had known that Mario was not himself and had developed this odd habit of retiring into his own thoughts, but I was chagrined to realize that it was not at all that he was jealous of my elevation to the bishopric. Instead, it had been because of some great change within himself with which he was preoccupied; it had nothing to do with me.

I had spoken so sharply to Khánum when I said that Communism is the Devil's game. I am sure it is, yet there was no reason for me to speak so harshly to this gentle woman who has been so hospitable. No wonder she made a joke; how else to turn away my pique? I heard myself sounding much like my own father, and that troubles me no end. Of late, my anger seems to be leaping out at odd moments without true provocation; at the small sins of those who confess to me, at ideas that disagree with established doctrine or, as the other night, at Khánum when she failed to see the simple truths of the Church's mission.

I find I am more and more defending Church dogma—which is, of course, a good thing, isn't it? After all, this is why I became a priest in the first place, to serve her all my days. And yet, I am not pleased with myself. My patience wears thin so easily. More, over and over I hear myself repeating the doctrines of the Church as though I were one of those colorful birds sailors collect in the tropics and teach to speak, even though they don't know what they are saying—those parrots. I ask myself why. I certainly believe in the doctrine of the Church—have believed all my life.

Perhaps it is the added responsibility on my shoulders from the work that accounts for it. If I ever *do* become an archbishop, I shall no doubt be the most unpleasant old man in the entire clergy. But this is surely not what I bargained for in those long-ago days when I prayed to my Lord Christ to serve Him, when I felt in my soul His acceptance of my prayer . . . and when I first began experiencing that infernal dream.

I think I understand what Khánum was talking about when she spoke of women hitching their carriages to the stars of men, but what did she mean by saying that men do the same thing . . . that they merely have different stars?

I suppose she has a *small* point. I suppose there are *some* men who value themselves only for what they do . . . as financiers or scholars might. But I think most men are just what they are, and would be no different no matter what they did. I am relieved that I am a priest and do not have to be concerned for my own value. So long as I can serve the church, I know my worth.

I comforted myself with this thinking and went off to bed that evening, but not without a prayer asking God to help me understand all this. It was in the middle of the night when I woke and suddenly sat bolt upright, again having trouble breathing. To begin with, I had had the dream again.

This time when the voice said "sleep not," my response was to literally waken. Suddenly I had heard—in my sleep I think—what I had said earlier: "So long as I can serve the church, I know my worth."

There, in front of me, like the words on a page, was an understanding of the whole puzzle. Do I believe my only value lies in my service to the Church and that God will love me only if I do this work? Is this what Kh́ánum was asking that had so threatened my composure? Was this behind my desire to rise in the hierarchy of the very institution that Mario and I had criticized so often? Is this why I sometimes hate Mario for defaulting?

I had no sooner asked the questions before I knew the answer to all four was a resounding "Yes!"

I suddenly saw that my need to vindicate myself in the eyes of my father had led me to the Church in the first place. That while my desire to serve God and my Lord Christ was real enough and my vocation a true one, it was only through the Church that I could be vindicated over and over as I rose in her ranks and gained the power for which I had yearned. To prove to him! To show him that he was not anywhere nearly as powerful as he would have us believe—he with his damnable birch rod and his paternal rages! To show him that I could be powerful, too, and even more than he, because I would have God's own power to uphold mine! I saw that my desire to become an archbishop (if ever realized), would give way to a desire to wear the red hat of a cardinal, and then what? Would I hope for the papacy? And if I did *not* become pope, would I then be nothing in my own eyes, and more especially in the eyes of that angry spectre that had driven me all my days? My own carriage, I realized, was hitched to the ghost of my father.

There are so many loyal and dedicated priests who find great joy in serving their small parishes and make the lives of their people their own *raison d'être*, and I had always thought myself terribly deficient in some way because I could not serve with such fervor. But now suddenly, I saw that I had disliked the simple duties of a parish priest because there was, to my thinking, no reward or honor in it. As I am sure I have mentioned earlier, it is not that I did not care about my parishioners, it was that their condition never changed, and my service led neither them nor me anywhere. It kept me, what is more, forever reminded of the poverty of my childhood and the powerlessness of my father's household. It kept me reminded of who I truly am.

For I am, after all, my father's son; the son of that man who had been so burdened with fear and weary with labor that he hated the world. Had I not chosen the church, would I have become him in my own eyes and in the playing out of my life? To some extent my brothers have, fighting the same battles for sustenance, fearing the same fears of a hopeless future. Would I, too, have ended up beating my children? Perhaps. I had always believed myself so much better than my father because I was not like him. But who was I now beyond a bundle of anger at a past long gone and ambition for an uncertain future? How then, am I so different from him—and not only him, but my brothers as well? And to think I had guarded my heart so carefully all these years, terrified lest I see this . . . and in the end the "great terrifying spectre" was . . . nothing.

For peasant or priest, I am none other than myself . . . and more like my father than I would ever have thought.

I am certain that Pius's belief that he must save the temporal wealth and power of the Church to bequeath intact to his successor was sincere. But it was wrong. His need to recover what had been lost and to rule the Christian world became more important to him than his need to shepherd the faithful, and now I saw that I, too, had wasted my life on a lie and called it truth. What had the Prisoner said? "Guard thyself, lest darkness overtake thee and fold thee away from the light." All these years of dutiful obedience had been without heart, and I realized it was as though I had been sleepwalking. Oh my God—the voice in the dream! I had been asleep!

I left my bed and, kneeling, began to pray. Over and over, I asked my Lord Christ for His forgiveness and made the most sincere confession of my life without, I might add, the assistance of a priest confessor. (How Mario would have loved that!) The tears of remorse that bathed my face changed into tears of release as the burden of shame fell away and, finally, to tears of joy at the knowledge of His forgiveness.

I rose and climbed back into the warmth of my bed, where I was able in my new freedom to see things I had never seen before. Not only had my father given me the gift of life, but he had bequeathed to me his aggressive nature that, though it kept the flame of my hatred for him burning, had also enabled me to undergo the rigors of my childhood and adult life. More, he had taught me the discipline of hard work that had served me so well in my vocation and brought about my advancement.

Even the wounds of his cruelty, which had driven me to prayer early in childhood, had provided me with my life in the Church. I am a bishop today largely because of that man.

At last I understood the Fifth Commandment—that we are to honor our parents. I had always wondered why we should be commanded to love one who is so impossible to love, but now I realized that God does not tell us to love them. He commands us to honor them . . . and I saw why. For the first time in nearly fifty years, I was able to pray for his soul and mean it. So, in the early, early hours, I lay listening to the clock tick the night into morning. And I forgave my father.

Then I fell asleep and dreamed a rather nonsensical dream—that Khánum and Mario and I were sitting together in a large roomful of people, listening to someone deliver a talk, and we were laughing together.

33

HILLHOUSE PAPERS: 1911

John and Carolyn Hillhouse were sitting in their parlor on a late August evening in 1911. It had been nearly a year since Carrie had attempted to take her life, and while she had recovered her health nicely and there had been no more crises of that nature, she had not yet returned to her naturally cheery self. John did everything he could think of to make her laugh, to keep her happy. Although for his sake she went along with his jokes, there was something gone from her personality, and it looked as though it might never return. It was as if the night Maggie had lost her puppies, Carrie had lost whatever last hope she harbored to have the children she longed for, as well as her joy in life.

Outwardly, she appeared to have accepted it. Still as pretty as ever, she was also as good-natured, friendly, and sociable to the neighbors as before, but the little spark of almost naughty humor that had danced in her eyes (especially when decorum demanded that she be especially proper) was gone. John missed his darling companion of their early years and was often at his wit's end wondering what more he could do.

Otherwise, it had been a good year for them. The business had been more successful than usual, as two of their sheep had won championships, and sheep farmers, anxious to improve their stock, were getting in touch. The stud fees were helping immensely. Maggie had had a second litter, and all had gone well this time. Kept until they were well-trained at sheep-handling, the pups had sold for good prices. Many of the old debts were being paid off at last.

As for Rob Roy, he had walked away with the Grand Prize at the field trials, and the stud fees from this champion would be a great help. His own price, if they sold him, would be a great boost to their exchequer, but they wouldn't hear of selling him. Mac was aging, and they knew that Rob Roy would sire wonderful pups for them in future. Besides, they loved him.

On this mild summer evening, they sat in some contentment. Autumn was waiting impatiently behind the Malvern Hills, and already there was a little color in the oak trees near the house. Carrie was busily knitting a sweater with thick yarn made of wool from their own sheep. She was making it for John to wear up on the hills when he was out with the flock. Even in summer, the winds coming across the land could be cold. "What are you working on now?" he asked her.

"A new jumper for you. You wear them out, one after another. I just don't know how you manage to do it," she said, with mock exasperation. "You're worse than a boy."

He heard in her remark the ever-present longing. If she eased it somewhat by making him out to be a child, he wouldn't dissuade her. "I like that natural color. I hope you are not going to dye it later."

"No. If I were to dye it, I'd have done so before I began the knitting."

"Oh, right. Of course you would have done, wouldn't you?"

They fell quiet then, and John took up his pipe, filled it, tamped it, lit the tobacco. He leaned back in his chair and sighed contentedly.

What with Carrie's illness and the never-ending work on the place, it had been a long time since John had looked at his father's papers. He had determined to finish them tonight. Now, he took up the last one and began to read:

1895:

"All these impressions I've gathered over the years regarding that long ago, amazing—not to mention shocking—experience in Persia, when the blood of the Báb's followers literally ran in the streets, soaking the ground and turning the dirt deep red, seem to be coming into some kind of fruition now.

"Had anyone suggested to me in those days that not only would I hear of the Báb in Europe and England but that the influence of his story would even reach the new world in America, I would have scoffed at such unlikely nonsense. That his successor—that is, the one he foretold, Ḥusayn-'Alí Nurí, or *Bahá'u'lláh* (The Glory of God), as he is called now—would survive the bloodbath to land in prison in Palestine and from there advise and warn the kings and rulers of the civilized world, would have seemed even more unimaginable, but I have lived to see this occur.

"Unlike our Queen, who, these days, is a constitutional head of state, these kings and rulers were all absolute monarchs. That means, of course, that to presume to advise them, let alone summon up the effrontery to *warn* them—of anything, let alone the consequences of their own decisions—could almost certainly cost one his head.

"Yet the Prisoner lived!

"He lived while the Emperor Napoleon III, the most politically astute ruler in Europe, destroyed his own character with women and arrogance, lost his wisdom in the maelstrom of ambition that cost him his kingdom and, sickened by self-indulgence, died.

"The Roman Church, once the greatest ruling power in the Western world, is politically powerless, materially impoverished, and spiritually diminished in influence. Pope Pius IX, the brilliant and almost saintly man who began his papacy with such tenderness for the faithful souls in his care, yet who ended it with arrogant authoritarianism and as hated as any pope in history—he who reigned so long he seemed almost indestructible, died.

"Alexander II of Russia, whose reign began with such high expectations—setting free the serfs and toying with the idea of a constitutional government—in the end failed his people, his family, and himself. And now he, too, is dead from an assassin's bomb. He was the best and brightest of the Romanovs, Russia's best hope for entering as a full partner into European political life. His brilliant young heir, who could have carried on his father's illustrious beginnings, died some years ago, and so Russia is left with the dullard, Alexander III.

"The Prisoner of Acca wrote also to the Emperor Franz Josef, of the Habsburg holdings; the Kaiser of Germany; and our Queen. It can be argued that the emperor and the kaiser are still quite alive and their nations flourishing, but perhaps their stories are not over. In England, we have been pleased to see the unification of the Germanys, as the Germans are a talented and organizational people and should be good for Europe. Surely, they are better than France, who cannot, since her own revolution in 1789, get her government in order or her people stabilized.

"As for our Queen, I am told He wrote to her, saying that because she had entrusted her government to Parliament and the people and outlawed slavery, she would be well-rewarded.[1]

"I can hardly imagine any reward that would mean much to her, however, as she wishes for only three things: that her throne will be safe from overthrow and that her 'dear Albert,' as she always refers to him, will be remembered. She has never been happy since Albert died in 1861. Over thirty years is a long time to mourn and may account largely for her third desire—the return of Christ.

"'I wish he would come in my lifetime,' they say she once remarked to the Archbishop.

"'And why is that, Madame?'

"'Because I would so love to lay my crown at His feet.'

"But she lives and rules and grieves . . . and bides her time until she can join 'dear Albert.'[2]

"He wrote to the rulers of the American republics as well, which brings me to my point about the fruition of the bloody years of the Bábís. I had not heard about this until Margaret and I visited the Colonies a year ago or so. A brash and unmannerly people, the Americans are nevertheless filled with energy and optimism. They have an almost childlike way of doing what they believe needs doing without doubting their ability to do it, and one cannot help but admire that.

"Margaret and I attended, as part of the British delegation, the 1893 Columbian Exposition, held in Chicago. Chicago is largely an industrial city, not unlike Liverpool but larger, and set in the middle of the prairie country. It is surrounded on three sides by huge grain farms, larger than any farms I have ever seen in England. The city is a sort of oasis of civilization set in the middle of the wilderness, although we did not see any Indians. Margaret was relieved, as she had been afraid we might be attacked by them, even though I had assured her over and over that most of them were gone now to lands well west of the prairie country.

"The other thing about Chicago is that it sits on the shore of one of the Great Lakes. They are certainly aptly named. There are five of them, and when viewed from a map, one gets no idea of how large they are. We stood on the strand one day and looked eastward and could not see the other shore. It was a windy day, and the waves crashed against the shore just as the ocean waves do at home. It seemed like an ocean, and I see now why they are sometimes referred to as the Sweet Water Seas. Margaret could not believe the sheer size of the country—and we saw only the eastern half of it. Having traveled in Russia, in my earlier years, I was not as impressed as she with either the lake or the size of the country.

"At any rate, we enjoyed the Exposition. There were huge areas made up to be foreign lands, and so we "traveled" one day through "China," "Japan," "India," and "Siam"; another day we "visited" "Spain" and "Italy."

"They were selling beautiful lithographs of scenes from the various exhibits. We bought one in bold colors called "The Return to Mecca"—three men in Middle Eastern dress riding on camels. Margaret said if only they wore crowns it would be reminiscent of the Magi, but it reminded me somewhat of my stint in Persia. I shall hang it in my study. We also bought another of George Ferris's great wheel in which we had ridden. This one is in pastel colors and will be nice in our bedroom. We passengers—there must have been over a thousand of us at once—rode in chairs, thirty to a chair, (fifteen facing each other), fastened to a huge wheel close to fifty metres high. It turned on an axle, and when our chair reached the top, we could see for miles. We saw the grounds of the entire Exposition and even much of the city beyond. It was truly quite adventurous.

"But the *most* adventurous was when we visited the "American Wild West" and actually panned for gold in a simulated river. The children of the fair-goers loved that and dogged their poor parents, begging to be taken back again and again to the "Wild West" for another try at gold seeking.

"There was a Wild West Show at one point, and Margaret finally saw the much-dreaded Indians and cowboys shooting at one another, but of course it was all staged, so she soon overcame her fears. We were sorry our Johnny and the girls could not have come with us, but I felt fortunate the home office allowed me to take Margaret. Besides, at age eighteen, John was busy with his studies, as he was to enter my old college, Pembroke at Cambridge, that fall.

"The industrial part of the Exposition was reminiscent of Prince Albert's Crystal Palace Exposition in London (though not nearly so impressive).

"But my reason for including this in these notes is because of what occurred at the Congress of Religions, one of the groups of exhibitions at the fair; that fruition I have already mentioned. The purpose of the congress was to explore the differences and similarities in the world's religions and suggest ways in which they might help to bring about world peace. There were Buddhists, Hindus, Jews, Zoroastrians, and Christians of various denominations represented and speeches given by all sorts of clergymen.

"One of the ministers, a Scotch Presbyterian by the name of Jessup (if I remember correctly), could not attend but sent along his talk, which was delivered by someone else. He commented:

This then is our mission. That we, who are made in the image of God, should remember that all men are made in God's image. To this divine knowledge we owe all we are, all we hope for . . . In the palace of Bahji, just outside the fortress of Acre on the Syrian coast, there died a few months since, a famous Persian sage, the Bábí saint, named Bahá'u'lláh—the Glory of God—the head of a vast party of Muslims who accept the New Testament as the Word of God and Christ as the deliverer of men, who regard all nations as one and all men as brothers.[3]

"He went on to say that Bahá'u'lláh had been visited by a British scholar. That would be E. G. Browne, of course, of Cambridge. I had met him a time or two at reunions and that sort of thing at Pembroke—he turned out to be a rather good orientalist.

"But I was flabbergasted, to say the least. It was the first I had heard of the death of Bahá'u'lláh, and I was surprised that he had finally succumbed. At the same time, I was almost equally surprised that he had lived into his seventies after half his life spent in prison. I had not thought of him for a long while, but thinking of him now, naturally I also thought of 'S' and wondered if she had heard. I had seen her briefly in Paris in her daughter's establishment, a few years back, and though silver-haired and in her seventies as well, she was yet energetic and looked to me as though she were still the young woman I had known and remembered so well."

John thought to himself, *"Father never really forgot that woman! I wonder what she was like. What attracted him so?"* He continued reading:

"Because we had been so fascinated by the sight of the Great Lake Michigan, we decided to return to New York by way of steamship going north from Chicago, through the straits of Mackinac south down Lake Huron, east across Lake Erie, and thence by rail to New York City from Buffalo. I would have preferred to continue east on the Erie Canal, through to Lake Ontario, but Margaret, being the ardent suffragette she is, would not hear of bypassing the little town of Seneca Falls, N.Y. It seems that in 1848, the Women's Movement began there at a gathering in a little church. So we laid over a day in Syracuse and hired a horse cab to travel the twenty-some kilometres to the site and back.

"There was nothing to see but the church itself—a very small building, I must say—and hardly worth the extra trouble and expense. To Margaret, however, Elizabeth Cady Stanton and Emma Willard are true heroines, and it was as though she were standing on holy ground. While we were there I told her about Ṭáhirih.

"Long ago in St. Petersburg, on the night we had all seen the play about the Báb, 'S' had told me about her teacher, and I was surprised to find that the day Ṭáhirih appeared without her veil in front of a group of men and announced her act as symbolic of the establishment of the equality of women and men in the new message from God, occurred one month before the gathering in Seneca Falls. I remember the date only because the former coincided with my grandfather's birthday.

"'So,' I told Margaret, 'the Women's Movement actually began not in North America at all but in Persia.'

"'Maybe,' she said, 'but I'm sure the movement couldn't get very far—from way over in *that* backward country.'

"'It got to Seneca Falls, New York,' I said, teasing Margaret. 'That's quite a distance, don't you think?'

"'Oh, you!' Margaret said, laughing, and slapped my shoulder.

"Here, then, is the summary of my exposure to this series of events if, in the future, anyone ever cares to read these remarks of mine.

"The main body of Islam is the huge Sunni branch that converted the world from Arabia to the borders of China, to the Atlantic shores of Spain, to oriental provinces of Russia, and to Central Africa.

"In Persia, a smaller branch of Islam had flourished, the Shias, and from that lesser group, an obscure sect arose early in this century. Persia, once a great light of civilization, had become the most politically corrupt and intellectually backward of any country in the world, and out of that unlikely soil grew this pair of divinely inspired Prophets, who taught a message so revolutionary, so beyond the thinking of even the most sophisticated of scholars or clerics or statesmen, that it would seem at first hearing acceptable to none.

"The most outstanding of their teachings were world peace upheld by a world federation of nations, the end of slavery, and the equality of men and women. More, they taught the essential agreement of science and religion and the basic oneness of all revealed religions—each brought in its own time by its own Messenger of God. (So I believe Jessup was mistaken about their being Muslims; they are called *Bahá'ís* after their Founders, the Báb and Bahá'u'lláh.) They have taught that those Messengers—Abraham, Krishna, Moses, Zoroaster, Buddha, Jesus, Muḥammad, and now these two latest ones—are essentially one Messenger, as they speak with a single voice, the voice of the Holy Spirit.

"It seems so terribly visionary, so daunting, that it cannot possibly ever come to pass. And yet, I wonder. It has certainly fascinated me since those early days in Persia, and I think if I were younger, I would be tempted to look into it more.

"The first of those two Messengers was imprisoned and killed within six years. His inheritor of the mission was imprisoned and exiled for life, and yet his message reached the kings and rulers of the entire civilized world—almost all of whom have lost not only their thrones and their power, but their lives within the Prophet's lifetime. One wonders what will become of the rest of them.

"The people themselves have been hearing of the message in Europe since the days of the Báb. 'The divine Sarah' Bernhardt even commissioned Catoule Mendez to write a play for her on the life of Ṭáhirih. As for the New World, within one month of Ṭáhirih's announcement of the emancipation of women, the women of the West arose and called for equality. Within a year of the Prophet's expiration in his prison, his message was given to the New World at the great Colombian Exposition. (I cannot help but think of the biblical promise of Jesus, 'As the lightning cometh out of the East and shineth even unto the West; so shall also the coming of the Son of Man be.')[4]

"Before the Prophet's command to cease the practice of chatteled slavery was ever made public, the practice was outlawed throughout the civilized nations.

"I only recently heard that the telegraph was invented by Mr. Morse within twenty-four hours of the night the Báb declared his mission to Mullah Ḥusayn (flashing from east to west again, you see). "What hath God wrought?" Morse tapped out, quoting from the Book of Numbers—what indeed!* And since that night, an explosion of technology has leaped like that very lightning from the minds of men, filling the world with technical wonders beyond one's wildest imagination. The telegraph, the steamships, and railroads are making the world so much smaller than it was. These same engines can accomplish almost anything they are adapted to. One wonders if there is anything left to invent."

John smiled at that comment and thought, "*Now there is not only the telegraph but the telephone; not only railroads but automobiles; and most recently—though it is doubtful if they can ever be put to any practical use—even the flying machines that are the latest craze among the more daring of the experimenters. I understand the army has bought fifty of them and is playing about with them, hoping to make use of them somehow, though I certainly cannot imagine how. Perhaps they wish to observe troop movements.*"

His father continued:

"It is interesting to me that Bahá'u'lláh, writing from his prison in Acca, promised the kings and rulers that by following his advice, they could now bring about the long dreamed of peace on Earth—what we have always called the Millenium—which has been promised by the Founder of every major religion.

"Perhaps they could have—but they did not. Instead, each has suffered not only death but the disintegration of his throne.

"Now he has promised the peoples of the world, that if they will spread his message of peace and reconciliation among nations, races and religions, peace is still possible.[5]

* Numbers 23:23.

"If he first wrote to the kings in 1867and died last year in 1892, surely there is time enough for the people of the world to act. But what if they do not? What if the people who have been charged to deliver this message fail to deliver it, or the people of the world—like their kings before them—refuse to listen. What will happen to the human race then?

"He has written, 'The world is in travail, and its agitation waxeth day by day. Its face is turned towards waywardness and unbelief. Such shall be its plight, that to disclose it now would not be meet and seemly.'[6]

"If Bahá'u'lláh is Who he claims to be, then I close these notes at last, and that with a bit of a shudder when I think of what may be coming. In any case I shall not be here, and I do find that a comfort."

* * *

John laid his father's papers down on the floor beside his chair. After a thoughtful silence, he said, "Carrie, do you remember my telling you about that prisoner my father had been writing about in his papers?"

"Yes, Love, of course I remember."

"I read in the Times that his son is coming to London in September. I want to go to see him. Would you like to come along?"

"Oh, I don't think so, dear," she said absently, recounting the stitches in her knitting.

"We could make rather a jolly week's end of it. We could have a nice dinner at the hotel and maybe see a play—something good doing at the Haymarket that week, I've read. Come along, Old Girl, what do you say?"

"John, we really shouldn't spend the money."

"Sweetheart, I truly plan to see this man, so the money's spent whether you come or not. It would get you out, be good for you. Do please change your mind."

"Who would take care of the animals?"

"I'll get the veterinarian's lad to look in on them." After a brief silence, he coaxed, "Carrie?"

Carrie sighed. "Alright, John" she said, capitulating. "If it will make you happy."

"But it is you I want to be happy," John thought to himself. Then, remembering that she had consented to come along, and that at least this was a small victory, he rose from his chair, and with a heartiness he did not truly feel, planted a kiss on the top of her blonde head, saying, "That's my girl! We'll have a grand time!"

On the ninth day of the month, they took the rail into London, where they were to see and hear 'Abdu'l-Bahá the next day. He had recently returned to Palestine from Egypt, and now had come to England.

Two years before, the Young Turks Rebellion had taken place in the Ottoman Empire. 'Abdu'l-Hamid, the son of 'Abdu'l-Aziz—that sultan of Turkey who, along with Náṣiri'd-Dín Sháh, had sent Bahá'u'lláh into prison forty years earlier—suddenly found himself deposed. All the political prisoners of the Turkish regime were set free. Among them was 'Abdu'l-Bahá. He had been twenty-seven years old when he had entered the citadel of Acca with his father and their companions. Now he was sixty-eight. His had, from the time of his early childhood when they were driven out of Persia to Baghdad, been a life of physical and mental hardship. Now, his health was precarious. Immediately, he undertook a journey to Egypt to rest and to recover somewhat in its milder climate.

He stayed for some months, then undertook the first of several journeys.

On September 4th, he traveled to England. On Sunday the 7th, he gave the first public talk of his life in City Temple, and it was there that Carrie and John came to hear him. John had persuaded Carrie to try one of the horseless cabs that were now beginning to fill the streets of London. They traveled from the hotel at ten or twelve miles an hour, and at first Carrie was frightened at the speed and found the engine noise unpleasant, but by the time they had arrived at City Temple, she was beginning to be used to it and actually to enjoy it a little.

The crowd was large and had gathered early. The huge church hummed with the murmur of voices as they waited for the service to begin. At last the organ was played, and this quieted the conversations of the curious. Wearing a cream-colored robe and a low taj wrapped in white linen,

'Abdu'l-Bahá moved to the pulpit of City Temple. His hair and beard were silver, and his face was lined with the creases of a lifetime of suffering. But his step was firm, his eyes bright, and most of all he radiated a power that moved everyone in the great sanctuary.

As 'Abdu'l-Bahá rose to speak, with his translator beside him, a hush fell over the congregation as though it held its collective breath.

> "Oh Noble friends," he said, "seekers after God! Praise be to God! Today the light of Truth is shining upon the world in its abundance; the breezes of the heavenly garden are blowing thoughout all regions; the call of the Kingdom is heard in all lands, and the breath of the Holy Spirit is felt in all hearts that are faithful. . . .
>
> "This is a new cycle of human power. All the horizons of the world are luminous, and the world will become indeed as a garden and a paradise. It is the hour of unity of the sons of men, and of the drawing together of all races and all classes. You are loosed from the ancient superstitions which have kept men ignorant, destroying the foundations of true humanity.
>
> "The gift of God in this enlightened age is the knowledge of the oneness of mankind and of the fundamental oneness of religion. War shall cease between nations, and by the will of God the Most Great Peace shall come; the world will be seen as a new world, and all men will live as brothers.
>
> "In the days of old an instinct for warfare was developed in the struggle with wild animals; this is no longer necessary; nay, rather, co-operation and mutual understanding are seen to produce the greatest welfare of mankind. Enmity is now the result of prejudice only. . . .
>
> "This is today the teaching for the East and for the West; therefore the East and West will understand each other and reverence each other, and embrace like long-parted lovers who have found each other.
>
> "There is one God; mankind is one; the foundations of religion are one. Let us worship Him, and give praise for all His great Prophets and Messengers who have manifested His brightness and glory.

"The blessing of the Eternal One be with you in all its richness . . ."[7]

After the service ended, the sanctuary was nearly silent. Most people rose and left quietly, and the only sounds were the rustle of clothing and an occasional voice in a low tone. Carrie and John left without speaking. John hailed an open horse-cab to take them to the hotel. On the way, John said, "I wonder in what manner the peace his Father promised will come about. Surely, with the wars we have seen in the last several years, he can't mean that this will come to pass any time soon. My father seemed to think that it might come in a hundred years. What do you make of it, Carrie?"

"What?" she said, absently. "What did you say?"

"I asked you what you thought of what he said."

"I don't know, dear. I thought it was all lovely, but I found it hard to keep my mind on it, what with him speaking in Persian and then the translator taking over."

"You were bored?" John was incredulous.

"No! Not at all! I was so happy I just couldn't keep my mind on what he was saying. John, the minute I looked at him, I was overtaken by the most intense feeling of happiness. And then, all at once, he looked at me."

"Yes, he included everyone. He's a very good speaker."

"No, John, it was just after he said, 'The breath of the Holy Spirit is felt in all hearts that are faithful.' Then when He said, 'you are loosed from the ancient superstitions which have kept men ignorant,' he looked deliberately and directly at *me*! And I don't understand it, but suddenly I knew that God loves me . . . loves us all! I've thought that maybe God doesn't love me very much because of what . . . what I tried to do, but when 'Abdu'l-Bahá looked at me, it filled me with such joy that I forgot where I was or what he was saying. I just felt happy to be alive and so peaceful, a peace such as I have never . . . well, you know, 'the peace that passeth understanding!'" Her eyes were shining! "God takes care of us, and will give us what we need in this life, John. He gives and yes, He takes away, but whatever He does, He does out of His love for us. So whatever happens from now on . . . whether we ever have children or not . . . is alright. She looked intensely at her husband, "John, it is *all* alright!"

John watched her face, saw the long-missing brightness in her eyes and was silent a moment, remembering that terrifying night he had sat beside her barely breathing form quoting, as though in a prayer, "*All shall be well, and all manner of things be well.*" "Oh, Carrie," he said, "My own sweet Carrie! You have come back to me!"

Then with the horse's hooves clopping in the background and in the full sight of the city of London, he folded her in his arms and kissed her.

34

CONFESSIONS: 1913

JMJ

My life changed after the long night that had ended with my forgiveness of my father. Oh, not immediately. But slowly I began to realize that something in me had been sad all my life—I had always known I was angry, but not sad. I found the sky bluer and the sunlight sweeter and life in general to be an altogether more pleasant experience than I had ever thought it might be. Little things—thunderstorms, nesting birds, and the laughter of children—were now pleasures that brightened my hours and brought unbidden smiles to my lips. My prayers were more sincere, my Masses said with more emotion, and my interaction with other souls more forgiving and compassionate.

The strangest part of all this is that it had never occurred to me in all my nearly fifty years that I was *not* forgiving and compassionate. It was after all, my life's work to offer forgiveness and commiserate with those who were in sorrow. But, of course, that is the whole point, isn't it? The words of absolution had been repeated from a ritual, and expressions of compassion had come, for the most part, from a sense of obligation (if not superiority)—but not truly, deeply from my heart. I realized that I had always thought of the phrase from the "Our Father"—"as we forgive those who trespass against us" as merely a difficult condition imposed by

God as payment rendered to secure our own forgiveness. Never, until the night of "awakening," had it occurred to me that it was, instead, a great gift from Him, a gift that not only insures our forgiveness but sets us free of anger and fills us with joy.

In 1888, I made a visit to the Emperor Franz Josef. I had not seen him for years, not since he had made his long desired pilgrimage to the Holy Land and had stopped by Rome on his way. He had received a second letter from the Prisoner in those days and was, I understood, chided by him for coming to Palestine without even inquiring of the Prisoner's whereabouts, a mere courtesy he had callously neglected. As the years had gone by, he became more autocratic than ever out of his fear of the loss of control, I believe, which would ultimately mean the loss of the empire. The result was that his is the most absolute despotism ever maintained among men. He has even been heard to say to a professor, "I want obedient subjects, not men of learning."[1]

Poor Franz Josef was growing older, and his marriage to "Sissy" had long ago gone sour. As for Sissy herself, she had gone mad. All of value that was left to him by then was his only son, Prince Rudolph.

Now, I had the unpleasant duty of calling upon him in his latest sorrow. It seems that Prince Rudolph and his mistress were dead. Since they were unable to marry, they had made a lovers' pact, and he had murdered her and committed suicide one day in his hunting lodge. This left, as the only heir to the great Habsburg throne, the emperor's nephew, the Archduke Frances Ferdinand. He was married to a commoner named Sophie, universally disapproved of by the citizens, and the emperor was in despair that his throne would be lost by some kind of royal default. His entire life had been, in my view, a series of tragedies—one following upon another. I couldn't help thinking that had Mario been around, he would surely have found a connection between the emperor's tragic life and the prisoner's letter. Moreover, no doubt, he would have surely pointed it out to me.

In 1899, I was elevated to archbishop. I feared, at first hearing of it, that it would necessitate my leaving Paris, which I had come to love with my whole heart, but was relieved to find that Paris was my assignment and that I would be there more or less permanently. I bought some new things for my apartment, now that I had hopes that this would be my permanent home, and made it more comfortable and inviting. It had a nice view of the city, and during the next four years, I enjoyed watching from my window the construction of Mr. Eiffel's strange looking tower—the tallest man-made structure in the world, they were saying. It appeared to be made of bare bones, and I kept waiting for them to clothe it with some kind of "skin," but it seemed as though they were just going to leave the thing that way.

I had yearned for this day so long because it was the final step before the red hat of a cardinal, which I had coveted since my youth. Now that my ambition was nearly fulfilled, I was surprised to find that my strongest reaction was that I should not have to leave my chosen city. The man I once had been felt guilty for feeling more love for a French city than for Rome, but the man I was becoming said a hurried act of contrition and shrugged the guilt away.

My friendship with Khadijah and her mother, Shirin Khánum, had continued to deepen over the years. Khadijah was very wealthy now and gave large sums to the church—always, she said, in gratitude for her many blessings: the life of her daughter, who is happily married with several children; the health of her now aging mother; and her love of her own calling in this world—the art of design.

In my new freedom of soul, I realized how much I missed Mario, and knew I would have to go about finding him. A year or so before, I had attempted several avenues of inquiry, with no results. One evening, I read in "Le Monde" that the son of the Persian prisoner who had so entranced Mario was coming to Paris to visit and would be speaking in a number of places. *If Mario is alive and in Europe,* I thought, *he will be here for that!* I felt sure that if I should go to where this 'Abdu'l-Bahá was speaking, surely I would find Mario there.

I mentioned it one evening to Khánum. "Have you ever heard," I asked her, "of a Persian called Bahá'u'lláh, who was exiled to Palestine and died there as a prisoner a few years ago?"

"Indeed I have!" she said, her face lighting up, "In fact, as a very young woman, I once saw him. He was visiting my employer."

"You saw him? You actually saw him? What was he like?"

"He was not at all tall and wore a long beard. He was exquisitely courteous, impeccably clean, and dressed well. Beyond that it is impossible to describe him."

"Because?"

She looked off into the distance for a moment and finally said, "I don't know. He was gentle and had a wonderful sense of humor, I remember. But he was more—majestic in his bearing and possessed of much personal power. He had a look of great intelligence about him. Yet, none of this quite describes him. But you must remember that I saw him only once and that so briefly and from some distance. I know only how deeply he impressed me and that I have never forgotten it. In fact, I almost never think of home—that is, of Persia—without remembering that moment."

"Interesting," I thought.

"I would not have thought *you* would have heard of him," she said.

"Oh. Well. I heard about him in Rome some years ago," I said desultorily. "I mention it only because his son, 'Abdu'l-Bahá, is coming to Paris to speak later this year. I thought because he is Persian, you might wish to hear him. I would be more than happy to escort you."

"I should be most pleased to go with you, Monseigneur," she said.

I smiled at her. "Don't you find 'Monseigneur' a little unwieldy? Please, Khánum, we are old friends. 'Father' will do nicely."

"If you like, Father," she responded. "I think perhaps he might like to see someone here in France who had seen his father, don't you?"

"I do," I said, smiling.

We found he was to speak at Number Four, Avenue de Camoens on November 10th, and we were able to go to hear him. My first concern was to find Mario—if he were there—and I spent a good deal of time looking for him, but alas, he appeared not to have come.

There was an air of expectancy in the room, and soon the Persian man entered in a robe and turban. He radiated such power and kindness that the people gathered there were all but breathless. As for me, my mind had been on Mario, and I had not planned to pay much attention to anything he said, but found myself listening in spite of myself.

He was speaking about the search for truth.

He said that we must, first of all, shut our eyes to all the superstitions of the past. Jews, Buddhists, Christians, and Muslims—in fact all religions—have become bound by tradition and dogma. All consider themselves the only guardians of truth, and every other religion is composed of errors. He said that in so doing, they limit themselves. I thought of how much Mario would agree with that and of how often we had spoken in the old days of that very thought.

'Abdu'l-Bahá went on to tell us that we should remember that the forms and practices of religions were really only the garments which "clothe the warm heart and living limbs of Divine Truth."

In order to find truth, he told us, we must first empty ourselves of preconceived notions and give up our prejudices, because if our chalice is full of self, there is no room in it for the Water of Life. I found that an amazing statement; in fact, I had discovered its truth that night of my "awakening." That we imagine ourselves to be right and everyone else wrong is the greatest of all obstacles in the path towards unity, and unity is necessary if we would reach truth, for truth is one.

By now I was beginning to scribble notes. I was able to get this much:

> "Science must be accepted. No one truth can contradict another Truth. Light is good in whatsoever lamp it is burning! A rose is beautiful in whatsoever garden it may bloom! A star has the same radiance if it shines from the East or from the West. Be free from prejudice, so will you love the Sun of Truth from whatsoever point in the horizon it may arise! You will realize that if the Divine light of Truth shone in Jesus Christ it also shone in Moses and in Buddha. The earnest seeker will arrive at this truth. . . . 'Seek the truth, the truth shall make you free.' So shall we see the truth in all religions, for truth is in all and truth is one!"[2]

Later, we all took tea together in a nearby reception room and had nice conversations. Seated on my right, I noticed Khánum speaking with someone. He was in his early thirties, I imagined, and he and his wife seemed pleasant. They were English, I gathered, as their French (not unlike mine), was heavily accented.

The atmosphere was quiet and decorous, yet there was good cheer all around and much soft laughter. Khánum and the young couple seemed engrossed with each other, so I occupied myself looking around at the many types of people who were attending this function. They were comprised of the obviously very wealthy and some not so wealthy, as well as Frenchmen, Englishmen, and Easterners. In fact, one Eastern man was a strange fellow. Small and energetic, he limped when he walked. He was rather old and of a homely countenance—almost ugly really; his nose had been broken at some point, and even his jaw seemed a little misshapen. Yet, in spite of all this, his eyes were bright and intelligent, and he had almost all of those around him laughing. A comical fellow, perhaps, I thought, but singularly lacking in dignity. I asked someone about him, and he said only that his name is Hamid and that he loves the Master very much. He also said that the Master is much amused by him. I couldn't imagine why, but then I am one who is not comfortable around cripples.

Khánum's young acquaintance, begging my indulgence, asked me if we would be returning for more of the series of talks. Khánum looked at me with a question in her eyes, so I said we definitely would come again. She seemed pleased, and besides, I was still hoping to find Mario.

After I had taken Khánum home and returned to my rooms, I poured myself a glass of Port and thought about Mario and how much I missed him. I thought, too, about what the Persian had said and how Mario would have loved the discussion we might have had about it all.

Jesus has said, "The truth shall make you free." When I had realized, that long and difficult night, the truth of who I (*and* my father), actually was, one facet of that truth had surely set *me* free—free of my anger and its attendant ambition, and the long unacknowledged sadness of my life.

Though we had known the words of our Lord all our lives, we had never understood the corollary—that truth is one. We had accepted only those scientific truths that had not disagreed with religious truth. But if God is one, then truth can only be one, and true science and true religion must meet somewhere at a point of oneness. Could it be, I wondered, that we do not know enough about either science *or* religion to make the judgments we have always made?

These thoughts were becoming much too heavy for my weary mind at this late hour, so I drained my glass and went to bed.

35

SHIRIN: 1911

Khadijah, known to the fashion world as "Madame Catrine," had become extremely wealthy. Women from Paris, Rome, London, and even some from the United States paid exorbitant prices for her designs, and the original shop in our house on Rue de Rivoli had been returned to a parlor, though she still designed at home, in Katherine Shaydah's old room, adapted now into her studio. The new La Maison de Catrine was located in a building she owned not far from La Gallerie LaFayette, where she employed a sizable staff of seamstresses, an elegant showroom, and comfortable fitting rooms to pamper the wealthy customers.

Our house now was sometimes the scene of gay gatherings and soirees, as she was socially in much demand, but never again was she impressed with all the wealth and finery as she had been in her youth.

Katherine had three children—Marcel, Rubin, and Gisele—who were now all grown up, and we all spent a great deal of time together. The oldest, Marcel, had married a young woman named Cecile when he was twenty-five. They have a little boy, Jean Michael, who is nearly four now. We still see Rubin often, as he has continued to be close to his three children, and is a doting grandfather. He had a difficult time adjusting to the idea that his grandson was to be named for him while he was still alive.

"Jews don't do that, Katherine," he had said. "Why don't you just wish me dead?"

But Katherine merely laughed at him and said, "Oh Father, you may be Jewish, but we're not, so you shall just have to get used to it." He grumped about it, but I think he was secretly pleased. Now, of course, he is a doting great-grandfather to Jean Michael. He and Khadijah, thank God, have moved into a friendly old age.

And I am a proud great-great-grandmother! It seems impossible to me that I have grown so old. I certainly do not feel old in my mind and heart, but at ninety-seven, my body reminds me with each passing month that it is growing exceedingly tired of its job. The stairs are considerably steeper than they used to be, and the days longer. Neither do I get about as well as I used to, with these thickening cataracts, and I am developing some difficulty hearing. And of course, it goes without saying that there are now daily assorted aches and pains. I sometimes need help walking in strange surroundings because of my vision, and then too, everyone is afraid I may fall. That is to say, everyone but me. The most difficult part, of course, is that I can read for only a few minutes at a time, and I know that soon now I will no longer able to read at all—my favorite thing! With a little good luck, I may leave this tired old stick of a body and go on to something better before that happens.

It was not long ago that Padre Vittorio came over one evening, as he often does, to while away the evening with us, and invited me to accompany him to hear the son of the late Mírzá Ḥusayn-'Alí Nurí. It seems he is coming to Paris to speak to his followers and others who may be interested. I was excited to go, because 'Abdu'l-Bahá will speak to me in Persian, which no one does anymore except Khadijah and sometimes Katherine. Then too, perhaps I can do a small kindness for him. After having spent his entire life as a prisoner with his whole family suffering so, I am sure he must be a very sad man, and meeting someone who has seen his father may bring to him a little bit of cheer.

Padre says he wants to attend to see if he can locate his old friend, but I think it is a little more than that. He has a fine mind, and we enjoy our long discussions. There are moments when I am reminded of my old friendship with dear Zhukovsky, yet, I find the Archbishop Vittorio something of an enigma. At times he seems rigid and proselytizing in his beliefs, then he evinces an interest in this new movement that has come out of an Islamic nation. When he was made a bishop, he was very insistent that he be addressed as Monseignour, but now that he is an archbishop, he laughs and says "Father" will be title enough. Perhaps, like most of us, he is beginning to mellow as he approaches old age.

At any rate, we went to hear 'Abdu'l-Bahá speak. So as not to offend him, I wore again one of my old head scarves, but I thought later that perhaps it had not been necessary. He spoke entirely in Farsi, and his words were translated sentence by sentence. I was so delighted to hear it. It sounded like music to me. He looked at me once and smiled. I think he knew how much I was enjoying the familiar sounds.

His talk was wonderful! He said that we need to accept the truths that can be found in all the religions. It comforted me a great deal, as I have worried over this division of beliefs all my life. All consider themselves the only guardians of truth, he said, and every other religion composed of errors. He said that in so doing, they limit themselves. The moment I heard that, a great hope rose up in my breast, and I began to wonder if the amity of religions might actually be possible. I understood, suddenly, what a driving quest this had been for me.

I was disappointed that I did not get a chance to speak with him, however, because he was very tired and retired as soon as he had finished his talk. I did so want to tell him I remember his father. However, I had another opportunity a few evenings later.

Also, something else occurred that evening that was, for me, momentous! Seated in soft chairs near me was a young couple, an Englishman and his wife. They had come from England just to hear 'Abdu'l-Bahá. After the talk had ended, we began to speak with one another. He introduced himself, saying, "My name is John Hillhouse, and this is my wife Carolyn. May I ask who you might be?"

"I am called Shirin," I answered, "but you are English, are you not?"

"Yes—from a small village on the River Wye, near the Welsh border."

"Is that so? I once knew an Edward Hillhouse, of Her Majesty's diplomatic service. I don't suppose there is any connec . . ."

His eyes grew wide and he all but jumped from his chair. "My father!" he said. "You knew my father? Carrie! This lady knew my father!"

"Mr. Hillhouse is your father? How wonderful to meet you!"

"*So this is Edward's beloved little Johnny!*" I thought. He resembled him in face, but he had Margaret's coloring. In a moment I asked him how his father fared, and he was forced to tell me that Edward had died in nineteen and aught nine. A wave of sorrow constricted my throat for a moment and moved from there to my breast.

"I'm sorry," I said.

We talked about him for a long while, and I told him about meeting his father in Russia so many years ago and of the gay times we all had shared with the Dolgoruky's. Just to be able to speak freely of him set free my spirit in some way, and my heart was singing.

"Your first name is Shirin? Is that correct?"

"Yes."

"With an 'S,' I should think . . . well, of course."

"Of course."

"Madam, it is such a pleasure to meet you! I never thought I would ever see you . . . that is, meet someone who knew Father in Russia. He often spoke fondly of those days."

"I met your mother here in Paris some years ago. She was so warm and friendly. I hope she is well," but he said she also had died, a year or so earlier than Edward. I expressed my sympathy for his losses.

With Father Vittorio's agreement, we made arrangements to meet again on the 12th, when 'Abdu'l-Bahá was to speak again.

That night after we had returned home, I was able to think about Edward and his passing. I wept a few tears, of course, but I had known that day in the shoppe when he and Margaret walked away that I would never see him again. Too, I am very old and have outlived almost everybody I have ever loved, so this was hardly unexpected. I saw then that my love for Edward had been my third sorrowful journey—and that it was over. I was relieved that, at my age, I would not have to "travel" anymore.

I realized that this latest loss, though real, was not burdensome. It seemed I had come to see death altogether differently than once. When I thought of all those I had lost—beginning with my childhood friend Maria, a Christian child whose presence in my life set me on this very quest for agreement between religions—it was a long list indeed. I saw that each one of them, more than merely being someone I loved, had brought me a great gift; that each had become a part of me, indeed that we had *exchanged* each other. When the Christians marry, they say that "the two are become one." It is true, but not only in marriage. We become a part of whomever we love, and the exchange is real and irretrievable.

And how enriched I was! My mother; Uncle Firuz; 'Alí Taqí; my sweet baby girl and bright son Hasan; the Lady Shaydah and Mírzá Abbas; my dear friend Zhukovsky; my revered teacher, Ṭáhirih; my wise and funny friend Too-Tee; and now my forever beloved Edward; none of them had been lost at all, because—for a moment I almost said, "they live in my memory," but that is not accurate, for memory is simple and cerebral, as in "2 + 2 are 4." No, they are within me, and I see their faces in my heart's eye, and as with Hasan, hear their laughter in my dreams. They live in my center, as constant as artesian wells, forever trying my patience, making me laugh, hurting my feelings and nourishing my soul, flowing with a vitality as real and alive as when they were clothed in their flesh, and I am never without them.

'Abdu'l-Bahá had said that we had entered the great age of unity—of oneness, and I saw suddenly that the oneness applied not just to the oneness of religions but to all those things we sometimes believe are so different, even in opposition. I was reminded of the day so long ago when I remarked to Rubin on the beach at Cobourg that the striations in the sand and the striations on the Chambered Nautilus seem so similar that I sometimes felt as if there were a oneness—an invisible but nonetheless real connection—to each of us and to all creation, a oneness that, in spite of its antitheses and variety, binds it all together.

It occurred to me that night that the oneness is total, involving the entire universe, and that it is no wonder we may come to understand that all is one, for God is one, and not just man but all creation is made in His image. The Christians say that God has "reconciled the whole world unto Himself."[1]

I have always felt that Islam believes that in her own fulfillment, she will bring about the oneness of the world . . . and of course, it is true, because if the Revelation of Bahá'u'lláh is true, then His Revelation *is* the Fulfillment of Islam even as it is the fulfillment of all the other religions as well, and so *will* bring about the oneness of the world! Or rather *has* brought about the oneness of the world . . . we have just not recognized it yet.[2]

Jesus is correct, and Muḥammad is correct; in that sense, the two have already become one. So it is certain that sooner or later all differences will be reconciled. No wonder 'Abdu'l-Bahá has said that the East and the West will come to embrace like long lost lovers!

With this discovery a huge contentment came over me, and as I drifted off to sleep I thought, "Oh, Edward, your favorite poet, the late Mr. Thompson, put it perfectly didn't he? 'Thou canst not stir a flower, without troubling of a star.'"

36

CONFESSIONS: 1913

JMJ

Two evenings later, I again picked up Khánum, and this time Khadijah came with us. We returned to the house on Rue de Camoens and prepared to hear the man they are all calling "the Master."

This time he spoke on science and religion and how they are essentially one. Again, he offered the idea that Truth is one—indeed, that all things are one in what he calls this "age of Unity."

He went on to say:

> "There is no contradiction between true religion and science. When a religion is opposed to science it becomes mere superstition: that which is contrary to knowledge is ignorance. . . . The true principles of all religions are in conformity with the teachings of science. . . . All religions teach that we must do good, that we must be generous, sincere, truthful, law-abiding, and faithful; all this is reasonable, and logically the only way in which humanity can progress.
>
> "All religious laws conform to reason, and are suited to the people for whom they are framed, and for the age in which they are to be obeyed.

> "The spiritual part never changes. All the Manifestations of God" [what I take him to mean Divine Messengers] "have taught the same truths and given the same spiritual law. They teach the one code of morality. There is no division in the truth. The Sun has sent forth many rays to illumine human intelligence, the light is always the same.
>
> "In the time of Moses, there were ten crimes punishable by death. When Christ came this was changed; the old axiom of "an eye for an eye, and a tooth for a tooth" was converted into "Love your enemies and do good to them that hate you."[1]

So it is that the practical aspects of religion suit the needs of the age, he told us, but the spiritual law never changes. Truth is one, and the essentials of all religions are one. Then he went on to say that religion and science are like the two wings of one bird and that if a bird tries to fly with only one wing, it will fall. So it is that we need both science and religion. A child cannot understand that the earth revolves around the sun until he grows older, he told us. In the same way, we do not always understand either scientific truth or religious truth, but the truths themselves are never contrary to one another. I was excited to realize that this was the answer to the very question I had posed to myself the other night.

Truth is one. I like that concept. No wonder Mario joined these people.

After his talk, he stayed and people came up to speak with him. One woman handed him a huge bouquet of roses. He thanked her graciously and then immediately began to give them away one by one. I saw that he gave the first one to that odd little ugly man—that Hamid.

I watched as Kh̲ánum greeted 'Abdu'l-Baha and that he took her hands and spoke to her with a sweet smile. He gave her a rose. She returned to her chair afterward, holding the rose against her cheek and smiling but with tears running down her face. She was not alone, however; many who spoke with him returned weeping . . . weeping and smiling! How does he touch their hearts so?

I thought I might speak with him as well. I approached him, and he looked up at me and took my hands. It seemed as though he knew who I was. Oh, not that I am the archbishop for this area; everyone knows that, of course, but as though he had known me from my boyhood, had known my long history of pain at the hands of my father, of my long hatred and my unholy ambition—known and understood. I was merely going to thank him for his talk and tell him that I had long believed that science and religion might be agreeable, but I never had the chance to tell him. I had noticed that he wore a white rose tucked into the sash around the waist of his robe, and with a twinkling smile, he tucked one of the gift roses into my purple sash of which I have been so proud. It was bright red and clashed with the purple, as the holiness of his spirit clashed with my ecclesiastical ambitions, and I felt ashamed. I, who no longer truly believed in "the rite of confession," wanted to confess to him, longing for his absolution and his guidance, but again he seemed to anticipate my thought.

Smiling at me and patting my shoulder, he told me the world needed men who could help bring her into the future, that the Revelation of Bahá'u'lláh was for all humankind, and that if I chose, I could help her to grow into this understanding of oneness—the oneness of science and religion, the oneness of faiths, the oneness of the human family. It made me so happy to hear him say these things to me. I had all but forgotten the bliss I had sometimes experienced in my boyhood prayers, but here with this man, I felt it again—that sweet burning that filled my breast and moved from there out into all of my being.

And then he said the strangest thing to me. I don't recall the exact words, but it was something about it being a long time since I had first heard the call of God, and that it is good that, at last, I am awakening from my sleep. I am almost certain that what he said must have been coincidental. Otherwise, how could he have known?

During the reception, after the talk, while we were all having tea and little cakes, I heard someone softly calling my name from my left. I looked up to see a couple walking toward me. At first I failed to recognize him, in trousers and with a woman on his arm, but then I burst into a great grin, because of course it was Mario! We embraced, and now *I* was in tears. We stood holding one another by the arms and staring into each other's eyes, then embraced again, then stared, repeating this odd little dance a number of times.

At last Mario introduced me to his companion—his wife, Francesca. She is dark, as opposed to his blond complexion, and quiet, though rather frank and strong—a perfect foil for my emotional friend. I took to her immediately. I introduced them to Khánum and Khadijah, and to John and Carolyn Hillhouse. We all sat together and had tea and the little cakes. Suffice it to say that the seven of us somehow became instant friends and have since spent many a happy hour together, often having evenings at Khánum and Khadijah's.

Another evening, when we had gone to hear 'Abdu'l-Bahá, Mario introduced us to the little Persian man, Hamid. I found it difficult to be around him. I may have already mentioned that his face was misshapen, nor had it been handsome to begin with. What is more, because his mouth was twisted, his French was terrible, and he tended to spray when he spoke. We all had trouble understanding him. Khánum, being Persian, had less trouble and was able to help us considerably. He said very little, except to make occasional remarks that seemed to delight everyone but merely succeeded in getting on my nerves. I was polite, of course, but, I must confess, his presence took some of the pleasure from my evening.

I do not have notes of what 'Abdu'l-Bahá talked about that evening, but he said several things that were amusing, and we all laughed. I realized then that my dream of Mario, Khánum, and me, sitting and listening to "someone" give a talk and laughing had literally come true. That déjà vu and 'Abdu'l-Bahá's earlier comment about my "awakening" made two strange events. These experiences left me feeling . . . umm . . . somewhat unsettled.

His subject was something about seeing only the best qualities in one another and ignoring the not-so-good qualities. It was about doing our very best to serve one another. I thought that, as a priest, I had spent my life not only in service but in forgiveness of sins. If, as it seemed, he had understood my ignoble and ambitious striving, then he would no doubt see my service as well and, I hoped, would at least approve of me on that score.

After his talk, he began serving tea to the guests with his own hands. Since he was the honored guest at this gathering, it seemed to me someone ought to be serving him. Nevertheless, he came to me first. Since becoming an archbishop, I am often treated with deference and served first, but this was something of a surprise. I confess I felt rather flattered as he approached bearing two cups of tea, and as I reached for one of them, he asked me if I would be so kind as to serve it to his friend, Hamid. I could hardly refuse. As Hamid reached out for the teacup with both hands, the sleeves of his robe fell away, exposing his wrists. How shocked I was to see them! They were scarred and red, and the marks were dug so deeply into his flesh that I couldn't help wondering why his hands had not been severed. We all noticed it, and Carolyn even gasped. He looked up at her and smiled. "Don't fret about these," he said, eyes shining, "These are as precious gifts to me. I received them in prison, in the service of my Lord."*

The entire group of us fell quiet. *"Gifts!"* I thought. "*No wonder the man acts strangely and jumps about so; he is mad!*" Then I realized that not since St. Peter had asked to be crucified upside down because he felt unworthy to die as our Lord Christ had died had I heard of this kind of devotion—except, perhaps, for several of the saints. I began then, for the first time, to wonder seriously just *who* this Bahá'u'lláh is to inspire men to such passion.

John and Mario pressed Hamid to tell us about more about it, but he would say very little—only that he had been a follower of the Báb and later Bahá'u'lláh since childhood.

Later we heard his story from one of the Paris believers, a woman named Blanche.

He was born in Tabriz in 1844, she told us, the year both of 'Abdu'l-Bahá's birth and of the Declaration of the Báb. His parents believed the Báb to be a heretic and took Hamid, at the age of six, to watch the Báb's execution. Later they became believers. During the years of the thousands of martyrs, his parents, who were farmers, were burned to death in their own house.

"Why wasn't he burned?" Carolyn asked, "Was it because he was a child?"

---

* The conversations related between Vittorio and 'Abdu'l-Bahá are fiction and based on what is known about the nature of 'Abdu'l-Bahá's interactions with people in real life.

"Being a child would not have saved him," Blanche said. "Had they seen him, he would have been killed as well. Rather, he was in the field fetching the goats for the evening milking and saw it all from a distance where he had hidden behind a rock. He was about eleven years old.

"He knew he could trust no one, so he lived on his own. He spent his childhood living in Tabriz, sleeping in barns and outbuildings, making his living cleaning boots and shoes, going from house to house. Later, when he had amassed a little money, he bought charcoal and sold it. He walked to the Holy Land, and finally, at the age of twenty-six, realized his desire to kneel at the feet of his Lord."

She continued, telling us that after a while, Bahá'u'lláh sent him back to Persia to teach. He was soon caught and imprisoned for four years. He was tortured and bastinadoed, which injured his one foot so badly that it never healed correctly and accounted for his painful limp. His nose and jaw were broken, and he was told he would be set free if he would divulge the whereabouts of the Bahá'ís in Tabriz. He refused, and they informed him he was to be killed. He prayed to Bahá'u'lláh and asked if he wanted him martyred or teaching; that either was acceptable to him, as his only desire was to be of service.

"Apparently," Blanche continued, "Bahá'u'lláh chose service for him, because he was able to escape in the night. He left Persia and, over the years, made his way back to Acca."

Our informant went on to tell us that at sixty-seven years, he is as energetic as we see him, and the moment his name is mentioned, people break out in smiles and chuckles. Because having known him for only a few minutes, one forgets his appearance and finds him delightful. "He moves so quickly, almost jumping about like a child," she said.

'Yes," responded Francesca Santini. "He reminds me a little of an organ grinder's monkey. I've never known a man so filled with good spirits and humor."

"'Abdu'l-Bahá loves him so," Blanche said. "He followed 'Abdu'l-Bahá to Paris because he wished never to be separated from him, but the Master has told him to remain in Paris for a year, to live among the Bahá'ís and help us become deeper in our understanding of the Faith."

John opined, "That must have made him very unhappy."

"It hasn't seemed to," she answered. "He is happy doing whatever the Master wants of him."

We were able then to understand better what he had been saying that night, when he had told us proudly while sipping his tea, "Now, I serve 'Abdu'l-Bahá as best I can. And that," he had added with his eyes flashing brightly and a delighted laugh, "is a joy worth all the days in prison!"

And as for me and my repugnance at Hamid's presence—it disappeared from that hour, and for a while an intense shame took its place. To think I had served him tea with such condescension! It passed in time, however, but I shall always remember how 'Abdu'l-Bahá so gently taught me about acceptance of those who may be different from ourselves and about whom and how to serve.

Now, I find that when Hamid speaks from his deep well of happiness, I too cannot help but laugh with him.

I think sometimes this 'Abdu'l-Bahá will cause me to lose my mind! After all, I know what I know. I know that the Church has been my best parent, and I do not think I could ever desert her. I know that my life has been one of service, but with purity? Hardly. Not with my ambitions. Yet, he has vindicated so much of Mario's and my thinking, and more, made me think of things that even we, with all our secret doubts, had never even approached. I know that since meeting him, I am seeing myself as never before. More, I am seeing all of life as never before. Strangely, he mentioned that I am, at last, awakening, as though the process were not completed that long night when I wrestled with my father's ghost. Could there be more? Was he saying there is more?

These Muslim believers, like Hamid, for instance, I have always "known" are doomed to certain perdition. It is, after all, what Holy Mother Church has taught. But Khánum? She is a Muslim of sorts, and what kind of Heavenly Father would damn her? Only a cruel god who enjoyed punishing, as my father enjoyed beating us. It occurred to me in this moment that, somewhere in my heart, I had equated, somewhat, my heavenly Father with my earthly one.

Further, the Church has taught also that any so-called Christian who is not within her fold is likewise doomed. Yet, neither Mario nor I have ever been able to truly accept that. We have seen too much sincerity outside the Church—too much "saintliness," if you will. She teaches that Mario is doomed because of his defection and apostasy. Mario has not truly apostacized, as he loves our Lord Christ as much as ever, but he loves Bahá'u'lláh as well and seems to find no contradiction in that. I find that for the first time in my life, I am wondering if there truly is a place of fire where we suffer forever for our sins. What would that accomplish? Would it not be similar to my father beating me for an infraction—not just a single punishment to teach me, but forever, without ceasing? What would I learn? And to what end would I learn it? It occurs to me as well, that even back in the days of my most intense hatred of my father, I would never have wished to condemn him to such a place. Not since my early strivings against unchastity have I struggled so with my Faith and its teachings.

I also know this—that though I may also burn forever for my doubts and disagreements and for my interest in this strange new teaching, I cannot stay away from it.

And now, there is this final knowing: that burn or not, damned or not, I believe there is a new day coming—a day when all human beings will be seen as included among God's beloved, a day when nationality will no longer matter, nor race, nor faith. If God sent Jesus to us, could He not also have sent Buddha to the East, as he sent Moses to Isaac's children and Muḥammad to Ishmael's? That perhaps we Christians may not have been totally correct about these things is my belief, and as an archbishop, perhaps I can attempt to help the Church grow into this. If this is my new and secret sin, then so be it, and I can only hope God will forgive me.

Because it is in my heart now, and it will not be removed.

37

SHIRIN: 1911

The second time we went to hear 'Abdu'l-Bahá, he remained with us after his talk, and I had a chance to meet him. I approached him, along with a large group of eager people wishing to speak with him. I suppose, because I am ninety-seven years old, people allowed me to go up to him ahead of many others. He reached out for me with both arms and took my hands, while a broad smile lit up his entire face.

I had intended to tell him how much I enjoyed his talk, how much it meant to me to know someone was actually teaching the idea of oneness . . . the oneness of religions and of nations and of races. But most of all, I wanted to tell him that I had seen his Father. I had expected that since he had spent his entire adult life in prison, he would be a man of great sadness. I had thought this bit of information might cheer him a little, but 'Abdu'l-Bahá was, without a doubt, one of most joyful souls I have ever seen. Further, I believe he not only knew what I was thinking, but more.

I received the surprise of my life, when, eyes twinkling, he said to me something about welcoming me "home." I wasn't sure I understood at first.

Of course, the moment I had seen him that first evening, I'd experienced an unforgettable sense of the power of his spirit. I knew then, immediately, why I could never think of Persia without remembering, Mírzá Ḥusayn-'Alí Nurí, whom I now know as Bahá'u'lláh. The Master has about him much the same aura as his majestic Father, a sweet-stern manner and an all-forgiving love, and it took me back to that moment in Mírzá Abbas's compound. I had hardly realized that I had been lonely for that sensation all my life since and had recognized it again in His mysterious son. In that second I understood. My soul, as my dream of Ṭáhirih had promised, had found her home.

He told me my life of service and sacrifice was acceptable to Bahá'u'lláh. I was very confused at that, because I cannot think of any service I have ever rendered anyone. On the contrary, everyone seems to have served *me*, from Uncle Firuz to Mírzá Abbas and the Dolgorukys; from Zhukovsky to Rubin. Even dear old Popov did so much for me, and I could never return anything to him. As for sacrifice, what have I ever sacrificed, aside from Edward, perhaps? But that was not truly a sacrifice—it was simply the right thing to do.

Then 'Abdu'l-Bahá gave me a rose. I have pressed it and will keep it always. More, I have asked Khadijah to bury it with me.*

As for this business of burying: Khadijah and I were both saddened to read a letter I recently received from Fareshteh. She usually writes long long letters, but this one was very short. We soon understood why, as her message was not a joyful one. She was terribly ill, she wrote, and not expected to live much longer. I found that hard to believe, because she was, after all, considerably younger than I, and I have always pictured her as the young girl she was when Ṭáhirih taught us to read at Mírzá Abbas's.

She was not sorry to die, she told me, but happy to be rejoining those she had loved, and to be forever nearer to Bahá'u'lláh. She wrote:

---

* The conversations related between Shirin and 'Abdu'l-Bahá are fiction and based on what is known about the nature of 'Abdu'l-Bahá's interactions with people in real life.

"The Master has assured us that we continue to live and to grow forever in the spiritual worlds. That we have lifetime after lifetime there, from world to world in 'the realm of the placeless'; that this world (and that first world when we are yet in our mother's body), are the only worlds in which death is a mystery and so can be somewhat frightening to contemplate. From this life on, growth and development continue, for as long as God's sovereignty will endure, until we reach some kind of spiritual maturity that none of us, with our present limited understanding, can begin to imagine.

"So this will be, after all, the last letter you will receive from me, but I am so happy to have heard from you, again, and to know you are still alive and apparently well; to have all the news of your life and family, of your grandchildren and great-grandchildren. Needless to say, I am overjoyed that you have been learning from 'Abdu'l-Bahá, Himself, and that you believe in Bahá'u'lláh!"

She was too weak to write more, she told me, and ended:

"I close now, after these few pages, loathe to say good-bye, but of course it is not truly a good-bye at all, as we *will* meet again in our Beloved's Kingdom, and so I sign myself in this final letter, as I have always signed to you, dear Shirin.

Forever—through all the worlds of God—your friend,

Fareshteh"

It is true, I *have* written to the Master here in Paris, and asked him if I would be acceptable as a believer. He answered me with the same sweetness as when he spoke to me at No. 4 Avenue de Camoens, assuring me again of his love, and sent me a little prayer to say, which I recite morning and evening now.

Of course, we went back again and again to hear 'Abdu'l-Bahá. It was strange how the little group of us had become friends almost instantly. We were all amazed to notice that whenever we gathered, even though the subject was religion, the entire house sparkled with gentle laughter. The older Bahá'ís, the ones who had formed the first tiny little group in Paris, were more than friendly to us, almost as if they were family, and they went well out of their way to help those of us who were trying to understand what had happened to us.

Our lives had changed, irrevocably and forever. Whoever we had been in the past, that person was—as it were—gone now. Each of us now knows he is not only a child of God but, as the Master has told us, a *friend* of God, and that we have a mission to help bring into being a world of peace and oneness of nations, races, and religions, and to educate our children to this mission also. So we have taken to referring to one another as "the friends." I was amazed at the variety in our little group. John and Carolyn Hillhouse are young, English, and members of the Church of England. Mario and Francesca Santini are Italian, as is Father Vittorio who, while still an archbishop in the Church and filled with doubts about the new Revelation that challenges his dogma, cannot seem to stay away. Sometimes even Rubin joins us, with his Jewishness very proudly admitted in this group. There are a number of French friends, as well as two Negro friends who came with a group of visiting American Methodist believers. Finally, there are Khadijah and I, who had been reared as Muslim Persians, and, of course, Hamid. I had not thought there to be a group like ours anywhere else in the world, but I soon learned that little groups like this are flourishing wherever the news of Bahá'u'lláh has traveled.

In fact, Rubin told me not long ago, "After all my years as a so-called Christian, I've come to see things a little differently. All Christians don't hate us, Khánum—only those who have had that hatred drummed into them by preachers, priests, and families who need to feel superior to someone or can accept nothing different without blaming some real or imagined villain. And as for Jesus, I am no longer so sure He was *not* our Messiah—he was certainly wise and kindly enough—and surely as much a victim of mankind's hatred as the rest of us Jews.

"But whatever the truth about him is, I cannot forget that our scripture promises a second great one to arrive in due time. In my mind, I keep hearing Psalms 24:7–10: '. . . be ye lift up, ye everlasting doors; and the King of Glory shall come in. . . Who is this King of glory? The Lord of hosts, he is the King of glory.' I had always thought that 'The Lord of hosts' referred to the creator, Himself, but now I have to ask myself, Khánum, 'Could it be that Bahá'u'lláh is the King of Glory? His very name means *Glory of God.* Could He not be the promised Lord of Hosts? One Lord for all? It is only a thought, but it keeps going around and around in my brain."

At last, 'Abdu'l-Bahá left Paris. We were heartbroken, and I now understood why people had traveled across the sea to be near him. I had met him so briefly and know I will not see him again in this life, and that leaves an empty place in my heart that will not be filled until I can join him in the spiritual world.

I can explain it only in this way: He is the reflection of his Father, Bahá'u'lláh, just as Bahá'u'lláh manifests God Himself. 'Abdul-Bahá is the moon, as his father is that biblical "Sun of Righteousness, who shall arise with healing in his wings."[1] And once having seen the Sun, we know all else to be darkness.

The group of Paris believers meets regularly in various homes and sometimes at ours. Some evenings, we are joined by the French Agent to Palestine, Louis Catafago, who first translated Bahá'u'lláh's second letter to Napoleon III. He was stationed in Acca at the time and became a believer after translating the letter.[2]

Hamid became far more than a comical figure as he told us stories from the early days in Persia and Acca. Also having been in Acca for a long while on two separate occasions, he had heard a good many of Bahá'u'lláh's teachings. He had been present when the revelations were coming on a number of occasions and told of how He spoke so rapidly that two or even three secretaries were hard pressed to keep up with Him; of how the light that radiated from Him blotted out the light from the sunny window behind Him. He said the power that filled the room made some of them tremble.

Hamid told us that Bahá'u'lláh had revealed, "Soon, will the present-day order be rolled up, and a new one spread out in its stead."[3]

He had a number of little hand-copied papers that contained some of Bahá'u'lláh's writings. One of my favorites, so much so that I begged him to read it over and over until I had learned it by heart, went like this:

"The All-Knowing Physician hath His finger on the pulse of mankind. He perceiveth the disease, and prescribeth, in His unerring wisdom, the remedy. Every age hath its own problem, and every soul its particular aspiration. The remedy the world needeth in its present-day afflictions can never be the same which a subsequent age may require. . . . We can well perceive how the whole human race is encompassed with great, with incalculable afflictions. We see it languishing on its bed of sickness, sore-tried and disillusioned. They that are intoxicated by self-conceit have interposed themselves between it and the Divine and infallible Physician. Witness how they have entangled all men, themselves included, in the mesh of their devices. They can neither discover the cause of the disease, nor have they any knowledge of the remedy. They have conceived the straight to be crooked, and have imagined their friend an enemy. Incline your ears to the sweet melody of this Prisoner. Arise, and lift up your voices, that haply they that are fast asleep may be awakened. Say: O ye who are as dead! The Hand of Divine bounty proffereth unto you the Water of Life. Hasten and drink your fill . . ."[4]

Carolyn Hillhouse told us one evening that her favorite was this one: "'I am the royal Falcon on the arm of the Almighty. I unfold the drooping wing of every broken bird and start it on its flight.'[5] I like it especially," Carolyn said, "because that's what he did for me."

Mario teased her, "Were your wings drooping, Carrie?"

"Yes, they were," she answered very seriously while reaching for John's hand. "Terribly. You see, we thought we would never have any children, and it made me . . . well, very sad for a long time. But 'Abdu'l-Bahá looked at me, just *looked* at me, and I've not been sad since. And now . . . " She blushed and looked down at her feet. We all were curious.

"Carrie, are you saying what I think you are saying?" Francesca, who is not hampered by British reticence, asked.

John grinned and said, "Yes, indeed she is saying what you think she is saying! E. J. H. Hillhouse the Fifth is on the way!"

And I thought, "*Oh! Edward's grandchild!*"

We were all delighted and gave them our congratulations and best wishes. Then Mario said, "Now, John, what if this miracle child is a girl? In that case, have you thought of a name?"

"Of course," John said. "She will still be E. J. H. the Fifth."

"And just how do you plan to work that out, my friend?" Mario asked.

"She will be called Edwina Joanna Henrietta Hillhouse, that's how," John said firmly.

"Oh, surely you're joshing, John," Vittorio said, literal as always.

A conspiratorial exchange sparked between the eyes of John and Carrie, and John said, "Y'think so, do you?" and wouldn't discuss it further.

One evening the talk turned on a very serious note. John was telling about his father's papers and how Edward had believed we still had time to accept Bahá'u'lláh's revelation and establish world peace. "My father seemed to think it might be rather unpleasant if world peace is not established," John said with typical British understatement.

"It's looking 'rather unpleasant' already," Vittorio commented. "I have just returned from Vienna, where I spoke with Emperor Franz Josef of Austria. He's very worried about the Balkans. He's afraid of war, and in the very near future."

"Yes," John said. "Our government is talking about it as well."

I commented, "It seems to me there is always a war somewhere."

"I know, Khánum," John said, "but while many in power in England don't think there truly will be a war, because we are—some are saying—too civilized for that nowadays. This war, if it *does* erupt, will be a huge affair. England is worried about it, as we would probably become involved—and France as well."

"Yes, Clemenceau is terribly concerned, I know," Katherine's husband Marcel commented. "He feels that Austria should never have annexed the Balkans. It is a Muslim area; it just doesn't seem right."

"At least the emperor is considering sending the new heir to the Austrian throne—his nephew, the Archduke Frances Ferdinand—to Serbia the third week in June on a goodwill tour. He is hoping that if he and his wife Sophie visit Sarajevo, it might help calm things down and ensure peace."*

---

* The archduke and Sophie were assassinated during their visit, which exploded into World War I in August, 1914.

"What do you think, Vittorio? You know the Habsburgs."

"I don't hold out much hope for it, myself. The archduke is not popular, and the people hate Sophie. I think war will come, and when it does, it will be huge and ghastly."

"Worse than the Crimea?" I asked him.

"Oh, much worse. The Crimean war took place over one little peninsula. This will involve all of Europe, I fear."

"But if God wants peace in this age, why will He let that happen?" Francesca asked.

"It is up to us to make the peace, Francesca," Hamid said. "He tells us it is now time for the nations to make peace. If we choose war instead, that is not the fault of God, is it?"

There was a silence then, and after a moment Hamid said, "The Pen of God* has written: 'We have a fixed time for you, O peoples. If ye fail, at the appointed hour, to turn towards God, He, verily, will lay violent hold on you, and will cause grievous afflictions to assail you from every direction. How severe, indeed, is the chastisement with which your Lord will then chastise you!'"[6]

Francesca persisted, "But I understood that Bahá'u'lláh has *promised* the long dreamed-of age of peace *truly is* to begin."

"It is hard to imagine how that will ever come about," Khadijah said. "I've lived eighty-five years, and it doesn't seem to me that humanity changes very much, and certainly not very fast. How can we expect to ever not have war?"

"We can't," Vittorio said decisively.

"'Abdu'l-Baha indicates that we will outgrow it, just as a child outgrows his temper tantrums," Hamid assured us. "Why, already, there is talk of universal peace among some of the nations of Europe."

Louis Catafago, the French agent who had translated the Prisoner's second letter to Napoleon III, said, "Even Louis Napoleon, before he died, came to believe in disarmament and a European central government to keep peace. That's never been proposed before. Perhaps the central government is an idea he got from Bahá'u'lláh."

---

* One of the titles for Bahá'u'lláh.

"It *will* come," Hamid said. "It has been promised for thousands of years in God's good time, and God keeps His promises. Remember, 'a thousand years in thy sight are but as yesterday when it is past, and as a watch in the night.'"[7]

Rubin responded, "That's from Psalms," and he quoted further, "'They shall beat their swords into plowshares, and their spears into pruninghooks: nation shall not lift up sword against nation, neither shall they learn war anymore.' Our prophet Isaiah said that."[8]

Hamid nodded, smiling.

"Bahá'u'lláh has announced that that very Promised Day is beginning now. First, though, unless humankind changes greatly, we must go through a period of terrible suffering throughout the whole world, until we see that there is no other way. Then we will make peace."

"The whole world!" Carrie said. "I don't see how the whole world can suffer at once. After all, a war in Europe won't affect the people in Africa and America and the far East."

Mario said, "I don't know, but I believe that when the time comes, there will be no hiding place."

After a short but thoughtful silence, we all confessed that we had no idea how it could all come about, and we saw that though God may have His plan to bring enduring peace to the world, we were not yet able to understand it.

All in all, it was a sobering evening, and the Archbishop Vittorio finally ended it by pronouncing in his authoritative way, "It will never happen. One might just as well try to go to the moon!"

38

SHIRIN: 6 APRIL, 1914

Father Vittorio, though somewhat confused, seems much happier than when we first met him. Certainly, finding Mario has a great deal to do with it. Mario works in the university library, so while he earns a rather meager salary, he is content with his living, and he and Francesca are so dear together. Each had a long period of loneliness before they met; Mario, robed, celibate, was all but locked in the Vatican library, and Francesca was trapped in her childhood home caring for an aging father until he finally died. They have a true appreciation of each other that is rare among married people. They love it here in Paris, although some day, they say, they will return to Italy.

But the main reason Father Vittorio is happier is that he now values his service for its own sake, rather than for the elevations it can bring him. I know this because he told me so. More specifically, he told the same thing to Mario and Francesca one evening when they were at our house. Only he and the Santinis had come for dinner, so there were just the five of us. Afterwards, over sorbet and coffee, he told us his life story about his long ambition, spurred by his wish to simultaneously please and triumph over his late father. Now he laughs and says that he hopes he does *not* become a cardinal. "I should probably have to leave Paris, and I would be little more than a glorified secretary to his Holiness, which would keep me busy doing tasks I have little interest in doing. Here, at least, I can touch hands with the people and bring a little hope to this increasingly desolate world."

"Hope?" Mario grinned at him, "I thought you had no hope."

"*Au contraire,* Mario. There is no longer any question in my mind that Bahá'u'lláh is a true Messenger from God. Whether or not he is the return of Christ, as some of you seem to believe, I am not prepared to accept—at least not yet. There are too many unanswered questions in my mind. After all, He is to return from the clouds, is He not?"

"*In* the clouds, not from," Khadijah said, "and we are the ones who, with our superstitious dogma and our imitations, put the clouds in the way of our sight." Then suddenly remembering she was addressing an archbishop, she added timidly, "Ah . . . perhaps . . . wouldn't you think, Father?"

"Perhaps," Father Vittorio said. "I admit I had not thought of it that way. The other thing is, we have always been taught that He Himself is to return."

"Then why, Vittorio, did He say that when He returned it would be with a new name, and that His followers would be called by his new name?"

"He did, didn't He? Why does no one remind us of that?"

"Why, indeed?" said Mario. "These are the clouds we were just talking about."

"H'mm, perhaps. Still, much of my reluctance has to do with my love of the Eucharist. It seems to me that if Bahá'u'lláh were truly the return of the Messianic Spirit, then he would have outlawed the celebration of the Eucharist, because Jesus said, 'Do this when you meet together *until* I come.'

"Vittorio," Mario said, "if the world accepts the message, then there is no need to outlaw the Eucharist. Hasn't there been enough of forbidding harmless activity in the name of God? If it is no longer loved and needed, it will die of its own accord, and even if it doesn't, remembering Jesus could never be 'wrong' in the sight of God."

"True enough, I suppose, but more, I can't match it up with the appearances of the Holy Mother at Fatima these past years, though their messages are not dissimilar. At the same time, Bahá'u'lláh was able to foretell the fate of the kings and rulers with an uncanny accuracy, and it will be interesting to see what becomes of the Habsburgs, the old emperor, the kaiser, and even Germany herself in the future."

Father Vittorio frowned in his puzzlement, and I had to smile at it. I've seen a good many babies born in my lifetime, and some of them fairly leap into life, as though they can hardly wait to try out this world. (They told me I was one of those, and my Hassan certainly was.) Then there are those who move a little bit toward birth, then wait for a while, then forward a little, then halt again as though they were timid about leaving the safe haven of the warm, dark nest. His reluctance to believe, which could possibly result in the loss of the safe haven of his beloved Church, sometimes reminds me of one of those. I think, though, that he might possibly allow himself to be born in time.

Almost immediately, he vindicated my thinking by remarking, "But of this much I feel certain: When 'Abdu'l-Bahá gave me to understand that the Revelation of Bahá'u'lláh is for everyone in the world—not just Muslims or Christians or Jews—and, in fact, even for those who believe in nothing, I felt again, for a moment, the old bliss of my boyhood prayers. And I saw where I belong. Holy Mother Church needs to come into the twentieth century. She is stuck in her past; she yearns for her past glory from before the revolutions, but our Lord Christ's message was never about earthly glory. If God approves, I will do my best to help bring her His latest Revelation—the oneness of religions and races, the equality of women and men, the acceptance of true science, and a world federation of nations."

Francesca said, "But what if the Church will not listen, Vittorio? What then?"

Vittorio looked sadly at the floor for a long moment and said, "Then I suppose I shall have to leave her, shan't I?"

Mario smiled at him for a moment and then said *very* softly, "Bravo, my friend. Bravo."

* * *

We all miss John and Carrie, and I especially will miss seeing them at the party tonight, because not only did we discover the fullness of our belief at the same time, but John is my only remaining link with Edward. Still, their life is in England. We hear from them occasionally by post. Carrie's health is excellent, and the baby—whatever its gender and name might turn out to be—is due late in the year. They tell us the Faith is growing there, and they are in a lively group.

Khadijah has had a letter from Shahane Dolgoruka. She had sent to her an invitation to my 100th birthday celebration with a note saying that, while she knew Shahane could not attend, she still wanted her to feel part of it. Shahane included a special greeting for me, which I am not to be allowed to see until tonight, and wished us all well.

All the Dolgoruky's we knew are gone now, even Natasha. Shahane and her children and grandchildren are the only ones left. Even our General Dimitri has died, but his grandson is serving Tsar Nicholas II as a Cavalry officer.

Gracious God, I have outlived everybody in the world!

Given that, I am relieved to have heard what 'Abdu'l-Bahá has told us about death. Life is an eternal journey, he explained, from one world of God to the next, never ending. We move from our first life in the uterine world, to the earthly life, to life in the ever-more refined spiritual worlds of God, and in each one, we are more truly conscious than in the one before. Our true life, the life of the spirit, goes on evolving forever, as Bahá'u'lláh's gift of our daily prayer proclaims, ". . . a fountain of living waters whereby I may live as long as Thy sovereignty endureth, and may make mention of Thee in every world of Thy worlds."[1]

I miss them all, but I am not truly bereft because I know that somewhere in God's universe, they fare well. My only true loneliness, oddly enough, is for the one who is still very much here in this world—the Master, and I know this emptiness will not be filled while I live.

From that day so long ago in Mírzá Abbas's courtyard, when I first caught sight of God's ancient beauty reflected in human garb as the sun is reflected in a mirror, something within me recognized that I was in the presence of God. Once having been in God's presence, from that moment on, no matter where we go, we are exiles on this earth. No wonder I could not find a home in any of the established religions, nor in any country.

One of the things I have taken note of in these long years and many places is that no matter what religion one belongs to if one is sincere, one will wish to somehow honor God. So, to that end, some give up family life and serve an institution, as Father Vittorio has. Others build cathedrals to His name or, like the Dervish Muslims and Hasidic Jews, dance to His honor. Some of us write music that reverberates through the cathedrals and through our souls, some paint and sculpt like Michelangelo, some even design, as Khadijah does. At the very least, we give money.

One evening, Hamid told us of an event the Master had related to him, which seems to me to illustrate our need to serve God. As Bahá'u'lláh was leaving Baghdad for Constantinople on the first leg of his five year journey to the Holy Land, various tasks were allotted among the friends who were accompanying Him. Several men did most of the cooking and the cleaning up. One was a barber, who took care of the needs of the travelers; another was the purchaser, who went ahead to buy supplies for the caravan; and so forth. The most coveted roles, however, were those of walking along beside Bahá'u'lláh's howdah when he was not riding His horse.

How to convey the unutterable bliss of those twelve days in the Riḍvan Garden that had burst the throats of nightingales, the Master had asked? How to convey the joyful spirit of those who traveled the long and difficult road with their Lord to Constantinople?

'Abdu'l-Bahá walked always on one side of his father's howdah; and a youth called Munib, who walked on the other side, at night or in the dark of early morning, was privileged to carry the guiding lantern. 'Abdu'l-Bahá told us, "The young man had been known in Persia for his easy and agreeable life and his love of pleasure; also for being somewhat soft and delicate, and used to having his own way. It is obvious what a person of this type endured going on foot from Baghdad to Constantinople."

His father was so upset that Munib had become a follower of Bahá'u'lláh's that he had actually made arrangements to have his son killed if he did not recant this "Bábí nonsense" and return to the "true Faith."

'Abdu'l-Bahá had said, "Now Munib, like the others, had learned the true identity of the teacher. He was none other than the one who had been foretold by the Báb—'He Whom God Will Make Manifest.'" Munib and the others were privileged to go with him to his next point of exile. "Our joy," 'Abdu'l-Bahá continued, "defied description."[2]

Laughing and singing, young Munib would lead the way with the sun by day and his little lantern by night. One pictures him—dancing on aching legs, skipping on blistered feet—and can all but hear his youthful voice reflecting the joy of the entire company, chanting his ecstatic phrases: "*Come let us scatter these roses! Come let us pour out this wine!*" [3]

So, it seems to me, we need to find God, and having found Him, we are enjoined to follow Him. The result of that loyal obedience is joy. And the result of joy is this need to honor.

I think again of Ṭáhirih's prophecy for me and of how it bore out so truly.

I remember, too, that terrible bloody night, when I begged Too-Tee to live—how I felt almost angry with her for appearing to love God more than life, and how she seemed almost joyful to depart. I understand, at last, her dying attempt to explain, "all life ends in death." She had known, after all, Who the Báb was, and I had not.

I know now what she was trying to say to me—that while our death may take us away from all we have known, afterwards we still have Him, and in Him is all we thought we had lost.

* * *

In our Muslim world we have a dance called the Dance of the Seven Veils. Westerners think it is only an erotic dance. It *is* erotic, because the love of God is a seduction and a coaxing toward a mysterious and wondrous fulfillment, but the dance is far more than that. It is a dance of growing; of learning to see. As we move through life, one by one the scales of blindness fall away and with the dropping of each veil, our excitement increases and our vision of Him becomes clearer until we, like that ancient man of Jerusalem upon meeting the Christ, cry out in our delight, "Wherefore I was blind, now do I see!'

We all jest with one another about the failure of memory in us elderly. Yet, I think it is not so much a failure as it is that as we age, the days go faster and faster until, like the spinning Yin and Yang, they become indistinguishable one from another; more, one's labor becomes indistinguishable from one's pastime. The same is true for our sorrows and joys. As with the lines in our faces, we can only wonder which lines came from our weeping and which from our laughter. And in the end, it hardly matters, as the whole purpose of it all along was this evermore illumined awakening, this eternal journey.

The world is going to become a terrible place before this new Revelation of God will triumph over the forces of evil let loose in our modern age, but we need only believe and persevere. The Most Great Peace will come, Bahá'u'lláh said, "ere long." I suppose that could mean one hundred years or five hundred years. But as one who has lived one hundred years, I can say with some authority that a hundred years is no time at all. The Book of Revelations says that in these days ". . . the devil is come down, having great wrath, for he knoweth that he hath but a short time." In a Tablet called "the Fire Tablet," God said to Bahá'u'lláh, "When the swords flash, go forward! When the shafts fly, press onward!"[4]

He did. And so must we.

I am so happy! To think that—after all the years and the suffering with the pain of loss and the burden of loving, after all the wandering with no home of my own, after my three sorrowful journeys—at the end of my life, I have found this! All my broken pieces are come together like the seamless robe of Christ. Sometimes I feel it is immoral to be so happy when the world is so filled with suffering—but then, with my own ears, I heard the Master say, "Be happy, Be happy!" Also, Hamid told us that Bahá'u'lláh has written, "Rejoice in the gladness of thine heart, that thou mayest be worthy to meet Me."[5] *Worthy,* He said! And surely, no one knew more about suffering than the Messengers of God.

The Master himself has said that we are to be patient yet not idle; that we are not to yield to the power of tyranny and despotism but serve the cause of democracy and freedom; that we are to be valiant and courageous even while all around us men are cringing with fear. Even now, the nucleus of the new race of man is forming.

There are moments when I can hardly contain my joy, for, in these latter days God has, in a mingling of justice and mercy, visited upon this dark world an avalanche of knowledge and a Noah's flood of grace, and my soul is all but swept away! We have, it seems to me, a choice; we can see these currant upheavals as a time of total destruction of all we have known and believed and be plunged into a soul's black night of despair, or we can see it as I believe it truly is—a sweeping away of the useless and worn, making way for the supernal creation of a new world, a springtime of growth and new life. The Apocalypse it seems, is at last upon us! And it is light upon light!

Speaking of honoring God, I often think of Munib, the spoiled boy who walked at Bahá'u'lláh's side all the way from Baghdad to Constantinople. Though my body can no longer manage much, our souls—that part of us that *truly* lives—must step into the world's approaching darkness with its feeble lantern. And even as the nations rage and nature goes mad, even in the torture of grief and the parching thirst for truth, how better to honor God for His great gifts of Teachers, knowledge, and the ever-refined renewal of Creation than to press on across this inhospitable terrain, singing with Munib.

How better—even in our searching and sinful stumbling, though sticks lacerate our feet and stones bruise our heels—that we should go laughing and singing, go leaping and dancing, on our way.

* * *

And now I hear my sweet Cecile and our little Jean Michael coming to help me down to the party, so my long reverie is over. I can hear Jean Michael bark his shin against the stair, say "Ow!" and whimper for a moment at the pain, then laugh with his mother at his own clumsiness.

And I say to myself, "Oh, yes, my children, you have it right. That is the way to live!"

The End

Notes

3

1. Nabíl-i-A'ẓam, *The Dawn-Breakers*, p. 330.
2. Ibid., pp. 330–31.
3. Ibid., pp. 358–59.
4. Ibid., p. 361.
5. Ibid., pp. 363–64.
6. Ibid., p. 365.
7. Ibid., p. 381.
8. Ibid., p. 384.
9. Ibid., pp. 386–87.
10. Ibid., pp. 399–400.

4

1. The account of the Seven Martyrs of Tehran is taken from Nabíl-i-Aẓam, *The Dawn-Breakers*, pp. 446–58 and 494–95.

5

1. Anís, quoted in Nabíl-i-A'ẓam, *The Dawn-Breakers*, p. 512, note 2.
2. The Báb, quoted in Nabíl-i-A'ẓam, *The Dawn-Breakers*, p. 514.
3. Zaynab, quoted in Nabíl-i-A'ẓam, *The Dawn-Breakers*, p. 552.
4. Shoghi Effendi, *God Passes By*, p. 70.

5. Ṭáhirih, quoted in Nabíl-i-A'ẓam, *The Dawn-Breakers*, p. 296.
6. Ṭáhirih and Quddús, quoted in Nabíl-i-A'ẓam, *The Dawn-Breakers*, p. 296.
7. Ṭáhirih, quoted in Shoghi Effendi, *God Passes By*, p. 118.

13

1. Pius, quoted in Martin, *The Decline and Fall of the Roman Church.*
2. Ibid.

18

1. Bresler, *Napoleon III: A Life.*
2. Bismarck, quoted in ibid.
3. Shoghi Effendi, *The Promised Day is Come*, p. 83.
4. Bahá'u'lláh, *Summons of the Lord of Hosts*, "Súriy-i-Haykal," ¶137.

20

1. Romans 13:1.

21

1. Bahá'u'lláh, *The Summons of the Lord of Hosts*, "Súriy-i-Haykal," ¶102.
2. Ibid., ¶103.
3. Mathew 26:11; Mark 14:7; John 12:8.
4. Bahá'u'lláh, *The Summons of the Lord of Hosts*, "Súriy-i-Haykal," ¶105–6.
5. Ibid., ¶106.
6. Ibid., ¶107.
7. John 16:12–13.
8. Bahá'u'lláh, *The Summons of the Lord of Hosts*, "Súriy-i-Haykal," ¶107, ¶110, ¶113, ¶114, ¶115, ¶123, ¶125, ¶126.

22

1. Bresler, *Napoleon III: A Life.*
2. Ibid.
3. Ibid.

23

1. Andreottie, *La Sciarada di Papa Mastai.*
2. Hennesey, *The First Council of the Vatican: the American Experience*, p. 174.
3. Dessain and Gornall, *The Letters and Diaries of John Henry Newman*, 25:169.
4. Andreottie, *La Sciarada di Papa Mastai*, p. 29.
5. Ibid.
6. Bahá'u'lláh, *The Summons of the Lord of Hosts*, "Súriy-i-Haykal," ¶102.
7. Ibid., ¶105.
8. Ibid., ¶106.
9. Ibid., ¶113.

24

1. Mathews, *Muhammad: Defender of Christians*, pp. 18–19.
2. Koran 2:257 and 10:99–100.

25

1. John 10:10.
2. Koran 29:45.

27

1. John 10:10.
2. Koran 29:45.

28

1. Bahá'u'lláh, *Gleanings from the Writings of Bahá'u'lláh*, ¶105.1, ¶105.5–¶105.6; Bahá'u'lláh, *The Summons of the Lord of Hosts*, "Súriy-i-Mulúk," ¶2, ¶11; Bahá'u'lláh, *The Summons of the Lord of Hosts*, "Súriy-i-Haykal," ¶179, ¶181, ¶182.

30

1. Bahá'u'lláh, *The Summons of the Lord of Hosts*, "Súriy-i-Haykal," ¶158.
2. Ibid.
3. Ibid.
4. Ibid.

31

1. Bahá'u'lláh, interview with Edward Granville Browne, quoted in Shoghi Effendi, *God Passes By*, p. 306; Habakkuk 2:14.

33

1. Bahá'u'lláh, *The Summons of the Lord of Hosts*, "Súriy-i-Haykal," ¶172–73.
2. "Theology and the Coming Christ," Seventh Day Adventist publication, pp. 23–24.
3. World Parliament of Religions; Columbian Exhibition, 1893; Parliament Book, 2:1125–26.
4. Matthew 24:27.
5. Bahá'u'lláh, *The Summons of the Lord of Hosts*, "Súriy-i-Haykal," ¶180.
6. Bahá'u'lláh, *Gleanings from the Writings of Bahá'u'lláh*, no. 61.
7. 'Abdu'l-Bahá, *'Abdu'l-Bahá in London*, pp. 19–20.

34

1. Mackenzie, "The Nineteenth Century: A History," p. 341.
2. 'Abdu'l-Bahá, *Paris Talks*, no. 41.9.

35

1. Colossians 1:20.

36

1. ‘Abdu’l-Bahá, *Paris Talks*, no. 44.2–44.5, 44.12.

37

1. Malachi 4:2.
2. Shoghi Effendi, *The Promised Day Is Come*, ¶123.
3. Bahá’u’lláh, *Gleanings from the Writings of Bahá’u’lláh*, no. 4.2.
4. Ibid., 106.1–106.3.
5. Bahá’u’lláh, *Tablets of Bahá’u’lláh*, p. 169.
6. Bahá’u’lláh, *Gleanings from the Writings of Bahá’u’lláh*, no. 108.1.
7. Psalms 90:4.
8. Isaiah 2:4.

38

1. Bahá’u’lláh, in *Bahá’í Prayers*, p. 10.
2. Balyuzi, *Bahá’u’lláh: The King of Glory*, p. 177.
3. Ibid.
4. Revelations 12:12; Bahá’u’lláh, “Fire Tablet,” in *Bahá’í Prayers*, pp. 317–18.
5. Bahá’u’lláh, The Hidden Words, Arabic no. 36.

Selected Bibliography

Works of Bahá'u'lláh

The Hidden Words. Translated by Shoghi Effendi. Wilmette, IL: Bahá'í Publishing, 2002.

The Summons of the Lord of Hosts: Tablets of Bahá'u'lláh. Wilmette, IL: Bahá'í Publishing, 2006.

Tablets of Bahá'u'lláh revealed after the Kitáb-i-Aqdas. Compiled by the Research Department of the Universal House of Justice. Translated by Habib Taherzadeh et al. Wilmette, IL: Bahá'í Publishing Trust, 1988.

Works of 'Abdu'l-Bahá

'Abdu'l-Bahá in London. London: Bahá'í Publishing Trust, 1912.

Works of Shoghi Effendi

God Passes By. Revised ed. Seventh printing. Wilmette, IL: Bahá'í Publishing Trust, 2010.

The Promised Day is Come. 1st pocket-size ed. Wilmette, IL: Bahá'í Publishing Trust, 1996.

Compilations

Bahá'u'lláh, the Báb, and 'Abdu'l-Bahá. *Bahá'í Prayers: A Selection of Prayers Revealed by Bahá'u'lláh, the Báb, and 'Abdu'l-Bahá.* New ed. Wilmette, IL: Bahá'í Publishing Trust, 2002.

Other Sources

Andreotti, Giulio. *La Sciarada di Papa Mastai.* Milan: Rizzoli, 1967.

Balyuzi, H. M. *Bahá'u'lláh: The King of Glory.* Oxford, UK: George Ronald Press, 1980.

Barrows, Rev. John Henry. *World Parliament of Religions: Vol II, Colombian Exhibition.* Chicago: The Parliament Publishing Company, 1893.

Bresler, Fenton. *Napoleon III: A Life.* New York: Carroll and Graf Publishers, 1999.

Crankshaw, Edward. *The Fall of the House of Hapsburg.* New York: Viking Press, 1963.

———. *The Shadow of the Winter Palace.* New York: Viking Press, 1976.

Dessain, C. S. and Thomas Gomall, eds. *The Letters and Diaries of John Henry Newman.* Volume XXV. Oxford: Clarendon Press, 1976.

Esselmont, John. *Bahá'u'lláh and the New Era.* Wilmette, IL: Bahá'í Publishing, 2006.

Hennesy, James. *The First Council of the Vatican: The American Experience.* New York: Herder and Herder, 1963.

Mackenzie, Robert. *The 19th Century; a History.* New York: T. Nelson and Sons, 1893.

Martin, Malachi. *The Decline and Fall of the Roman Church.* New York: Putnam Publishing, 1981.

Mathews, Gary. *Muḥammad: Defender of Christians.* Knoxville, TN: Stonehaven Press, 2001.

McMillen, Sally G. *Seneca Falls, and the Origins of the Women's Rights Movement.* New York: Oxford University Press, 2008.

Nabíl-i-A'ẓam. *The Dawn-breakers.* Translated by Shoghi Effendi. Wilmette, IL: Bahá'í Publishing Trust, 1932.

"Theology and the Coming Christ." Article in a Seventh-Day Adventist Publication.

Tuchman, Barbara. *The Guns of August.* New York: Ballantine Books, 1990.

BAHÁ'Í PUBLISHING AND THE BAHÁ'Í FAITH

Bahá'í Publishing produces books based on the teachings of the Bahá'í Faith. Founded over 160 years ago, the Bahá'í Faith has spread to some 235 nations and territories and is now accepted by more than five million people. The word "Bahá'í" means "follower of Bahá'u'lláh." Bahá'u'lláh, the founder of the Bahá'í Faith, asserted that He is the Messenger of God for all of humanity in this day. The cornerstone of His teachings is the establishment of the spiritual unity of humankind, which will be achieved by personal transformation and the application of clearly identified spiritual principles. Bahá'ís also believe that there is but one religion and that all the Messengers of God—among them Abraham, Zoroaster, Moses, Krishna, Buddha, Jesus, and Muḥammad—have progressively revealed its nature. Together, the world's great religions are expressions of a single, unfolding divine plan. Human beings, not God's Messengers, are the source of religious divisions, prejudices, and hatreds.

The Bahá'í Faith is not a sect or denomination of another religion, nor is it a cult or a social movement. Rather, it is a globally recognized independent world religion founded on new books of scripture revealed by Bahá'u'lláh.

Bahá'í Publishing is an imprint of the National Spiritual Assembly of the Bahá'ís of the United States.

For more information about the Bahá'í Faith,
or to contact Bahá'ís near you,
visit http://www.bahai.us/
or call
1-800-22-unite

OTHER BOOKS AVAILABLE FROM BAHÁ'Í PUBLISHING

ALI'S DREAM
The Story of Bahá'u'lláh
John S. Hatcher
$15.00 US / $17.00 CAN
Trade Paper
ISBN 978-1-61851-068-6

A stirring work of young-adult historical fiction revolving around the life of an eleven-year-old boy with a mysterious dream that inspires him to investigate his heritage and spiritual destiny.

Ali's Dream is the story of Ali, an eleven-year-old boy living in 'Akká (present-day Israel) in 1912, whose life becomes a quest for the meaning of a mysterious dream. This dream leads him to carefully study his Bahá'í heritage, and sets him on a course to discover his own spiritual destiny. Author John S. Hatcher has woven scenes and fascinating details of the history of the Bahá'í Faith—stories of heroism and heartrending drama—drawing from them universal truths about sacrifice, suffering, and the spiritual qualities required in growing up. *Ali's Dream* is an adventure into which readers may enter with Ali to seek those qualities and ideals that result from commitment to a cause greater than themselves. It will give readers a relatable and personal window into a fascinating piece of history as well as a coming-of-age story about what it means to grow up and find one's place within one's cultural heritage.

PEARLS OF WISDOM
Illustrated and Compiled by Constanze von Kitzing
$12.00 US / $14.00 CAN
Paper Over Board
ISBN 978-1-61851-069-3

A beautiful, full-color, illustrated children's book containing simple yet profound passages from the writings of the Bahá'í Faith arranged around themes of spiritual significance.

Pearls of Wisdom is a beautifully illustrated book of passages from the Bahá'í writings presented in a manner that will appeal to children of all ages. Arranged around themes such as God, the soul, prayer, friendship, and love, all passages are accompanied by vibrant full-page color illustrations by award-winning illustrator Constanze von Kitzing, whose work strikes the perfect balance between playful and reverent. *Pearls of Wisdom* is an ideal book for the whole family to enjoy together, and it is hoped that it will lead to rewarding discussions about important spiritual topics in the home.

SELECTIONS FROM THE WRITINGS OF 'ABDU'L-BAHÁ
'Abdu'l-Bahá
$23.00 US / $25.00 CAN
Hardcover
ISBN 978-1-61851-065-5

A timeless collection of writings, containing spiritual and practical guidance for all aspects of life.

Selections from the Writings of 'Abdu'l-Bahá is a compilation of correspondence and other written works of one of the central figures of the Bahá'í Faith. The book covers a wide range of topics including physical and spiritual health, death and the afterlife, the reality of man, the oneness of mankind, and the elimination of prejudice. 'Abdu'l-Bahá was the eldest son and appointed successor of Bahá'u'lláh, the Prophet and Founder of the Bahá'í Faith, and is considered by Bahá'ís to be the authorized interpreter and the perfect exemplar of the Faith's teachings. The wisdom imparted in this volume of his writings remains as timeless and relevant today as when it was first committed to paper.